SOUL Keeper

CATHRYN MARR

ebook ISBN- 978-1-7329336-3-7
Print ISBN- 978-1-7329336-4-4

Edited by: Elizabeth MS Flynn http://emsflynn.com/
Cover design ©2018 Fiona Jayde Media http://fionajaydemedia.com/
All graphic images ©2019 Fiona Jayde Media http://fionajaydemedia.com/
Book Design by Tamara Cribley of The Deliberate Page

Printed and bound in the United States of America

First Printing April 2019

Published by Brokenoggin Books L.L.C., PO Box 10, Philo, California 95466

Visit website https://cathrynmarr.com

To Mom and Dad, who inspired me to follow my dreams and never give up.

To my husband, Ron, who's supported me every step of the way.

*And to Terese Ramin, special thanks for joining forces
with me and making this dream reality.*

Thank you all from the bottom of my heart!

*With heartfelt thanks to Dawn Johanson, my Gateless '16 sisters, my niece
Stacey, and always, always to my children Brynna and Nathan. I am so
grateful to you for your constant belief in me.*

Disclaimer

This book is set in a contemporary but alternate version of San Francisco. The authors have deliberately used colloquial grammar and regional dialogue and spelling in many places. The lexicon at the end of the book includes a list of words, phrases, and definitions that will hopefully help to dispel any confusion.

Hell is empty
And the devils are here.

—William Shakespeare, *The Tempest*, Act 1, Scene 2

A dull roar shook the scrubby hillside around Dr. Michael Beck, causing the earth to roll beneath his feet.

"Yes!"

Elation coursed through him. He'd done it—begun the process by which his Watcher ancestors might escape their tomb and rise to take over the world, beginning with the western half of the United States. Glee filled him as he watched the Visitors Center collapse in on itself, sending up a gout of flame, followed by a plume of dust-filled smoke.

A shuttle bus, flung sideways by the blast, spilled screaming tourists every which way from its open sides before it was dashed against a field stone wall then swallowed when the earth cracked open beneath it. Beck crowed when the majority of the passengers were gobbled up with the bus. They would be the first souls his forebears would consume on their journey to resurrection.

Movement at the periphery of his vision drew his attention. Two of the bus's female passengers—a short, squashy redhead of indeterminate years and a tall, elegant middle-aged blond—had been thrown clear of the explosion. They struggled upright where they'd landed in the scrub and turned to each other, looking shocked. Before they could move or speak, a wraith-like fog issued from the fissure into which the bus had disappeared. It moved swiftly to cover the women, drowning their cries in seconds.

A sense of triumph ran through Beck. After years of preparation, he'd finally done it—fired the first salvo in a war no one but him had known was coming. Soon, the Watchers would rise, and he would become a god…

Chapter One

Any battle between "good" and "evil" intended to culminate in either a "day of reckoning" or an "end of the world as we know it" scenario necessarily involves four things: agents of darkness who have no idea WTF they're trying to bring about; agents of light and right who say "WTF!" and oppose them; The Creator, who will deal out the reckonings regardless of who "wins"; and the shadow-bound agents of reason who understand too well what a Day of Reckoning might entail—and fear it. It's worthy of note that an "End of the World as We Know It" endgame is unlikely to work out well for anyone...

—from *The Lightway Codex, Introduction: Overview* by McCleron O'Connell, Indigo Lightworker

The unearthly quality of her singing assaulted him even before the sound reached Luc's ears. Doubling over in pain, he gasped and ducked into a flower-shadowed corner near the entrance to the lime green painted cinderblock storefront that housed his destination. Breathing into the pain in an attempt to contain it, he wrapped his arms about his head and ears.

The protective move failed. It was more than the actual sound that hurt him. Pitch, tone, and an indefinable otherness also came into play. The angelic essence—the sheer crystalline brilliance of the light, the power behind each note—drove wormlike fingers into his too-sensitive Ekoa Krillu brain, pierced every nerve in his system, rattled his teeth, then ripped free.

Shit! He fell to his knees. Since Kartchner had ruptured, the Brotherhood had been looking for ways to stop the oncoming threat by getting rid of anyone the Watchers would be most likely to feed on—and from whom they could gain strength.

To that end, Luc was being sent to "secure" all known "special" kids and adults. Senn Lawton, the liaison between them and the Council of Light, had suggested he might know someone who could help. He'd also said the woman he was sending Luc to could dance, but the bastard sorcerer had utterly failed to hint at Aurora Montgomery's ability to incapacitate a potential enemy by singing a medley that ran from emo to hard rock to pop to country western, and show tunes to—Luc winced his eyes shut and wrapped his arms more tightly about his ears when her voice soared—a fucking sixteenth-century madrigal, for God's sake. No wonder his search for the source of the temblors ended here. If her singing could fell him, it could no doubt disrupt the earth's seismic core, too.

The song broke off as though interrupted by something or someone. The pain that ran through every vein, pore, and nerve lessened but did not entirely abate. Still, it was manageable. Grimly, Luc stumbled to his feet. No wonder Senn had told him *this* woman was the only one who could help him to rescue the child that underground whispers referred to as the Sixth Element. He owed the damn sorcerer a holiday in hell for not cluing him in on the full extent of Miss Montgomery's abilities. Still, if those abilities helped Luc to protect the youngster he'd been tasked with finding…

Well, then the disturbing extent of discomfort she caused him in the process would be worth it.

He stepped through the building's iron security gate and into the open door of Sunshine Dance Studio.

Aurora Montgomery sensed him and the pain she'd caused him before he placed a foot in her doorway.

Skin crawling with the urge to flee from some kind of predatory presence, she abruptly stopped singing while she danced and pivoted to face the incoming threat. The sight of the huge, dark man paused at her threshold caused the air to leave her lungs in a rush. Easily over six and a half feet tall, he menaced the room by his existence in it. Aurora's breath went shallow.

Sexy and disturbing.

The thought skirled upward through every nerve ending, scorched its way from her toes to the base of her spine the moment he set foot on the scarred hardwood of her studio floor. From the base of her spine, the notion skittered into the fine hairs at the nape of her neck. *Sexy and…*

Disturbing.

She caught her breath when the word pulsed erratically, erotically, in her veins.

Disturbing…disturbing…disturbing…

It vibrated through her, speared unexpectedly to the tips of the breasts that plumped against her brightly colored dance bra. The word—the promise—plundered her lungs before it plummeted into her belly.

Wariness flitted through her. At the age of twenty-six, she'd never experienced anything that came close to resembling this sensation. And now that she was…

Mate…couple…breed…

On the other side of the room, his nostrils flared. He turned and took in the dim room with a single glance before settling on her. His eyes flashed, lips parted, tongue flicked out to taste the air.

Her breath shuddered in her lungs. He took an involuntary step toward her, caught himself, and stopped dead. His eyes narrowed. Aurora struggled to capture her runaway breath as her first impression of him revised itself. He was not merely sexy and disturbing. He was sexy, disturbing, and *dangerous.*

She'd put money on that last being his most prominent characteristic, especially among those who knew him.

She didn't.

It felt like she did.

Very, *very* well.

I don't do demons, hell spawn, some part of her whispered.

Shocked, she slapped the notion down, but not before he lifted a scarred black brow and shot a thought back at her: *Have you ever* done *anyone, angel?*

Aurora stopped breathing. Damn. He'd heard her. He'd *heard* her. She'd always been able to "hear" others, to project thoughts back for them to take in on some unobtrusive, internal level. But other than some of the disabled, disadvantaged, or challenged children with whom she worked, she'd never met anyone able to hear her the way she "heard" them, as though carrying on a mental conversation.

Telepath, something deep inside her said. Only not, exactly. Intuition informed her he was far more.

She swallowed. *Crap.*

Beneath the studio's floor, the earth rolled gently, as though in portent. *Psi. Inhuman. 'Krillu.*

Fallen.

Throwing up her mental and psychic shields, she backed deeper into the studio, away from him. Maybe he'd come to the building that housed her dance studio to see someone else.

He hadn't. She knew even before he took a second, determined step toward her that he hadn't come into the Haight for anyone but her.

Luceire took in the lithe form of his quarry, and the first thing that flared through the lingering pain of her song was a savage growl of satisfaction.

Mine.

He squelched the disquieting hunger to possess, to conquer—and to be conquered by, which unsettled him—the petite but voluptuous creature. The well-defined muscles of a dancer enhanced her curves, accentuated breasts, thighs and buttocks he wanted to fill his hands with.

He winced when his cock hardened, reminding him of just how long he'd been without. Members of the Brotherhood of Shadows took an oath of celibacy along with the vows they made to cleave only unto their mission to protect humanity. That meant that psi vamps—and specifically the Ekoa Krillu—like him did not mate at all. Not permanently, anyway. They fed on the life force of anyone or anything willing—and sometimes unwilling—to share with them. That included the emotional energies exuded by individuals and mobs as well as the residual energies that lingered any place that had seen vast amounts of passionate activity like dance halls, theaters, poverty-stricken neighborhoods, and battlefields. They definitely did not pair off with anything they considered *kine*, or food.

No, if a psi vamp was wise, he maintained a herd of willing partners, alternating among them in order to keep his resources healthy and available—much the way experienced sanguine vampires kept a coterie of chattel willing to regularly donate blood. This woman definitely impressed Luc as the energy source to end all—if he could figure out how to get close enough to feed from her without dying. Except...

She turned toward the mirrored wall behind her as though searching for an escape. The movement showed him her nipples through her neon pink sports bra. Again, the musk that soaked her dance shorts drenched his nostrils, saturated his taste buds; his already engorged cock swelled to embarrassing, agonizing proportions. He hissed in a breath.

She was not merely sustenance, he realized with sudden clarity. She was downfall, sure as the moon, bright as the sun. She was the stuff of life itself, the substance every 'Krillu since the Fall craved. Life energy, pure and simple. Every fiber of his being wanted—no, *needed*—to possess, protect, surround, and invade her.

Mine.

Even as he fought against the knowledge, his feet took him toward her.

She danced gracefully, agitatedly, another foot away—and started to glow.

Stunned, Luc checked his instinctive pursuit, shielding his eyes with a hand. *What the hell?* Even as he watched, her aura intensified, surrounding her with vibrating shades of pink, yellow, and indigo. The concentration strengthened until it was almost opaque. Then a sudden burst of power flung him backward, across the studio threshold, through the lobby door, and across the sidewalk to land flat on his back on the cracked asphalt of the San Francisco street while every fire hydrant within a thousand yards blew open and spewed water down around him.

Mouth agape, Aurora stared after the airborne man. She looked at her hands, held out in front of her in a warding gesture she didn't remember making. Waves of lightning-like energy pulsed around her fingers, flaring between her and the studio entrance in a visible stream. Her mouth worked. *What the—*

No. Whatever had happened, whatever that was, it hadn't come from her…

Had it? No. It couldn't have. Not ever. Such a thing wasn't possible. Perhaps for one of the special children, the "crystal ones" she'd lately started to work with at her day job at Kate Cavanaugh and Associates, Pediatric Therapy, could have done it, but surely even that was unlikely. Had to be. And yet…

She looked from her hands to the still-vibrating double doors on the other side of the room. The track of pulsating sparks was beginning to subside, but the implication was undeniable. Just as Kate and Solaya had told her, apparently, she had *gifts*.

And they were coming into their own.

He hadn't realized Luceire Garard was back.

For the space of a breath, consternation flooded Savitri Nousaine. He was the underworld master of the city—and had been since before San Francisco had been the Spanish settlement Yerba Buena. Nothing and no one got within a thousand-mile radius of his city without his knowledge—especially no one who bore the unique energy signature that came with having trained with him. And Garard had trained more closely with him than anyone before or since.

Which had made his break from Nousaine's patronage and his subsequent admission into the Brotherhood of Shadows a betrayal of proportions equal only to Mephisto's original break with heaven.

He switched his senses outward, toward where he could feel Garard's presence. Faint seismic activity centered on the site, causing him to narrow his eyes. Garard had found the girl Nousaine had been feeding from since her energy had appeared on his…radar…six months ago. At the moment, she was seriously agitated. But until she'd reacted, he hadn't known Garard was anywhere near the city.

It disturbed Nousaine to realize that the Brotherhood seemed to have worked out a means to mask their energy signatures so thoroughly. Still…

He placed his fingertips on a north-facing window of his vantage point at the top of the Transamerica Pyramid. Shutting his eyes, he reveled in the burst of energy that had kicked Luceire Garard out the entryway of Sunshine Dance Studio onto his keester—a move that was surely responsible for causing the 'Krillu to drop his guard, bringing him to Nousaine's attention.

The ability to keep an eye on San Francisco in its entirety was only one of the advantages of owning space at the top of the city's tallest building. The greatest benefit, however, came from the building's design itself. The energy absorbed by the quartz crystals embedded in the surface of the pyramid's concrete pillars and blocks acted as a tuning fork of sorts, amplifying everything that came to him—especially when he was able to physically touch the stone. The amplification allowed him to control the metropolis, feed some of his hunger without having to make one-on-one contact with his victims the way most psis had to.

Sometimes, yes, he did that for the sheer pleasure of the hunt, the incredible high that came from descending on his prey and consuming it whole.

But that was the basest part of his nature. The part in which he reveled, in the rare event that no one was looking.

On the other hand, he never made contact with the building's quartz-encrusted exterior when it came to feeding, even from a distance on the woman who'd just pitched his greatest enemy into the street. The power she hadn't yet realized she carried would have been too much even for him to safely absorb.

Nousaine had been spying on Aurora Montgomery since the death of her father six months before. That was when she'd first come to his notice—the first time she'd experienced emotions strong enough to shock him into an awareness of her.

The first time, he'd quickly realized, she'd gone unshielded by the force of her remaining parent's love.

Her grief allowed him to prey psychically on her, absorbing her vitality by attacking her dreams with nightmares and feeding on the life-giving energy the traumatic visions created as she fought them. The force with which she'd expelled the strongest and most accomplished of his former protégés was formidable, sweeter than anything he'd ever tasted—and he'd sampled a lot of *prana* through the millennia. It kept him intensely alive, made him stronger than any other existing vampire, psi *or* sang.

It made him hungrier, too. That was why he'd fastened his attentions on Aurora the minute she had come to his notice.

The pleasure of devouring the nearly manic vital forces of his wealthier clients had long since diminished in value for Savitri. The energy he pulled from their pretty, petty lives sustained him, of course, but the flavor palled. His clients' essences lacked spice, spirit, vigor. The longer he fed on them, the more like him they became. He'd fed on many of them for so long that their souls had shriveled and blackened to a point near nonexistence. In order to fully satiate his appetites, he would need to completely drain them of life.

Getting rid of the bodies of prominent persons, however, was problematic. Savitri had been forced to seek sustenance elsewhere—specifically, from the misery that lived in the nighttime streets in some of the more extreme parts of the city. Like some of the clubs inside the Tenderloin or within the violence of Little Saigon. But the energies of indigents and whores, street urchins and partiers, and even the do-gooders who trolled for them in an attempt to provide them all with better existences were stop-gap at best. The altruists were generally passionate about their cause, at least for a while, but the energies of the other night cattle were too often polluted by drugs or alcohol, the potency of their spirits sapped long before Savitri went near them. If he didn't watch himself when he fed from them, he could easily go through five or six a night. That many dead or dying bodies led to questions and investigations Savitri had no desire to encourage.

But Aurora Montgomery…

Again, Nousaine savored the flow of emotion, of power, that came from her. Feeding from her chi could sustain him for centuries if he could keep her alive that long. It could make him the most powerful Ekoa Krillu who'd ever lived. Would ever live.

In ecstasy, Savitri flattened both hands against the windows in the four-sided, quartz-caked pyramid that faced in her direction and sucked her in.

A few miles away, a boy wearing a troubled expression, a bright blue super-hero cape, and a knitted orange slouch hat looked across the bluff to where the narrow pyramid scraped the city's sky. Hair so fair that it appeared white haloed his head when he plucked off the cap. Troubled, he scrubbed a hand through his flyaway hair, trying to ease the static electricity itch. His insides jittered, making him feel squirrely. He hated being exposed like this, hated being out in the open where anyone could pick up his thoughts, maybe find him. He didn't want to be what *they* told him he was. Warrior. Protector. Guardian. *Indigo*. But he couldn't *not* be those things, either. That thing in his head that scolded him about right and wrong, said he had to do this. Didn't have to like it, just had to do it.

Anxious, he slanted another glance at the pyramid's spire. Something evil watched the world from that building, and he didn't want whatever it was to notice him before his work on this plane was finished.

Hunching into himself, he took an uneasy sideways step along the grassy headland. A low rumble signaled an oncoming earthquake, and he shifted his weight, riding the earth's roll the way surfers might a wave. As the temblor subsided, an unhappy huff of exertion caused him to turn his attention downslope. A few feet below, a heavily pregnant girl somewhere between fourteen and sixteen slouched against the hillside, attempting to catch her breath.

"C'mon, Mag," the boy said, his tone anxious. "Medics leave the Care Village early. We have to move. Need to get safe before the locusts come out."

"'S'not easy haulin' this belly around these hills, Fish." The girl called Magpie sounded irritable. She patted her stomach then tilted her head back to look up at him. "You got any water and some candy? Baby wants French fries, but the other might help."

Fish glanced from her to the distant triangular tower with misgiving. The "baby's" constant desire to binge on French fries was a danger no one had cautioned him about when he'd stumbled into this assignment. Not only were French fries not healthy for Magpie, but they cost money he often didn't have. Some of the locust-like vampires and the others, the ones that fed on energy, had set up outdoor, banquet-style canopies in parks the city's homeless frequented. The food tents were available later than anything run by human providers, but they always reminded Fish of a docu-vid he'd once seen of farmers feeding livestock, fattening them up before leading them to slaughter. French fries and other forms of potatoes were usually available at those places, but it was a trick to get in, grab some while they were hot, and get out without the bloodsuckers or energy feeders catching him and eating their fill. Most of the vampires adhered to a "catch, feed on, and release" philosophy in order to maintain the food supply, but there were a few…

Fish shuddered. He hated vamps, more now that he was tasked with keeping Magpie and the baby she carried safe. Carefully, he patted the various pockets stitched into his cape until he came up with half a Kit Kat bar and a piece of hard candy, then walk-slid down the hill to hand them to her.

"Can't stay here."

"I know."

She shoved the chocolate into her mouth. Chewed and swallowed before unwrapping the hard candy and popping it onto her tongue. Then she dug her heels into the incline and attempted to hoist her ungainly self erect. Failed.

Sighing, Fish reached down and locked elbows with her, then pulled her up. The faint tremor of an aftershock caused them both to stagger. After an unsteady moment, Magpie was on her feet. She supported her belly with one hand while steadying herself against Fish with the other.

Torn between carrying out the task to which he'd been born and running far away fast, Fish stood still for a moment, listening hard. There it was. Beyond the threshold of human hearing, out of the range of even dogs, someone screamed.

And screamed and screamed.

Frightened, he grabbed Magpie's hand and dragged her up the slope. No way could they risk going to the mobile shower units in the Haight today. Something was coming, and it was big, dangerous, and final. He had to get Magpie and her baby out of sight, out of hearing, out of peril, and keep them there.

No matter what.

Chapter Two

The difference between psychic vampires (psis) and sanguinary
vampires (sangs) is simple: psi vamps feed on human energy;
sangs require human blood. If a psi is able to control its needs,
it can distill the anger from mob energies as well as heal illness,
emotional imbalance, and pain in the humans it feeds on.
Sangs who can likewise control their feeding urges are capable
of injecting healing antibodies into those suffering from often-
fatal human ailments, including cancer. With these rare and
notable exceptions, all Fallen Angels are monsters.

—from *The Lightway Codex, Appendix i: Defining the Players*
by McCleron O'Connell, Indigo Lightworker

Blinking, Aurora staggered and sat down hard on the studio floor. It was
as if every bit of energy had suddenly been extracted from her. If this
was what coming into her "crystal powers" meant…

But no.

She swallowed and sank full-length across the floor. Turning her cheek
to the oak planks, she closed her eyes and fought a nauseating wave of
weakness. Whatever had just happened—whatever she'd just done—the
weakness she experienced now was not new, merely greater than what she'd
suffered with increasing frequency since her father's death. It was as though
something or someone was draining not only her emotions but sapping her
energy and her will, as well.

It's not unusual to lose yourself when someone you love dies, she assured
herself in the same way the doctors Solaya had taken her to see thirty, sixty,
and ninety days ago had done when they'd found nothing physically amiss
with her. *Give it time and you'll be fine.*

But she'd given it six months. Instead of getting better, every time she felt like she might be getting some of her energy back, she felt weaker still. Now, for example. She'd never felt so drained that she kissed the floor and wanted to die.

"Rory!"

Aurora's nickname jarred her aware to the clacking of high-heeled shoes across wood.

"*Rory!*" Solaya Lawton sounded unnerved. Aurora felt her friend's hands shaking as she touched her face.

Aurora blinked, and tried to open her mouth and shape words with her sluggish tongue. Instead, not even a thought formed.

"Dear goddess, what has he done?"

Aurora heard, rather than saw, Solaya plop her huge, omnipresent, leather purse on the floor and open it to paw through.

"Don't worry, sweetie, we'll get you up and moving in no time."

"No, you won't." The baritone that accompanied the tromp of heavy-soled boots across the room was harsh and worried. An enormous male silhouette dropped to Aurora's other side. "Let me have her, Laya."

"No, Luc," Solaya said anxiously. "You'll make it worse—"

"Trust me," the man Solaya had called Luc said. "I've got her."

Then a shadow obscured what light there was and gentle fingers turned her head, tilting it back. A broad thumb pressed her chin downward, opening her mouth. Warm, cinnamon-scented breath touched Aurora's lips before his mouth descended on hers.

Luc breathed out, forcing not air but energy into her. The pulse that had been thready beneath his searching fingers thrashed and started to race. He slid an arm under her knees and shoulders and sat down to draw her into his lap. She raised a lethargic hand and tried to smack him away. He pulled her in tighter, pressed harder into her flagging chi.

"Luc, stop," Solaya ordered, grabbing at him. "You'll kill her."

No. He shrugged away from Senn's twin, who was sometimes his ally but more often his foe, and continued to breathe his own energy into Aurora. Though a portion of the psychic residue in her was unfamiliar to him, he recognized the major source of the drain on her stamina as well as he recognized himself. Savitri Nousaine had mentored him when he was new to this world, tutored him in control, predation, and survival. Shared both energy and prey with Luc at the same time he'd imprinted himself on the Fallen. And the same way bite marks on a rape victim could identify a rapist, the master psi's feeding signature was all over this tiny woman.

If Luc didn't do something to replace what Nousaine consumed, and quickly, Aurora Montgomery would be taken away from him before they had even met.

Who are you? What are you doing?

Muzzy but determined, the thought filtered into his mind from the woman in his arms.

It didn't occur to Luc to wonder how she was able to communicate telepathically with him. She'd freaking tossed his butt into the street without touching him. The "she's more than human" thing kind of went without saying.

Putting back what was taken from you, he thought back. *Protecting you.*

By kissing me? Derision was palpable.

I'm not… Luc began, but it was a lie because suddenly he was.

Kissing her.

Thrusting his tongue between her lips and teeth like it had a right to be inside her.

Framing her face and the back of her head in one big palm to anchor her to him while the arm around her shoulders lifted her higher, tighter against him.

Feeding on the intense flow of unimaginable energy between them.

Gasping, Luc tore his mouth from hers. In horror, he met the frightened indigo of her eyes. God, oh God, what had he done? Partaken of the incandescent prana that radiated about her when all he'd set out to do was protect her from the master psi vamp who'd nearly devoured her alive.

It had been *that* close, and Luc had felt it. Taken that psi's killing residue into himself until…

Fear shuddered through him. Until he'd felt himself becoming Savitri Nousaine. Until she'd diverted a burst of the same power that she'd used to fling him across the room *into* him.

Instinctively fed him to prevent him from killing her.

He didn't think she knew what she'd done.

He thrust her at Solaya. "Take her."

"You *noshed* on her." The fury in Solaya's voice was scalding. It accused and condemned, cursed him without quarter.

"Not intentionally." Denial arrived more swiftly than confusion. He'd condemned himself already. *Never feast on the ill, the unaware, the incapacitated, or the disinclined* was both the spirit and the essence of the code by which he lived. It had been nearly five centuries since he'd broken it. He should have been strong enough for anything—especially for warding off Savitri Nousaine, his one-time Guide to All Things Psi.

Except he wasn't. Not when the energy was slammed into him before he knew what was happening. Not when the life force she hurled into him was so untainted and pure.

Baffled, he watched Solaya drag the petite, powerful woman away from him—and plant herself between them.

"How did she—*what* is she?" *More than human.* The knowledge that he'd so readily accepted when he was trying to heal her bowled through his mind, knocking everything he'd understood for millennia sideways. Humans might possess a flair for clairvoyance and other things most commonly attributed to the "sixth sense," but this was...

Extraordinary.

No wonder Senn had sent him to her for help.

Uneasy, Luc peered at the woman on the floor. Her weakened aura fluttered in a visible effort to regenerate and shrank close about her body. Away from him.

"Special." A female grizzly with a cub, Solaya placed a protective hand on Aurora's arm and bared her teeth. "She's not for the likes of you, *strike dog.*"

Anger carved red fissures into Luc's brain. Solaya's bigotry against who and what he was despite the Brotherhood's shared connection with Celeste Fury and the Council of Light was ancient, ingrained. He caught provocation in an iron grip and manacled it to the floor.

"Nor you, either, I think, sorceress," he returned mildly, "no matter how much good you've done in this incarnation."

Solaya's hands cupped, filled with crackling balls of blue-white flame. Luc considered the orbs with misgiving. Technically, the light wouldn't harm him. On the not-so-technical side, absorbing the light's unadulterated energy would make him ravenous for more. Sort of like potato chips. Consuming too much salty goodness was bound to be bad—eventually. He just wasn't sure *how* bad. Or how eventually.

"What do you want, Nephilim?" she asked him.

Her, his entire being responded instantly. He shut the traitor down.

Ignoring Solaya's inaccurate use of the term "Nephilim" when it came to him—he was a full-fledged fallen angel, not a crossbred, giant, human-angel hybrid like those the Watchers had spawned—Luc narrowed his eyes. "You realize there's a master psi tracking and feeding off of her." He gestured with his chin at the woman on the floor. "He's left a dynamic signature—"

The flaming energy balls in Solaya's hands got larger. "If it's not your backwash, then it's none of your concern, 'Krillu," she told him. "Tell me why you're here."

Beneath his breath, Luc swore. *Everything about her is my concern*, the part of him that recognized that Aurora Montgomery belonged with him insisted. *Especially since one of my kind is draining her.* His mouth, however, had temporarily attached itself to his wiser side. "I'm here on joint allied Council business," he told the sorceress. Honestly, because Solaya could spot the hedge he wanted to hide among a field of them. Truthsaying was one of her most potent gifts. "Senn sent me. He told me your friend there could help me locate a missing child. She is Aurora Montgomery, isn't she?"

Solaya glared at him. She'd spotted the evasion. "Aseneth would never deliver Rory or a child to a member of the Brotherhood of Shadows."

"No, that's true," Luc agreed, though doing so hurt. Too many people equated his kind with *demon* because the Brotherhood of Shadows lived, by necessity, outside the laws of man and the Council of Light alike—that whole "dirty job, but someone has to do it" thing. Though he was no angel, he was nowhere close to *demon*, either. "Not if there was anyone else who could help them." He glanced again at the woman with the blinding aura. She had propped herself up on her hands to look at him. Uncomfortable under her disquieting regard, he looked away, back at Solaya. "There's not."

"There's always—" Solaya began, but Aurora interrupted her.

"Senn sent you?"

Face averted, Luc nodded. "He thinks you can help me find the child I've been sent to protect." He badly wanted to look at her. To feast on her. To get just one more taste of the pure vitality she'd poured into him moments ago.

To breathe the incredible scent of her—she smelled of night blooms at the first waft of evening, of bergamot, jasmine, white roses, and blackberry blossoms, heady and intangible and glowing with the light he lacked—into his lungs and soul while he took everything she was and fed himself back to her. To—and this desire shocked him—meld with her until there was no end to him, no beginning to her.

Mine. The thought slithered through his nerves, flooded his cock with blood.

They hadn't, in point of fact, officially even yet met.

Not yours came the instant response. *Not anybody's. I belong to myself.*

Mine. Luc's beast lunged against its shackles, trying to get loose. No way in hell would he let the Council know she was capable of causing earthquakes. He would protect her from them at all costs. *Always mine.*

Aurora's breath caught, the mounds of her breasts rising into the chest-baring scoop of her tight-knit bra. Her *No* resonated through him.

Want mine. Need. Mine! He sucked air and brought his gaze to hers.

Hers sidled away.

No, her mind said again, but this time the sound of it was curious, tentative. Then, cautiously, *what child?*

Luc's inner beast growled with something close to satisfaction. *Gotcha.*

He needed her help to find a child.

That single piece of knowledge floated through Rory, fixed her attention despite the almost crushing lethargy in her brain and limbs. Children were her purpose, her *raison d'etre.*

When she was a child herself, she'd been misdiagnosed as a nonverbal autistic. Doctors had wanted to put her on medication to *even out* her mercurial temperament, brought on by her inability to make the world around her understand what she wanted to get across. Her parents had resisted for years, trying one thing after another to grab and focus her attention, make her *want* to express herself in a language that didn't sound like gibberish.

When she was four, in an attempt to do something normal, her mother had enrolled her in a dance class.

There'd been no looking back after that.

Music was a godsend. Rory felt everything through the soles of her feet. Rhythm entranced her. Vibration was a tactile experience, something she could touch. Movement was expression. It filled her, exploded inside her, lit her up both day and night. She could articulate it.

Kinetic illustration became words.

It had taken another two years and a speech therapist with telepathic gifts to work out how to translate mental pictures into speech. She was eight before she could finally speak without impediment.

It was this experience that led her to open her dance studio two years ago, shortly after she'd graduated from college. Backed by Senn and Solaya, and with the help of her former therapist, she'd connected her studio to after-school programs throughout the city, so those in need would have somewhere to go, something positive to do—a place to express themselves when their home lives and the streets outside threatened or overwhelmed them.

When they needed someplace to hide.

When she finally got her master's degree, she'd kept her studio, but also taken her dance movement therapy program to Kate's clinic a couple of days a week. She wanted to give disabled, traumatized, and at-risk children with no way to express themselves a means to articulate emotion.

Now this *guy*, who spoke with Solaya as if they knew each other fairly well—and didn't like it—needed her help to locate a child who was in danger or distress. Her, Aurora Montgomery, who'd never done anything that remotely resembled…well, detective work. She thought she'd met most of the Lawtons' colleagues and acquaintances. She didn't remember ever meeting him. And he was pretty unforgettable.

"What child?" she repeated—aloud this time.

She was pretty sure hunkly Mister Huge, Dark, and Dangerous winced.

"Ahm," he said, and puffed out a breath. "I'm not entirely sure. That's why Senn sent me. He said you'd be able to help me work out that part."

"Not a chance—" Solaya started, but again, Rory interrupted her.

"That doesn't make sense. How would I know how to locate a child someone like you"—she made a gesture that took in his floor-to-ceiling physique—"can't?"

Luc snorted and made a show of slapping street dust off his pants. "Mad telepathic and psychokinetic skills, perhaps?"

"But I don't…"

Her voice trailed off. Because, of course, she did. As illustrated moments ago, she was both intensely telepathic and possessed potentially killer tele-kinetic skills that scared the life out of her.

There'd been a few minor…incidents…over the years when things around her had seemed to move of their own accord. When they were kids, Solaya had said Rory was "emotionally trashed," but Rory had never associated the events with a psychic ability. She'd already been different enough and hadn't wanted to. But when Luc had walked in on her dance practice, there'd been an immediate disruption in the rhythm and flow of the energy around her. In a split second, it had coalesced into something with which she didn't know how to deal: *him*. Her agitated mind hadn't been able to cope, so she'd—

Hooked up to the hum of whatever it was that went on in her head, harnessed it, and thrown him out.

She'd always been connected to a comforting but indistinguishable buzz of voices. When she'd first learned to speak, she'd talked about those voices, certain everyone could hear and communicate the way she did. But they couldn't. At school, teachers and students had labeled her a lot of things she wasn't because of it. And now this Luceire Garard, who clearly wasn't quite human himself, wanted her to…

What? Tap into the buzz so she could help him?

"That's the one," he told her quietly, as though by simply watching her face he'd pegged the direction of her thoughts—which, given their earlier unspoken conversation, he no doubt had.

"But I'm not sure if I—"

"There's always a first," he assured her.

"Not always," Solaya said darkly.

He ignored her, his intense gaze focused on Rory.

Eyeing him warily, Aurora levered herself into a sitting position then moved to propel herself off the floor. The effort stole her breath, made her dizzy, but she had to get up, had to help him, despite her uncertainty. If Senn thought there was a problem where a child was concerned, there was a *big* problem.

Except she felt so freaking *feeble*. If it had anything to do with that burst of…*power* that had coursed through her moments ago, she didn't think she wanted to experience the attendant thrill of rightness, of being whole in and of herself ever again. If she did, she was pretty sure she'd never survive the subsequent energy drain. Newborn calves finding their legs for the first time had more strength than she did right now.

Her legs shook and her arms trembled. It took everything she had not to fall flat on her face again. If she didn't sit down…

She plopped back onto the hardwood and put her head between her knees. Although not quite as incapacitating as it had been, the strange weakness still plagued her.

Peeking up, she regarded the enigmatic object of her confusion and unaccustomed lust. He was everything a man should be and a thousand times more. Powerfully built and big enough to double as a wall she could hide behind. Tall enough to reach things on any high shelf she cared to imagine, and…

Sinfully breathtaking. As in quite unforgivably beautiful. Women would weep and pay thousands of dollars to acquire eyelashes like his. Not to mention the eyes the lashes surrounded. Intense, gorgeous, dark, they were the murky, turbulent blue of San Francisco Bay during a lightning storm. The neatly tied-back fall of his mahogany-chestnut hair almost reached his shoulder blades, glinted with highlights of tawny red-gold, black, and brown in the sunshine that filtered through the foliage outside her studio windows. She wanted to run her hands through that hair, feel it on her breasts and belly. Play in it.

She sucked in a wary breath. What was *that* about? Her attention span sucked, even when it came to doing her own hair. She'd never even played hairdresser with Solaya as a child. Applying her somewhat "Ooh look! Shiny" lack of focus to Solaya's spectacular fall of nearly black hair would have been a travesty. But this… The strands of his hair looked so *thick*. She wanted to learn each of them by touch.

To learn *him* by touch.

She'd already had a taste of him, and all that had done was cause her to want another.

And more…

So much more it made her lightheaded, trying to process the longing.

A new surge of dizziness washed over her, and her entire body crumpled in on itself without her saying it could.

Woozily, she twisted to peer at Solaya. Her oldest friend-cum-sister made a harsh sound of combined fury and anxiety then slid an arm beneath Aurora's shoulders to help her up and over to the narrow wooden table that served as Sunshine Dance Studio's office.

Depositing Rory in one of the folding chairs at the table, Solaya cast a look of utter revulsion at Luceire.

"You are so dead, Garard," she told him flatly.

Being a member of the Brotherhood of Shadows meant that even an Ekoa Krillu like Luc was possessed of a conscience. It also meant that guilt was something he'd long ago been forced to come to terms with. The fact that he couldn't actually be killed, only ritually imprisoned for eternity, didn't count. He nodded.

"Seems fair," he agreed, his troubled gaze on the woman Solaya's brother was certain could help him—if Luc could stop Nousaine and his disciples from stealing her energy. Trouble was, the woman was a walking smorgasbord of energy. Anything she felt, she projected—meaning that at the same time she'd thrown him, a perceived threat, into the street, she'd alerted every psi vamp in a fifty-mile radius to her whereabouts.

A series of runic tattoos might help to mask her and her uncontrolled outbursts from those who would feed on her until she learned some control, but she still needed to learn to shield herself on a psychic level, too. He cast a speculative glance at Solaya. "Riddle me this before you plan my demise, witch. Why haven't you and Senn taught Aurora how to shield herself from us energy suckers? She feels *everything*. I could feed on her from the moon."

Solaya's smile was fierce. "About that…"

"Back off, Laya," Aurora interrupted weakly.

Luc and Solaya looked at her.

"What?" Solaya's tone was sharp.

The look Aurora sent her burned with surprising intensity. "Back. Off." She made a flicking gesture that caused a surprised Solaya to stagger.

"What the…" Solaya stared at her. Aurora had lived next door to her and Senn since she was born. She had lived in their house since her father had died only a few months ago. Her mother had been gone for the better part of ten years. "What the hell was that?"

Rory gave her fingers an appreciative glance. "So that's what you and Kate meant about my *powers* coming in. Nice."

Luc smothered laughter. "That was a nudge," he told Solaya. "She gave me a full shove when I came in and I wound up in the street on my ass."

Solaya glared at Rory while pointing a *"you damn well better stay* waaay *over there where I can keep an eye on you"* finger at him. In a huff, she swung about and crossed back to where she'd left her purse, retrieved her phone, and punched a number. The connection appeared to go through almost immediately. "Senn? What the *fuck* were you thinking, sending a fucking Brotherhood striker—a 'Krillu, for God's sake—to get help from Rory?"

She stalked to the opposite corner of the room, the constant clack of her heels as she moved restlessly about inhibiting even Luc's preternatural abilities to eavesdrop on the conversation.

Making sure Solaya's back was to them—he wasn't afraid of her, but she seemed hell-bent on preventing him from talking to her friend about his mission—Luceire crouched in front of Aurora. She looked so innocent. So delicate.

She was the epitome of the guileless human creature with which his kind had been entrusted to guard, guide, and serve before the Fall. That had been their purpose from the moment of their creation, their entire reason for being.

A hollow sensation of guilt riffled through Luc. If each angel was charged with a single human to protect, she might have been his.

Beyond a shadow of a doubt, she *was* his.

Dumbstruck by a realization that had nothing to do with carnal craving, Luc shut his eyes against the otherworldly glow that emanated from her despite her damaged state.

She. Was. His. Purpose, reason, cause.

His.

The ache inside him receded, replaced by a call more feral than any he'd experienced in the long millennia of his existence. He opened his eyes.

Again, he was struck by the insubstantiality of her, by the desire to safeguard her at all costs. Her skin appeared pale and almost translucent, the blue lines of her veins visible against the backs of her hands and tops of her feet. Were he a blood vamp, he'd have been salivating—one more thing he had to shelter her against. Those damn locusts.

He shuffled position, feeling suddenly vexed and uncomfortable. Vexed because no way should Senn have suggested a woman who appeared so breakable to help with the sort of mission Luc was engaged in. And uncomfortable, because…

Hell. The way she'd thrown him across the room then caused Solaya to stagger with a twitch of a finger…

Aurora Montgomery might not be at one hundred percent strength, but she was far and away stronger, tougher, and more powerful than Senn had led him to believe. Luc wanted to see what else she was capable of.

He was so totally screwed.

Not to mention as dead as any "cursed to live forever while suffering great torment" immortal could be if Senn ever learned what he was thinking.

If Solaya learned it, he'd spend eternity hanging by his thumbs over a pit of molten lava that burned off his skin and smoked him until he was nice and tasty for the pit demons to feed on. Either way, not worth contemplating.

"I'm sorry about what happened—what I did. Are you all right?"

Aurora Montgomery offered him an anemic smile. "Not really," she said truthfully. "But it's not your fault. I haven't felt like myself in quite a while." Tiredly, she tipped her head back against the wall and looked at him curiously. "Solaya called you"—her features crinkled wryly—"a lot of stuff that made no sense. You said you were part of a-a brotherhood that's working with 'the Council,' and that Senn sent you to me about a child. What is it you need me to do?"

Touch me, believe in me, redeem me, the greedy thing inside Luc pleaded. He wrapped a mental fist around it and slammed it back into its box, buried it in rubble. Gruffly, he held out a hand to her, palm up. "I need you to help me find an endangered child," he said, "but first, let me try to help you."

Neon Boneyard, Las Vegas, Nevada

Bluetooth firmly attached to his ear as he listened to his twin sister rant at him from San Francisco, Aseneth Lawton, better known as Senn, made his way among the vintage signs in a closed portion of the Neon Boneyard.

He'd known Solaya wouldn't take him sending Luc to Rory well. But he could see what she, for all of her preternatural talents, could not—the various directions things could go wrong. Usually, he believed the future was what you made it and he didn't interfere with or try to redirect the visions he had of things going wrong. But this time… His gift of second sight had showed him something he couldn't unsee, couldn't allow to happen. So, he'd sent Luc to Rory in an attempt to do just that.

Dust plumed out from under his feet, rose in mini-dervishes around his knees as he hunted for what he knew didn't belong—here or anywhere. Pausing to run his tongue across his bottom lip, he sampled the hot, dry air.

The flavor of old ozone from long-dead signs touched the exposed membranes on the underside of his mouth first. Almost as an afterthought sat the tang that had brought him to the Boneyard in the first place: salt layered beneath the metallic suggestion of iron and copper.

Blood.

Damn. He couldn't be too late. Not again.

Grimly, Senn rotated, tasting the air as he moved, trying to locate the blood's source. In his ear, he could hear Solaya tap against the speaker, demanding his attention. He didn't have time for this.

"Damn it, Laya," he snapped, "I'm workin' here. The Brotherhood and the Council gave him a mission—life or death. I sent him to Rory because she needs more help than we've been able to get her. Luc can read psi trace that we can't, pick up the signature of whoever is draining her, and stop it. She has abilities you and I can't imagine, and she can help him find and protect the kid Falken and Celeste sent him after. It's time to let her go, let her *wake up* to what she's capable of."

A high concentration of iron-copper tang arrested him mid-turn. He spun back, one step, another half. There. *Shit.* He was going to be too late.

"Crap, Laya, can't do this now," he barked as he broke into a run. "Find me the Las Vegas healing team and get them to the Neon Boneyard on Fremont. Fast."

Ripping the receiver from his ear, he skidded around a pair of huge casino signs that had seen better days maybe eighty years ago.

And stopped.

The pair of small bodies propped against a mermaid made out of neon tubes told him everything he didn't want to know.

He was already too late.

Chapter Three

Led by earthbound cherubim Celeste Fury, the Council of Light is a network of like-minded individuals from both the dark and light sides of the immortal and human realms. Their mission is to protect Lightworkers, also known as earthbound angels, when their lives are in danger. They also track down immortal beings who actively prey on Lightworkers and the humans they protect. Though of opposing philosophies, the Council often works with the Brotherhood of Shadows when their interests are allied.

—from *The Lightway Codex, Appendix i: Defining the Players*
by McCleron O'Connell, Indigo Lightworker

"Senn? *Senn!*" Solaya shrieked. When her brother didn't respond, she hurled the phone across the studio. It bounced three times in its rubberized case and skidded to a stop in the center of the dance floor. "Fuck, fuck, fuckity *fuck!*" Nothing good ever came of Senn requesting a healing team. Especially lately. Meaning maybe Luceire Garard really was here for a reason, possibly even a good one. "Shit."

For the hint of an instant, she ground her teeth. Then she stalked toward her phone. Each step caused her stilettos to *screek* furiously across the studio's scarred-but-cared-for hardwood.

"Gosh darn it, Solaya," Aurora grumbled. "You're ruining my floor. Take off your blasted shoes!"

"Senn's in trouble."

Luc jerked involuntarily, and spun toward her. "What kind of trouble?"

The intense disquiet in his voice made Solaya eye him sharply before she bent to retrieve the phone. It was unbroken, thanks to its protective case. Frustrated phone throwing was a habit she'd long intended to break. Unfortunately, with a brother like Senn and a roommate like Rory, *intention* was about as far as she ever got. "Healing team kind," she said.

God *bless* it. They had better be in time.

Luc swore softly and rose from his crouch. "Where?"

Concentrating on scrolling through her contacts to find the one she wanted, Solaya waved him off.

Swearing, he crossed to her and grabbed her arm. "God *damn* it, Solaya. I can help if I know where he is."

"There's nothing you can do from here, Garard, so get over yourself." Not bothering to look at him, Solaya found the name she sought and hit CALL. "Keile," she said into the phone, "Senn needs healers—"

The violence that seemed lately to be Luc's constant companion reared up and caused him to snatch the phone out of her fingers. Shocked, Solaya tried to snatch the instrument back. "You're too bigoted against my kind to know fuck all about what I can do," he said hotly. Into the speaker, he said, "I've got this, Raeburn."

"Garard?"

"You bastard," Solaya ground out. "If anything happens to my brother because you're dinkin' around—"

"Solaya?" Keile Raeburn shouted. *"What in thunder—"*

"Where. Is. Aseneth?" Luc asked with soft menace, enunciating each word carefully.

At his back, he felt a prickle of energy, low key and tentative but somehow sure, like the sun rising to burn off fog. Beneath the studio floor, the earth trembled.

"Tell him, Laya." Aurora's voice vibrated with worry—and power.

Solaya's head snapped around. Her eyes went wary, causing Luc to swivel and look at the woman behind him.

Light and authority radiated from Aurora, haloed her in a lower-wattage version of that same crackling aura that had slammed him into the street. He felt it nudge Solaya backward toward a corner of the room even as the air around her whispered at the edge of hearing, *"Tell him, tell him, tell him… Now!"*

"Crap! Rory…" Solaya gasped, and Luc saw her struggle against the overwhelming push to do what Aurora asked, at the same time as she fought the knowledge that it was indeed the younger woman compelling her.

"Tell him tell him tell him…" the air murmured.

In the distance, at the other end of the phone connection, as though he, too, could hear her, Keile Raeburn shouted, *"Screw him. Tell* me*!"*

Neon Boneyard, Las Vegas

Senn had just finished covering the small bodies with a tarp he'd salvaged when a concentrated wave of healing energy flooded the Boneyard. He glanced up, wondering how the healing energy and retrieval team—H.E.A.R.T.—had managed to arrive so quickly, and without him hearing them.

But there was no one there.

Surprised and alarmed, he looked at the tarp above which the power had coalesced. It was visible to him now, a weft of pulsing violet-white light that effervesced with streaks of pink, yellow, and blue lightning.

Why did both the auric appearance and its energetic signature seem familiar?

He watched as a sliver of essence edged out from the whole, appeared to reach down through the tarp as though seeking the young victims beneath. It recoiled almost immediately, turning a greenish yellow-gray in what Senn interpreted as grief. For a moment, it hovered, as though uncertain what to do. Then anger flooded it—violent hues of red, orange, charcoal—before it turned on Senn, punched him hard in the chest, and sent him sprawling.

Shit, he thought, recognizing the aura's signature now. *Rory.*

Rory? Since when—

Before the question finished forming, the wave of light struck him again—like small fists beating at him in outrage and sorrow. Then the force blazed yellow, orange, and pink, turned back toward the tarp—and flung it aside to settle protectively over the lifeless children.

"No, no, *nooooo!*"

Gulping back sobs, Aurora sank back onto the studio floor and folded in on herself. Luc was already striding over to drop to his knees beside her while Solaya stood nearby, eyes wide with consternation and fear.

"How many?" Reflex made Aurora flinch from Luc's presence. Throat clogged with tears and anger, she directed the question at Solaya.

Solaya crossed to crouch beside her, put out her hand.

Rocking back and forth in an attempt to contain the agony, Aurora shrank from her.

"Don't *touch* me."

Inside her, the world screamed and battered at her. Everything came in—every sensation, every sound, every emotion experienced by every person between her studio and the dusty open-air museum in Las Vegas. It felt like every nerve ending, both physical and psychic, was raw, burning. It *hurt*, physically, mentally, emotionally, and she had no filters to shut out any of it. Especially the lingering sensation of fear and horror she'd gotten from the children in the Boneyard as they'd died. What was happening to her? Why couldn't she filter them—it—out?

An ululating chorus of keening rose in the ether that connected her to others like her. Every inch of her skin, her organs, her being throbbed in agony.

"Don't either of you touch me."

"Rory, I…"

"It hurts. Oh God, it *hurts!*"

"I don't understand." Again, Solaya reached for her, then withdrew. "Rory, please, tell me what's happening. I can't help if I don't understand."

"They're dead, but they're still dying, Laya." Aurora lifted her face and let the full impact of her distress hit Solaya. "They're not the first. They're all still out there *dying*, and no one will make it stop, just let them be dead so the pain will *stop*. Laya, please, *make it stop!*"

A shriek of unbearable pain escaped her, causing Solaya to turn tear-filled eyes to Luc without thinking. "I can't… I don't know what's happening. Can you help her? Help her."

He shook his head, feeling equally helpless. Balanced on his heels behind her, he was already as close to Aurora as he dared get until he could figure out how to touch her without hurting her. "I need to know what's happening first." He framed the crown and back of her head with his hands, not quite touching her energy field. "If she ever had any shields, they're gone, and she has no filters." He glanced sharply at Solaya. "She's taking in everything anyone throws off. Is she empathic?"

Solaya nodded. "But I always thought it was limited to the kids she works with. The ones who can't communicate with or talk to anyone else. I don't think she even realizes what she does."

Luc frowned. "She doesn't know she has abilities? You never told her?"

"We told her as much as we thought she could handle." Solaya's jaw worked. "That she's unique, special. That once she learned to accept and harness her energy, she'd be capable of doing things other people can't. That…" She looked at Aurora, who was still rocking with pain. "She didn't believe most of it, and she's never done anything remotely like this."

"So, nothing like, say, throwing someone across a room without touching them. Nothing like dusting you back with a gesture. Nothing like…" His hands brushed the faint glow of Aurora's shrunken aura. Pulled back when she stiffened, as though him simply touching the atmosphere an inch from her skin hurt her. His lips thinned. "Nothing like sending her already depleted energy almost six hundred miles to help out your brother when he calls for a healing team?"

Neon Boneyard, Las Vegas

Senn stared at the yellow blanket of energy that covered the small bodies like a quilt. He'd only ever seen Aurora generate this kind of presence and passion when she danced, and then it simply radiated from her, showering vitality upon her audience. But that generosity of spirit was tempered by joy, colored with the discipline of choreography. It didn't shriek with pain and protectiveness and the sound of a soul shattering beyond repair. *Holy freaking Mother of God, what the hell?*

"Rory?" he whispered. He'd known that when her abilities finally manifested, they'd be out-of-control awe inspiring, but this…

Damn. This was dangerous. This was…

He blanched as realization hit. His honorary baby sister was working on instinct alone. She couldn't have any idea she'd sent the majority of her life force here, to the bodies of these children, instead of fully returning to her physical self when she'd reached out with her whole spirit to protect them. If she didn't withdraw the bits she'd left behind…

"Shit, *Rory!* Please," he exclaimed.

He slammed to his knees and spread a helpless hand over the intense hues that belonged to Aurora alone. He had so much power and magic at his disposal except when it counted for someone he loved. For this, he had nothing. *Nothing.* From six hundred miles away, he could not teach her to undo something he'd had no idea was even possible. He'd heard of astral travelers leaving their physical bodies and getting stranded when something or someone else moved in or borrowed the unprotected flesh. He'd never heard of anyone who was able to parse out pieces of her energy in order to send a single part so far from home while leaving a physical, sentient presence behind.

"Rory, you've got to go back. I can't help you do that from here. Please, Rory, no one can help these kids now, you've got to withdraw—"

The phone in his pocket buzzed. He started to reach for the Bluetooth receiver, before realizing he'd removed it when he couldn't get Solaya out of his ears. Cursing, he whipped out the phone, tapped it on, and pressed it to his ear. As he did so, the hand he'd raised above Aurora's aura involuntarily dipped and made contact with it. As thick and tangible as gel, it oozed over his fingers, up his wrist, and clung. Horrified and afraid to remove his hand lest he strip necessary substance from Aurora herself, Senn stared at the auric discharge as he spoke into the phone.

"Laya?"

"Senn, it's Rory—"

An agonized scream broke the air in stereo, coming not only through the phone at him but from the gelid substance around his hand. He jerked, and the keening cry went higher, harsher, making his skin crawl to get away from it even as he forced himself to go still and calm. The shriek's intensity subsided to a tortured sob on both sides of the connection. Grimly, Senn watched the matter encasing his hand turn a muddy, sulfuric yellow tinged with dirty white and gray.

"Senn." Solaya's apprehensive voice filtered through to him once more. "It's Rory, and I don't—"

"She's here, Laya," he told his sister bleakly. Guilt battered a painful *You should have taught her how to protect herself years ago* tattoo against his conscience. "I've never seen anything like this. I can't help her either. Put Luc on. He's going to have to psi up and pull her back."

Luc, however, was having his own problems. He'd never been anything remotely resembling human, but the keening sound of Aurora's pain triggered something primitive in his brain. Some instinct told him to protect what was his, find what threatened her, and kill it.

The psi vamp in him only wanted to make it stop.

Folding himself over her in an effort to reinforce her psychic shields with his, he'd wrapped his arms about his head the moment her cries ratcheted into the higher octaves. The pain in his skull, through every nerve, was paralyzing. If she didn't stop soon, his brain would implode and leak out his ears, but he couldn't move away from her. She needed help—he had to give it.

When Aurora's agony notched down to tormented sobs and whimpers, Luc raised his throbbing head to look at Solaya. Frightened, she stared back, jaw working as she gripped her phone.

"Senn says you have to psi up and pull her back," she told him.

Luc started to shake his head but winced. Any movement intensified the ache, caused nausea—which he'd never experienced before. He didn't want to imagine what Aurora was experiencing.

"I don't know if I can," he whispered. "I don't know if there's enough left to pull back. Ask him—"

Underneath him, Rory stiffened and cried out. Luc moaned and crouched lower over her. If he could get himself to put his hands on her, he might be able to draw off some of her pain, take it into himself—*psi up*, as Solaya put it—and literally carry a portion of the weight in a non-physical fashion. But touching her might also do more damage, send her deeper into the raw misery that already appeared to be destroying her by increments.

"Aurora," he murmured, "you've got to help me help you. I can't do this if I don't know what's happening... *Augh!*"

The breath hissed painfully from his lungs when Aurora suddenly opened her eyes, threw up her hands, and gripped his face so that her fore- and middle fingers dug into his temples. He was barely able to think *Vulcan mind meld* before he found himself looking into eyes that had gone all-pupil black. Then it was as if she somehow dragged him into their deep-space emptiness and he *saw...*

At first, there was nothing but a cold, menacing darkness—an undulating, fluid, jet silk of nothing.

There was no sound, but he felt the void as pressure against his ears, experienced it in the suffocating weight of a thousand universes pressing down on his chest, and squashing the air from his lungs.

Then a web of lights swept around him, a million stars strung together by a lattice of spider silk. They winked in and out of the emptiness in hues of amethyst, pale rose, and brilliant, clear quartz. Crisscrossed around the globe that cocooned him, converging at a single, radiant flash of color that sparkled with pink and yellow, violet, and a translucent white. He could feel that glimmer calling to him, protecting him, binding him…

Belonging to him.

His sunshine against the darkness, his warmth and salvation, his—

Abrupt awareness followed by fear seemed to cleave his soul in two. *Aurora*. And then he felt her—exposed, screaming, fingers bleeding and raw as they scrabbled for purchase against the metaphysical cliffside over which she'd been pitched. He gasped and clawed his own way to the edge of the vast vacuum—

Where he plummeted abruptly out of the teeming nothingness into the hell where dead children screamed.

Chapter Four

There are two important schools of thought when it comes to psychic vampires. The first, from the psis themselves, is that they are misunderstood creatures who are not nearly as bad as the reputation they've been given—especially when they are fully awakened to their energy sucking natures. Their rationale is that energy of all kinds vibrates within and around "lesser mortals," and much of that energy is unforgivably negative; it must be siphoned off if an individual or group of individuals is to survive and thrive. The second school of thought comes from the angels, psychics, psi-ops teams, and healers called upon to deal with the horrific side effects of an untrained, unethical, or simply gluttonous psi vamp's feeding habits. That school of thought can be summed up in five words: Just Say No to Psi Vamps.

—from *The Lightway Codex, Chapter 4: The Ekoa Krillu and Psychic Vampires* by McCleron O'Connell, Indigo Lightworker

Luceire Garard had been around since the dawn of man, give or take a day out of the original Biblical seven that the Book of Genesis suggested it took the Creator to fashion the world. In that time, he'd witnessed everything from his own Fall, to the births of Christ, Muhammad, and Buddha, death, religion, fanaticism, and destruction. He'd whispered in the ears of those who'd produced Holy Scripture, including the Talmud, the Bible, and the Qur'an. He'd experienced every emotion known to humankind and then some, participated in events of great joy and those of sorrow. He had, in short, lived more lifetimes than anyone should have to. He'd seen and felt everything—or so he'd thought.

He was, of course, wrong. He realized that the moment he'd entered Aurora Montgomery's studio and she'd psychically thrown him out. That had never happened to him before. But that event was nothing to the help-lessness and horror she dragged him into now. Everything she suffered, he suffered, too. What she saw, he witnessed. In gray scale and sepia tones, he could see Senn and the pitiful remains he knelt over. Saw in vivid, high-defi-nition color the bilious gel-like substance that blanketed the too-still forms and oozed around Senn's hand and forearm.

It was then that Luc discerned the long strands of dirty, clotting color attached to the children like umbilical cords. Visible only on the etheric plane, the tethered lines appeared to slurp power directly from the souls trapped within the children's lifeless bodies. What precisely trapped the spirits and prevented them from crossing the veil after death, Luc couldn't tell. That their souls remained imprisoned on this plane was clear. Which left the children, in Aurora's words, "dead but still dying"—horrible, drawn-out deaths that allowed the parasitic thing that had killed them to continue to feed.

Similar tap-like lines had attached to the fluid, sunny yellow substance Luc knew was part and parcel of Aurora. The ropey strands were slowly infecting the auric material, spreading filth through it as they milked the life from her, as well.

A distant part of Luc wondered if he could follow the siphons back to their source, or if it would be better to simply cut the cords from here. But that would mean severing the dark energy that not only bound the chil-dren's spirits within their lifeless shells but fed directly from the substance that contained Aurora's self, too.

Something primitive twisted in Luc's gut. He didn't know how to stop this from his position on the plain Aurora had dragged him into, but he could not let this thing happen. Could not allow the children's spirits to suffer at the whim of the beast that would use and keep them like cookies in a jar to snack on a little at a time.

Could not allow the monstrous filth to infect and wipe out the extraor-dinary light that was Aurora Montgomery.

From a great distance, he heard himself roar. Without giving himself time to think about *how* it should be accomplished, Luc reached through the ether as though wielding a knife and simply sundered the children's and Aurora's connections to those life-robbing tubes.

Instantly, the children stopped screaming.

For the merest hint of a breath, Luc saw Senn start in surprise as the viscous yellow stuff blanketing the children and his hand brightened for a moment and ebbed away. At the same time, and somewhere not *here*, he felt Aurora quiver, go rigid then deathly still. Then he felt washed in ice. Slid backward into the overwhelming darkness of the void he'd traversed with her to reach Senn and the corpses.

Then that link too dissolved, and Luc was flung violently out of the murky plane onto the floor of the San Francisco studio where Aurora lay limp and heavy across his lap, her cornflower blue eyes wide open and unseeing.

A stinging slap and Solaya's frantic "*Luc!*" brought him back into the frame. Sucking in a heavy breath, he lifted his gaze from Aurora's still form to the sorceress's frantic face. It took a moment for his eyes to fully focus, his brain to process not only what he saw, but sensed.

In the flick of an instant, he slid Aurora flat onto the floor, placed the back of his hand near her mouth. She wasn't breathing. Quickly, he checked for a pulse at her neck and wrist, felt for a heartbeat. *Nothing.*

Emptiness filled him. In seemingly less time than it took to cross a street, he'd found her and lost her.

"Rory," Solaya sobbed, dropping to her knees to touch her friend's cheek. Then steel replaced grief. She looked at the air above Luc's head, made a snatching gesture at an insubstantial *something* that seemed to have coalesced there. "Aurora Jane Montgomery, get the fuck back into your body this instant, or I will whack your heart into next year to start it."

Startled, Luc tilted his gaze upward, caught sight of a faint, amorphous, mustard yellow shadow lurking above him. His wandering faculties snapped together in a flash as realization struck: Aurora wasn't dead, just…

Disconnected from the incorporeal lifeline that tethered her spirit to her body.

Astral warriors and travelers utilized the otherworldly bond to keep the spirit connected to the physical self. Like Hansel and Gretel's breadcrumbs, the bond ensured the out-of-body traveler a safe and easy return when the trek was finished. While the traveler was "away," it also acted to protect the body against uninvited takeover. An inexperienced traveler—or one shaken involuntarily from the body by shock or trauma the way Aurora had been—sometimes lost the thread. The road home was more difficult then, sometimes requiring external help to prevent the temporary out-of-body experience from turning into a more permanent one.

This in mind, Luc bent and placed his lips against Aurora's ear. "If you don't follow my voice back into your body right now," he told her firmly, "I'll be forced to kiss you until you *wake up*"—this last said as he reached up and stuck his hand into the shadowy mass hovering above his head—"which will probably be painful for me, because"—he glanced once at Solaya, then brought his hand down with a hard *thwack!* to the center of Aurora's chest that made her entire frame jump—"you don't impress me as the Sleeping Beauty type."

For an instant, the studio was still as both he and Solaya held their breaths. Then with a harsh gasp, Aurora jerked upright, flailing wildly. Gulping as though air had never tasted so good, she slumped, weeping, against Luc's chest.

"Thank you," she whispered. "Thank you."

Unable to help himself, Luc wrapped his arms around her even as he eyed Solaya over the top of her head. "Tell Senn he'll need the forensics retrieval unit. Those bodies need to be fine-toothed."

Solaya shut her eyes for a moment but lifted the phone to her ear. "What happened"—she waved her free hand—"out there?"

Luc shook his head. "When I sort it out, you'll know." He scrubbed his chin over the top of Aurora's head to get her attention. She mumbled something unintelligible through her tears, wrapped a hand in his shirt front, and fitted herself deeper into his embrace. His face softened. "We should get you home," he said. "Where are your street clothes?"

She gestured toward a door to the right of the entry with a sign on it that read LOCKERS. With a glance at Solaya, he eased Aurora aside and headed in that direction.

"Tonight, you sleep," he told her. "Tomorrow, we need to do something about protecting you from yourself."

"Don't you need a bigger car, all the crap you carry?" he asked Solaya thirty minutes later after they'd closed up her studio and gotten into the sorceress's

Mini for the drive home. They'd all be more comfortable in his kitted-out Range Rover, but Solaya had declared she couldn't be without her car, and since he was the interloper, tough beans.

Solaya gave him a toothy smile in the rearview mirror. "It carries anything and everything I want it to."

Luc grimaced, his big body hunched and contorted deep into the backseat with Aurora, his head and neck bent at an odd angle against the Mini's roof, and his legs angled awkwardly sideways across the vehicle. "Great." Clearly, Solaya's magic didn't want the car to carry *him*. He shifted beneath Aurora, trying to find a better position for his legs.

"What did you mean, protect me from myself?" Rory's sleepy voice distracted him. "Laya and Senn have been trying to do that for years, but nothing's worked. Something always"—she hesitated—"falls apart inside me and they have to start over."

"That's because no matter how much good meditation and focusing exercises do, they're not specifically geared at fastening *your* spirit to *your* body." He did his best to twist around so he could smile at her. "You're not like the other kids, Aurora."

"Rory," she said automatically. "And I know I'm not, never have been, let's not dwell on it. Also, not telling me *how* you can fix me." She turned to place a hand on the side of his neck, instantly relieving the crick developing there. "You're not comfortable back here, so why didn't you take your own car and just follow us?"

Luc regarded her silently. Because he didn't want to let her out of his sight now that he'd found her, that was why. He needed to look after her, keep her safe, almost as much as he needed to get on with his mission. Knowing this about himself and reconciling it with the less than cooperative aspects of his personality—like the part that said he had to be glued at the hip, *guard her at all costs, you moron*—was going to take some doing.

"Because you need a keeper," he told her dryly and shifted a foot so it kicked the back of the driver's seat, "and the witch isn't it."

Solaya started to flick a middle finger arcing with witchflame over her shoulder at him, but Rory leaned forward and swatted the back of her head. "Drive," she told the sorceress. "Semantics later." She switched her attention back to Luc. "Explains nothing," she told him peevishly. "I want specifics."

In spite of his discomfort, Luc grinned. Aurora Montgomery was nothing if not direct. "Runes," he said. "I'm going to tattoo you with runes."

"Tattoo?" For a moment, horror wrinkled her brow. Then she sighed and sagged tiredly against him. "Sorry, daddy," she whispered, yawning. Then to Luc she said, "Okay. If you promise it'll work. When?"

"As soon as possible," he said, but she was asleep.

It was almost dark before they reached the house that had been in the Lawton family since it was built in the mid-nineteenth century.

Located on Alamo Square, it was a tall, narrow, forest green Victorian with a first floor that started below ground level and a square, turreted attic awash with light from the windows that ran along all four sides. The front windows on the walk-up main floor were currently covered with a white bedsheet with the words NO TO HOMELESS FEEDING FOR ALAMO SQUARE spray painted on it in black.

Seeing the sign, Luc found himself grinning. It didn't take a genius to figure out who'd put up the sheet. Even for the brief but freakily intimate amount of time he'd known Aurora Montgomery, he recognized her handi-work. He shifted her restlessly sleeping form higher in his arms and glanced sideways at Solaya. She winced tiredly, grumbling something about "people who hang their agendas on bedsheets" that made him smother a laugh.

"Damn it, Rory," she said. Solaya's housemate had opinions when it came to local politics and expressed them freely—usually against both her and Senn's advice. Solaya wasn't sure if the current statement advocated against a recent move to pay homeless residents to move into shelters in exchange for them acting as live blood donors to sanguine vampires or if it referred to the alternatively suggested movement to allow the blood-feeding Dugo Balang free run of the parks after dark in an effort to keep down the homeless populations that inhabited them. Solaya had an idea that Rory was against both suggested programs, but *for* one that would collect and distribute still-good food that was scheduled to be disposed of by local restaurants. But with both sang and psi vampires infiltrating local watch groups and municipal councils, food distribution was the least likely to pass.

Rory's willingness to display her political colors made it difficult to guard her against the plethora of things starting to go bump in the city. "We agreed. Have you no sense of self-preservation?" Solaya asked.

Aurora blinked sleepily and tapped a middle finger against Luc's chest.

Solaya heaved an exaggerated sigh that belied the look of concern she cast from her friend to Luc. He returned the look with a shrug and a tip of his head at the door.

"Right," she said and unlocked it. She pushed it wide and stood aside to usher him and his burden inside. "Living room to the left."

He nodded and slipped sideways through the indicated doorway. Dark hardwood floors and framing met him on the other side, absorbing the last of the daylight that still filtered through the large front and side windows. A glance showed him the heavy leather sofa and chairs scattered comfortably around a Persian area rug stretched in front of a hearth on one side of the room. On the other side, another Persian carpet sat beneath a large coffee table that appeared to be made from a slice of redwood. A flat-screen television hung on the wall in front of the table, a comfy-looking love seat and chairs around it.

Luc carried Aurora to the sofa in front of the fireplace and laid her on it while Solaya headed for the kitchen to find Aurora something to eat. Quickly, and as impersonally as possible, he stripped Aurora down to her cami and boy shorts. The thin fabric of her undergarments left even less to the imagination than what she'd been wearing at the studio, and his fingers itched to touch. To know. She grumbled at leaving his warmth and clutched his shirt to make him stay. Gently, he disentangled her fingers, grabbed a colorful fleece throw from the back of the couch, and covered her with it.

"Rest. I'll be back soon."

She offered him a crooked smile. "Yay, tattoos." Then, softly, "Who *are* you? You're so familiar, but I know we've never met."

With a twist of his lips and a troubled exhalation, Luc knelt and tucked the blanket around her shoulders and beneath her chin. "Just the guy Senn sent to you for help. Things…"

He hesitated, glanced up at the click of Solaya's heels as she paused in the doorway. Worry for Aurora and dislike of him radiated from her in such powerfully emotional waves that it was like being buffeted about in a ship at sea. The events in the studio had depleted his ready stores of energy, but he could not allow himself to succumb to the temptation to gorge on the emotional overflow without Solaya's consent. He shut his eyes and did his best to ignore her.

"Things got out of hand," he told Rory, turning to her. "I need your help, but we can talk about that later. Right now, you need to rest and get your energy back, and I need to feed."

She lifted a hand, made a vague gesture toward the back of the house. Movement lifted her scent into the air, sent it drifting into his nostrils and straight to his groin. "There's food in the kitchen. Solaya could—"

"No." Luc rocketed to his feet, damning the instant clutch of desire. "No. Thank you."

When she started to protest, he shook his head. "You need to rest," he said. "You'll do that better without a stranger in the house. I'll come back in the morning so we can get you tattooed and talk about why I came to see you."

Troubled, Aurora studied him a moment. "All right," she agreed. "If you're sure it can wait."

He licked his lips, trying not to taste the sleepy sweetness of her energy or give into the unexpected yearning to taste her chi again or his cock's plea for him to crawl under her blanket and sink into her.

Struggling not to hear again the souls of the children who lay amid the gaudy neon bones in Las Vegas crying out for death.

Reminding himself once more that until the woman on the couch could protect and replenish her own spirit, she could do no one, including herself, any good.

"I'm sure," he lied.

Without a backward glance he got the hell out of range of temptation.

Two hours later

The sense of something left undone zinged across her awareness and dragged Rory from sleep. Disoriented, she eased herself erect and warily looked around the almost unnaturally silent house. The events of earlier in the evening tortured the edges of her consciousness, filling her with sadness and loss. She hadn't been able to help the children—hadn't known *how* to help them—but *he* had. Rescued them and her by releasing the children's souls. By shielding her and drawing her back to the living when she would have followed the children…

Home.

The thought prickled at her awareness. She cupped the side of her head, massaged it with her fingertips. If *he* hadn't stopped her, she'd have let the essence of herself wander out into the astral ether in search of a home she didn't remember while her body died.

Home.

Without being fully aware of what she did, she closed her eyes and touched the air in front of her. Immediately, a three-dimensional image of the Earth appeared against the backdrop of her eyelids. She made a circling motion with her finger and a haloed grid appeared around the globe. A second flick of her finger filled the grid with star-like sparkles connected to each other by bright purple-white lines.

She tilted her head, spinning her finger to make the globe turn, watching the network's links as she did so. When she reached the western coast of the North American continent, she paused to study a feeble pinprick of illumination as yet unconnected to the grid. Weak lines of amethyst emanated upward, toward the crisscrossed global latticework as though *it*—whatever or whoever *it* was—was trying to link into the matrix.

A wave of dizziness struck as she watched the amethyst lines. She turned to press her face against a cool spot in the leather of the couch. An image of Luceire Garrard, looking frighteningly fierce, forearm lodged hard across the throat of someone she couldn't see, rose vividly in her mind. She drew a rough breath, then raised mental fingers to his savage features and stroked gently. He drew back, startled, loosening the pressure of his arm on his opponent, who disappeared before Rory could see who he was.

Again, her fingers whispered across Luc's brow, down along the bristly stubble that framed his jaw, brushed back his hair. Uncertainty crossed his face before he appeared to look directly at her for the space of several heartbeats. Then, as though he couldn't help himself, he shut his eyes and leaned into her feathery mental caress—turned his head and planted a kiss in the center of her palm, making it tingle.

Making *her* burn.

Panicked, Rory opened her eyes and jerked upright, severing the connection. Dear God, what was she doing?

She moaned at the recollection of her first sight of him. The memory of the kiss they'd shared when he'd tried to replenish her disintegrating energy with his sizzled through her. A spring coiled low in her belly, vibrating at the thought of his touch, and her veins pulsed with heat.

With a gasp, Rory clapped her hands together, shattering both the grid's image and her connection to it. Even so, he overwhelmed her senses, tortured her body to drenching wetness—she touched two fingers to a painfully puckered nipple and closed her eyes—and left it hanging, taut-strung and unfulfilled, begging for a release she'd never achieve on her own. Senn had said the children she'd tried to protect with her essence were only two of many who'd disappeared lately, and she…

All she could think about was having Luceire Garard come up behind her, put her on her hands and knees, and slam his hard, hot cock deep inside her. Ride her until she screamed from the pleasure.

Made her his vessel, his receptacle.

His.

With a whimper of frustration, she dragged a pillow over her face, trying to smother the erotic images. *He* wasn't there. Yet she could feel the imprint of him on her skin as if he were.

Groaning, she sank back into the buttery upholstery and crossed her legs, wrapped her arms over her breasts. The high-intensity clit-kit she'd given herself for her last birthday was about to get the workout of a lifetime, or she'd never be able to concentrate on anything important like those kids again.

Swearing, she rose on trembling legs and headed for the stairs to her bedroom.

Council of Light Regional Offices—ME, Forensics, and Pathology Suite
Carson City, NV

Celeste Fury ran both hands through her hair, turning the already spikey mass into short, spiny clumps. Frustration and anger marred her delicate Asian features, flattened her mouth into a grim, determined line. She was used to giving orders that brought about results. She was not used to waiting for the Council of Light's crypto-forensic enigmalogist to figure out What The Hell Went Wrong.

Expression grim, she eyed the bodies lying on Keile Raeburn's gurneys, then glanced at Senn, who acted as the liaison between the Council of Light and the Brotherhood of Shadows, and who'd found and escorted the dead children from Las Vegas. She'd issued the kill order on the "new" and "special" young humans in order to prevent this…travesty.

If the Nightkeepers had done their jobs, none of these children would have suffered the horror of having their souls trapped inside their lifeless bodies. They'd simply be dead, their parents would be able to bury them and mourn them properly, and the morgue gurneys would be empty.

"How many does this make?"

"Nine."

"*Nine?*" Celeste stared at him. "Whiskey Tango Foxtrot, Lawton?" No one outside of the allied congress's chambers knew she'd issued an order to slaughter the special ones. Neither Lawton nor Raeburn had been party to that meeting. "We're supposed to be keeping an eye on these kids, keeping them safe. Where are their guardians? Who was watching them?" *And why didn't the Nightkeepers get to them first?*

"I don't know."

"Find out," Celeste snapped. "I want heads on plates." She cast another glance at the children on the tables, and flinched. She'd issued the order to the Brotherhood's black ops Nightkeepers in service to The Greater Good, but the result wasn't supposed to look like this. Anguish and remorse filled her, but she couldn't back down now. Her voice was hard and determined. "I also want the who, when, why"—her voice turned ugly—"and most of all, *how.*"

Senn nodded, jaw working. Something was off with the Council's leader. Looking at her gave him the impression that however real her anguish might appear, her tears would be better suited to crocodiles.

Keeping his suspicions to himself, he turned when the Council's enigmalogist shut his eyes and flattened his hands, palms down, about three inches above each child. Head tilting back and forth as though listening to something no one else could hear, Keile passed his hands along the bodies, feeling, Senn knew, for whatever residual energy the killer might have left behind. Like fingerprints, auric signatures were unique to an individual. Once identified, Keile would not forget the idiosyncratic characteristics. Senn had once seen the *mal'akh*, or messenger angel—in this case, one well-versed in the forensics of both the human and spiritual planes—create a profile and near-photo quality image of a rogue blood sucking Dugo Balang from a lingering impression picked off a cadaver.

Such was not to be the case this time.

"I'm sorry." Lips tight, Raeburn looked from the bodies to Celeste and Senn. "There's nothing, not even a remnant of the spirit Senn described."

He tapped the steel table. "It's as though someone or something wiped away all trace."

Celeste eyed him sharply. "How is that possible?"

"I'm not certain."

Keile raised a brow at Senn, who shrugged. "No idea. Solaya was aggravated when I spoke with her. I don't think she's sure what happened, either."

Between them, the gurneys that contained the children's bodies rattled.

Eyes bright with anger, Celeste blinked at them. Again, Senn received the impression of more going on behind the cherubim's dark eyes than she wanted him to twig to.

"Gentlemen, I suggest you work this out, pronto. These children would be better off dead than lingering in this…limbo while God knows what feeds on them." She started toward the door with quick, angry steps. "If we can't prevent harm to the children entrusted to our care, we'd better find someone who can."

Chapter Five

Legend tells us of a being born of a union between a fallen angel and the seraphim he corrupted shortly after his descent from heaven. Born of corruption, this creature is thought to be both immortal and immoral; it thrives in shadows and darkness, and it should not exist.

—from *The Lightway Codex, Appendix i: Defining the Players* by McCleron O'Connell, Indigo Lightworker

After leaving the Lawtons' residence, Luc walked downhill away from Alamo Square in search of public transport. Troubled, he sought refuge from the blossoming streetlights in the deepening shadows of the trees and bay windows overhanging the sidewalks.

Aurora Montgomery disturbed him—*all* of him, physical, mental, emotional—that was all there was to it. What unsettled him even more was that Senn, her lifelong protector, had sent Luc the Fallen, the hell-kind, to her. Why?

She was light and airy, a creature of sunshine and song, a dancer who could—if the photograph Senn had given him was any indication—fling herself into the air and hang there longer than should have been humanly possible.

He, on the other hand, was a beast of darkness and shadow, born among angels and sent down by his own considered actions to dwell among devils. He had not wanted anyone, human or not, in more millennia than could be easily counted, but he wanted her. Craved her warmth, her light, no matter how badly her song, her radiance, could hurt him. And she *could* hurt him. Her abilities were raw and untrained, but she had more power in her fingertips than he'd ever dreamed of possessing. And he'd dreamed, once, foolishly, of becoming the equal of the Almighty who'd created him.

More uneasy than he'd ever felt, Luc caught a taxi for the Wharf.

Though most longtime San Franciscans avoided the touristy shops and attractions of the Fisherman's Wharf/Pier 39 area on the Bay, Luc loved it. It was a constant movable feast of free emotions, clatter, and sea lions. When he was troubled and drained, as he was now, it was his destination of choice.

Hands open at his sides, palms outward and fingers splayed wide, he moved through a huge crowd of teenagers dressed in party finery. They were giddy and restless, boisterous and eager, waiting to purchase ferry tickets to one of the islands. Careful not to touch any of them, he sipped gently at the overflow of emotions, letting his fingertips trace the air, gathering sensations. Within the throng, a group of boys laughed and joked, shoving each other about. Luc edged toward them, drawing off their excess energy before it went beyond simple rowdiness and exploded into something more. The boys calmed almost immediately without losing any of their animation and Luc moved on.

Ambient or "light" feeding was an unusual way for an Ekoa Krillu to sate his need for vital energy, but for Luc, it was both effective and restorative. As he'd done with the boys, he had the ability to abstract the surfeit emotion from a situation, whether that emotional glut was from a hostile mob or a euphoric one.

He preferred not to indulge in feeding on a crowd too often. Ingesting too much of a throng's energy, whether exultant or aggressive, tended to make him energy-drunk, and that made him dangerous. It was difficult enough sometimes to control his baser urges to extract the life out of those around him. The last time he'd been energy-soused, he hadn't bothered with restraint. He'd simply devoured.

Not far away, a street musician flooded the air with soulful jazz. Luc stepped inside the saxophonist's musical energy field, shut his eyes, and breathed in the music's power. It vibrated through him, heady and rejuvenating. When the musician finished the piece, Luc stepped up, chatted for a moment, then purchased each of the available CDs by way of thanks.

A movement deeper along the boards heading toward the sea lion docks distracted him. He paused, watching a hooded figure made shadow by both dusk and clothing. Like Luc, his hands were open, fingers splayed. Unlike Luc, he jostled into whomever passed, touching and grabbing in order to feed. Voices—loud, angry, and disturbed—washed his wake.

Luc's mouth flattened. For a moment, he watched the young psi vamp incite his victims into displaying the emotions he wanted to absorb—anger, trepidation, annoyance, fear. Negative emotions were stronger and therefore easier for both human and inhuman psis to feed on. The stronger and more overwhelming the target's response, the greater the high for the psi, the bigger the drain on the victim. It was unethical to feed this way, but Luc had seen it before among psychic vampires who either didn't realize what they were, or who refused to acknowledge the destructive aspects of their needs.

Ahead of him, the fledgling psi had latched onto a small group of what appeared to be college students and was toying with them. Clearly fed up with his taunts, a pair of young women peeled off and headed into a darkened passageway between closed shops. Luc flowed after them, knowing with certainty that this was what the other psi had been angling for: the headier rush of power brought on by an up close and personal encounter with the girls' fear.

Sure enough, the moment the girls reached the edge of the gloomy passage, the younger vamp went after them. Before Luc could reach them, the three of them were out of sight amid the murky shadows. He picked up his pace.

The short *shurh* of a spray pump, a vicious curse, and the sharp, agitated sounds of a woman soundly cussing out someone made him break out into a run. He skidded into the walkway in time to hear an unearthly growl issue from the other energy eater at the same time as he appeared to grow to twice his original size. Both girls screamed.

Shit, Luc thought, wincing when the cries battered the inside of his skull. The other energy eater wasn't a human crazy-maker type psi, which would have been bad enough from the victims' standpoint, but a full-on Ekoa Krillu monster like him.

Grabbing hold of the breeze off the Bay and twisting until he was part of it, he surged forward between one heartbeat and the next, grabbed the other psi, and threw him out onto the boardwalk.

"Run," he ordered the girls as the other vampire bounded to his feet.

"*My* souls," the 'Krillu shouted at Luc, striding after the retreating girls.

Luc got in his way. "No." He planted a hand against the other immortal's chest. "You've fed. Leave them."

The energy eater looked down at Luc from his manifested height. A nasty smile curved his mouth. "Or what?" he asked. "What will *you* do, human?"

"Stop you," Luc said—and sank his fingertips through the fabric of the younger psi's hoody and shirt, and into his skin.

Startled, the psi vamp looked down at where Luc's wrist protruded through his clothing. Then, with an agonized gasp, he deflated back to his normal size and staggered against the nearest shop window. Breath rasped in his lungs. His face tipped toward Luc's. "Who…*what*…are you?"

"Your master," Luc started to snarl but stopped when the other psi's hood slid aside and revealed his features. "Athan?" he managed before the past rushed forward and swallowed him whole.

Dr. Michael Beck prowled the Tenderloin, looking for fresh victims with which to feed himself and the Watchers. He tended to think of his ancestors as "waiters" rather than "watchers," since that's what they did—waited for him to feed them. Waited for him to give them new life. Waited, really, for him to resurrect them. Which technically made him more powerful than they were, even though who and what he really was needed to be enhanced by them. But he was patient. He could wait.

Laughing to himself over his unintentional pun, he looked around. Groups of people hung around outside several of the area's more popular taprooms, but he wasn't looking for professionals either schmoozing or shaking off the residue of a hard day. He wanted something special—a bar that would suit the evening's appetites. Any of the many vampire hangouts throughout the city would have welcomed him as Erra, the Akkadian plague god he pretended to be during his hunts. Privately, he loathed the posturing human "vampires" to which these bars and clubs catered. The only good thing he'd ever found about humans who defined themselves as vampires was their willingness to let him feed deeply and often intimately from them. After the energy he'd expended that day in his practice as a pediatric psychiatrist, however, he required something sweeter and more brutal than welcoming.

Given his muscular, blond good looks, the sort of prey he was after was usually easy enough to acquire. Tonight, however, he wanted the kind of violently orgasmic, sexual feed that was best found in anonymity and conducted in private—especially when the sort of partner he sought was sure to be less than willing. A college bar filled with virginal freshmen would have suited his needs admirably. Virginal first years or even high school students with fake IDs who were out slumming for the first time would be even better. For both him and the Watchers he fed.

Filled with purpose, he crossed the street and headed for Blood Simple, a vampire hangout that did double duty three days a week as The Voodoo Roost, a New Orleans-inspired jazz club that inhabited the space Tuesdays, Fridays, and Saturdays. On Mondays, Wednesdays, and Thursdays, Blood Simple catered to the under twenty-ones but unintentionally specialized in students from all-girl schools. Beck didn't mind the occasional boy virgin—they were singularly delicious in their arrogant "take but can't get taken" attitudes—but uncorrupted girls contained something indefinably special: a place to plant his seed.

Impregnation allowed him to feed on the innocent from both within and without. Brutalizing their bodies as well as their emotions by turning sexual consent into terrified subjugation provided him with a meal that could sustain him for days. Getting his conquests with child at the same time granted him continued access to their minds and psyches, permitted him to feed on them for nine months at a time—or until they terminated the pregnancy.

Planting his sperm in their untried bodies was like coupling a live feed directly from them back to him. They couldn't shake the thought of him and the horror he'd caused, which meant they thought of him constantly, sending their anguish his way. If they carried to term and survived the birth of his issue, they were his for the life of his spawn, irrevocably tied to him by things over which they had no control. Together, a little at a time, he and his offspring would consume them.

He reached Blood Simple. As usual, there was a queue of eager wannabes outside waiting to be selected for entry. Most nights, they'd all get in—eventually—but cruelty and anticipation were part and parcel of the vampire mystique. A little desperate uncertainty never hurt anyone.

Unless Erra was around.

Sliding effortlessly into his assumed persona as the plague god—it was amazing what a little eyeliner and some pancake makeup did to disguise an identity—Beck slithered along the logjam, occasionally brushing against one or another of the wishfuls. So intent were they on admission to the club that most didn't notice him. The few who did edged closer, drawn to his aura of tormented hunger, the vampire mystique he wore with practiced ease. He smiled mockingly at them, showing a hint of expensively sharpened fang in the process, and moved on. Looking only for underage girls who smelled fertile.

When he'd finished casting his net, he returned to the club's narrow entrance. With a nod to the bouncer, he slipped inside.

Savitri Nousaine's attention sharpened the moment Dr. Beck switched directions toward Blood Simple. Smiling, he relaxed in the backseat of his limousine for the late evening drive to his home in San Francisco's Cow Hollow/Pacific Heights district. The smile widened when Beck chose a boy and two girls from among the adolescents and college freshmen waiting in line. So, it was to be one of those nights, was it? Excellent. He'd feed well, if distantly, on the reactions the sociopathic psychiatrist elicited from his prey as he led them down the garden path to—

Nousaine straightened at the sense of something new in his protégé. Beck intended to suck the life out of one of the girls and the boy—to kill them outright and feed on their terror as they watched each other succumb. The extreme emotional effect the first two deaths would generate in the other girl should be enough to feed Beck and every psi around him for a fortnight or better, especially if he held her captive for a day or two, forcing her to anticipate the final curtain drawn on her short life.

Disturbed, Nousaine sat back. Rummaging around in Beck's psyche was too often akin to wandering down a dark alley without a flashlight. He didn't object to Beck killing human cattle—far from it. It saved him from having to go out and find his own victims for at least another day or two. But taking and killing too many youngsters from the same club on the same night was foolish. The deaths would not and could not be overlooked in the same way homeless fatalities might be, unless…

Through his darkened passenger window, Nousaine watched the city's lights wink on as the night got deeper. Though of Nephilim descent, Beck was more human than Repha'im, the product of generations of adulteration of another, long-entombed species—the Watchers. Despite the many talents that had caused the master Ekoa Krillu to promote the doctor as his second, Beck's worst human characteristics were cause for concern. He was without conscience, hungrier and more ruthless than the full-blood fallen Luceire had ever dreamed of being.

In simple human terms, Beck was a sociopath, born and not made.

He was not, of course, Luceire's equal in either intelligence or power, but normally Beck's proclivities suited Nousaine well. Just not quite so much all in one night. It was unfortunate, but Beck would have to be stopped—or at least strongly encouraged to spread his feeding about.

Nousaine had just flicked on the limo's intercom to tell his driver to change direction and take him to Blood Simple when a waft of taint filtered through the vent on that side of the car. Movement arrested, he turned toward it and sniffed.

The taste of corruption soiled the membranes of his parted lips and tongue, made him gag. Eyes narrowed, he twisted, trying to get a bead on the direction from which the pollution came. Within seconds, he'd pinpointed the location—Alamo Square, Lawton residence, the girl.

Once again, he tasted the vent's draft then hit the button to lower his window in order to sample the breeze directly. The same tang smacked him in the face, sickening him.

Someone had tampered with—and contaminated—Aurora Montgomery's energy, coating it in a protective barrier. Someone like…

Fury filled Nousaine. He tasted the wind again. Yes, he was correct. The arrogant bastard had interfered with his food source.

Beck's activities forgotten, Nousaine turned his senses to the night. This time, he would find Luceire Garard and kill him permanently.

"Athan?"

Uneasy, Luc stared at the son he hadn't seen since shortly after the Great Fire of London. Though history said differently, Luc had long suspected Athan had had a hand in starting that tragic blaze. The fire was only one of many reasons Luc and another member of the Brotherhood of Shadows had captured Athan. Like his father, Athan could not be killed. That hadn't stopped Luc and the Brotherhood from ritually imprisoning Athan in an iron-wrapped coffin in the North Sea.

Half seraphim, half fallen, Athan was a creature that should not exist. The product of Luc's successful effort to tempt and seduce his mother, Sophiel, Athanarius carried attributes inherited from both his parents. He was brilliant and mercurial, dangerous and cunning, deceitful and honest in one—a great deal like Mephisto, the cherubim's highest-ranking member, before arrogance and rebellion led to the fall. Neither creature had an ounce of humanity in him.

Luc had been a ranking warrior member of the Order of Principalities and Powers, many of whom had deserted heaven with M—as Mephisto was better known—before he'd been cast into the abyss to become more than human, less than divine. Athan was Luc's greatest regret and ultimate motivation in his quest for salvation. If he could somehow save himself from perpetual damnation, he might also be able to save his son.

"What are you doing here?"

"Feeding." Athan raked him a scornful glance. "I would have thought that was obvious, given you're here for the same purpose...*Father.*"

Luc's mouth flattened. Three and a half centuries with no contact and they were still parent and teenager going at it, tooth and nail. At what age did a child finally outgrow the need to best the parent—or did he?

Of course, Athan's predilection for death and violence didn't help.

Bearing that in mind with the fact there were hundreds of mostly innocent humans about, Luc said, "What are you doing in San Francisco?"

Athan nodded in the direction his prey had gone, twisted Luc a grin, and shrugged. "Feeding. Great city for it—so much fresh emotion. Intense." He pointed his chin at Luc. "I wouldn't think it'd be much to your taste."

Luc stared at him without responding. His fingertips itched. He pulled his hands slightly away from his sides and let the prickly sensation coalesce into something he could read. Insight was swift. Athan was here for more than a night on the town—not in itself a major revelation. Tilting his head, he read his twice-cursed son. Athan smiled and nodded.

He was after Aurora Montgomery, too.

Wrath skidded through Luc. Before he was aware of moving, he pinned Athan to the walkway walls and planted a forearm across his throat. "Not one inch toward her," he said.

Athan's rough laugh sandpapered Luc's face. "I guess now we know what punches your buttons, don't we," he wheezed.

Ignoring the taunt, Luc leaned on Athan's windpipe as he bent forward to snarl directly into his ear, "Not one inch or I will kill you."

"You might have to," Athan rasped back—and grinned.

Disquieted by the cavalier amusement and underlying tone of "*Well, if you must,*" Luc relaxed his hold on Athan's throat. Laughing, the creature his son had become slid out from underneath his sire's forearm and was gone.

A few miles across town, Aurora Montgomery dashed up the stairs in her sleep.

Fleeing the flickering images and panicked whispers of children crying out to her even in death, her somnolent body launched itself up the three flights of stairs to her tower garret, skidded into the center of the hardwood floor, and began to stretch, twirl, spin, gyrate—fold into supple, impossible shapes, and then leap free.

Around her sparkled the same earthly sphere formed by the interconnecting matrix she'd drawn Luceire Garard into that afternoon. Voices—loud, soft, muted by distance—swirled around her in the grid. Face twisted in horror, she occasionally paused in mid-spin to put the tip of a forefinger on a web-like connection, cocking her head to listen before twirling on.

When the ceiling began to feel too low, the space too confining, her still-sleeping form flung itself back to the first floor and out the front door, down the steps, out through the wrought iron gate, and across the street to the faery ring formed by a circle of spreading and slanted pine trees in Alamo Square Park. The earth-shaped matrix-grid went with her, surrounded her, inescapable. Within the sphere's tangled lines, anguished voices pleaded with her to find them, rescue them.

Reckless and despairing, her body contorted, bare feet pounded the earth, gathered speed—ran gracefully up the tree trunks, using them as platforms from which to launch herself end over end in moves both elegantly acrobatic and frenetically expressive.

Her feet bled, scraped raw by the rough bark, and the ring of trees grew too confining.

Frantic for space, for movement, her unconscious form flew across the park, past the vampires—both psi and sang, human and not—that fed on the homeless persons who'd slipped by the vigilant neighborhood watch and sheltered in the buildings on the playground.

Hungry, but with blood-filled kine already in hand, the Dugo Balang and their human counterparts watched her go.

Hungry, but unsatisfied by the low-energy signatures the homeless sent off even while the sangs fed on them, the Ekoa Krillu and the human psis reached out and latched onto the burning spill of vitality she put off, gorging on it.

Weakened, she stumbled, picked herself up, and ran on, still sleeping.

Luc felt her nightmare panic the moment he left the pulsing energy sphere surrounding Pier 39.

"Fuck!"

The cabbie he'd hired to return him to his car in the Haight eyed him in the rearview mirror. He shook his head. "Forgot something," he lied. "Just drive."

He should have risked hunger and lust, should have stayed with her—should have covered her in protection sigils the moment he realized she'd never survive her own abilities without them.

She had to survive.

He *needed* her to survive.

Sometimes being earthbound but not the least bit human really sucked.

The voices in the network of violet lines waxed and waned as Rory ran, filtering down to a single strong, fearful murmur of *"Help me, please, somebody, don't let anything bad happen, find me,"* and a much thinner, staccato chant of *"I'm here…here…here."*

In an effort to escape both, Rory's feet instinctively carried her west and south, through Lower Haight and into Haight Ashbury, the length of the Panhandle. Within ten minutes, she'd arrived at the folding gate across the front of the building that housed her dance studio.

The gate was locked.

Still asleep, she fumbled wildly at her clothes. The skimpy boy shorts and flimsy camisole contained no pockets and no key. Hadn't she worn a coverup home from the studio? She didn't remember that—or being stripped out of it.

"Are you all right?"

The voice, unknown and sinister, slid underneath the veil of slumber and into her nightmare. She hooked her fingers into the edge of the gate's metal cagework and cringed into the overhanging shrubbery that framed the building.

"You must be freezing," the voice coaxed. "How about you come with me and we'll get you a blanket."

"*No.*" The word was half scream, harsh and unintelligible. There was something wrong with the suggestion, with the person behind it, but she didn't know what. "Stay away from me."

The voice came closer. Persuasion gave way to command. A hand wrapped her arm. "Let me help you."

"No." Guttural but firm. The muscles in her arm pulsed, and the stranger's bruising grip loosened and fell away.

"The hell?"

He looked at his hand, back at her. Something in him turned from sinister to predatory. His lips twisted in a parody of a smile. He grabbed at her again.

Fright vanished. The sleep-induced distortion left her voice. "Stay away from me."

Enunciated. Clear. A threat to be heeded.

He laughed and took a step into her energy field. Drew a breath and tried to suck in her vitality, leech it away from her. She opened and closed her fingers on the metal mesh, getting a better grip, then poured the strength of her dancer's body into her hand.

The iron grating grew hot and started to glow.

Fascinated, she looked at it, concentrated on it. Power coursed through her, into the spark of crackling radiance, slid along the black latticework and into the lock. With a soft *chink* it opened. The iron hinges creaked softly and the gate yawed. Her lips curved in triumph.

Against the night-dark backdrop of dream, she looked at her opponent. Threw both hands out toward him in a hard, mental *shove*. When nothing happened, he started to laugh—

Until Rory bared her teeth and repeated the motion, and he found his head hitting the cement block wall of the tapas restaurant across the street.

The taxi disgorged Luc on Haight at Shrader at the very moment the blond man with the shredded physique became a sack of potatoes striking concrete.

Like the few other late-night passersby, he gaped at the sight in momentary surprise. Then his lips twitched. He glanced down the street. As he'd anticipated, Rory stood outside her studio in the same insubstantial *Dancers Do It Better* camisole and skimpy pants she'd worn when he had pulled the fleece blanket over her.

There was something disconnected and uninhibited about her that made him think she was probably sleepwalking, but that clearly didn't matter. Conscious or not, her *sub*conscious had learned that particular move fast. He should have realized. If she could defend herself so emphatically from *him* when she was wide awake and oriented, she'd also be well equipped to champion herself from those who meant her harm when her inhibitions were on hold.

As long as she sensed the danger.

Moving forward, he watched her open the studio's gate then close her hand around the lock. The gate shut behind her when she moved to the building's door and cupped her fingers over that lock, as well. Within seconds, the door popped open to admit her. If he wasn't mistaken, she was channeling a controlled version of the power that had allowed her to fling both him and the blond guy away from her, using it to burst the locks then seal them behind her.

If she could do all of this while dream-walking, retrieving the child he'd been sent to collect should be a breeze—once said child was located.

The problem, as it were, in a nutshell.

He waited until Rory had slipped into the studio before crossing the quiet street to have a look at her latest victim.

Dr. Michael Beck's evening had been, in a word, delicious.

The two plump fifteen-year-old girls and the acne-spotted sixteen-year-old boy were clay for Erra's molding. After inviting them through a hidden door and into a Gothic-styled room not even the club's owner was aware of, he'd pulled a bottle of absinthe from the stash he kept on hand and suggested they all "taste the vampire difference." Trying for adult indifference even as his eyes went tellingly big, the boy said, "YOLO," and the girls agreed.

In his guise as Erra, Beck explained both the mind-liberating and transformational symbolism of the *la louche* ritual as he'd poured the liquor known as the green fairy into traditional glasses and balanced slotted spoons containing sugar cubes atop them. Then he'd perverted the time-honored ritual by pouring absinthe instead of iced water over the sugar cubes and lighting them on fire.

When he removed the spoon and raised his glass to his lips, they followed suit. The boy tried to copy him sip for sip while the prettier, heavier girl screwed up her face over the liquor's anise flavor, but drank up anyway. It didn't take much of the original recipe, hallucinogenic-imbued alcohol before the inexperienced adolescents were floor-wiping drunk.

It was then that he'd begun to toy with them, "accidentally" touching them in inappropriate places, teasingly chastising them if they shrank from his advances, and playing them off each other to see what might get a rise. As anticipated, the boy's emotions built first, turning him alternately aggressive and confused as he not only got drunk for what was likely the first time in his life, but also succumbed to the drink's mind-expanding effects. That was when Beck, as Erra, began to pursue him both sexually and psychically.

Clothing and modesty loosened quickly after that, and Erra feasted.

Later—when he was temporarily sated but the young still clamored for the pleasure of his attention, for the punishment and abuse he visited upon their bodies and psyches—he ushered them through another secret door into a disorienting warren of narrow alleys that ran beneath the club. In no time at all, he'd imprisoned them in separate, reinforced cells. They were tasty morsels and would grow even more succulent once they realized they were alone with no one to hear them scream. Tomorrow, or perhaps the next day, he would return to feed in earnest.

The minor uncertainty they were already beginning to feel underneath the drunken daze was heady.

Beck was surfing that confusion-enriched high when his drive home brought him within range of Aurora Montgomery's panicked flight into the Haight. Like the majority of other psi vamps in the area, he detoured to grab a taste.

The stench of the fair-haired man's origins and feeding proclivities reached Luc in nauseating waves, teasing the ever-present craving he'd only managed to take the edge off of by visiting the Pier. Psi but not 'Krillu. Human but not quite mundane. The athletic thirty-something stank of gluttonous psychic corruption—

And Savitri Nousaine.

In spite of himself, Luc recoiled and looked quickly about, tasting the air. Nousaine had a habit of personally keeping track of his chosen, especially after-hours when they stank of depravity the way this one did. The 'Krillu master was out there, alert and aware, but not nearby.

Close but no cigar.

He let his gaze rove the shadowy area, where vampires—both psi and sang, human and not—gathered in twos and threes. He understood why the psis had come. Aurora Montgomery's emotional leakage sparked his basest hungers, too. The blood locusts, on the other hand, disturbed him. Their presence meant she was probably injured and bleeding as well as spilling enough grief-stricken energy to power the city. He could handle the psis without problem. The sangs, however…

"Jinx?" He telepathically hailed his closest friend, Jinx Falken, a Dugo Balang who'd fallen from grace with him.

Almost immediately, and in typical Jinx fashion, a graphic novel dialogue balloon containing only a question mark appeared in Luc's mind. The corners of his mouth lifted as he replied, *"Locust problem, my location. Can you deal?"*

The derisive snort Jinx sent in response made Luc's grin widen. *"Fuckin' A."*

"Thanks." He waited until the first sang clutched his head in pain and reeled off into the night. Then he returned his attention to the well-built man who'd peeled himself off the sidewalk to stare curiously after Aurora. The interest raised Luc's hackles. His nerve endings sizzled with aggression. *No*, he thought possessively. *Mine!*

Territorial much? he asked himself derisively. Especially over a woman he barely knew.

You know her, body and brain argued. *Very*, very *well*.

In the long and short runs, it didn't matter how well Luc knew her. The blond scum who stank of Nousaine's depravity and a perversion that was wholly his own could not be allowed near the dance therapist.

A few swift strides took him into the street in front of Rory's building where he planted himself, feet spread, hands loose at his sides, a giant shield that would have to be breached before anyone got near *his* dancer. In response, the smaller blond man looked directly at him, then took three steps toward him. And grinned.

Junkyard dog, Luc thought. Anger at the conceit whispered along his nerve endings.

Don't, he cautioned himself. But dealing with Athan had depleted his energy reserves despite the overflow of vitality along the Wharf. Temptation pestered him. He bared his teeth. Reached out with a pulling gesture that gathered up the other man's chi and flung it into the night, all in one move.

The cluster of Ekoa Krillu and their human counterparts pounced on it like manna.

The blond man staggered. His knees buckled, taking him to the pavement. Hoarse laughter wheezed out of him as he regarded Luc, but he stayed down. "Keep her while you can," he rasped. "I'll be back for her—and you, too."

"That would be a mistake," Luc responded softly—and once more made a seizing and twisting motion with his fist at the air surrounding his opponent.

The other man went down flat on his face. This time, he did not get up.

Turning, Luc flicked the mass of tainted energy at the feeding psis and crossed to the security gate. A single, quick yank broke the solder-like seal open and allowed him in. Another swift tug and he was through the door.

Tomorrow—today—he would repair both locks, but tonight, the only thing that mattered to him was getting to Rory.

Stemming the flow of both her emotional and physical bleeding.

Making sure she was safe.

Chapter Six

According to what we currently know, "Crystal Children" are of the Divine. Part of their purpose is to form a psychic communication network. This crystal matrix is similar to a cyber-grid used to open or shut down various pathways of human interaction using thought transference—in this instance primarily to channel love and healing wherever they are needed. It is possible these "Crystals," as they are known, are examples of Darwin's theory regarding man's natural evolution. In any case, there is no denying these children are more than human.

—from *The Lightway Codex, Appendix i: Defining the Players*
by McCleron O'Connell, Indigo Lightworker

Even in her sleep, Rory felt him coming.

Fast and hard she danced, hurling herself from one end of the studio to the other in higher and more complex bounds. The floor grew distant, became ocean against the horizon, then rose up lightly to meet the soles of her feet. Fell away when she leapt again.

Hang time became flight as the voices in the lattice-worked communication matrix grew more insistent.

Twisting in the air, she dove for the burnished planking, somersaulted upright, and stretched into the next move. Sprang one-footed onto the plié bar, balanced for a moment, then hurdled off to wheel the length of the room. Swiftly, she ran up the cement block wall at the far end, and soared for the rafters. Hovered.

Just as some part of her was deciding whether to return to earth or remain aloft, *he* came in.

As he came toward her, massive but tattered black wings spread skyward from between his shoulders like the shredded sails of a pirate ship. Black jeans, tight black T-shirt, mahogany hair that appeared black in the dim light did nothing to alleviate the image of what he was.

Fallen. Irredeemable. Unrepentant.

Cursed.

Heat pooled between her thighs. The tang of her own desire filled her nostrils.

She wanted him.

His body inside hers, destroying the remains of her virginity. Filling her beyond her capacity to take more of him. Taking all of him anyway.

Riding her until she screamed and her body imploded. Until his exploded into her.

Again, and again and again.

Without thought, she reached for him—and fell.

He caught her, settled them safely back onto the studio's hardwood. "Rory."

Sighing, she folded her arms and legs about him—

And ceased to dream.

He meant to check her over, find out where she was bleeding before he did anything else. He meant to staunch the bleeding and take her home. He meant to be *good*, to be cool and impersonal, to be sheltering.

He meant to keep his priorities in order—to remember that members of the Brotherhood did not succumb.

When she wrapped her legs around him and ground her cleft against his arousal, he forgot all of it. Hell, he could barely remember she was in the throes of the most vivid and passionate parasomnia experience he'd ever witnessed. If he gave in to her body's fiery quest for sleepsex, the after-guilt for her would be unparalleled. She had no idea what she was doing—and wouldn't remember it in the morning in any case. He. Could. Not. Take. Her.

Could not give in.

When—if—they came together, he wanted her awake. Aware of every move in the dance they shared.

She drove a hand the length of his torso and into the waistband of his jeans. Before he could pull her off him, she'd found the head of his cock, stroked it. Without permission, it betrayed him. Went rigid and thrust into her curling fingers.

"God, *Rory!*"

Precum moistened her palm, lubricated his cock when she pushed deeper inside his briefs and rubbed. His shaft pumped mindlessly into her palm. Her hand tightened on the expanding member. Her body rose and sank against the swelling, saturating the front of his jeans with her wetness.

The scent of her arousal nearly drove him mad.

"Rory, *stop.*"

He might have been cast out of heaven and into the pit, but if he let this go where she was leading, he'd wind up confined to hell for sure.

She's in pain, his last shred of coherent thought suggested. *This is about Vegas, about the children. Feed, Luceire. Siphon away the dream so she can sleep…*

Listening to his own advice for once, he cradled her face and leaned his own down to hers. Planted his mouth on her avidly seeking lips. Breathed in her excess fear, her uncontrolled energy, as he gently brushed his fingers along her forehead and temple. Swept away the dense fog in her aura and cast it aside.

Her body went limp and heavy against him.

Three more passes and several more sipping breaths and her hold on him slackened. Her legs slipped from his waist. The hand in his pants curled laxly in on itself and withdrew, tucked itself beneath her chin. On a sigh of relief and regret, he skimmed his palm once more across her face.

Then he slid his free arm beneath her knees and sat down when he discovered it was her feet that were bleeding. He tore off his shirt, ripped it into strips, and wrapped her wounds. He wanted to wash them and coat them in antibiotic ointment, but that would have to wait.

Finished, he hoisted her against his naked chest. Walked out of the studio, and sealed the door and gate behind them.

A few 'Krillu loitered in the street outside. A look from Luc sent them fading into the darkness like cockroaches exposed to light. In a mood like this, he was dangerous, and they knew better than to mess with him—or anyone he claimed.

When they were gone, he carried Aurora to his Range Rover. Drove her home, put her to bed, and climbed in with her. Wrapped an arm around her and tucked her securely against him.

It was the only way to safeguard her from herself. And from *them*.

The Brotherhood and the Council. Psis and sangs. Blond bastard. Savitri Nousaine.

Him.

In her sleep, she spooned her perfect backside into his loins. They responded.

Luc groaned.

Perchance to dream but not to sleep…

For approximately three and a half hours, Rory slept like the dead—if the dead were able to butt-knock a guy's stick and balls every few minutes—and Luc slept not at all. Then she stretched awake, felt him behind her, shrieked, and fell out of bed.

From that, he surmised that she remembered nothing from her sleep-dancing episode.

Luc hadn't really expected her to. Hope was a different animal altogether, but he was used to working without it. No, it was the look of vulnerability and wariness with which she'd regarded him after crabwalking backward into a corner that made him feel like the serpent in the garden—or the poisonous snake someone had flung into her bed.

He didn't remember anyone ever undoing him with a look before.

He didn't like it.

And that was before Solaya had dashed in, gone all she-bear at finding him in Rory's bed, and tried to pitch him out the garret window. Before he'd said anything about wanting to look at Aurora's feet.

That was the point at which things got a little surreal—and he was *Fallen*, for pity's sake. "Surreal" was pretty much his middle name. But aside from a few already fading white stripes across the soles, Rory's feet were healed.

Solaya looked at him. "I thought you said they were shredded."

He gave her a flummoxed *don't ask me* look. "They were. But her…gifts… have manifested. I'm guessing this is part of them."

"But healing like this is…" Solaya searched for a way to put it but failed. "She doesn't have this kind of control yet."

"She did in her sleep." He shrugged. "Controlled, fine-tuned, used."

"*She* is right here. Not knowing what you're talking about. Explanations required."

Exasperated and now completely awake, Aurora jerked her feet away from them by hiking her knees under her chin and covering her toes with her hands. The move plumped her breasts into the armholes of her cami. It also caused her already scanty boy shorts to ride up, exposing more of her exquisitely toned rump than Luc's libido was able to withstand. His already denied and engorged cock swelled painfully against his fly. He winced.

Solaya socked him in the arm when he grabbed a pillow from the bed to cover his lap, then glowered at Rory. "No explanations until you're mummied up. I mean sleeves, baggy turtleneck, palazzo pants."

Automatic rebellion flashed across Aurora's features. "All grown up, Laya. I have a business, boobs, and everything—"

Catching himself looking at the display of said grown-up "boobs" spilling over the sides of her camisole, Luc choked.

"—and you're not my mom." She made a sound of disgust. "You're only two years older than me, for Pete's sake."

"I don't need me to be your mom, just your keeper," Solaya retorted. "Put something on before his eyes fall out and he strangles himself, 'cause that would be messy."

She strode out of the room when Aurora stuck out her tongue and Luc hung his head, laughing. "God, I need coffee," he said.

Fifteen minutes later, he sat at the Lawton kitchen table, a cup of extra dark brew at his left hand. Stickied across the table in front of him was an array of 3x5 Post-its on which he'd sketched the runes he planned to turn into tattoo stencils.

Already dressed to the nines in a lace-up, black leather bustier, a short red leather jacket and pants—practical, she said, for what she had to do that day—Solaya clacked about the room on six-inch stilettos shooting dagger-like looks at him. He did his best to concentrate on Aurora and ignore the sorceress's continued desire to dispatch him at once and with extreme prejudice.

It wasn't difficult. Across from him, Rory was beautifully sleep-tousled and haphazardly dressed in a brightly patterned, vintage silk kimono that kept falling off her shoulders to display the *Dancers Do It Better* camisole beneath.

The whole idea of "doing it" was one he couldn't eject from his head. Even though he'd managed to control himself last night, he was pretty damn certain that at least this dancer did—or would—*do it* better than anyone he'd ever done it with. Or considered doing it with.

Hell, he ached to do it right now.

Distracted by his wayward libido, he watched her sprawl forward to plant her chin on the table. Her fingers twitched toward one of his drawings and unstuck it from the surface. She scrutinized the Post-it. "What will tattooing me accomplish in real time?"

Unable to keep his mind on his work, he crumpled the sticky note beneath his pencil and regarded the object of his discomfort. "What?"

"Tattooing." Her restless fingers tapped arpeggios on the table. "Real world applications. Why does it have to be done?"

Drawn back to the task he'd set himself, Luc bit back a grin. She'd asked the same question in a variety of forms since he'd snatched the magnetic pad of Post-its off the refrigerator, picked out a pencil from a nearby basket, and started sketching. He'd given her the same cryptic response each time.

"Symbols carry power among the damned."

It wasn't the best answer, but it was the one he hoped she'd pay attention to until he could offer her a better one. But she kept asking.

"'Symbols carry power among the damned.'" She rolled her eyes. "What on God's green does that even mean?"

"It means that if you're going to astral project when you're not even aware of it, your body needs to be marked out of bounds so nothing…" He paused. "So nothing *uninvited* sees it as some sort of tacit invitation to"—he winced when she raised her brows—"make off with you. Writing something down makes it more tangible and permanent. Hell." He sighed, stumped for words. "I don't know how else to explain it, but you need to be able to—"

"For heaven's sake, Rory." Solaya stopped her incessant prowling and leaned across the table between them. "Someone needs to do something to keep you in your body and stop the astral you from wandering across the galaxy"—a glare at Luc—"or running through the city in your sleep."

Sputtering, Rory waggled a finger from herself to Solaya. "I—you— we… *You!*"

Solaya grimaced. "Yes, all right, okay, *me*. I didn't think it was time to tell you what was happening to you or to teach you how to work with your abilities. Senn thought we should. I won. My bad, okay? Can we get on with it?"

Rory stared at her. "You? Wrong? What a concept. Refreshing, but still."

Luc smothered a chuckle. Senn's sister admitting she was wrong about anything was a first in his experience.

Ignoring Rory, Solaya cupped a hand around a suddenly available ball of crackling pink-orange flame and scowled at Luc. "Don't. Say. Anything." She hefted the witch fire when he spread his hands wide in a pacifying "*who me*" gesture. "It might not kill you, but it *will* sting."

With a huff of annoyance, Rory smacked the ball of light flat in Solaya's hand, surprising them both.

Solaya's turn to gape. "When did you learn to do that?"

"In my sleep, I guess." Rory dusted her hands free of her friend's magic. "Like so many other things, according to you two."

"Yesterday, you had trouble acknowledging you might have special abilities. Today…" Solaya shook her head.

Aurora shrugged and pointed at her wrist. She didn't wear a watch, but the implication was clear. "Don't you have to be somewhere?" She sent a sideways, deliberately provocative glance toward Luc, and back to Solaya. "He's hot as sin, no lie, and there'll come a point where I want to jump his bones, but really, right now?" She flopped melodramatically across the table and looked sideways at Solaya. "Drained."

Solaya sent her a dirty look when Luc choked, spun out of his chair, and left the room. Short, sharp explosions of poorly stifled laughter filtered back to them from the front of the house.

"You are incredible," Solaya told Rory in disgust. "And *really* weird."

Rory grinned.

Mostly sobered, Luc returned and leaned against the counter. "I'd call her lethal," he said, lips twitching with amusement.

Solaya made a motion that effectively put his comment beneath her shoe. He grinned.

Ignoring him, she glanced at the stove clock. "Shit." She stuck a manicured red nail between her front teeth, gaze fixed on nothing while her eyes darted back and forth as she thought. She tapped a few more paces around the kitchen then scrutinized Rory anxiously. "I should go, but it *could* wait until Luc does your tats. You need a chaperone." She winced when Rory frowned at her. "Fine, someone to make sure you don't do anything you don't mean to." The younger woman's scowl deepened. Sighing, Solaya gave it up. "Fine. Keile has autopsy results." She looked at Luc. "You're supposed to be there, too."

Luc nodded. "As soon as possible." He glanced across the table at the woman whose aura, despite the outward show of silliness, was wrapped in disquiet. His fingers jerked toward her, wanting to comfort. Instead, he fisted them tightly behind him. *Too soon*, intuition whispered. *Don't spook her.* "Once the stencils are done, it shouldn't take more than two or three hours to do the tattoos. Then we'll both be there."

Solaya regarded him for a long moment. Then, exhaling, she nodded and gave Rory a kiss on the cheek. "Be careful," she whispered into her friend's ear, but she looked at Luc when she said it.

A few seconds later, she'd gathered up her bag and keys and was gone.

"Where do you want me?" Rory asked him an hour later.

They stood in the cool, dark stairwell that led from the garage under his house to the main floor.

In my bed, Luc thought with a slanted glance upward toward the enclosed porch where his swing bed hung, overlooking the Marina and San Francisco Bay. *Under me.*

The object of his lust tilted her head and gave him a sloe-eyed look that told him she'd heard his thoughts as clearly as if he'd spoken them. When she sent back the thought, *I'd like that*, he inhaled sharply. Blood pounded so painfully through his cock he thought he might be the first man to have an erection actually burst his zipper.

Turning away, he fought for control before indicating a door opposite the garage entry. "Through here." Opening the door, he ushered her into a quietly appointed room done in dark sage and cedar. "Meditation room." He pointed at a closet in the near wall. "Towels are in there. I'll need to get at your back."

"Okay."

Unselfconsciously, she peeled out of the sweatshirt she'd worn against the morning chill, crossed her arms at her waist, and skinned her tight T-shirt up her torso as she moved into the room. Her nipples made stiff peaks in the black of her sports bra.

Luc's groin tightened again. Apparently, the only body issues here belonged to him. "Ahm…"

She raised her eyebrows. "Go or stay," she said with a shrug, turning her back and crossing her arms to pull off her bra. In the bank of windows above the harbor, the reflection of her left underbreast escaping the Lycra made him groan. "Dancers get changed where they have to."

Tossing a mumbled "Be right back" over his shoulder, Luc fled.

Upstairs, he closed the door of the master bath and pressed his back to it. Tried to collect himself.

Failed.

What the hell was the matter with him? He felt like a fourteen-year-old who'd just had his first glimpse of the girls' showers.

He was dawn-of-time ancient, and he'd never been fourteen. Even when newly born, he'd never been any age but what he was now.

Blood thumped violently through his cock. He shut his eyes and clamped a hand over the bulge in his pants, trying to make it stop. The image of a dusky aureole cresting the edge of Aurora's bra was burned on the inside of his eyelids. He opened his eyes hoping for relief, but instead found the picture stayed with him. The intoxicating remembered scent of her late-night arousal joined it.

Kid stuff.

His body trembled against the lie.

"*Shit!*" If he didn't get a handle on this, he'd never be steady-handed enough to draw the protection sigils and runes he wanted to stencil down the center of her back, let alone manage the needle so he could tattoo them.

Cursing, he snapped open his jeans and flipped up the lid of the toilet. How long since he'd had to go to these lengths to relieve a woman's effect on him?

Never.

Grimly, he shoved aside his briefs, leaned one hand against the wall behind the toilet. *Get a grip.* The corners of his mouth kicked up without humor as he took his straining member in hand.

Rory looked around Luc's meditation room. Easily twelve by fifteen feet, the retreat was spare but comfortable, invitingly masculine. An open yoga mat lay toward the room's end, a few feet in front of the wall of full-length windows. Shoved against the inside wall behind it was a low oak table decorated with a substantial, free-standing crucifix, a laughing Buddha, a large quartz and amethyst cluster, and a prayer shawl. White pillar candles stood at each back corner. An incense burner filled with incense sticks was in front of the Buddha, a small bronze gong to the side. Prayer beads lay atop the prayer shawl while a heavy black rosary dangled from the crucifix's crosspiece. A brush of owl feathers at one edge of the table would be used, she supposed, to waft smoke and prayers toward the heavens.

Idly, she wondered if he frequented a confessional, a sweat lodge, or both.

Covering his bases, she decided, half amused and half saddened—until an image of giant, tattered black wings superimposed itself. Startled, she went motionless. Turned her head away until the vision was gone. The wings reminded her of a ship with wounded sails or an eagle grounded by shredded feathers. The wings also seemed faintly familiar—she'd seen them recently, but couldn't remember when, where, or why.

Uneasy, she crossed the room to the windows, hoping light would chase the cobwebs from her brain. The massage table positioned against the far end of the window wall called to her. Curious, she held out a hand toward it. A gentle wave of vibrations whispered across her fingertips. She smiled, recognizing the amethyst that lined the pad of the Healing Flame table. The stone had been used on her often enough in the energy-balancing sessions Solaya and Kate Cavanaugh—head of the pediatric therapy clinic that had commissioned her to lead dance therapy classes at the clinic a couple of days a week—had gotten her to try.

The theory was that using a warm, amethyst-charged table or bio-mat during a massage or energy work would benefit—and balance—the entire body and anything that ailed it. Luc had both a table and a mat, and instinct assured Rory there had to be a reason for that, however redundant it seemed. She wasn't sure about the claims surrounding the equipment, however, since she was pretty sure she was as "unbalanced" as ever, despite the many times Solaya or Kate had urged her to "just lie still" on the table in Kate's clinic. But she loved the sensation of the rock crystals' aliveness as they pulsed in her hands.

She ran her fingertips across the table's purple leather upholstery. The embedded amethysts caressed her senses, beckoning to her.

Smiling, she finished pulling off her bra. She spread her sweatshirt over the leather and lay on it, facedown, wondering what was taking Luc so long to return. There was something about him that called to her. Without yet knowing him, she *knew* him, deep down, body and soul.

The desire she felt to give him what she laughingly called "my virginity" both puzzled and intrigued her. It didn't count that, while she'd been using a vibrator since starting college, she'd never been penetrated by a cock. Right? But the intensity, the craving, she felt to have *him* was something she'd never experienced. She'd gone tingly around guys before, but a majority of the men who'd seen her naked in dancers' changing rooms or who'd plumped her tits into costumes were gay. This…

Her belly took fire and her nipples hardened painfully, prickled at the thought of his touch. He hardly seemed like the safest or wisest bet for someone with whom to share her body for the first time, but she wanted to just the same.

Restless, she squirmed and tried to adjust her aching breasts more comfortably. It was no good. With him on her mind, all her own touch did was to stiffen the already tight buds into throbbing pebbles that begged for his mouth.

Gritting her teeth against the need to relieve the ache, she turned her face to the window and squeezed her eyes shut. *Think of something else*, she told herself, *anything else. Find the grid…*

As it had yesterday, the soft purple lines of the psychic communication grid appeared on the screen of her eyelids. Sighing, she let it come, focusing on the bright, familiar point that was San Francisco and home.

Disjointed chatter immediately filled her head with the voices of children and young adults she'd never met but with whom she'd carried on numerous conversations. She listened for a moment, trying to sort one fragmented voice from the next before sending out her own query. *Are you safe? Who's doing this?*

An urgent jumble of thoughts came back at her, more distorted than before. *Don't know don't know can't find find find…*

Disturbed, she eased out of the nexus and severed the connection.

As a child, she'd loved the sense of never being alone that the voices provided. It had been comforting to not feel isolated before she'd learned to vocalize. Once she'd learned to talk, however, the doctors her parents had taken her to before they'd found Kate had made her think that she was somehow broken, unhealthy, and maybe dangerously abnormal because of what she heard inside her head. Yesterday was the first time she'd ever been shattered by what she heard.

Trying to push away the memory of the screaming, she pressed her forehead into the amethyst table, looking for escape and release. The tips of her fingers caressed a nipple, eliciting a pleasant thrill. With little encouragement, her other hand slipped down her belly, past the waistband of her yoga pants, and into the folds below her pubic bone to touch her clitoris. Gently, she toyed with herself until moisture coated her fingers. She took a breath as her body tightened and began to pulse. She slid her hand deeper into her pants to push a finger inside herself, in and out, more and more quickly. The dream she'd had last night—rather, she'd thought it was a dream, but after what Luc had told her this morning about her sleepwalking, she wasn't sure—came back to her.

Dancing like a mad woman. Landing in his arms. Wrapping her legs around him. Finding his fully clothed cock fitted between the lips to her vagina. Wanting him, *craving* him…

She pushed another finger into herself, ground against her hand as his desire filled her mind and the sensation of riding his enormously rigid cock took her. Moisture coated her hand as her body imploded and she came, biting back a moan. Holding onto his name.

So, she thought when she was able, *still a virgin, right?*

Snorting at the irony of that question and the realization that she was glad she'd put fresh undies in with the streetwear in her go-bag, she let her breathing slow. After a few minutes, the soft judder of the stones and the table's warmth lulled her until, little by little, she relaxed. She tucked her arms along her sides and wiggled herself into a comfortable position.

And drifted…

Straight to him.

The air around Luc thickened, tingling with *otherness.*

Luc…

His name was an unspoken moan in his ear, a rush of lava-level heat through him. Startled, he straightened, allowing his still hugely engorged member to bob freely. Nonplussed, he started to pull up his shorts and jeans.

The phantom sensation of slim fingers on his stayed the move. Breath whispered along his throat.

Luc.

The breath shuddered from his lungs. "Rory?"

Yes.

He winced. Hell and damnation. Her spirit was out of her body again. She must have fallen asleep. He'd thought leaving her alone for a few minutes while she was awake would be fine. Clearly not.

He inhaled sharply when he felt her…*presence*…slip behind him and press against his back. Strong arms slid around him. The phantom fingers that had stayed his trailed the length of his cock. His member bucked upward, hard.

A wicked chuckle warmed the fabric between his shoulder blades.

"Rory!" An admonition to stop. A plea to continue.

Shh. The sensation of her fingers skimming his member, wrapping around it. *Let me.*

"No, wait…" he ground out.

Too late. She stroked him, squeezed him. His shaft thickened and went rigid. His body jerked and bowed into her hand. His seed spumed out of him, a violently intense jet that seemed to go on forever. She lubricated him with it. Brought him to a powerful second climax that sent him spinning and made his head burst with light.

Still her hand clasped and unclasped around his cock, and it responded. When the third explosion hit him, he shouted something unintelligible and collapsed to his knees.

When he finally slumped forward onto the bath mat, spent, her essence folded protectively around him for a moment. Then, in a glimmer of sunlight, she was gone.

Downstairs, Aurora slid back into her body. It greeted her with a relieved snuggle. Sighing, she stretched and opened her eyes, sat up. Looked curiously at her sticky hands. Remembered exactly how they had gotten that way—left, her juices; right, his. The power she had over him even in ethereal form…

She was pretty sure she should feel embarrassed by what her spirit had done without her permission. Instead, she grinned. So *that's* what that felt like—both the sensation of traveling to and from her body on her own and the act of pleasuring a man she desired. Discovering that as badly as her body wanted his, his wanted hers even more. *Cool.*

And a little intimidating. His cock was huge. She was pretty sure that, even given the size of a couple of the dildos she'd tried, her channel wasn't. How would he ever fit?

You can birth babies, the imp in her brain told her slyly. *He'll fit.*

Her body urged her to get him to help her figure out *how*, right now, before his body worked up another giant head of steam. She chuckled even as she fidgeted, both self-conscious and turned on by the thought. Aware that if the moment presented itself, lust would shut out any cautions her brain came up with. Bury restraint and never go back for it.

Hearing footsteps overhead, she cast her eyes toward the ceiling. She slid off the table and headed for the doorway to await him.

Carnal vertigo, just one more thing he'd never experienced. One more thing that, even in the world of impossible things that surrounded him, Luc hadn't believed possible.

It took a while for him to pull himself together enough to get off the bathroom floor. Pleasure still spasmed through him in waves, making his blood shimmy in his veins. Good Christ! If she could bring him to this with an incorporeal hand job, the real thing would kill him—and he, for fuck's sake, was immortal. No one, *no one* had ever… Not physically, not psychically…

He shivered. The knife-edged hunger to feed on human passions that had twisted through him since he'd fallen to earth as an Ekoa Krillu—since he'd joined the Brotherhood and vowed to spend eternity in undistracted celibacy—was gone. Vanished.

He'd never expected to feel replete again, yet here he was, satiated to bursting. The amount of energy she'd poured into him in spirit form was impossible, but she'd done it and thrived on the sharing. He knew that because he could sense her downstairs as she reclaimed her body and woke. She was curious, then pleased as all get out over something. He was pretty sure it was because of what she'd done to him—and because she'd found her own way back into her body.

Laughter huffed out of him. She learned fast.

She was also a danger, both to herself and to him. His pulse took a quick tumble, came up hammering. He could feel her curiosity over how he might be able to help her body scale passion's heights even now.

His cock, so recently sated, rose to the occasion once more.

Stifling a curse, he grabbed a washcloth off the towel rack and ran cold water into the sink. Slaking her curiosity—and his own carnal cravings—couldn't happen, not in any more real sense than it already had. He'd made a vow, he'd…

"Members of the Brotherhood will refrain from engaging in sexual congress unless The One to whom their souls are bound appears…"

Luc sucked in a hard breath when the words of the oath he hadn't thought of in five hundred years came back to him. Soulbound. He could feel his heart twist. Holy… Was that what this was? His soul and Aurora's had been trussed together at the dawn of time and, without even realizing it, she'd just claimed him?

What was it Solaya had said yesterday? Oh, right. *Fuck-fuck-fuckity-fuck.*

He shut his eyes as hope assailed him. He had an *out* sanctioned by the Brotherhood.

A sigh of frustration shuddered through him. That would have to wait.

At least for a while. If whoever was using psychic kids the way the two in Vegas had been used found the child he'd been sent to locate…

Hell would come for them all.

Breathing deep and looking for calm, Luc ran the terrycloth square under the tap. He could use a shower, but leaving Aurora alone longer than strictly necessary read like a bad idea where his sanity was concerned. She was like the kid who'd just learned to work the secret lock on the candy store—where his cock was the lock, his cum the candy. There was no telling what else she might try on for size if he didn't get back to her soon.

Quickly, he washed and dried his genitals, then stuffed himself back into his pants. The bathroom needed a good scrub, too, but he settled for wiping up the biggest drops of seminal fluid and folding up the bathmat to drop in the washer on his way to the kitchen.

When he got there, he opened and downed one large bottle of room temperature spring water and grabbed another couple. Energy work of any sort was draining, and he was certainly drained in more ways than one. Opening a second bottle, he headed downstairs.

He choked and nearly dropped the water when he reached the third step from the bottom and realized Aurora stood in the meditation room doorway, topless.

His recently depleted cock raised a salute. Her nipples tightened in response. "Um…" he stammered.

She took a step toward him. Her nipples pouted, breasts swayed with the movement, making his palms itch and his mouth water. Like the rest of him, his hands were large. She would fill them to overflowing.

The beast inside him stirred. Drooled.

"Is there somewhere I could wash?" She held out her hands. "I never knew semen was so sticky."

Oh hell. She'd not only given him an invisible hand job, she'd brought the physical evidence of his orgasms back with her? Speech eluded him. He'd never met anyone like her before on any plane of existence. Had she no shame or body-consciousness at all? His jaw dropped. He caught it, snapped his mouth closed. She knew what she'd done…for him.

Her hard-tipped breasts and the scent of her arousal told him exactly how much she wanted him to do the same for her.

Carefully, so he wouldn't stumble—his knees felt damned wobbly all of a sudden—he took the final steps to the landing. Gestured a bottle at the room behind her. "In there…" he croaked. Shit. He'd been a big bad since the dawn of history and now, because she was half naked, he couldn't speak. He cleared his throat. Took a swallow of water.

Tried to shift his mind and gaze off her begging nipples.

Or perhaps that was merely his cock doing the begging.

Pestering him to slide it into her wetness until they were both coated in it.

"In there." Still kind of raspy. He moved to point at a closed door at the back of the room. Caught her staring raptly at the flexing and burgeoning bulge behind his fly when she didn't immediately move out of his way. Her shoulders seemed to go back, and her chest strained toward him.

Fuck, his demon whispered, *she wants it as bad as you do. She belongs to you*—with *you. You both know it. Take her. Get it out of the way, out of your head, and done.*

No, the hard-edged enforcer, the guardian warrior in him snarled. *Not happening, not now. She needs to be protected from her own energy leaks. Work first, fuck later. Time and place, fool. Time and—*

Getting the distinct impression that the beast in him was about to make a case for both, Luc slammed the door on that particular discussion. Forced himself to lift his gaze over her head, away from the invitation her...*assets*... issued. Sucked in everything he could to inch by her without touching, since she clearly wasn't going to get out of his way.

"Washroom is right here." It contained a shower, as well as a sink and toilet, but he wasn't going to think dirty girl/dirty boy thoughts right now. Would. Not.

Visuals came to mind anyway. He compelled himself to think about children in danger—*dead but not dying*. They *needed* a lot more than his carnal *wanting* could justify.

Wanna bet?

He pictured himself catching his demon and throttling it. "Fresh towels are in the rack."

The smile she gave him was blinding. "Thank you."

Struggling to keep his mind on his mission and the child he needed her help to find, he fled across the room to retrieve his tattooing supplies. If he could come up with a sigil that warded her from him, it had to be all good.

Chapter Seven

Years spent dancing in company and changing costumes in crowded unisex dressing rooms had left Rory unselfconscious about nakedness—whether it was her own or someone else's. It felt odd to suddenly feel awkward about a state of undress she'd long taken for granted.

It wasn't that she didn't know how to be modest—she didn't wander around the house nude or semi-nude when Senn was home, for example—it was that she simply didn't think about it most of the time. Now…

Sighing, she finished washing sex from her hands and plucked a towel from the rack, winding it tightly around her chest. Then she returned to climb back onto the amethyst table. Visibly relaxing, Luc settled onto a rolling stool at the fold-up drafting table in the far corner of the room. Moments later, he was immersed in turning the rune sketches he'd drawn earlier into stencils he could position along her spine and tattoo.

She swiveled onto her belly to watch him. There were so many things she wanted to ask—like exactly who he was, where he came from. Why she felt she knew him even though they'd barely spoken. Whether or not covering up her breasts really put them out of his mind. She was pretty sure it didn't because having his back to her didn't keep her imagination from picturing the sheer size of his hard-on or the strength of his climax. Climax*es*. Plural.

Rory's mother had never told her much about sex or what to expect from it. Perhaps because she'd been taken too soon, or been too uncomfortable to speak about it. Her father had been too embarrassed by the subject to explain anything. Solaya had flat out refused to discuss the subject with Rory, so Senn had been the one to explain just enough to make it clear why Rory needed to "watch out for boys." He'd also been the one to hand her a copy of *Cosmopolitan* that had helped to fill in some of the blanks in Rory's education.

It had been in that magazine that she'd first read about supernatural men—*fallen*—who were capable of multiple comes during a single sexual encounter. Most of the tabloid magazines had ecstatic articles on the subject written by journalists who'd allegedly experienced the phenomenon. Rory had never given the subject much thought, though the idea had excited her inexperienced libido the same way reading erotica did. Now, however, her curiosity—ah hell, who was she kidding? Her lust—had gone into overdrive. She wanted to ask Luc if he could bring her to the prolonged multiple orgasms she'd read about but never managed to achieve on her own, even with the use of special clitoral stimulants and her best vibrator. Was more than one orgasm at a time the kind of thing only a man like him could give a woman? Give her?

In an uncharacteristic display of prudence, she kept the question to herself. That thing inside her that had linked them telepathically when he'd first entered her studio—was it only yesterday?—told her that chattering questions at him while he worked wouldn't serve either of them, the child he'd been sent to find, or the children clamoring for help in the nexus. Still, she felt the electric sizzle of connection, the empathic link that snapped into place between them. It was as though he'd left his mind open to her so she could see what he intended.

She pressed gently into the boundaries of their mental bond. Drew back uneasily when she realized the link went two ways.

She was used to connecting telepathically with children whose communication skills were stunted. Some of them were seriously ill, victims of childhood leukemia, heart defects, or worse. Some had been labeled autistic by traditional developmental standards, then later, "crystal kids" (healers) or "indigos" (warrior/protectors) by more discerning people like Kate Cavanaugh. She'd assumed since childhood that she could connect with them because she'd been diagnosed as on the autism spectrum, too. Senn, Solaya, and pediatric psychologist Kate Cavanaugh had always told her she was not autistic, that she simply possessed a developing set of skills that made her unique. Until Luc had stepped into her dance studio and she'd telekinetically thrown him out the door, she'd never believed them.

Again, she tentatively touched the link she shared with him. Again, he opened wide, invited her to make their tie two-way. Again, she retreated. Dark things lurked in the alleyways of her psyche, memories both recent and long past that she didn't want to aggravate, let alone share. She might have unintentionally dragged him with her through the psychic node yesterday, but that didn't mean she knew him well enough to trust him.

No matter how much her body wanted to get busy with his.

Or how much fun her astral self had had pleasuring him.

She felt his strangled laughter before his shoulders started to shake with it. He sent a wicked glance over his shoulder at her. *You'll get yours.*

Flushing, she turned toward the window, but not before the impudent elf in her subconscious shot back, *Promises, promises.*

The startled guffaw from his corner made her squirm. She closed her eyes on the principle that what she couldn't physically see would go away and leave her alone. Her spirit-self might be ready to play with him, but the fleshy bits were bashful.

A picture of her standing in the doorway half naked, waiting for him to come down the stairs, formed in Luc's thoughts. Her face went hot. Okay, so only mostly not bashful.

It took awhile for the masculine chuckling in the drafting corner to subside. When it did, silence reigned as Luc let the work absorb him.

Once again, Rory drifted, sinking into the grid where the babble had grown shrill and anxious. Restless and uneasy again, she turned over and sat up. Swiveled to the opposite end of the table and lay down again, trying to separate the gibberish into distinguishable phrases. Looking for the source of the distress. Taking in a harsh breath and retreating at the sight of dark, ominous tentacles spreading into the psychic web, dousing the pinpoints of light one by one.

"What is it?" Luc's stool squealed away from his slanted table. A couple of strides brought him across the room to her. He caught her shoulders. "Are you all right?"

Wide-eyed but not seeing him, she cringed and shook her head. "What is it?" she whispered. "Who's stealing them?"

"Rory," Luc said sharply, "talk to me. What do you see?"

"I don't know." She raised her hands, trying to identify what she didn't understand, attempting to get a sense of it. "It's not… It doesn't belong." Troubled, she craned her neck to look up at him. "It's bad, Luc. Really bad."

The first time she'd said his name aloud. He didn't let the sound of it, the desire to hear it moaned or screamed as she came with him inside her, distract him. "Can you describe it?"

"Dark. Stealing all the lights." She shook her head. "Whatever it is, I don't know how to stop it." She looked over at his desk. "You said tattooing runes on me will help keep me grounded. Do you have one that will help me keep my balance if I walk the grid to get a better look at what's happening?"

He hesitated. The first rune that came to mind for this was *Ehwaz*, which bothered him. Not only would this rune bring harmony to her as it allowed her to communicate better on various levels, but it could allow her to travel between different levels of awareness as well as different worlds. Given the ability she already possessed to astral travel, he was hesitant to add anything further to it. Her face was so worried and earnest, however, that he abruptly nodded.

"Yes." Releasing her, he returned to his stencils. "Give me a minute to draw it out."

Ten minutes later, he sighed and stretched, scooped up the designs, and turned toward her. "You ready for this?"

In response, Rory reached around and peeled the towel off her back. "No, but let's do it anyway."

Chapter Eight

According to experts, psychic vampires are mortal people whose need for energy metaphorically connects them to the bloodsuckers of legend. This is only half true. In fact, there are mundane persons whose need for vital energy is so intense that they seem to wring it directly from anyone with whom they come into contact. The technical term for humans like this is "drama queens" or "crazy makers."

—from *The Lightway Codex, Appendix i: Defining the Players* by McCleron O'Connell, Indigo Lightworker

Sucking in a breath of good intentions, Luc wheeled his tray of instruments across the room. Went back to snag his stool and an adjustable, high-intensity lamp that he switched on and angled to get the best light on her back.

He paused to collect his thoughts and resolve as he studied the satiny canvas her skin represented. A single freckle centered between her shoulder blades made him smile. There was truth in the old adage about freckles being angel kisses. He would use this one as part of the harmony and balance rune he planned to draw there, entwined with his own personal sigil. If this quest took them where it appeared it would, she'd need every bit of protection available. Adding his particular mark to the mix would be like permanently installing a GPS tracker on her. Wherever she went, whether it was in the physical or psychic worlds, he'd be able to find and protect her.

Only marginally uncomfortable with his decision to mark her this way without first getting her consent, he studied the line of her spine. It seemed a crime to mar the creamy perfection with ink, but it was the only way he knew to quickly tether her spirit so it couldn't leave her unprotected. He'd tattoo the protective rune, *Algiz*, just below her hairline, finish with *Sowelo* to combat dark energy in the small of her back where the flare of her hips and buttocks formed the shape of a perfect, inverted heart. Between them, he'd fit *Ehwaz* (communication and traveling between worlds), *Laguz* (the traveling of the soul and the unconscious mind), *Uruz* (union of energy and mind), and *Perdhu* to keep her down to earth.

Over her heart center, intertwined with *Gebo*, for harmony and balance, he'd place his personal sigil to mark her as under his protection. Once activated, the symbols would give her a permanent trail of breadcrumbs to follow, so no matter what she did or how far she traveled outside it, she would never again lose her way back to her corporeal self.

Recent experience in his bathroom notwithstanding.

The circumstances there had been unique, contained within the boundaries of his house and playfully erotic rather than traumatic. His body thrummed with awareness. The gleefully generous but ghostlike nymph who'd tormented him to exquisite release would come to him again at the slightest encouragement, he feared. She'd chosen to follow him and, he suspected, her own body had been as engaged in what she'd done as her spirit—which was precisely the link that had allowed her to find her way back to her physical self.

"Will it hurt?" she asked, bringing him back to what he was doing.

It took him a moment to pick up the train of her question. "Getting tattooed along the spine is more painful than other places, yes." He brushed her hair out of the way, scrubbed an alcohol swab over the base of her neck. "This one on your neck will probably be the most painful." His lips twitched. "If you survive it, the rest should be easy."

"Okay." A thoughtful pause. "You and Solaya say this needs to be done, so I don't"—she searched for words—"jump out of my skin again and…go someplace—"

She hesitated, troubled lines etching her face. Images of the bodies in the Neon Boneyard flashed through Luc's mind, as vivid and immediate as her struggle with the memory. She didn't want to, but she would revisit the scene again and again until she knew how to change the outcome for another child. Until she could make it stop.

"—so I don't go someplace not *here* without meaning to again. I don't get how tattoos will stop that. Are they magic?"

Luc grimaced. "Magic" was a volatile term when it came to angels—Fallen or not. In the mundane world, the term suggested that a wave of the hand or the wiggle of a nose could change things in whatever manner the wielder chose. Even in the world he'd come from, it couldn't. Angel, demon, Fae, or human, the only way to get what you wanted was to work at it.

In some instances, however, there *were* both practical and symbolic shortcuts.

"Sort of, but not exactly." He picked up the transfer paper with the first rune, held it where she could see it. "Essentially, runes are an old form of written language. They represent various concepts to the ancients—the beings—you need to be guarded against."

His eyes narrowed and his mouth worked as he considered explanations, staring at the stencils in front of him. "Humans with special abilities have always been around, but those who are truly gifted are rare and usually reviled, even in modern times. You're one of the new breed, the next step in the human evolutionary process—"

"I'm *what?*" Rory turned halfway over to look up at him incredulously. "What the *hell* are you talking about?"

"Human evolution." Grinning, Luc gently nudged her to lie flat again. It occurred to him that he had laughed, lusted, and lived in abject terror for someone more in the thirty-six hours or so since he'd met Aurora Montgomery than he had since… Well, probably ever. "Moving from one stage of evolutionary development to the next. Kind of like homo erectus evolving into man as he is today. Except the aspect of evolution we're talking about here is more of a fine-tuning. It's happened before, and it'll happen again, so why not here, now, and with you as part of it. Here, turn face down"—he indicated the face rest—"and lie still so I can get at your neck."

Muttering something about "crazy people" and not being "named Alice," which meant she didn't "have to believe in impossible things before breakfast," she did as he requested. Laughter, unconstrained now and freeing, roared through Luc. Disgruntled, Rory hoisted herself on her elbows and sent him a killing glare before she flopped back onto her face.

Laughter exploded, causing the dark places he'd carried inside him since the day of The Fall to start to splinter. Light, so long missing from his soul, bled through the widening fissures in a sheer white radiance he found both fascinating and blinding. He reached one long-fingered hand toward it, toward Rory…

Something stabbed at his chest, reached for his heart—

Much as he'd done to Athan at the pier.

Gasping, he jerked sideways, fell. Felt the snatching fingers slip out of him, thrust again.

"Luc, what's wrong?"

Frightened, Rory rolled off the table and tried to help him up. He shoved her away—from him and from the grasping thing that must not ever touch her.

So cold. So damn cold and dark.

Blindly, he flung out a hand, hoping to catch the edge of the darkness that bound him, rip it away. He didn't want to descend back into the hell he'd finally started to crawl out of. Did not want to lose his fragile grip on the light.

What thrives in darkness cannot survive the light.

The axiom sifted through him on the wind of malevolent laughter.

Nousaine, he thought. Peering down at him from the glassed-in catwalk of the tall house two streets deeper into Pacific Heights and away from the Bay. Briefly, it occurred to Luc he might have miscalculated by purchasing this place above the marina with the idea of keeping track of his former mentor while putting himself in Nousaine's face.

Then he felt Rory anchor her heels to the floor behind him, fling one slim arm over his left shoulder and sling the other around his ribs beneath his right. And haul him *hard* backward, away from the fist that threatened to yank whatever soul he still had from his chest.

"No, Rory, don't—"

He gripped her hands, tried to disengage her from him. Tried to tell her that if the fist in his heart plunged all the way through him and into her, she'd be done, every last ounce of her energy claimed, absorbed by the shadows in which his kind lived.

Dead—or worse, catatonic. A vegetable.

His tongue wouldn't work. The words couldn't form.

She wasn't listening anyway.

Instinct rode her, drove her to propel him beneath the gem-charged table, to reach up and grab the amethyst bio-mat. To use her insignificant weight to flatten his big body and lie prone atop him, haul the amethyst mat over them like a shield.

In less time than it took him to draw a breath, light filled him. The sensation of having his heart, lungs, soul, and tonsils yanked out by the roots at the same time faded.

For a moment, he simply lay there, breathing harsh, grateful breaths, wondering how Aurora had intuited her way through this one.

Then fury took hold. His encounter in the bathroom with Rory's astral self had shocked him to the extent that he'd dropped his personal wards, given anyone who wanted it psychic access to him. Left not only himself but Rory and his mission vulnerable.

"Are you all right?" Sliding herself and the amethyst-lined mat sideways off of him, she swept her hands quickly over him, checking for damage.

"No." Gravelly, needy. He couldn't allow himself this kind of *need*. Ravenous, craven. A soul-deep entreaty to replenish his energies from the primal life source he knew she was.

Catching her hands, he pushed her away. It physically hurt him to do so, but even the lightest touch of her fingers fed her energy into him, made him crave more. Heightened his need to drain her into himself and devour her.

"But you—"

"I don't want to hurt you. Don't touch me," he managed. Damn Nousaine anyway.

But the virtual fist in his chest had held the signature of another psi vamp, too. One who barely registered on the supernatural scale, and with whom he'd recently come into contact.

The fair-haired man from the street outside Rory's studio.

"*Shit*!" Of course. The man had to be Nousaine's newest protégé. That was why his energy signature had seemed familiar. Nousaine was linked through his acolyte directly into whatever the man fed on, and right now, they were jointly feeding on *him*. Looking, after the taste they'd gotten last night, for Rory. And now that they knew Luc was back and could track him…

They could find *her*. Easily.

Luc sucked in a breath when he realized what he should have understood from the moment she'd thrown him out of her studio, the second she'd fed back to him the energy he'd expended in replenishing hers.

She was the energy mother lode the Ekoa Krillu craved.

Nousaine and his locust-like army of energy freeloaders would never stop until she was imprisoned somewhere they could keep her—

Dead but not dying.

Fuck-fuck-fuck!

Luc rolled away from her and got to his feet, horrified. Darkness roared through him with the understanding. The search for the special child he'd been sent on. The missing children who were in the same shape as the ones her spirit had tried to protect in the Neon Boneyard. All of it, on both sides of the light/dark war, was about one thing.

Getting to the woman whose very name proclaimed what she was.

The dawn that ended night. The light that pierced the darkness. The flame that lit the way.

Aurora Montgomery. Human evolution's new beginning. A freaking banquet of energy enough to feed them all.

Anger filled him. He couldn't allow it. Couldn't let any of them—not the Brotherhood, the Council, nor the creatures of the night—take her and use her. Not on his watch.

And where she was concerned, it would always be his watch.

Save the children, protect the girl.

He didn't know if he was capable of both, even were he not Fallen.

"Luc? Luceire?"

His full name from her lips. He craved the sound of it, would have preferred to hear it as a needy, breathless whisper in his ear, an ecstatic cry when he brought her to molten orgasm rather than filled with the concern he heard in it now, but…

She sat upright, naked from the waist up. "Luceire, are you all right?"

"No." Jamming his hands into the pockets of his pants to prevent himself from reaching for her breasts, he backed away from her. "It was a mistake to bring you here. Why did you have to"—an inadequate gesture toward the fly of his jeans—"You shouldn't have… I shouldn't have let you."

She was in danger because he hadn't known how to—hadn't wanted to—stop her. Because Nousaine and his protégé had sensed—and wallowed in—the surge of energy he'd released as he came.

"It was a mistake. All of it."

"You were in pain." Her cornflower blue eyes were wide, earnest. They held him captive in a way that should be outlawed. She rose, bringing the mat with her. Keeping it between her—them—and the window. "I wanted to help." She moved to place her palm over his heart center. "You…" She paused, puzzled. "You…belong to me. I don't understand that, but I have to…" Another pause wherein she seemed to question what she was about to say. "I *need* to—" A click of her tongue accompanied by a roll of her eyes. "It's weird, but I need to…take care of you. You need a keeper."

Laughter huffed from his lungs, sharp and incredulous. "*I* need a keeper? *You're* the one who hasn't got a clue what she's doing. *You're* the one who jumps out of your body and dashes off to points unknown, dragging me with you, then doesn't know how to get back. And *you're* the one running around the city in the middle of the night attracting every psychic vampire and blood locust in the vicinity while they all try to feed off you."

He stepped forward into her hand, leaned down until his face nearly touched hers. "You're the one," he said softly, "who jumped ship down here to jack me off in my bathroom, leaving your body empty and vulnerable to any astral traveler who happened by in the process."

His nose and forehead touched hers. "And you're the one who left me so blown by making me come three times by spirit touch alone that I dropped every ward and defense I put around us and left both of us wide open to attack by the 'Krillu master of the city."

She snagged her lip between her teeth but didn't back away. "Is that what happened?"

He lifted his face from hers and nodded. "That's what happened. And it's not going to happen again."

"Oh, it probably will," she said matter-of-factly, then hoisted the amethyst mat and squared it back on the massage table. "We just have to take this mat everywhere we go so you'll have body armor when the unexpected happens to you. See"—she drew lines across the pad with her finger—"if we cut here, here, and *here*, we can make you a psi-proof vest with a high collar and a crotch guard."

He gaped at her.

But wait, she wasn't finished.

"And maybe we can make a sort of hat thing to wrap around your head so no one can get into your thoughts—"

As it had so many times already in the past thirty-some hours, laughter snorted out of him. "A sort of hat thing? Like an aluminum foil helmet?"

She nodded. "Full body armor. Protection against alien invasion." She tipped her head and narrowed her eyes, giving him a thoughtful once-over. "Or at least full over the vital bits. I'd suggest an amethyst- and crystal-crusted jacket and chaps, too, to protect your arms and legs from an onslaught of psychic vampery by whomever is trying to jack you up, but that might be a bit much, even for you."

"*Jack me up?*" He choked. "Psychic *vampery?*"

She tossed up her hands and gave him a look that said *if the shoe fits…*

He lost it. *Let Nousaine and his minions try feeding on this.* Doubled over and howled.

No wonder Senn had sent him to her. He'd always said Luc—and every other reforming Fallen involved with the Brotherhood—should just die already and get out of Dodge, considering their angst-filled, seen-it-all attitudes. Luc had lived in one form or another since the dawn of time, but this tiny, shapely blonde who'd been alive for less than an nth of his lifespan was going to kill him. With laughter.

And he'd follow her down whichever horrifying garden path she led, happy for the first time in…ever.

He'd have to send Senn a thank-you card.

If they survived.

The thought sobered him. He looked at Aurora. "You are a menace."

She gave him mock wounded. "Except for a couple of spiders that one time, I have never—"

He held up a hand. "Let me amend that. You are a menace to me, my sanity, my ability to think straight, and my priorities. By now, you should be tattooed, we should have been to the meeting about the children's bodies—"

Her eyes went wide. Her guard went up, effectively shuttering the connection between them. She backed away from him.

"—and be on the way to finding this kid who's my mission—"

"*Our* mission," she whispered. "Isn't that what you tried to tell me yesterday before I got…distracted?"

Shit. She hadn't forgotten or recovered from thinking about the children in the Neon Boneyard or what had happened to them. She was just…

Managing.

Had probably been *managing* stuff like yesterday for years without anyone realizing—including Senn, Solaya, and the parents who'd tried so hard to protect her from the very things happening to her now.

Without thinking, he took a step toward her. That protective something that had reared its head the moment he'd first laid eyes on her made him wonder if taking her to the morgue was the best idea. He didn't think he could avoid taking her, not to mention that by taking her with him, he'd be able to keep an eye on her, but… "Who do you go to when things get rough like they did yesterday?"

She made a face. "Usually, when the voices in my head get too loud, I talk to Kate, at the center where I do pediatric dance movement therapy a couple days a week. My parents started taking me to her when they noticed I was *different*. They were told I was autistic when I was little because I didn't talk clearly until I was nearly eight. They were told I had some sort of apraxia and needed therapy, but that wasn't quite it, either."

"Rory, you don't have to tell me."

"If we're going to work together and stuff like us talking without speaking and me wandering around without a body keeps happening…" A wrinkle of her nose. "Yeah, I probably do."

He stifled a smile. "Tell me about the voices."

She sighed. "I've always heard voices. It just always sounds like someone else is talking in my head. I mean, you know how your own voice sounds when you're thinking, but this is different. There's always this kind of constant murmur, but lately, they're louder, more desperate."

She shrugged. "When I was younger, my parents didn't like seeing me teased or bullied or *anything*, so they were super protective. They first took me to Kate when I was maybe fifteen because it got so bad they wondered if I might be schizophrenic—except the voices never told me to do anything. It was more like being in homeroom in high school—a constant buzz in the background. They never told me exactly what Kate said after that first meeting, but they seemed relieved and frightened at the same time. Their overprotectiveness got worse." She worried her lip.

"Hearing other people's thoughts mostly stopped when I got into college—maybe because I was so distracted by everything that was going on in front of me that I just stopped listening. The voices came back the minute I started working with kids at my dance studio, and at Kate's center. That's when Senn finally told me about him and Solaya and the things they're able to do." She grinned suddenly. "He's also the one who told me I might be a crystal something. Which is weird, but it made sense to me, given that crystals have always been used in radios to amplify sending and receiving." A glance at him was accompanied by a wry twist of her lips. "And I do."

"You certainly do." Luc chuckled because she needed him to. A life spent swaddled in bubble wrap so no one could drop and break her sounded less than ideal—and also far more loved than he could comprehend. It also meant he had to make sure she could protect herself from Nousaine and his minions.

Although it was becoming more and more clear to him that he might be the one in need of shielding rather than Rory. He gave the amethyst-charged massage table and bio mat a considering glance. Maybe she was right about the body armor.

Or at the very least, some kind of shield stone. Perhaps one that could be embedded in his skin. Or worn on an eyebrow bar, or possibly even a nipple ring.

The thought made his mouth curve. He glanced at Rory, wondering what she'd think of—or, more to the point, *do*—if he got his nipple pierced.

On a whim, he lifted the table and planted it in the middle of the room, then went to rummage in the meditation room's closet. A moment later, he'd retrieved four sizable mixed quartz and amethyst clusters.

"Here." He handed two to Rory. "Help me with—" he started, but she'd already moved to place a cluster at each end of the window wall. In turn, Luc consigned the others to the opposite corners of the interior wall.

The atmosphere in the room changed instantly.

Luc splayed his fingers and reached out mentally to touch the air, testing the energy field's protective boundaries. The barrier didn't extend beyond the meditation room's four walls, but within the room itself, it was solid.

Giving Rory a speculative look, he asked, "How did you know the amethysts would help?"

"I'm not sure." She offered him a negligent one-shoulder shrug. "But since amethyst is both protective and healing, and quartz crystals collect light and warmth and amplify them, it just seemed obvious." Her mouth curved in a self-deprecating smile. "I mean, light chases dark, right? If a room is dark—"

"Flip the switch." He glanced at the stencil transfers on his desk, then at the closet from which he'd taken the amethyst and quartz clusters. "Turn on the light."

She nodded.

"Okay," he said, striding to the closet to retrieve a small coffee can that rattled when he picked it up. "I can work with that."

On the glass-fenced widow's walk surrounding the upper floor of his home, Savitri Nousaine clutched his chest and staggered. Catching hold of the balcony railing, he steadied himself and peered over the rooftops to the steeply angled street on which Luceire Garard's new house sat. He'd never before had a psychic connection to one of his former pupils severed so fully.

Eyes narrowed, he mind-probed the area, searching for the link that had existed only moments before. Since coming into being and establishing himself as the god-like high priest of the West Coast, he'd created a solid—if parasitic—mental bond with each member of his immortal caste as well as a majority of the human psychic vampires within San Francisco's confines. The bond he'd used to remind Luceire who was superior between them was gone, as though it had never been.

A small flame of displeasure ignited inside him, followed almost at once by a sucking-draining sensation. He gasped, then caught himself again. Someone challenged his supremacy—and from nearby, given the strength of the connection.

Unaccustomed disquiet gripped him.

Closing his eyes, he pulled up a mental picture of the city and scanned it. All the usual suspects in all the usual places, exactly as it should be. Except…

The small flame of displeasure and unease erupted into a conflagration. Except for Beck, his mostly human minion, who would do everything possible to overthrow him, seize his power, and become a god. And Garard, the *recovering* Fallen—as though joining Satan's war against God was an addiction to get over in twelve steps—who'd long ago vowed to destroy him.

Anger rising, he probed each of his remaining psychic connections in an attempt to tap the nexus and find Beck or Garard that way. Perhaps he'd gotten too sanguine about his superiority in recent decades—

A faint fissure near the Embarcadero–Beach Street tourist area caught his attention. Eyes narrowed, he cocked his head, testing the feel of the unfamiliar player on his board. 'Krillu…but not. Dugo Balang…but *definitely* not. The flavor was of something other.

His attention sharpened, and his lips curved into a savage smile. *Athanarius. Of course.* And over there in the south…

His smile turned ferocious. Over in the south within the darkness of the underground cells, Beck's teen conquests would be the doctor's downfall.

Chapter Nine

Though their paths often cross, the Council of Light does not trust the Brotherhood of Shadows. Members of the Council work for right and crave light. Members of the Brotherhood come primarily from among the Ekoa Krillu (psychic vampires) or the Dugo Balang (sanguine vampires). Both of these vampire classes originated from the ranks of the Fallen angels who were cast out of the divine realms and cursed to an eternity of darkness. Led by sanguine vampire Jinx Falken, the Brotherhood's primary purpose is to keep order in the universe. It is composed of three classes: warriors (culled from among humans who are immortal only in that they are able to reincarnate or incarnate again and again); enforcers or "strikers" (who are sent out to assess a situation, determine the threat, and take care of it); and Nightkeepers (who remain so deep in the shadows that no one but the Brotherhood's leader is aware of their existence).

—from *The Lightway Codex, Appendix iii: Relationships*
by McCleron O'Connell, Indigo Lightworker

While Rory watched, Luc embedded a two-inch amethyst shield stone in his left pec. It was a painful process, but the sensation of being protected against someone like Nousaine was immediate. By the time he was cleaned up and ready to move on to Rory's tattoos, the wound site was mostly healed and only mildly tender.

At instinct's insistence, he added blue aventurine to the quartz and amethyst crystals for more specific protection against his Ekoa Krillu brethren.

He ground the stones into a fine powder and mixed it with thrice-blessed henna-colored ink—a unique, little-used blend created by the Brotherhood and consecrated by its highest-ranking members—to create the glyphs he tattooed along Aurora's spine.

"*Audiuro vos in te*," he muttered. I bind you within yourself. "*Te inimicos tuos.*" You defeat your enemies. "*Te vinci…*" You defeat…

By the time he was finished, it was late in the afternoon and Rory felt strangely light-headed but grounded, stronger, and better than she had since her father's death—though the plastic film along the center of her back over the new ink pulled a bit every time she moved. There was little pain, but occasional twinges and itchiness caused her to want to wriggle her shoulders in an effort to loosen the tape. Instead, she leaned forward against her seatbelt on the drive from Luc's to the forensics and pathology suite of the Council of Light's San Francisco stronghold and ordered herself to be still.

The stronghold was situated on the lowest level of a large Victorian home in the Panhandle, on land Luc had told her the Council owned and had deployed for use as a tent city and hospital in the wake of the 1906 earthquake. It wore an air of history overlaid with modern accoutrements. While he conferred with the woman he'd introduced as Celeste and the pathologist, whose name was Keile, Rory wandered about until she came to a set of sealed hospital-style doors. Intuition she didn't understand but didn't question drew her forward. She touched a flat, square button on the wall that read PRESS TO OPEN and stepped through.

Inside, the temperature seemed to drop twenty or more degrees instantly. Shivering, she wrapped her arms tightly around herself. If she'd known where they were going, she'd have brought along something more substantial than the lightweight peasant skirt, camisole, and flimsy sandals to wear after the tattoo session.

She glanced around. White-tiled walls backdropped antique dark oak and glass-fronted cabinets that held a collection of modern stainless steel and old-fashioned enamel basins and other equipment. The overhead lights were bright and contemporary, the visible lab equipment state of the art, but the majority of the gurneys appeared to be leftovers from another era.

Unable to stop herself, she moved toward the ancient tables, nine of which were covered with pristine white sheets that hid pitifully small human forms. The same deafening clamor that had beaten her temples from the inside before she was sucked out of herself and to the bodies in Las Vegas throbbed in her head again now.

Dead but not dying. Dead but not…

She clutched her head, trying to press out the uproar with her fingers. *I can't understand you when you all talk at once,* she thought at the voices.

Help-help-help, they wailed. *Trapped. Dead but not dying…*

I'm trying, she whispered.

She whimpered. The pain in her head increased to migraine proportions. Without warning, heat ran the length of her spine, seemed to run straight through to her heels and glue her feet to the floor. Inside her head, the racket quieted, and calm flowed through her. The runic tattoos at work. Cautiously, she looked up.

The same sort of mustardy-gray threads of energy that she remembered seeing attached to the bodies in the Neon Boneyard appeared to be bleeding through the sheets covering the small forms on the gurneys. The strands formed a single, braided nexus that disappeared into a corner of the room.

Follow it, a voice in her head urged.

Sharply, she glanced around. There was something about this voice that didn't belong in the psychic network as she'd always known it. It was coming through too clearly, too adult, too commanding, too—

Dizziness struck hard before she could complete the thought. She staggered and tried to catch herself on the edge of a gurney. Instead, her hand landed on a sheet-covered body. Immediately, the voice—the…entity—seemed to salivate, panting, eager. *Yeesss,* she heard it sigh at the same moment that she felt something or some*one* attempt to attach umbilical-like energy threads to her and *suck.*

Simultaneously, she experienced a disorienting and unsettling *yank* in the middle of her back—as though a harness she hadn't known she was wearing had been jerked. Then she heard Luc roar, "Rory!" and more than one set of footsteps thundering toward her.

She was sliding toward the floor when he burst through the double doors, Senn—when had Senn gotten there?—close on his heels.

The sense of *yank-yank-drag* in the center of her back increased the closer Luc came. The line of runes along her spine flared hot.

Irritation ran through her as she realized Luc must have somehow tied her to him without asking permission first. Then the wooziness was gone as though it had never been. The crystal grid snapped into place, more vivid than ever. The voices inside it were no longer a nearly unintelligible murmur, but clear and individually distinct. In chorus, they pleaded with her to cut the cords.

For a moment, she hesitated, repulsed by the thought of getting any-where near such corruption. But she couldn't just leave the souls of these children to *rot*.

Before she could bring herself to do anything, Luc and Senn reached her. Senn drew to a sharp halt, gaze shifting between her and the sickly-looking energy threads that ran from the bodies to an indeterminate point outside of the morgue.

Luc glanced at the space above the gurneys, then back at her. "They need your help," he said softly. "Can you release them?"

"Yes." She waved a finger between herself, Luc, and Senn. "You can see it? Both of you? That…hose thing?"

Luc nodded. "Not as clearly as I could when you dragged me into the ether, but yes."

Senn's lips twisted. "Yes. I can see."

"Then you know I have to do something about it—have to find out who or what their souls are tethered to so I can release them." Tears in her eyes, she said, "I want to bring them back. I don't want to kill them."

"Rory."

Arms open, Luc crouched to gather her up, but Senn slid between him and Aurora to put his arms around her instead. The look he turned on Luc was pointed and not friendly.

"You don't have to do this," Senn told her gruffly.

Rory drew his face down and touched her forehead to his. "If I can't bring them back, I do."

"I'll do it." Face grim, Luc straightened and put a hand on her shoulder, looking over her head at Senn. "It's what I'm here for, right?"

"No." Rory turned and wrapped her arms around him, buried her head against his chest. "I felt what it cost you last time. I can't let you do it again. I'll do it." She straightened, said more firmly, "I can do it."

Senn caught her hand before she could raise it. He stooped to look into her face. "I'm sorry you've been dumped off the deep end into this, kiddo." He grimaced. "If you were to follow those tethers and get caught…"

His voice trailed off as Luc stepped in to tower over them both.

"If she gets caught, what?" he asked, voice lethally soft. Rory stepped away from Senn and looked warily from the sorcerer to him. Luc's lips twisted. "Go on, Lawton. Tell her what you told me before you sent me to her." He moved Rory out of the way and stepped between her and Senn, got in the latter's face. "Tell her," he said, "what you don't think she needs to know."

Rory watched Senn work his mouth around something that appeared to taste bad. She'd trusted him since she was small—in all but genetics, he was her big brother. If he felt she didn't need to know something, then maybe… "Aseneth?"

He winced, shook his head. "Rory…"

Still aware of the buzz from the crystal network and the bodies on the gurneys, she narrowed her eyes. He and Solaya needed to quit being so overprotective. If she needed to know something, she needed to *know* it. Their responsibility for her well-being was long past its sell-by date.

"Senn."

Her surrogate brother sighed. He cast a sidelong glance toward the doors through which Celeste and Keile entered. Returned his gaze to her. "If you get caught following whatever's binding these kids, I don't know what might happen. I don't know if what you want to do will help or hurt them. Whatever's holding them"—he gestured toward the gurneys—"you might be playing into its hands, giving it what it wants—you. If it gets hold of you…" He swallowed, regrouped. "Actions, even actions committed with the best intentions, have unintended consequences. I don't know if there's a way to save these children other than to let them go. I don't know if we should try."

For a long moment, Rory studied him. His eyes pleaded for her to understand whatever it was that he couldn't tell her.

Through the tattoo ties that seemed to bind them, she felt the large, solid presence at her back that was Luc. Conscious of the intimidating woman called Celeste watching them, she took a deep breath and tilted her chin once in an almost imperceptible nod. Then she made the same slashing motion Luc had made to sever the etheric ties to the bodies in Las Vegas. Quickly, she plucked apart the few lingering wraithlike strings and tossed them aside.

Within moments, the mood in the grid calmed to a gently pulsing amethyst streaked with the darker violet of deep mourning. The fearful atmosphere in the forensics suite also subsided. Grimly, Celeste stepped forward and gestured for Keile to check the bodies. He did so quickly, laying a hand over the heart center on each and bowing his head for a moment in silent communion. Then he eyed her sadly.

"They're gone," he confirmed.

Celeste breathed a sigh of relief, gave Senn a clipped nod, and left the room. A moment later, Keile glanced at Rory, then followed.

The moment they were gone, Rory turned on Luc. "What did you do when you tattooed me? That...*jerking* thing I felt in the middle of my back—that was you, wasn't it? Trying to psychically haul me out of here?"

Senn caught her shoulder. "He did *what* to you?"

Rory slapped his hand away. "You told me nuthin' 'bout nuthin'," she informed him. "Needed to know. Stay out of this."

Senn's jaw tightened, but he turned to Luc. "Tattoos?"

"Back. Off." Rory got between the men and smacked Senn in the chest. "He asked, I consented. Solaya thought it would be a good idea. Done." She half-turned toward Luc, who backed up a pace. She moved with him, jabbed him in the chest. "But there was no mention of whatever extra you might have done while you were at it." She turned to Senn. "When did you get here, anyway?"

He tipped his head toward the gurneys. "I came with them."

"Oh." She swallowed when the clamor in her head rose again. *Help-help-help...*

Even as she glanced about in an effort to locate the source, she knew that whoever cried out was not here in the morgue. As though in response to that knowledge, her new tattoos flared to life, radiating heat that seemed to wrap around both her and the new voices. She pressed her fingers to her temples and imagined a stillness in which she could understand what was being said without blocking it out entirely. *Help-help-help. Find-find-find... them...her...them...baby...*

Again, she felt a tug in the center of her back, the region of her heart.

Chaos stilled. The image of glowing runes—much like the ones Luc had etched into her skin to represent her communication and heart chakras—appeared in her mind. The one over her heart didn't look exactly like the drawing he'd shown her. Instead it appeared as though *Gebo* had been combined with another symbol. That was where the slight wrench she'd been experiencing had come from. She turned to ask him about it, but a single, faint, tormented whimper stopped her.

Help me.

Startled, she turned to see where the sob had come from. Feminine and anguished, it seemed to echo about the room without coming from anywhere within it. She looked at Luc and Senn. "Did you hear that?"

Senn shook his head.

Luc canted his, listening. "Any of the kids the Council's keeping tabs on not check in today?" he asked the sorcerer.

"Not that I know of," Senn began, but Rory shushed him with a raised hand.

Please, help me.

Closing her eyes, she centered herself, turned her head slowly, listening. "Where are you?" she whispered.

Don't know… Tenderloin, Blood Simple… Just help…

An image of darkness and shadows, a flickering light at the entrance to an alley, the blurry, double-vision impression of a street sign flashed through her mind. Then depths no illumination could reach. She exhaled a fierce breath.

"On my way," she promised before she glanced at Luc and Senn and headed for the door. "Try to keep up," she told them.

Then she ran.

The teens' fear was delicious. Athan shut his eyes and sucked it in, ready to drown in it.

Not what you're here for.

The voice—his conscience or his handler, he could never be sure which, though he suspected his handler because he wasn't sure he had a conscience—buzzed about his ears, an annoying fly he badly wanted to swat away. "Fuck off," he told it.

The painful, hollow skull sound of a finger *thunking* hard against a screeching microphone answered him. *Get on with it.*

"Yes, master," he muttered and reluctantly released the taste of fear to follow its scent instead. It took him underground, somewhere along Market between the Tenderloin and Embarcadero.

The stench of rotten eggs assailed him the moment he hit the rusted access ladder into a no-longer-used sewage tunnel. Hopefully, the hydrogen sulfide levels weren't as great as the stink suggested, or the kids he'd come to find were in real trouble. He took a look around, glad he'd found an entrance in an empty alleyway, and took a deep breath of aboveground air. Then he used his hands and feet to guide him in a controlled slide down the corroded metal instead of risking the rotted steps. Hell, he might get an infection in a cut or scrape, but it would disappear in a day or so. A fall, on the other hand, would be far more painful and could be momentarily debilitating. It wouldn't kill him—nothing would, which was a pity—but the voice in his head told him he had no time to waste on broken bones.

The air at the bottom of the ride was a good thirty degrees warmer than the mild spring air aboveground, the humidity so dense he could have moved it aside with his hands. The darkness was absolute. He pulled a small Maglite from a tool pocket on his cargo pants, flashed it around the tunnel. A sign a few yards along an offshoot caught his attention.

WATCH OUT FOR VAMPIRES.

His lips twitched. Someone with a sense of humor—or better, someone with intimate knowledge of the dangers that lurked in subterranean passageways. He could see his father—Luceire; the bastard didn't deserve Athan's respect—putting up such a sign to warn people against true immortals like him.

On that unsettling thought, Athan returned to the business at hand.

It took long minutes of tracking, first in one direction then the other, before he was able to pick up the trail of teen terror within the pungent scent of hydrogen sulfide and general decay. After that, it seemed forever before he found the series of crude but tightly sealed doors that had been cut into the brick and concrete walls.

By that time, he'd been hearing voices in the constant trickle of water through the passageway for several twists and turns. Audio hallucinations were a known phenomenon, a side effect of spending too long breathing the underground tunnel's hydrogen sulfide. He did his best to tune out that eerie mutter. Unfortunately, he was too keyed up by the taste of the fear he wanted to feed on to be able to quiet his mind.

Being an immortal rejected by both heaven and hell was a pain in the ass. His only crime against heaven had been to be born to parents on opposite sides of good/evil borders. Hell rejected him for the same reason. If neither realm could deal with him, what the hell was the purpose? *His* purpose? He should have superhuman night vision, lungs that weren't bothered by bad air, the knack for not wanting to nosh on other peoples' emotions, and the ability to find what he was looking for without having to try, right? Especially if what he was doing was trying to save some kids' asses.

Snorting, he kicked self-pity into the blackness and resumed his search. A bleating whimper that was decidedly not the sound of dribbling water came from behind a door a few yards ahead and to his right. Athan listened. According to his handler, he should have heard at least three different heartbeats. A chill ran through him when he heard only the one. He took a shallow breath of sulfur mixed with the intense aftertaste of someone else's terror and stepped to the door.

There would be hell to pay if he'd arrived too late to recover at least one of the teens Michael Beck had taken.

Senn at his heels, Luc headed after Rory as fast as he could. He was plenty damn fast, but she was already out of sight by the time he hit the steps to ground level.

Fuck.

"Keep up," she'd said. How hard could that be, right? After all, he was probably a good two feet taller than her, plus vampire. That meant he had speed, agility, and mad skills she couldn't possibly possess. Keeping up with a diminutive human woman—with or without her own set of mad skills—should be a piece of cake.

Right?

Yeah, not so much. He should have been prepared after he'd seen the way she danced last night.

"Where'd she go?" Senn asked, gasping as he took the steps to the closest exterior door two at a time.

"Hell if I know," Luc responded. "Why'd you send me to her, anyway?"

"I thought she'd be good for you."

There was an odd reserve in the way Senn said it that would have bothered Luc if he had time to think about it. Since most of his mind was occupied elsewhere at the moment, it didn't.

"Are you fucking kidding me?" He stopped short. "You and your sister don't like or trust me, but you think the one person everyone has helicopter parented for twenty-six years would be good for me. I've known her for two days, I can't die, and she's already giving me heart attacks. Had to chase her halfway across the city last night and almost didn't make it in time."

Senn nearly ran into him. "What?"

Luc nodded. Something in Senn's tone concerned him, but until he had time to think about why, he let it slide. "She sleepwalked—or rather sleep *ran*—from your house to her studio, with every bloodsucker and emotion-feeder in the city trailing her. Threw one of them across the street without touching him when he got too close—*in her sleep.*"

"Fuck." The alarm in the other man's voice made Luc look at him hard. Senn waved it off. "I knew we should have told her she had gifts a long time ago. Prepared all of us."

For what? Concerned burrowed more deeply into Luc. He'd had the sense from the beginning that there was—or would be—more to this "assignment" than he'd been told. "She should have been better prepared, yes." He turned, trying to concentrate on locating Aurora through his connection to the sigil incorporated into her heart tattoo. "But don't kid yourself that you'll ever be prepared for what she can do. We'll be lucky if she hasn't disincorporated from here and reincorporated somewhere on Venus or in the Bay."

"The hell you say," Senn said, aghast.

Luc winced. This was exactly what had concerned him about adding *Ehwaz* to the chain of runes along her back. Intuition, however, had overridden him. He turned another few inches and stopped, finally catching her direction. "There." He pointed south then headed across the street toward where he'd parked the Range Rover. Tossing Senn the keys, he said, "The only way we'll catch her is if we drive and let her point the way."

Chapter Ten

When about to do something stupidly dangerous, it's good to be followed by your Guardian Thug.

—Aurora Montgomery, *Crystal Elder Philosophies*, from *The Lightway Codex, Appendix vi: Quotations* by McCleron O'Connell, Indigo Lightworker

Before he'd Fallen, Luc had had gifts—real, God-given powers meant to benefit the humans he'd been tasked with guarding and guiding.

As a warrior in the service of heaven, he'd been able to do incredible things, including smiting things, bilocating—or even multilocating, if necessary—if humans called his name. Like the rest of his caste, he'd been created to carry out orders, to protect and serve, to do whatever needed doing in the name of his creator and on behalf of man. In short, he and his fellows had been soldiers and point men, unthinking thugs in service to their Creator's human pets.

That had rankled.

His abilities and those of his fellows had altered when they'd been cast out. Though they were still immortal and far more than human, they were also far less than they had been—no longer divine. Their God-gifted capabilities had been stripped, and what talents remained were hard-won. They also now required special sustenance—like human blood or energy—as well as ordinary, everyday human food in order to keep up the preternatural aspects of their abilities.

In other words, they'd become parasites forced to feed on the very humans they'd once protected. The alternative was losing themselves and their remaining abilities entirely.

Among the gifts Luc had retained was exceptional strength, agility, and the kind of speed that allowed him to appear as though he "blinked" between one place and another. He also had a knack for pulling illusion from the air, the skill to manipulate certain elements, the ability to read the auras and energy signatures of humans and paranormals alike, and remarkable height. He could not, however, change, end, or alter things that he felt needed to be adjusted. Nor could he change the course of history or simply appear out of nowhere or travel between two points—tesseract—without physically making the journey. In the millennia since he'd given up working with the likes of Savitri Nousaine, he'd never missed those abilities more than he did now.

Jaw clenched, he gestured at Senn to stop the Range Rover for a minute. Rolling down the window, he shut his eyes, again seeking both Aurora's energy signature and the tug that linked him to his sigil. To her.

Keep up, she whispered in his mind. *You marked me, see if it does you any good.*

"Anything?" Senn asked anxiously.

"She's playing with me," Luc said, frustrated. They were entering the Civic Center area, several miles from where they'd started. Traffic was so thick that nothing moved. His attention was drawn to a colorfully dressed man who stood on one of the lower steps leading up to a theater, bullhorn in hand. Luc heard him proclaim a coming war on vampires of every stripe, calling for angels to descend and finish the battle that had begun at the gates of heaven during the Fall.

Worry ate at him. Something about the declaration rang true, but he couldn't fix on it while every instinct he possessed told him Rory was in ever-increasing danger. He opened the passenger door as an elegant, leggy blond woman and a shorter, more robust, spiky-haired redhead approached the herald. At the same time that Luc put a foot on the pavement, the crier's voice suddenly cut off.

"I can hear her, but she's masking herself, trying to stay off the damn grid so she can't be followed the way she was last night. She learns fast."

Curiously, he watched the two women move off, talking animatedly, while the man with the bullhorn started to fishmouth as though shutting up hadn't been his idea. Sudden onset laryngitis? Odd.

Luc squinted hard after the women, wondering why they seemed familiar. Then Senn slammed a fist into the dashboard beside the steering wheel in frustration, drawing his attention back to the moment. "Where's she going?"

Jerked unceremoniously back to where he was and what they were doing, Luc grimaced. "There's no telling. Told you. Halfway across the city last night, barefoot. Her feet were covered with cuts when I found her but completely healed this morning." He got out of the Rover and shut the door. Leaning in, he stared at Senn accusingly. "She's more than you told me—more than you can possibly imagine. Hell, if she *can* bilocate or tesseract—"

"That's not possible," Senn said, but he sounded uncertain. He also sounded frightened.

What haven't I been told? Luc snorted. Time was wasting. "For a guy who's known her all her life, you know fuck all about what she's capable of now that her gifts have come in. Nothing is impossible if people like you and I can exist."

"But disappear and reappear?" Senn asked, ignoring the insult. "Full physical body, not astral projection or—"

"Aurora being able to fold space and time in order to get somewhere faster is a stretch," Luc admitted, "but I wouldn't put it past her. Her ability to protect herself and those around her is growing exponentially, especially when she's startled, frightened, or passionate about it. If Nousaine or his people get hold of her and she doesn't destroy them, she'll be the feast to end all feasts. They'll feed on her energy for years. Even before her powers manifested, Nousaine and his people were already feeding on her. That's why she was always so weak."

"So, find her. You put that damn locator tat on her, use it." Senn put the Rover in drive and prepared to jerk it away from the curb. "When we're finished, I'm going to go talk to this guy"—he jerked his head toward the man on the steps—"see if I can get a read on him. Something's not right here."

Luc's mouth flattened. Nodding, he made a best guess about Aurora's direction then headed east as fast as his feet would carry him.

Rory looked around. At the back of her mind, she heard an indistinct whisper, like someone preaching or calling the masses around him to arms. She could also hear familiar voices. Luc and Senn. Their words evaded her, but the growing fear in her surrogate brother's voice bothered her. She'd never heard him sound like that before.

Luc, on the other hand, was more pissed than worried. A tiny smile curved her mouth. Served him right for doing things to her quite literally behind her back.

In front of her, the evening sun hung low in the sky, flinging shadows everywhere. Urban prairie butted up against broken sidewalks and freeway overpasses. Graffiti-covered warehouses were interspersed with a few boarded-up and equally graffitied houses. Everything smelled faintly of rotted vegetation, industrial leftovers, and decay. She was in a part of the city she didn't recognize and had no idea how she'd gotten there. One minute she'd been on the stairs, racing out of the Council of Light's morgue, and the next…

Well, the next thing she knew, she was here. Wherever *here* was. The voice in her head that had brought her here was silent.

"Do you live under the Bay?" a voice behind her asked.

Rory turned around. A teenager with a face like a vertical chunk of train track cocked his head and pulled a bright blue cape closer about his shoulders. An orange slouch hat lay low on his forehead, accenting eyebrows so blond they appeared nonexistent. His aura was a nimbus of indigo hugging him close. Rainbow-colored stripes emanated like sunbeams from his hands and haloed his all-knees-and-elbows, raggedy-man figure. He fairly reeked of not-quite-human essence and otherness. *Healer,* she thought without knowing why. Intuition told her she had nothing to fear from this quarter.

"Pardon?" she asked.

The kid rubbed the side of his head as though it hurt. "It's only that you sorta look like Carrie Underwood, and I know she's been living under the Bay so people can't find her." He gave her a puzzled look. "Are you her?"

"I don't think so." She shook her head, wondering why she couldn't hear his thoughts the way she usually heard those of other teens. Adolescents were often so emotionally charged that they had a tendency to broadcast even when they didn't intend to. This one was a blank, though the nearer she got to him, the louder the voice in her head that belonged to the evangelist Luc had seen on the steps became.

Wipe them out, that voice shouted. *Wipe them all from the face of the earth. Vampires, warmongers, psychic children, Fallen…*

A shudder of revulsion ran through her. *No!* her mind shouted. *Stop!*

Without thinking, she pictured him muted, unable to open his mouth except to feed himself. One of the runes along her spine seemed to ignite. Then, as though an invisible hand erased a school blackboard, the evangelist's voice faded. A vision of him fish-mouthing soundlessly into his bullhorn filled her mind. She took an unsteady breath and turned to the boy. He gave her a funny look. One that said he knew what she'd done and wasn't sure what it meant.

"I'm Rory. What's your name?"

The boy opened his mouth as if to tell her, then pounded the heels of his hands against his temples. "No, I mustn't." He looked anxiously at her. "You already know, you must. If I tell, they'll hurt me."

Instantly forgetting what had brought her here, she straightened. "Who'll hurt you?"

He drew himself onto his toes, danced nervously from side to side. "I don't know. They never said. They just hurt."

"How do they hurt you? What do they do to you?"

He jerked at his hat, glanced about, started to shove it up on one side, then pulled it back down over his ears as though it could somehow protect him. Gave his head a convulsive shake. "No. Can't. Hurts."

"Okay." Disturbed by that assertion, Rory changed tactics and made a gesture that encompassed the area. Inside her mind, the preacher started to speak again, but this time his voice was soften and distant. "Can you tell me where we are?"

"Bad place," he said, spinning apprehensively around. "You came here from out of the Bay. You have to know the bad places."

"I…" Nonplussed, she stared at him, still trying to work out who "they" might be. And why they might be in—or come out of—the Bay. Even in her work with Kate Cavanaugh, she'd never met a child quite like this one. His aura didn't go with the frightened person he presented to her. From an energy standpoint, he appeared heavily shielded and almost invisible…

The thought brought her up short. What were the odds that he was like her? She'd been overprotected by parents and friends alike, her energies masked to all but a very few until her father died. Maybe this boy hadn't had that kind of support system but had been ostracized and abused to the point where he'd gone inside himself to hide. Maybe that was why she couldn't read him the way she was normally able to read the marginalized kids with whom she worked.

She took a deep breath and closed her eyes, feeling for the runes along her spine. One of them had something to do with communication, right? When the one at the top of her spine warmed, she grinned. Communication and focus, traveling between worlds. Right. *Traveling between worlds.* Got it.

"I heard someone call for help," she said, opening her eyes. "Then I was here. Did you hear someone, too—or did you come here to bring me to them?"

The boy nodded. "*They* said you'd be here, that I had to come so you'd know you were in the right place."

"You talked to them?"

Another nod. "This morning, in the bathroom." He hiked his cloak higher around his shoulders. "They talk to me through the drainpipes."

The tat at the nape of her neck started to itch. She concentrated on it and the boy at the same time. As though he knew she was trying to read him, his aura shrank to a thin, protective layer around him. Zigzagging streaks, the dark, muddy gray of fear and uncertainty distorted the previously clear colors. She stepped closer and whispered, "Will you show me where you talked to them?"

The boy glanced furtively about and nodded. "They said to bring you when you got here." Then he turned and scuttled into the dusk, apparently trusting her to keep up.

Drawing a thoughtful breath, she stared after him. She couldn't be sure that following him would bring her to whomever had cried so desperately for help when she was in the morgue, but standing here wouldn't accomplish anything. Her instincts, always willing to side with a kid, told her to trust that following him would get her where she needed to go.

She took a step forward, into the waning light.

Immediately, whatever was attached to the tattoo at her heart center stretched taut, as though someone or something tugged on a heavy fishing line, attempting to reel her in. She jerked against the pressure, feeling as though she'd been chained to something solid and immovable. When that only increased the strain, she reached over her shoulder and plucked at the sigil through her shirt, trying to get hold of it. After a moment, she caught the invisible cord in one hand and gave it a good *yank*. For a moment, it felt as though she'd tried to tug the earth. Then, like an overstretched elastic, the thing she was chained to snapped toward her.

Grinning with satisfaction even as the remaining runes prickled along her spine, she chased after the boy.

Five miles away, Luc felt Rory wrench at the bond he'd created. "Shit!" He'd attached her to him so he'd have a link to her but had forgotten that the connection went two ways. Given she'd dragged him through the invisible web she had access to before they'd even been introduced, he should have remembered. Now she was doing it to him again—hauling him along without giving him a chance to think.

He had a moment to grimace at Senn—

—then he was stepping into the middle of a weedy concrete lot in front of a rundown warehouse, south of the slot.

Before supernaturals had come out into the open and San Francisco became a sanctuary city for preternatural beings, the city had been made up of distinct districts. The majority of the districts had been safe enough—meaning crime had been kept to a minimum in most areas to encourage tourism. Aberrant behavior had been tolerated as long as it stayed within the confines of the Tenderloin and a couple of places along Mission.

When normal people began to accept that "weird shit" existed whether or not they chose to believe in it, the lines between what was acceptable and what was anomalous behavior, and where those activities were tolerated, began to erode.

As a result, a new normal had been created. Where city officials had once pulled together random crackdowns in the more well-heeled neighborhoods in an effort to keep things clean and safe for wealthier taxpayers, they now had a more hit and miss approach to the problem. Since moneyed blood vamps and energy suckers alike were paying taxes and joining the ranks of government, it was difficult for well-meaning human bureaucrats to keep things even. They began to look the other way when the Fallen— psi and sang alike—started to cull meals from the runaways and homeless overrunning the city. After all, it was reasoned, vampires were citizens, too, and they had to eat.

Since the incursion and mainstreaming of the "weird shit" paranormal element, crime and aberrant behavior had pushed outward from the Tenderloin and into the areas that surrounded it. The scraggy, broken-concrete field in which Rory currently stood had once been part of a clean, crime-free, and heavily populated neighborhood that now was…not. She looked around at the empty warehouses and storefronts. Apprehension prickled through the hair at the nape of her neck. Something she didn't like the feel of, and couldn't see, was watching them.

She glanced at the kid who'd led her here and wondered if she was going to regret her decision to trust him.

"You coming?"The boy jitterbugged nervously back and forth on asphalt that looked like it had seen a fair amount of seismic activity. "We can't stay out here. They'll see us. They'll come."

"I can feel them coming," she said absently, wondering who *they* were, "but I have to wait for—ah." She brightened when the sensation she'd come to associate with having Luc nearby tickled the hair on her arms. Every particle of her being started to warm and tingle even as her spirit stretched away from her body, reaching for his. She pointed at the spot where the Brotherhood enforcer suddenly seemed to walk through a door in the air. Appearing perturbed and a trifle disconcerted, he squinted about until his gaze landed on her. "Here he is."

Grim-faced, he strode toward them. "What the hell, Rory?" he said. "Dragging me through the ether again—"

"Chaining me to you without asking first was a bad idea, Garard," she shot back. "I'm not sure what you did to my back, but I want the tie cut."

He loomed over her, all dangerous and badass. Instead of shrinking, her spirit chuckled with delight. *At last, someone to play with!* She felt herself start to glow.

"The minute you stop needing a keeper," he snarled, "I'll consider it." Reaching out with both hands, he captured the glowing energy around her, balled it into his fists, and stuffed it firmly back into her by clapping her between his palms like a cop might pat down a suspect.

"It's not like you really need a device to find me, is it?" She heard the challenge in her own voice.

"Satnav, GPS locator, bungee cord, whatever you want to call it, until we're finished with this and I can be sure you're safe, you're wearing the harness." Moodily, he turned to the boy and grimaced as though he'd smelled something bad. "Fish," he growled. "What the hell?"

"Fish?" Rory asked. She took another look at the youngster. The name fit. There was something goggle-eyed about him. His mouth was small, his lips full and protruding in his thin face. "Fish," she repeated, cementing the name in her memory.

The teen disappeared into his shoulders as he glanced sideways at Luc from underneath the edge of his hat. "You said to call if I heard something," he said defensively, "so I did."

"I told you to call *me*."There was an ominous edge to Luc's tone.

"She has better hearing." Fish gestured at Rory and tucked himself more deeply into the folds of his hat when the psi vamp glowered at him.

"Excuse me." Rory stepped between them to put a hand on Luc's chest, pushing him back. "Getting nowhere." He scowled at her. She fluttered her eyelashes and tipped the corners of her mouth up. "Solve the problem first, yell at people later."

Luc closed his eyes for a moment and shook his head, then grinned ferociously at her. "Looking forward to that." He switched his attention back to the boy. Fish. "Show me," he ordered.

Fish nodded, then turned to slink into the shadows spreading out from the nearest warehouse.

The door required a hefty amount of body English mixed with preternatural persuasion before Athan was able to get it open. Muttering invectives, he closed his eyes and imagined the door as a holograph that he could push a hand through. Then he made himself appear larger and beefier than he already was, shoved a boulder-sized fist through the reinforced iron-and-steel thing, and yanked the whole thing toward himself. With screeching, grinding reluctance, the door came free of the tunnel wall. He wrestled it aside, resumed his normal appearance, and retrieved his Maglite. Then he stepped into a humid darkness.

Fetid air filled with the musty aftertaste of mold and mildew assaulted him. There were no shadows because there was no light. Even the beam from his flashlight was swallowed up, illuminating only the area where he planted his feet.

He'd lived in such darkness once. That had been a bad time, but it had taught him unequivocally that he was a creature of light. He craved sunshine and shadow the way his father had craved the energy given off by a human soul—the way sanguine vampires craved blood. He could survive by absorbing psychic energy—a legacy from Luceire—but he was his mother's son, too. Sophiel—

Ahead and to his left, something *chinked* against the tunnel's stone surface. Attention arrested, he quickly switched off the Maglite and turned his head to listen. Another *clink*—something metallic striking stone. Tucking the flashlight into the narrow utility pocket on his thigh, Athan put the fingertips of his right hand on the wall to use it as a guide and eased forward as silently as possible. On the one hand, the move seemed silly since, technically, given his ancestry, he was capable of seeing through darkness even more absolute than this. Still, not using his dark-sight was a habit ingrained in him during millennia of living among humans. Appearing "not different" had proved useful on more occasions than he cared to count.

Strictly speaking, blending in wasn't necessary in present-day San Francisco where almost everyone understood that "otherness" was a reality. That didn't mean the supernatural population was completely accepted, however. There were still some factions hellbent on getting rid of them by whatever means necessary. And while lynching wouldn't kill Athan, it was still a damn nuisance, not to mention a frigging waste of everyone's time.

Another *plink* disrupted his thoughts. He tipped his head toward the sound.

"Please," a frightened voice whispered in his mind. *"Help me."*

"I'm here," he said aloud, hoping the voice would respond in kind. "Where are you?"

"Here."

He retrieved the penlight and flashed it floor to ceiling, looking for a door or even a crevice he'd missed in the darkness. Anger and irritation, seemingly his go-to emotions, flared through him. He took a deep breath, then exhaled harshly, just managing to prevent himself from pulverizing the Maglite to dust between his fingers.

"Tap again," he urged, trying not to sound impatient. He should have had his mother's ability to see through solid objects or to appear wherever and whenever she wanted to in the blink of a human eye. But he wasn't a guardian angel or even, strictly speaking, angelic, despite the maternal half of his heritage. He was a being that shouldn't exist, one of a kind, and the rules that governed his abilities were…

Infuriatingly unpredictable at best.

Thunk, tink, ching!

The metallic ringing came from farther down the passage. Athan scraped forward, guiding himself by feel as well as sound. When his hand encountered a corner in the passageway, he turned and followed the wall until it turned into patterned brickwork.

The clanking grew louder.

He played his flashlight over the tunnel walls until it caught on something flat gray and rust-free. Another door, this one double wide. He felt his way over to it, searched for a handle or knob. Instead, he found a slightly raised panel and keypad. He gritted his teeth. "Fuck."

Fitting the Maglite between his teeth, he ran his hands around the door's surface and edges. He could build an illusion of the portal in his mind and stick his hand through it the way he'd done with the iron door in the main tunnel, but he hesitated. This entry felt different—more solid, denser. More secure. If it had been built to keep out people like him—or as like him as other beings came—he wasn't sure what might happen if he used his abilities on it.

Likely the kind of bad thing he didn't want to have to deal with at the moment. Such as the teen or teens he was seeking winding up immolated.

Grimacing, he held a hand over the keypad to see if he could read the psychic residue off the last numbers that had been touched. It took three tries before he got it right, but he finally heard the edges of the door sough apart. He pried it open wide enough to slip through. The portal sighed shut behind him.

Chapter Eleven

Alleged to be the most human of the angels, the Watchers blended with humanity and interacted with mortals as near-equals while retaining their divinity. This very ability contributed to their fall from Grace—sometimes referred to as the "Second Fall." Not only did the Watchers "go native" by sleeping with humans and begetting children with them, they became corrupted by their stay on earth. It's said that there were those among them who were not corrupted by human foibles but were nonetheless exiled for failing to report the sins of their brethren. Thus banished, the opposing members of these groups of expats became what we now refer to as The Outcast, The Watchers, and The Illuminati.

—from *The Lightway Codex, Appendix i: Defining the Players*
by McCleron O'Connell, Indigo Lightworker

Brooding, uneasy gaze on his blond nemesis, Luc followed Rory and Fish toward a boarded-over warehouse. The loose, dancer's sway of her hips, the light but precise ballerina placement of her feet as she walked, mesmerized him. The laughing, almost smug glances she threw over her shoulder at him made him want to strangle her at the same time that he hungered to kiss her senseless.

He desired her body and soul—or with as much soul as he had left. But more, he needed her—her light, and her sunny, in-your-face attitude. He needed to keep her safe from the harm he instinctively knew she was rushing toward and that was rushing even faster toward her.

How the hell was he supposed to protect her if he couldn't keep track of her? Especially when the very runes he'd applied to keep her grounded meant that she could now run through a fucking *ripple* in space-time.

She was a riddle wrapped in an enigma wrapped in a package so bewilderingly bright and unselfconsciously sensual and sexy that he could barely think straight. Athan's mother had pushed his limits, but not like this. Though hardly his proudest achievement, he was pretty sure that he'd gone after Sophiel purely for the exercise. Who else, after all, had ever succeeded in corrupting—and impregnating—a seraph?

That aside, surely he'd come across other women in the span of creation who were at least similar in appearance and demeanor to the dancer who'd caused him to come all over his bathroom without even being physically in the same room with him. So why had none of them punched his buttons and tightened his trousers the way she did? Why had he not wanted to absorb them into his skin, his senses, his *life* the way he did Aurora Montgomery? And what the hell was that about, anyway? Being truly immortal rather than just exceptionally hard to kill, he'd never thought of himself as someone with a life to live, but rather with an existence to endure.

As though she'd heard his thoughts, Rory turned and started walking backward, gaze on him. "Mistake."

His guard automatically went up. "What?"

"Enduring existence rather than living. How boring is that?"

Luc snorted. It bothered him that she could read him—or more to the point, hear his thoughts—so easily, but it wouldn't do to give in to that idea. To recognize that he could no longer hear hers unless she let him. "You're barely a zygote on the end of a pin by comparison. Don't judge."

Rory shook her head. "Just sayin'. You live a long time, apathy sets in. Could be bad"—she waggled a hand in the air between them—"for someone not you."

Laughter huffed from his lungs. It had been decades—the 1960s, Woodstock, maybe—since anyone had taken him to task over the wages of indifference. God above, he was *old*.

A comic book dialogue bubble appeared in front of his face. *Don't engage.*

Damned Jinx. His lifelong friend might lead the Brotherhood of Shadows team and require 24/7 telepathic access to him, but that didn't mean Luc wasn't allowed some privacy. He saw Rory raise an eyebrow at him as he swiped the mental image away.

"What'd he say?" she asked.

Startled, he managed, "What—who?" *Communication*, he thought non-sensically. *Intuition and psychic or telepathic abilities.* The tats had probably enhanced her abilities there, too.

"Whoever's pissing you off."

"You could see that?"

She shrugged and gave him a lopsided grin. "Body language."

Luc stared at her, bemused. Damn. Outclassed big time. What the fuck had he done when he inked her? Or better, what the freaking hell was she, and what hadn't Senn and Jinx told him? About her *and* this mission?

Grimacing, he lifted his gaze over her head in time to see Fish disappear into some high grass then through a jagged hole in the side wall of the neglected building. Quickly, he caught Rory's arm and hauled her out of his way before she could stumble backward into the structure. She stuck out her tongue at him and fluttered her eyelashes when he had to stop long enough to rip off several of the rotting boards to make the opening big enough for him to get through. Ignoring her, he took her wrist and tucked her firmly behind him as he ducked through the enlarged entry.

Inside, the warehouse was dim and appeared mostly empty, smelled and tasted of rot and decay. The air was thick with dust motes that eddied and swirled in what remained of the light that filtered through broken windows and cracked walls. The silence was extreme—the atmosphere seemed utterly deadened to sound, the stillness deafening. No outside noise penetrated the dilapidated structure, making Luc wonder if someone with magical abilities had employed a dampening spell on it.

"This way."

Fish's whisper was an exhalation, disturbing the dust around him and interrupting Luc's thoughts. The boy twirled his hand at them to keep up as he crept forward with surprising speed. Keeping Rory tight behind him, Luc followed.

Since her out-of-body experience at Luc's before he'd tattooed her, Rory had had a difficult time keeping her mind on the tasks at hand. She was normally somewhat distracted by her awareness of the grid, but things had really gotten away from her the minute he'd walked into her dance studio and her abilities had awakened.

She wanted him. Bad. And diddling herself whenever she got home tonight simply wasn't going to cut it.

Disorienting glimpses from her sleeping run across the city flashed into her mind. Her frantic dash up the tree trunks in the ring of trees across from the house. The clawing, cloying sensation of half-breed Dugo Balangs targeting her, her blood, when her feet began to bleed. The sapping, deadening draw on her energies by the Ekoa Krillu who had invaded the square to prey on its homeless residents after dark.

The blur of porch lights and neon signs on closed businesses as she fled through the concrete streets. The deathly frightening sense of danger nearly upon her when she had reached the iron gates that protected the front of Sunshine Dance.

The disturbing but incredible rush of heat and power that had spilled through her when she melted the lock on the gates then threw yet another psi vamp away from her with a flick of her hand.

The dark, brilliant flood of strength and energy that had poured through her when she'd danced.

The vision of tattered black wings and the craving she'd experienced upon Luc's arrival, then when she'd landed in his arms and her cleft had come into contact with his straining erection.

For the first time in her life, arousal was something more than a momentary side effect of her profession. Many of her fellows viewed sex as just sex—another physical activity useful in relieving stress after a long day of rehearsals and performances. Though she'd chafed at her parents' and the Lawtons' tendency to overprotect her from the world, Rory had always known she'd never be able to view even the idea of any sexual relationship as merely casual, so she had steered clear of them. "No fucking where you work" was the rule by which she lived. Still it had been difficult, given that some of the more seductive shows she'd appeared in were little more than very sensual, highly arousing, dry-humping, clothed sex.

Not for you, something inside her had always whispered. She kept a few special toys on hand to relieve the worst of an after-performance ache. Still, her inability to simply let go and fully enjoy what dancing and being touched by a partner did to her body chafed sometimes. But even the most provocative dance had never caused her to feel like this.

Despite her anger over Luc's duplicity and the invisible harness he'd inked into her back, her body fairly wept with the need to be touched by him. Joined with his.

With the grid buzzing in the background, she tried to concentrate on anything but the massive and intriguing length of flesh encased behind the fly of his black jeans. And couldn't.

She wanted him to do to her what no one but she herself had done to her before—wanted his mouth and one of his hands on her tits, his other hand at her mound. Wanted his thumb on her clit, his fingers jammed into and pumping hard within her slit while she screamed herself hoarse from the pleasure of orgasming for the first time at someone else's—his—hand.

She wanted to go down on him, to taste his inhumanly sized cock, feel it swell and shudder, spume and erupt inside her.

She wanted that cock bumping and grinding inside her while she came and came and *came*, and his cum filled her.

She was pretty sure she wanted this more than anything she'd ever wanted in her life—

—and then he pulled her after him through the hole in the warehouse wall.

Immediately, the empty building started to whisper to her.

She did her best to keep her mind focused on the supremely tasty-looking shape of Luc's butt and the fact that she wanted to bite it, but the warehouse refused to be silenced.

Need, need, neeeeed, it murmured. *Feed, feed, feeeeeed…*

Unsettled by the intrusion, she removed her thoughts from the flood of carnal fantasies and turned it to the usually frantic, hive-like buzz of the grid.

An uncustomary silence greeted her. Attention sharpening, and trusting Luc to keep her from falling in the real world, she shut her eyes and called the lighted nexus to her. A few of the bright pinpoints appeared to pulse, but the hush was absolute. It was almost as though everyone connected to the network had drawn a breath at the same time and was waiting.

A sense of dread filled Rory. Uneasily, she opened her eyes and stopped short to send mental feelers into the stillness, searching for answers. Luc cast a questioning glance over his shoulder at her. Only half aware of his regard, she raised her eyebrows and looked around.

Need, need, need, something within the shadows and dust motes muttered. *Feed, feed, feed…*

"Do you hear anything?" she asked Luc.

Eyes narrowed on her, he canted his head this way and that, fingering the amethyst shield in his chest as he listened to the silence. After a moment, he drew a breath and nodded grimly.

"Something's lying in wait." He tugged her hand, tipped his head after Fish. "We need to go," he said softly, "but keep your ears open."

They followed Fish along a slight valley in the concrete floor. A grated drainage trench ran its length, ostensibly to catch runoff from water, chemicals, or other fluids that might once have been used inside the warehouse. Intuition sharpened, Luc studied the drain as they went. At one point, Rory stooped to touch the iron lattice, then shook her head at him, troubled.

"It's blocking me," she whispered.

Equally bothered, Luc nodded. Psychic ability was just one of the many skills supernatural beings possessed that iron tended to interfere with. Rory had melted the lock in the iron gate at her dance studio in her sleep, but he'd also gotten through the gate and into the dance studio itself before she knew he was there. The iron had prevented her from sensing the dangers outside it.

Thoughtfully, he watched Fish carefully put one foot in front of the other as he walked along the top of the grate, keeping his feet off the concrete. There might well be more to the kid than he'd realized. The trench took them past a maintenance pit covered with broken boards to another part of the building, where an intricate labyrinth of abandoned crates and barrels wove around to a surprisingly well-maintained freight elevator. Two levels down, they stepped out of the elevator onto a loading area where the distinctive sound of barking sea lions hit them. Pinnipeds lined a no-longer-used loading dock that extended into the Bay.

Overhead, cloud cover obscured the sky.

"This way," Fish murmured and guided them away from the dock, across more weed-riddled, broken asphalt and concrete. Shallow gullies formed by runoff populated a scraggly slope that ended at the water. Wild grasses, vines, and flowers caught at their feet and ankles as though the vegetation worked in league with something that didn't want them to get wherever they were going.

Fish looked anxiously back toward the warehouse, then skidded downhill.

Senses sharpened by suspicion, Luc also looked back the way they'd come. Again, he touched the crystal in his chest. Awareness niggled at him again. Something that he couldn't put a finger on raised the hair on his arms and at the back of his neck. He glanced at Rory. She cocked her head, gave the warehouse a calculating squint. Her fingertips fluttered forward to brush the air in that direction. Then her lips twisted. She gave Luc a curt nod and returned her attention to Fish, who'd stopped a little over midway downslope, apparently to peer *into* the hillside. When he looked up at them, Rory picked her way down through the rough grass, sand, and gravel, pointedly ignoring the hand Luc held out to her. He swallowed a grin with an automatic chaser of irritation and followed. Holding her hand had felt good, and he wanted to do it again. The contact had seemed somehow normal in a world where "normal" was outside his purview.

They joined Fish where a fissure in the hillside revealed a rusted, moss-coated concrete sewage pipe. Luc guessed it hadn't been used since the first part of the twentieth century. The very idea of it made him feel itchy. Since he'd hauled himself out of the pit after his Fall, he'd never been fond of enclosed places. He was a big guy, and even something wide and high enough to allow a pair of normal-sized humans to walk side by side felt cramped to him. A wash of sand and rocky gravel still decorated the downslope where rain and sewer water would have rushed down into the Bay. He watched as Fish flattened himself in the brush atop it and peered cautiously over the lip then looked back at them.

"The voices are in here."

Immediately, Rory slipped around Luc and down the incline to look into the tube. Luc barely caught her before she stole inside.

"There may be wildlife," he told her firmly. "You go *after* me."

She looked him over from the tips of his custom-size black Doc Martens to the width of his shoulders all the way up to his eyebrows, which were nearly two feet higher than the top of her head. Then she squinted at the pipe and laughed.

"You'll never fit," she said and slid under his arm and into the aperture.

Luc swore under his breath, glanced up, and caught Fish by the cape before the boy had a chance to get away. "Your escapade means you next." He plunked the youth into the pipe and entered after him, blocking the exit. Fish turned and tried to duck back outside.

"Too small, too dark." Fear filled his voice as he tried to shove Luc out of his way.

Understanding his panic all too well, Luc snapped his fingers. A faint illusion of witchlight appeared in his hand. The illumination was so dim that Solaya would have jeered at his ineptitude, but it was better than noth-ing. It was essentially the same sort of mind trick that had allowed Athan to appear larger than he was to the frightened girls on the pier. Luc didn't use the talent often and it showed, but it was all he had. A flashlight hadn't been on his list of "might needs" this morning.

"You called her, you make sure she's going to the right place," he said harshly, flicking the sphere of light into the tunnel ahead of them. He didn't like terrorizing the boy, but trying to cram himself into a space sized for smaller humans who'd lived more than a hundred years ago was making him cranky. More to the point, he couldn't risk letting Rory go in there on her own, especially given how quickly she could move. If anything hap-pened, he wasn't sure he'd be able to get to her in time in the cramped space. "Anything happens to her, happens to you."

To his credit, the boy didn't blink, only said anxiously, "I have to get back. They need me."

"*Who* needs you?" Luc asked sharply, but Fish had already followed the pathetic excuse for a witchlight into the culvert and didn't respond.

Feeling much the same way he had when he and Jinx had clawed their way through the claustrophobic tracks out of hell, Luc edged cautiously into the subterranean ductwork and followed.

A dense, fog-like thing rushed Athan, flinging him backward into the sewer channel. Dropping the flashlight, he caught himself on his hands and flipped upright to slide back through the portal before it could slam shut and seal itself against him again. Even so, the door whacked his trailing arm and caught the hem of his T-shirt as it closed. Ignoring the excruciating sensation of the bones in his forearm breaking and knitting themselves back together almost immediately, he jerked his shirt free. Cool, damp air touched his ribs when the material tore. He stepped forward, blinking, taking stock.

Darkness, Stygian and absolute, penned him in. A shudder of memory ran through him before he could stop it. He'd been incarcerated in an iron-bound coffin and dumped in the North Sea for decades in the mid-sev-enteenth century after London's Great Fire was blamed on him. He couldn't be killed, but he could be ritually imprisoned, which was *far* worse.

Determinedly, he left the past behind. The vaporous fog-thing wrapped around him, alive but not sentient. Almost nosey. He brushed the thing off, felt sticky moisture coalesce on his skin as whatever it was wafted to one side.

The clank of a chain drew his attention. He tried to orient toward it, but even with his extraordinary talents, it was difficult. Stone and gloom amplified everything, made it nearly impossible to get his bearings. He couldn't even sense energy signatures, which puzzled him. Even iron didn't usually mask things from him. Someone had set up the obscure-me ward at the door to guard something, but that shouldn't have had any effect on his abilities, either.

"Hello?" he called.

More weak chain rattling. He remembered that sound from dungeons of centuries past. Remembered, without emotion, the feel of shackles biting into his wrists and ankles…

"Hello," he called again. Anxious to rid himself of phantom sensations and deeds he didn't want to recall, he said, "I'm here to help. Where are you?"

The sound of breath rattling in human lungs made him turn to his left. Opening his senses, he got down on the floor and began to ease forward, sliding his hands carefully about as he went. A faint spark of energy came from behind and to his left. He turned, tasting the atmosphere and the stink of human waste and fear. Slowly, he inched forward until his searching hands came into contact with a thin arm encased in T-shirt cotton. Clammy film coated the arm, which twitched when he touched it.

The distant scoff of shoes on concrete made Athan lift his head toward what he thought was the door he'd entered through. Energy riddled with sunlight coursed along the tunnel on the other side of the imprisoning wall. A shudder ran through him with the desire to feed on that energy.

Instead, he bent low over the victim—a boy, he thought—and whispered, "Help's coming."

Then he rose, called up his ability to meld, and melted into and through the wall of the chamber, back into the corridor.

And ran.

After an uncomfortable number of twists, turns, and jogs that sloped gradually upward through the hillside, the concrete tunnel finally widened onto an extremely dank but roomier corridor. Gratefully, Luc stepped into it and straightened to his full height. He hadn't actually needed to stoop—much—in the tunnel, but mindset coupled with his mild claustrophobia was a powerful thing. Now, whether it should have or not, his entire body felt like it had been squashed into a Pringles potato chip tube the way joke snakes were stuffed into a peanut can. He stretched to work the crick out of his back, neck, and shoulders, and looked around for Rory and Fish.

The ball of light he'd created hovered near the tunnel's ceiling fifty feet away. Below it, Fish and Rory stood in shadow. The boy bounced on the balls of his feet, spinning nervously in place. Rory's head tilted first one way then the other, the indistinct silhouette of her hands cupped to her ears. Luc's senses keened, gut briefly clenched with foreboding. He edged along the corridor, listening.

A hollow *thunk* broke the stillness. In almost the same instant, Fish turned and bolted back toward the mouth of the passageway in a flat-footed run. Simultaneously, Rory ran forward and Luc felt a yank at his heart center—the damn "leash" he'd tattooed at the midpoint of her back working against him, tugging him along in her wake. Muttering epithets that called into account the lack of forethought that had allowed her to make the tether two-way, he hurried after her. The terror on Fish's face as he rushed past caused Luc to refrain from reaching out to catch him and force him to continue with them. Instead, he sent the almost-exhausted witchlight after the teen to illuminate his retreat.

Two more turns deeper into the underground labyrinth found them in another pitch-dark corridor. Luc sensed rather than saw the outline of heavy steel doors inset into the walls about six feet apart on either side of them. A hundred feet or so farther ahead, a thin beam of light lit the floor. Instinctively, Luc lengthened his stride to catch Rory and thrust her behind him as a rush of dark but familiar energy washed over them.

Athan.

His hands curled into fists and his gut twisted as he suddenly under-stood exactly what he and Sophiel had loosed centuries before.

The spike of energy ahead of them grabbed Rory's attention at the same time Luc's grip tightened on her arm. She winced.

"Ow!" She tried to jerk away when Luc put a hand over her mouth and hauled her to his side. "Hey!" she protested—or tried to.

Ahead of them, a vivid, lemony yellow aura brightened the darkness above the thin beam of a small flashlight someone had left on the floor. Ducking out from under him, she started toward it, only to have Luc snatch her back.

"It's benign," she whispered. But it wasn't entirely benevolent. Every sense she possessed stung with that knowledge. She couldn't get over the feeling of being watched that made the *Ehwaz* tat between her shoulder blades itch. "Leave off!"

His glare was a physical sensation in the shift of his grip on her arm. *Me first*, he told her silently.

Equally silent, she flicked her fingers impatiently against his hand. Reluctantly, he released her but didn't step out of her way.

Something bad in there.

Not because of whoever that is, she mentally shot back, gesturing at the receding yellow glow. The shade of the aura told her that the unseen person was new to and hesitant about the lighter side of things. How new, she couldn't tell.

Uneasy but holding her hands open to the darkness, she sidled around Luc, testing the atmosphere as she glided forward.

The sensation of being spied on increased, and the spot between her shoulder blades began to burn.

She'd always felt looked after and taken care of in one way or another, especially since the death of her parents. After they'd died, she'd experienced their continued presence as an almost physical thing—as though they stood at her shoulder with countless members of her ancestors and guardians, supporting her, and even occasionally guiding her toward or away from something she'd planned to do. But this was different. Unlike Luc's tracker at the center of her back, this *presence* seemed wrong. Intrusive. More than nosey. Like the thing that had been making her tired lately. The thing that had instantly sapped her energy the day Luc first appeared in her studio.

The thing that had physically drained her when she went into the psychic grid.

Something akin to the willies shot down her spine, making her look around sharply. Whatever or whoever it was, it was also making her feel anxious, and anxiety was not a place she lived. She didn't like it even a little. Whereas everything about Luc made her feel like something life-changing was lying in wait for her, this other thing felt like disaster and horror and no going back. She wished that whatever abilities she'd suddenly come into would allow her to understand what she sensed.

Something to work on.

She reached the light spill on the floor just as the yellow aura seemed to get sucked into the blackness further along the passageway. Beside her, Luc stooped to pick up the flashlight. He turned it over in his hands, sniffed it, and recoiled.

"Athan."

"What?" she asked.

"Nothing," he said almost furiously.

"You know who that is." Not a question but a statement, bold and accusing.

"Not now," he snapped, angry. "Let it go and let's get on with it."

Rory eyed his dark silhouette. It was clear that he knew the aura's owner, and that the knowledge made him angry—more so with himself than anyone else. She was just about to press the issue when a mewling sound caught her attention. She turned toward it, but Luc grabbed for her.

"Rory, don't."

She slipped out of his grasp and, before he could prevent it, took the light from him and stepped through the illumination-swallowing doorway it revealed. Luc joined her as she swept the torch around. The weak cry had subsided, but the impression of terribleness lying in wait got stronger. The sound of something sliding across the floor startled her and she shuddered. Luc ran a hand down her arm to squeeze her hand. Then he relieved her of the flashlight and pointed it at the floor in front of his feet.

"Let's see what we've got," he said grimly.

The overpowering stench of human waste and decay hit them first.

Rory tried to control her gag reflex against it and lost. When Luc tried to help her, she pushed him away, gesturing for him to locate whatever caused the horrifying odor. Then as quickly as possible without light to aid her, she stumbled to the side and vomited up what little she'd eaten that day. As her insides churned, the runes along her back burned and writhed—sent wispy, spider-like movements racing through her. She stiffened. It felt as though an electrical charge zapped her brain, winged painfully along every nerve ending in her body to the tips of her fingers and ends of her toes.

Something twisted inside her, shaped a facet of her personality she hadn't known existed. She'd always been a peacemaker, whether that meant brokering a peace between Senn and Solaya during their childhood squabbles or negotiating a temporary cease-fire between gang members who were students or siblings of students at Sunshine Dance. She'd never been prone to fits of temper, and anger was something she didn't do. But now, anger—bright, hot, and unfamiliar—surfaced to pull her shattered emotions together in a way nothing she'd ever before experienced had.

As though she stood outside herself, Rory watched herself straighten and wipe her mouth. Then she dropped her arms to her sides and spread her fingers wide. A sensation of blazing heat ran through her limbs and into her hands, lit a fire behind her eyes. And suddenly she could *see* the intricate pattern of the light-and-sound dampening charm someone had cast on the place. Her fingers plucked the air, pinching, pulling, unknitting the invocation. When she was finished, her palms glowed softly for a moment before she flicked her hands.

Light filled the room, revealing three teenagers—what appeared to be two girls and a boy—lying as close to the center of the chamber as possible. Each was manacled to a different wall by heavy chains that stopped short before the kids could touch each other. Everything inside Rory tightened.

"What the hell?" On the floor tracing a length of one of the heavy chains in his search for the adolescents, Luc slapped a hand over his eyes and peered up at her from between his fingers. "What'd you do?"

She gave him a grim smile and a one-shoulder shrug. "Must be something you did."

He rose. "Rory…"

"Don't, Luc." She shook her head. "Whatever went into those things"—another hand flap over her shoulder to indicate her new tattoos—"it's getting me through, so it's all good. I just gotta…" She hesitated and shrugged again. "I've just got to learn how to work them instead of letting them work me."

Bleak but determined, she went to assess the teens.

Luc reached them first. From the sound of the faintly beating hearts, he already knew that two of the teens were barely alive. He placed his fingertips at the third's throat. Judging by her cooling warmth, she appeared to be recently dead. He looked up, shook his head sadly at Rory. Despite his effort to keep her back, she knelt beside the girl and placed a hand in the center of her chest. Gave Luc a beseeching look.

"Help me," she said. Then she began to sing.

The instant she opened her mouth, agony tore through Luc, drove him to his knees. His throat ached with a scream without voice, and his head felt as though he was being battered to death by a sledgehammer from the inside. Instead of dulling it, the cavity in the tunnel resonated and intensified the song until the only thing he knew was pain, worse than he'd experienced the day he'd found Rory at the dance studio. The rune tats or the pulverized crystals he'd added to them amplified the effect of her voice a thousand-fold, minimum. He tried shutting his eyes against the throbbing, but his eyelids, along with the rest of his muscles, seemed to be paralyzed. He couldn't move, couldn't breathe. The amethyst shield stone in his chest burned.

"Rory." His voice was barely a rasp. "Please…"

Something about the timbre of her song changed, softened. As swiftly as the pain had come, it was gone. Luc drew a harsh breath. Rory's request for help echoed through him and, without thinking, he reached for her.

Power rippled through him the moment his hand contacted her back. Heat radiated up his arm and into his chest, made him reel all over again. He cursed himself and the weakness he wasn't used to. Pulled himself together and pushed every bit of energy he had available into her.

Nothing happened for a moment. Then there was an earthquake rumble and the entire tunnel pitched and rolled. A blast of energy ran through Luc and exploded into the cell, hurled him into the nearest wall, with Rory on top of him. Feeling drunk and giddy from the energy overload, he caught her close and wrapped himself around her, absorbing the excess power that coursed through her until the energy aftershocks subsided.

A low moan and the sound of a chain scraping the floor caught their attention. Rory scrambled off of him, and Luc's jaw dropped. He watched as the girl who had been dead moments before curled onto her side and coughed weakly.

Beside him, Rory made a small sound and slumped, drained. He turned to stare at her. "What *are* you?" he asked.

Sated by a late-night feed at Carpe Noctem, the club owned by the blood-sucking leader of the Brotherhood of Shadows, Beck once more dreamed of becoming the plague god Erra, bringer of mayhem and pestilence. He was still too human to be as thoughtlessly brutal as the god he emulated, but once his ancestors transferred their power to him, he would be merciless. He would find every special female child of the right age with the right amount of Nephilim ancestry and he would re-populate their race. Rebuild everything his ancestors had lost by being entombed for so many aeons.

Though security at Carpe Noctem was tight, and those waiting to enter were culled early and often to make sure no under twenty-ones were admitted, he'd still managed to pluck two ripe, underage coeds from the waiting throng, right under Jinx Falken's nose. Thinking of how the reformed Fallen would react when he learned of Erra's audacious play made Beck giggle in his sleep.

The coeds had been identical twins, beautiful, popular, and from a family that would miss and hunt for them—not his usual sport. But seducing them out of the clique of students they were with had been relatively easy. Successfully luring them into the tunnels where he'd spent the night alternately terrorizing them and forcing them to perform sexually deviant acts they'd never wanted to imagine had to be the sweetest thing he'd ever tasted. Draining the life force from one of them while the other watched and felt every single thing he did to her sister…

His cock hardened again.

A low rumble and roller coaster-like surge rattled him out of bed and sent him staggering into the doorway of his Glen Park apartment's bedroom. Bracing himself against what his ecstasy-addled mind assumed was a moderate earthquake, he clung desperately to the dream's pleasures even as they faded. His hard-on wilted. Reality set in as a brilliant flash of pure energy sent him sprawling across his Persian rug. He tried to right himself, but an exhaustion more profound than he'd ever experienced flattened him to the floor.

Weakness filtered through his limbs, made his head a dead weight. Again, he tried to move but couldn't. Not an earthquake. He had enough presence of mind to know that his energy was being drained by someone or something. A huge amount of energy had to have been expended to do this to him.

In an effort to reclaim his strength, he tried to tap his mental link to the teenagers he'd imprisoned in the subterranean tunnels. They should be cold, terrified, and despairing enough by now to bring his borrowed energies back in a flash. But the connection was broken. He could feel the frayed edges of the tie, understood with disbelief that someone had done what should have been impossible—permanently disconnected him from his energy source. Had stolen it…

He tasted the still-tingling air with the tip of his tongue…stolen it by freeing them.

Hunger and exhaustion raged through him. Without thinking, he attempted to mine his psychic energy link to Savitri Nousaine, Master of the City. Nothing, nada, zip, zilch. It was as though Nousaine had found out what he was doing—what he was trying to become—and somehow cut him off.

Some part of him understood he should be concerned about that, but the god he was becoming couldn't be bothered. He reached for the link between himself and his ancestors at the same moment they began to howl inside his head.

Fear ran through him, separating him from Erra. The Watchers, those angels sent to mingle with their human charges and then exiled to earth by *their* Creator as having become "too human" to return to paradise— those beings from whom he was, in fact, distantly descended—were spoiling for blood.

His.

The connection between them and their food source was gone, and their energies had been drained, too.

An intense eruption of light and energy flooded Savitri Nousaine's crystal tower, flinging him back from the windows. He landed with what should have been a bone-shattering *thump* against one of the office's interior walls. Bits of plaster dusted him when the wall and ceiling cracked from the force of the strike. Shouts and screams came from outside his door just before it burst open to admit two members of his security staff and his personal assistant.

"*Sir!*" the assistant shouted and ran to him.

The security personnel split to either side of the office, weapons drawn, searching for the source of the attack before Nousaine said faintly, "There's no one."

"Get the medic," his assistant shrieked, causing him to wince at the pitch.

He put a hand on her arm, claiming her attention while simultaneously drawing off her excess adrenaline to replace a little of the energy the power surge had drained from him.

"No," he said with such lethal calmness that the woman lurched to her feet and staggered back.

Clearly bewildered by her sudden weakness, she sank to the floor against an intact wall. Nousaine regarded her with something akin to regret—or as close as he ever came to it. He never fed on staff if he could help it. It was bad for business. Nevertheless, he'd have to finish draining her once things calmed down a bit. Staff would corroborate the earthquake or heavy, tremor-like occurrence and the assistant's subsequent collapse. Cause of death would not be able to be determined but would appear natural.

Discarding the thought with his momentary frailty, he pushed himself to his feet without help and touched the dent in the wall he'd been thrown against. Psychic residue tingled under his fingertips, burned upward into his palm. Wary, he pulled his hand back and looked at it. Nothing to see there—except the faint glimmer of something he couldn't identify.

Attention sharpening, he made his way back to the windows he'd been flung away from. The quartz in the building's façade was amplifying the energy burst, leading him psychically along an invisible nexus of pathways, showing him things he'd only previously suspected. Sunrise etched the baseball-size dent in the window at what must have been the point of the force's impact, spiderwebbed away from it in brilliant lines.

"Get this repaired immediately," he said absently.

Neither the security guards nor the other staff were brave enough to tell him that they saw nothing in need of mending. Instead, they simply watched as he put out his hand to touch the glass. He pulled back when an overwhelming flood of telepathic information spilled through him. The exchange was disjointed, but a few coherent words came through.

Beck. Betrayal. Two masters.

Watchers.

A shudder of unease passed through Nousaine. His eyes narrowed. He'd thought those "others" of ancient legend had been done away with centuries prior. That the unpleasant Beck was capable of deceiving him about something like this, and was also able to hide that deception…

Beck was not the sharpest mentee Nousaine had ever trained. Sometimes, however, ambition and delusion were enough.

Lips pursed, he stepped forward to touch the window just outside the spiderweb of cracks. Heat seared his fingers, seemed to sizzle on the skin.

Kidnap. Kill. Unsanctioned.

Anger made inroads into Nousaine's carefully cultivated demeanor. Though brusque and unsubstantiated, the anonymous communication bore the earmarks of truth. Enough so that Nousaine tapped the link between himself and his human second.

It took barely a moment for him to read the truth. His mouth etched a distasteful grimace into his cheeks. If the Watchers were involved, he'd have to swallow his principles and try for a temporary truce between his forces and those of the Council. An unholy but beneficial alliance would be the only way to bring his second and the "others" down.

Chapter Twelve

Stories are told about beings entombed deep within a place once known as Kartchner Caverns. There is anecdotal evidence suggesting that these beings may be what human folklore has termed the Watchers. The myths surrounding these banished creatures are many, but the most frightening is the story that speaks of a time when the Watchers will rise from slumber and invade the earth to consume all of humanity.

—from The Lightway Codex, Appendix i: Defining the Players
by McCleron O'Connell, Indigo Lightworker

There was no cell reception in the tunnels. Luc didn't want to leave Rory alone in order to return to the surface for help, but there was little choice. Iron and something else blocked his mental connection to Jinx, and even Rory's crystal grid seemed to be unavailable.

Though weakened by the extraordinary amount of energy it had taken to bring the second girl back from the brink of death, Rory was quiet but seemed fine. Luc wondered if he couldn't push some energy into her the way he had after her spirit had disappeared during their initial meeting. However, now that the crisis was past, the same block that prevented him from contacting Jinx also inhibited him from borrowing energy from an outside source to replenish either of them. The iron obstructions also made it impossible for him to drain off even a bit of the teens' extreme terror.

Reluctantly, he started back through the tangle of passageways to find help.

He hadn't gotten far when he met Senn, Celeste, and a full Council of Light healing team coming toward him. As Celeste and the H.E.A.R.T. team passed him, Senn halted and pulled him aside.

"Who called?" Luc asked. "I was about to, but there's no reception down here."

"Anonymous tip," Senn said tightly. "Your friend Fish showed us where when we arrived."

Luc looked down the tunnel to where the healing team and Celeste were entering the first cell. "Who told Fish how to reach you?"

When Senn merely shrugged, Luc worked his jaw around something more than mere irritation. He wished he could figure out what it was about the boy that bothered him.

Instead, he turned and headed back toward the chamber where Rory waited with the teens. Senn followed.

The healing team had already moved in and set up spotlights, working as quickly as possible to prep the three teens for travel. Senn wanted Rory to go, too, but she shoved him away and turned to Luc, silently pleading with him to understand.

He did, too well. The way she hovered over them, it was clear she wanted to make sure the kids were being taken care of. She needed help, too, judging from the wild-eyed look she gave him. She was wired, not weakened by the amount of energy she'd expended to resurrect the dead teen. Adrenaline fairly sparked off her, despite her near-frantic efforts to contain it. She needed to get rid of it somehow.

And he needed to feed.

He saw her recognize his hunger, felt her start to push the energy toward him. He shook his head. *Not here.*

She closed her eyes and ducked her chin slightly. *When? Where? Soon…*

He offered her a tight-lipped grin in response. It had better be soon. Because of the energy she'd drawn from him to do whatever the hell it was she'd done, he was as near to ravenous as he'd come since he'd first climbed out of the pit. Merely sipping the excess off a tourist mob wouldn't cut it.

A low growl purred in his throat. He needed energy, and as much of it as Rory could spare, as soon as Celeste and the H.E.A.R.T team were nowhere nearby. Something told him it would be a bad idea for anyone from the Brotherhood, H.E.A.R.T., or the Council—especially the Council's director—to see Rory in action. Particularly the part where she was capable of jump-starting the recently deceased with a little help from him.

As though she'd heard his thoughts, Celeste cast a sharp, penetrating glance at him, then Rory. Whatever she saw made her snap, "I want to see you both in the clinic tonight."

Rory gave her a side-eyed glance, then turned to look at her full-on as though perplexed by something in Celeste's expression. She opened her mouth.

A chill of presentiment rippled through Luc. The area along his back where his wings had once been itched and burned in a way it never had. The unease he'd been feeling since Senn had first sent him to Rory intensified to def-con levels. Every protective, guardian instinct he'd ever possessed switched into high. He stepped quickly toward her.

"You should at least have someone check you over," he told her. His gut warned him it would be bad for everyone, but especially Rory, if Celeste learned what Rory had done to bring the teen back. "You got thrown pretty hard in *the earthquake*."

He put subtle but emphatic emphasis on "earthquake," warning her not to give herself away. She responded with a slightly restless but killing look that made him stifle a laugh and had Senn physically backing up a couple of steps. Clearly, her inborn cheekiness remained undamaged.

"What about you? I think you hit a wall. I only bounced into you."

"I'm unbreakable," he said mildly.

"We'll see," she murmured in a way that made him certain they would.

And that he would probably come out worse for wear.

He cleared his throat. "Anyway," he said.

"Fine." Then telepathically, for him alone, *Something's wrong. Where's Fish?*

Luc sent a glance up the tunnel. *Afraid,* he answered. *Ran.*

We have to find him before someone else does. Rory turned to Celeste. "I'll ask Kate to look me over when I go to the clinic tomorrow. Or you can do it when I visit these kids"—she made a sweeping gesture that encompassed the teens ready to be wheeled out of the tunnel—"to make sure they're doing okay."

Luc heard the warning in the statement at the same time Celeste did. The director's lips pulled back tightly over her teeth in a travesty of a smile.

"As you like." Ignoring Luc, she eyed Senn. "I'm holding you responsible for seeing she does."

Rory shrugged. Luc rolled his eyes. Senn gave them both a *What the hell* look, but let it slide—for the moment. "As long as you promise to get checked out," he told Rory. He eyed the dark end of the tunnels. "I don't think we're finished here," he said cryptically and headed deeper into the passageway.

Rory at his back, Luc joined him in searching the remaining corridors around the cell in which the teens had been imprisoned. Three more iron-and-steel reinforced doors were located and broken down. One of the cells was empty, but between the other two, they found five more adolescents aged approximately thirteen to seventeen. Four of these five were long dead, the fifth barely alive.

Rory immediately rushed toward the dead, weeping. Luc caught her, pulled her to his chest. She struggled against him, straining toward the bodies.

"There's nothing. You can't…"

I can, she shouted in his head. *Let me!*

His gut churning, he reached out with his spirit to comfort her. Even if he had energy left to bolster hers, the bodies, bloated or desiccated, had clearly been in the cells for a long time.

They're too long gone, he responded. Nothing came back from a sleep so endless without a price. Hell, he couldn't begin to comprehend what price might be exacted for the child she'd already brought back. *Look at them.*

She turned within the framework of his arms and did. Covered her mouth and turned back. Anguish was a living thing, wracking her shoulders, leaving her with soundless sobs. He felt her wrap his spirit's offering around herself and hunker in for a few moments. When she pulled back, he released her to collect the child who was still alive before the Council's forensic retrieval unit moved in.

Hours later, in the sunlight of the following perfect May afternoon, the forensic team wrapped up its initial investigation. A Council investigative team had been dispatched to canvass the remaining miles of sewer pipes, just in case. All possible evidence had been collected, and the living had been ferried to a Council-run pediatric hospital. Keile Raeburn, the Council's enigmalogist, had removed the bodies to the Council's morgue. Now, only ghosts remained in the tunnels.

From the spot on the hillside that made up the long-unused sewer tunnel's entrance, Rory, Luc, and Senn watched Celeste and the remainder of her team negotiate the slope back to the Council vehicles.

"What was that about?" Senn asked.

"What was what about?" Luc asked.

"I don't know what you're talking about." Rory blinked at Senn, then looked upslope, the way Fish had led them to the tunnel entryway what felt like days ago. All those dead kids…

She shuddered. Instantly, Luc stepped in front of her, blocking her view of the tunnel.

Eyes narrowed, she worried her lower lip. A lot had happened that she couldn't reconcile, but for the moment, all she could think about was Fish and whatever—*who*ever—was frightening him. He had to be somewhere.

Distracted, she pictured the crystal nexus for the area, searching for the spark of light that belonged to him.

What is it?" Luc asked, scanning the hillside, too.

She scrutinized the hill, slid a glance toward Senn, and shrugged. Then said for Luc alone, *Something's wrong. Fish is afraid.* She glared at Senn when he snapped his fingers in her face to get her attention. "What?"

"Read me in." He sounded irritated. "I know you two"—a scowl and hand gesture that encompassed Luc—"are talking. What happened out here that you don't want Celeste to know?"

Luc tilted his chin down. *The fewer people…*

Rory gave him an impatient flick of her fingers. Luc sighed and nodded. Looked at Senn and said baldly, "With a bit of a boost from me, Rory can raise the recently dead. I don't think anyone should know, especially Celeste, the Council, and Solaya."

Senn stared from one of them to the other, uncomprehending for a moment. Then, aghast, "The fuck you say—"

He broke off when a high-pitched shriek rent the air. The escalating *no-no-no* in the cracking tones of an adolescent male trailed by a frantic "Help!" followed.

"Fish!" Rory called, starting uphill. Without thinking, she focused on the runes along her back, felt *Ehwaz* flare. The air in front of her undulated and a doorway appeared.

Follow me, she told Luc.

Then she pulled the door open and stepped through.

Luc saw a flash of light before the air seemed to ripple and form a door through which Rory disappeared. At the periphery of his vision, he saw Senn's mouth gape.

"Tesseract," he said, and swore. "She *can* do it."

Without responding, Luc reached for the tether between him and Rory and grabbed Senn's arm. "We're both going," he warned and stepped into the space-time fold Rory had left open in invitation, dragging Senn with him.

An opalescent nothing, similar to the indefinable space between worlds that Luc vaguely remembered from before the Fall, wrapped around them for a moment. When the pearly mist disappeared, they found Rory on her knees beside a makeshift pallet. Fish stood nearby, back pressed into the wall of a Quonset hut, hands scrabbling for purchase on the rusted metal. He looked like he was trying to keep himself in place—or prevent himself from bolting. His eyes bulged, gaze darted wildly around the shelter and back to the hugely pregnant girl who lay flat on her back atop the comforter she was using as a bed. Alternately moaning and screaming in agony, she rocked from side to side, clutching her belly.

"Jesus Christ," Senn said and stumbled forward, briefly disoriented by the trip.

Luc steadied him, then strode to squat beside Rory. He looked up at Fish. "Is the baby yours?"

Fish eyed him, terrified. He stuttered something that sounded like "Protect."

"Something's not right." Rory twisted, trying to ease herself behind the girl to prop her up. "The baby—we need to get her to a hospital."

"No." Fish threw himself away from the wall and onto the floor between them and the girl, babbling. "No. Magpie, no. Protect. Baby…baby…" He grabbed Rory's arm, pleading, "Have to. Can't. Watchers, no. Protect child. Save *child*!"

Watchers…

Senn grabbed Fish. "What did you say?"

At the same moment, Luc felt a wash of obscene energy gust into the space. The irritated, prickling sensation he'd been feeling off and on along his back since Rory had revived the dead girl in the tunnels intensified.

"Rory."

"Shh," Rory murmured.

"Rory!" Luc repeated.

"Shhh," she crooned again, stroking the girl's sweat-soaked hair. "Luc, this is Magpie. She needs us to help her and protect her and—" Her eyes widened. She looked at Luc. "And her child."

Luc swore and was on his feet in almost the same breath. "We have to get them out of here."

Senn hoisted Fish over his shoulder. "The Council—"

"*No!*" Fish screamed the word, terrified. "Mustn't. Dangerous. No Council, no!"

"Brotherhood." Luc caught up the girl—Magpie—and mentally called Jinx to alert him to the emergency. "Safehouse."

Rory rose, dragging the comforter with her to wrap around the girl in Luc's arms. "She needs a doctor or a doula."

"We'll get one," Luc assured her, "but right now, we have to *move*. Can you open a door again?"

She nodded. "Where to?"

Chapter Thirteen

Tesseract versus the Fae "Pop in". Tesseracting means creating
a fold in space-time, much like folding two pieces of string
together and stepping across the divide. By contrast, "popping
in" is something only the Fae can do. It is stepping through
a vacuum from one side of the "veil" between the Faery and
mundane worlds to the other. Breaching the vacuum creates
the "popping" sound.

—from *The Lightway Codex, Appendix xlvii: The Fae & Definitions*
by McCleron O'Connell, Indigo Lightworker

L uc directed them to Carpe Noctem, the multi-leveled supernatural
nightclub owned by his oldest friend, Jinx Falken. The club catered
strictly to over twenty-ones and specialized in food and drinks and
live music.

It also housed a variety of sex clubs frequented by the city's vampires.
Private entrances allowed members to partake of varying degrees of kink.
Here, humans could mingle with vampires and other supernatural beings
to dance, drink, eat, or take a walk on the wild side. Vampires, of course,
came to feed. Rory had never been, though she'd long been curious about it.

Solaya, who seemed to have been everywhere and done everything, had
told her it was "one of those places good girls don't go." Rory, who'd danced
in more sensually and sexually explicit shows than the sorceress was aware
of, had rolled her eyes—and planned to go at the first available opportunity. She'd just never expected the opportunity to present itself in such a
unique fashion.

Curious, she looked around.

Above the club floors were apartments. The first two floors of the apartments were available for long- or short-term rentals by clubgoers who wanted to continue partying after hours. The higher floors included both luxury apartments and meeting space and were for the exclusive use of the Brotherhood of Shadows.

There were two penthouse apartments, one of which belonged to Jinx. The other had been designated for use as a safe house by whomever Jinx decided to allow into it. Both were kitted out with the kind of security governments could only dream of—if they even knew it existed.

It was the second of these two apartments into which Luc had Rory "open a door."

Jinx was waiting for them. He was as not quite as tall as Luc and of a slighter build, with dark blond hair and a five-o'clock shadow in mixed shades of blond, brown, and auburn. The cleft in his chin seemed to deepen with the scowl he directed at Luc. His blue eyes darkened to gray when the Brotherhood's enforcer stepped around him without saying a word and headed down the back hall toward the last of the apartment's three bedrooms.

"I thought you said *you* were comin'," the blood vamp drawled. He'd done time in the American South, temporarily acquired an accent, and refused to give it up because, as he said, "The ladies like it." Jinx Falken was nothing if not sensitive to the longings of ladies, both supernatural and human, who forever sought his company.

Luc didn't stop until he'd carried Magpie into a bedroom decorated in dove gray, deep lavender, and a soothing shade of blue for which Rory didn't have a name. She turned down the bed so Luc could place the pregnant girl in it. Fish hovered anxiously at the edge of the room while Senn piled pillows behind Magpie's back. Rory went into the bathroom to find towels.

"I did come," Luc was saying to Jinx as she returned. "With company. We need a midwife…"

A petite, dark-haired, fairy-like woman literally popped into the room at his side before he could finish. Startled by both the woman's unexpected appearance and the literal popping sound that had accompanied her arrival, Rory took a step back. Quick and sure, the woman bent over Magpie and placed a hand on the girl's distended belly.

"Kessie," Luc said, not appearing in the least surprised by the woman's sudden appearance. "Good to see you."

The woman, Kessie, kept her attention on the girl in the bed. "Why isn't this child in the hospital?"

Distressed by the question, Fish jigged forward, shaking his head. "No. No-no," he whispered. "Danger."

The woman took a long, hard look at him, as though she could see exactly what he feared. She nodded. "All right. We'll do this here and no one the wiser." She turned to the rest of them. "Get a sheet to cover her," she snapped. "And slide those towels"—she pointed at the pile of fluffiness in Rory's hands—"underneath her." A finger directed Luc to lift Magpie so this could be accomplished. "Then all of you get out so I can see how she's doing."

Luc again lifted the patient and Rory rushed to make a towel pad as instructed.

Jinx leaned against the doorframe, head cocked, eyebrow raised as he studied the proceedings. His drawl thickened. "Y'all need anythin' else?"

Luc glanced at him, mouth opened to say something, but Kessie beat him to it. "Yes. Call Solaya Lawton and tell her to bring her kit."

"Ah…" Jinx winced. His accent all but disappeared. "I'm not sure that's wise."

"She's a healer, isn't she?"

"Yes, but…"

"Baby," Senn told her succinctly. "Solaya's afraid of babies."

Kessie snorted. "Tell her to get over it and get over here. Me 'n this child"—she looked at Magpie—"What's your name, child?"

Magpie gasped and cried out, clutching her stomach. Fish cringed more deeply into the corner but refused to stop keeping an eye on Magpie. He didn't speak, either.

One of the runes along Rory's spine flared to life, seemed to put a thin shield between her and the pain Magpie felt. She flinched then steadied herself. Took a breath.

"Her name's Magpie," she offered.

"Good name." Kessie nodded and patted the girl's arm, before continuing, "Tell Solaya that Magpie and I will do the heavy lifting, but we want her herb kit. She hands that off, she can probably leave with the rest of you. Maybe." Back to Magpie. "You're doing fine, kid, just breathe." She cast a sweeping glance about the group. "Go on. Get!"

She shooed everyone out of the room—after Jinx handed her the requested sheets. She was already shaking one out as the door shut behind them.

Disquiet slipped through Rory's bloodstream. Her insides jittered, over-taxed by the energy she'd not only put out but taken in over the last couple of days. Something told her that the more people who knew about Fish and Magpie, the more danger they were in. *It* was out there, circling, hovering, sniffing about—looking for them. For her, too.

A glance at Luc and Senn, both of whom seemed to have relaxed since the highhanded woman's arrival, made her do her best to squelch her nerves.

"Who *is* that?" she asked.

"That's—" Luc began, but stopped when the woman he'd called "Kessie" opened the door wide enough to stick her head out.

She ignored him, looking about until she found the boy who cowered against the nearby wall.

"You Fish?" she asked.

When he nodded reluctantly, she motioned him back into the room.

"She wants you." Then, to the rest of them, "First baby, she's a little thing. This is going to take a while. Hours. We'll need food for these children, and ice. Solaya here yet?"

Senn's features pretzeled into a look of disbelief. "Sorceress, not fairy. She can't just pop in like you or tesseract like…"

"Get her," Kessie barked and closed the door again. Re-opened it. "Who tesseracts?" Turned when a thin moan came from behind her. "Tell me later. Whoever it is, don't fold space again until we talk. *They* can track you that way."

"Ah…" Rory blinked at the door. The sense of unease increased. "*Who* can track me? Who the hell is that?"

"I don't know who can." Luc frowned at the closed door. Said almost to himself, "Or how, given the runes." He grimaced at Rory. "That's Kestrel Sundstrom," he said. "She's a woodland fairy."

"The poofing in." Rory nodded as the thought hit her that, being named for a bird herself, no wonder Kestrel liked Magpie's name. "Wait." She looked up at him. "Is she the Kestrel Sundstrom from Kids Kare?"

She'd heard that, apart from busing underprivileged or inner-city young-sters into the redwood forests to teach them about the earth and its creatures, Kestrel Sundstrom kept to herself. She had *not* heard that Kids Kare was operated by the fair folk.

"You know Karing Kids?" He looked surprised.

"More like heard of it. And her." Rory tried to sift through what she knew about Kestrel Sundstrom. "Midwife" wasn't on the list. "Some of my kids are in her environmental program." She didn't know much about fair-ies, woodland or otherwise, and Magpie and her unborn baby had suddenly come under the umbrella she labeled "kids I'm responsible for." She hadn't felt threatened by the fairy. More likely, she realized with chagrin, she felt usurped. "Why is she here?"

Luc shrugged. "She's an empath. She does that."

Rory worried the inside of her lower lip. The energy inside her was still building, making her feel just a little frantic. She didn't know what to do with it, how to get rid of it, without pushing it off somewhere. She could feel Luc's hunger through the binding rune in the center of her back. She couldn't ask him to take—accept—her shunting off some of the overflow onto him. Not here in front of Senn, especially. Because she had a feeling that trying to transfer even a little of this energy to Luc would turn into something hot and private. Carnal.

Not here, not now. Remember the child.

But later.

She took a breath and forced herself back to the topic. "Yes, but does she know what she's doing"—she waved a hand—"you know, for the baby. The *child*."

There was an edge in her voice he recognized, a surge of pent-up energy zinging through her that he couldn't avoid feeling through their connection. Aside from anything else it might have done, reviving the teen in the cell had played havoc with her equilibrium. Had heightened her energy levels to those of a partying mob in a single person. Knowing what he did about her, what she was capable of, he didn't think he could simply siphon off the excess and leave it there. Didn't think she would let him.

It was risky to touch her, but he nevertheless took her shoulders between his hands and stooped so he could look her in the face. Her incredibly open, speaking face. She put a hand on his chest and started to push her energy into him.

He shut his eyes. Tension shuddered through him. The tether between them made everything more intimate. Excruciatingly vibrant. Agonizingly sensual. Unbearably sexual. And he was hungry.

So very, very hungry.

As from a great distance, he heard Senn make a rumbling sound low in his throat. "Luc," he said. Then more sharply, "Garard."

At the same time, Jinx thumped him hard upside the back of his head. "Luceire."

Luc blinked. She could not feed him here. He couldn't let her, no matter how badly she needed to rid herself of that jittery, overwhelming excess. No matter how badly he needed to help her do just that.

Or how badly he needed and wanted to drag her to bed and mate with her, feast on her.

To share energy with her.

To *feed*.

She made him feel so damn *hungry*.

He heard her say something like, "Does she know what she's doing in there?" and took it as his cue to respond. "I trust Kessie," he said. "She wouldn't have come if she didn't know what to do." Then to lighten the tension between them, and only half kidding, "But she's fae. They're unpredictable. Don't get in her way."

"I got that." As though waking from a dream, she blinked at him then gave the bedroom door another dubious look before turning away. Though she was clearly distracted as much by what was going on inside that room as by what had just happened—or not—between them, a small smile formed her mouth and Luc heard her whisper, "She's a fairy. I met a fairy. That's so cool."

Wishing he could taste that mouth, spend time exploring it, Luc smothered a groan. He would trust Kessie with Rory's life if he had to, but he wasn't sure she came under the heading of "creatures cool to know." "Only if you don't have to work with them," he said drily.

"Or take orders from 'em." Jinx gave them a theatrical shudder. A buzzing sound came from his pocket. He pulled out his phone then glanced at Rory. "There's a phone in the kitchen so you can get hold of Solaya. I'll have food sent up from the club's kitchen for you."

With a jerk of his head at Luc and Senn, he sauntered back toward the main part of the apartment.

Senn narrowed his eyes and squared his jaw, then gave Rory a quick, "They'll be fine. You're safe here," and followed Jinx.

Rory put a hand on Luc's arm. Her fingers fidgeted with his sleeve, twisted the fabric and released it multiple times as she fought to contain the anxious energy pulsing through her. "What's going on?" Even as she tried to stand still, she was moving, up onto the balls of her feet, back on her heels, a step sideways and back. "What about the kids at the hospital?"

He put a single fingertip to her chin. She stilled. "Magpie and the baby will be fine," he told her quietly. "And the kids at the hospital are in good hands." He hoped. "I don't know what Jinx needs, but he wouldn't ask if it wasn't important. I have to go."

He didn't want to leave Rory here alone, even with Kessie a closed door away. He cupped her face and was nearly undone when she leaned into the caress. Quickly, Luc stepped back. "Call Solaya and then have something to eat. There are a couple more bedrooms"—he made a motion toward the end of the hall. "Why not choose one and try to get some sleep. I'll be back as soon as I can."

Reluctantly, he turned and followed Jinx and Senn.

Beck in his guise as Erra, the plague god, lay belly down in the brush on the hillside near the entrance to the ancient sewer tunnels. Fury and loss howled through him in equal measure as he peered through the weeds. Both above and below the entry, the Council of Light forensic team came and went with the most intense activity centered on the concrete maw in the hillside itself.

Not only had the Council found what was his, but they'd taken it all. His hoard of terrified teens. The energy he fed on. His means to become less human, less mortal, and more supernatural. More Nephilim.

More godlike.

Beneath his anger, he felt *them*. Heard *them*, the Watchers. As usual, they were ravenous, their hunger unassuaged. Just to keep them quiet, he had to supply them with a never-ending source of energy and power. The special children, the psychic and gifted kids he used his practice to find— this was their only source of sustenance. It had been enough to start with, but now they wanted more powerful prey—wanted what he'd felt coming off Aurora Montgomery.

Getting to her was more of a challenge now that Luceire Garard was defending her, but Garard was nothing compared to the Watchers since he'd lost his wings. If Erra continued to find and keep the children in a limbo state—dead but not dying—the Watchers would have an unending source of nibbles.

He considered his options. With his personal source of energy reduced to zero, those possibilities were reduced. He needed the power, the high, he got from kidnapping and imprisoning the adolescents. Perhaps…

He nodded to himself. Yes. He was a good and faithful servant. If they wanted him to procure Aurora Montgomery on their behalf, they surely wouldn't begrudge him a little of the stuff he fed them. Wouldn't fault him for consuming one of the souls himself.

Then he'd have both the patience and the energy to wait until Garard's guard was lowered. At which point, he would pounce on Aurora Montgomery.

And once he put her in his siphoning tanks and slowly fed her soul to the Watchers…

They would regain their full strength and complete their resurrection, finish erupting from the caverns in which they'd been entombed and reward *him* with the power he craved—a legacy that was his by divine right and bloodline.

That was the bargain he'd made with them. When the power came to him, he would no longer have to put up with or depend upon the likes of Savitri Nousaine for his abilities. No longer need to let that impure Fallen scum have access to him at all.

Once again, he raised his head to peer over the grasses. A painful niggle at the edge of his consciousness, like a tickle inside his brain, told him that Nousaine and the Watchers were both looking for him. Soon he'd be free. Until then, he was compelled to respond to both masters.

Even after all this time, it hurt when they called him. It was as though they could physically reach into him and yank, tear, pummel. Punish. Frightening the teens then consuming their fear helped to insulate him against that pain. Now that they were gone, his link to them severed, he needed to find some other way to nourish and shield his own energies before he responded to either Nousaine or his Watcher kin.

Tight-jawed and furious at the unfairness of it all, he scuttled backward across the weedy field until it was safe to stand. Quickly, he headed back to where he'd parked his vintage Corvette and got in. It started with a roar of power. Stamping hard on the gas, he squealed the car away from the curb and headed deeper into the hills.

Soon, he promised himself. *Soon.*

Chapter Fourteen

Earth, Air, Water, and Fire are the best known of the elements
and elemental beings. They are not by any means the only
elementals, however. Lately, we have come to realize that there
are at least two more types of indispensable beings—a fifth,
similar to the one depicted in the old human movie *The Fifth
Element* and representing unconditional love; and a sixth that
we have not yet seen "in the flesh," as it were. This element is
alleged to be the embodiment of awakening knowledge, and
the next step in human evolution.

—from *The Lightway Codex, Appendix i: Defining the Players*
by McCleron O'Connell, Indigo Lightworker

Left to her own devices, Rory prowled the penthouse apartment, restless and
disgruntled. It had been her new gifts that had led to finding Fish, who'd
guided them to find the kids in the tunnel. And it was her abilities that had
led to finding the pregnant Magpie, then deducing that the babe she carried
had to be the child she and Luc had been tasked with finding and protecting.
Now here she was, patted on the head like some precocious five-year-old who
was too young to be of further use. Told to call Solaya then stay where she
was, out of trouble, while the rest of them went off to take care of business.

Her business. Damn it. The business her gifts had clearly been designed
to deal with.

Even though she had no idea how most of those gifts worked. Or what,
exactly, they were.

This instinctive *doing stuff* then wondering what you'd done afterward—
and whether or not you'd done the good or right thing—was invigorating
but wearing.

She glared down the hallway to the rear of the apartment. As requested, Solaya had arrived thirty minutes previously, disappeared into what she'd termed the "birthing chamber hell hole," and had yet to reemerge. She'd looked pained and uncomfortable when she'd walked in, but when Rory had offered to deliver the herbal kit for her, Solaya had shaken her head and shut the door in the younger woman's face. A moment later, Kessie stuck her head out to tell Rory she wanted tea, water, ice, vegetarian sandwiches, and French fries sent in because Magpie was hungry, and Fish needed to eat.

Fuming, Rory called for the food, delivered it to the door of the off-limits bedroom, and saw the door once again shut in her face. She hated fictional heroines who ignored perfectly reasonable orders to stay put not only for her own safety but that of others, but…

Dammit! She wanted to *help*. She needed to *do*.

Let it go, she thought she heard her mother's voice whisper. *This is about that girl and her baby, not you.*

"Mum?" she asked aloud, wistful. It had been ten years since she'd heard that beloved voice. More than a decade since her mother had last chastised her for being petulant over the things Solaya could do—and was allowed to do—that Rory could not.

Yes. A sensation of warmth surrounded Rory with the brush of lips across her brow. *I'm here. I'm sorry I haven't come before and that I can't stay now. You need to let Solaya do what she trained for. You have other gifts. It's time for you to use them.*

"Use which gifts?" Rory started to ask, but the sensation of *presence* faded and she was alone again.

She threw herself onto the couch, tried to curl up, rose again immediately. A chair that looked as though it was designed for napping was no better.

A restless sigh escaped her. After the intense activity of the last few days, she was at loose ends. That scared her. Nearly everything she'd done so far with her new powers had been done by instinct and accident, without thought.

Her tongue flicked nervously along her lips. She cast another glance toward the bedroom hallway. What if she did something now, here, that made everything worse—that led whatever, *who*ever, was chasing her to *them*.

She shut her eyes and breathed. None of this—from Magpie to the once-dead girl in the underground cell—was about her. It was about *them*, the kids, the baby. The same way that the abilities that had manifested the moment Luc had stepped into her studio were about two things: saving

Magpie's child and making sure no one hurt the children she worked with or the ones she communicated with in the nexus. They were all, everything.

Which meant she needed to learn how to control her abilities, use them not merely by instinct but command. But how?

Letting her mind coast on the thought, she picked up a remote and flicked on the television. Images of earthquake damage around the city dominated the screen. Closed-caption emergency information crossed the bottom of the screen while a voiceover reported:

"The governor has declared a state of emergency across San Francisco County in the wake of a massive and strengthening earthquake swarm causing sink holes, power outages, property and structural damage, and an unprecedented number of fires in heavily populated areas. Residents in affected areas are advised to evacuate as quickly and safely as possible. The National Guard has been called in…"

Uneasily, she switched the set off again. The timing and strength of the most recent quake coincided with the moment she'd jump-started the girl. There'd been a quake when she'd thrown Luc out of her studio, too.

Her breath caught. It couldn't mean she was somehow responsible. Could it? Because she was something unnatural, doing something unnatural, both undisciplined and uncontrolled. Because she hadn't known what she was doing before doing it.

A tremor ran through her. No, that couldn't be right. Could. Not. Because if it was, then she was dangerous, not only to herself and those around her, but to the entire Bay area.

Memory tweaked, belaying guilt. But no. The quake swarms had begun well before her powers had kicked in. She remembered whispers in the nexus about sizable unforeseen temblors in unexpected locations—southern Arizona along the Mexican border; Missouri and throughout the Midwest— that went back at least a couple of months.

She closed her eyes, kicked off her shoes, pressed her toes into the floor, and splayed her fingers wide. There, insubstantial but nearly constant, the earth trembled, vibrating along her fingertips and the soles of her feet. Her insides, her bloodstream and nerves, keyed alert. Her tattoos pulsed with heat, sent premonition skittering along her spine. On the screen of her eyelids, the crisscrossed violet lines of the nexus appeared. A spot of orange blurred into existence, accompanied by a faint wail. She tilted her head back and forth, listening. Not the voice she'd come to associate with the child Magpie carried.

The sob came again, clearer, and with it the words *"Help me, please. Help."*

Startled, she opened her eyes. She knew that voice. She'd heard it in the cell just before she'd slammed energy back into the dead girl's recently vacated body. Her father had once told her that saving a life made her responsible for it ever after.

She'd witnessed exactly how seriously her father had taken that belief, seen more than once what that friendship, that responsibility, meant to him as well as the men he'd saved in Afghanistan. She took her responsibilities seriously, too.

Without pausing to think, she stepped out of her body and opened herself to the web.

The same starlit, impossible darkness that she'd experienced a few days ago, when she was weak and untried, engulfed her now. Everywhere she looked, points of light glowed or stuttered with varying degrees of strength. Without fully understanding how she did it—or knew to do it—she traced the distance between herself and the single growing red speck that indicated the cry for help. Just across the city, *there*. At the hospital, in the corner opposite the building that housed Kate's clinic.

Where the kids in today's dance movement therapy session would be arriving soon.

Damn. In the midst of everything else, she'd nearly forgotten.

She slid back into herself, gulping air. The last few days had been awash in new experiences, new abilities, new everything. Rushing into the web to get to the bodies of the children in the Neon Boneyard. What she'd done while waiting for Luc to tattoo her at his place. Her instinctive use of amethyst and quartz to protect him from his own demons. The "door" she'd opened in the world that had taken her directly to Fish, and later to Magpie.

This. Wandering about in the ether as though she knew what she was doing.

Maybe she did. If she could astral project herself the six hundred or so miles from San Francisco to Las Vegas, surely she could astral project herself the few miles across town to the hospital to find out what was happening there before meeting with her clients.

Or she could just open a door and be there. Physically. Unhampered by being incorporeal. Ready to do something in the flesh.

A draft from a vent in the ceiling raised gooseflesh on her arms. Rory shivered. She was still wearing the clothes she'd thrown on before leaving the house a couple of days ago. She snatched up and put on the buttery soft, teal leather jacket Solaya had shucked when she'd arrived. The canvas messenger bag Rory carried everywhere in order to be prepared for nearly anything lay underneath the jacket. She picked it up and checked to make sure it contained clean dance togs before slinging its strap across her chest so the bag hung behind her right hip. Looked down the hallway, where the door to the birthing room was still closed. She took a quick look at the digital calendar-clock below the TV screen.

"Damn."

She had less than three hours to get to the clinic's movement therapy studio for today's session. If she opened that door in the world again, she could get to the clinic early, leave her body where she could easily get back to it, then astral project across the street to the hospital to look in on the kids without being seen. And that, she gathered, from what Luc, Senn, and the sang vamp Jinx, was the point—to remain undetected. To keep anyone from finding Magpie and the child. To *not* lead them to the children here.

It took an instant for her to decide.

Something big, dark, and dangerous was coming, and she wasn't sure what to do about it, only that something would have to be done. She was responsible for the teens who'd been taken to the hospital. For reviving the one. She *needed* to see how they were doing. Talk with them. Find out *how* what had happened, had happened to them. Who.

And do something about it.

Twisting about, she looked over her shoulder, trying to see the glowing aura thread in the center of her back that tied her to Luc. Made a pinching, yanking motion with her fist. The tether thinned but didn't break. She nodded, hoping it would be enough to let Luc know what she was doing without letting him know exactly where she was doing it.

With a mouthed, "I'm going out" at the bedroom hallway, she eased open a door in the world and left the building.

Luc was in no mood to take prisoners. What he *was* in the mood for was thuggery, and a lot of it. Bashing heads. Punching minions and their evil overlords. Getting punched in return. Winning. He wanted a good solid dustup that culminated in him—and Jinx and Senn—getting the results they were looking for.

Unfortunately, what they got was somewhat less than that.

Savitri Nousaine's call to the Council of Light had resulted in Jinx dragging Luc and Senn with him to the master psi's office for a confab. The office looked like an earthquake had hit it—and a very neatly directed earthquake at that. Still, the building didn't appear to have been affected even though an almost continuous stream of rumbling and gentle rolling shifted through the area.

Cluster quakes, Luc had thought grimly. The very thing he'd been sent to investigate Rory for to begin with.

The very thing Senn was certain would cause the Brotherhood or the Council to order Luc to do away with her.

Yeah. Wasn't gonna happen. Not by his hand or any other. Which meant that the sooner he was back at her side, the better.

He regarded his former mentor. Nousaine had told them the teens had been imprisoned by someone human. The ancient psi vamp had refused to give up the name of the protégé he thought might be abducting and torturing teens. It was only something he *suspected*.

Luc had wanted to break Nousaine's head over his unwillingness to provide them with the information they needed. It hardly mattered that the damage would not be permanent, only that it got done. Because Rory. Because child. And he'd tasked himself with doing whatever he could to ensure their safety.

Jinx had stayed his fists, however, and simply offered to sink fangs into Nousaine to get to the truth. The city's master had instinctively put a hand to his neck before rallying and repeating his "I'm not moved" position. At the same time, Senn had eyed Jinx. Jinx had shrugged and assured him the rumors about Dugo Balangs being able to read a person's life, their memories, and their thoughts by drinking their blood were not exaggerated.

Luc had seen Senn's jaw visibly tighten as he mentally filed away that bit of knowledge for future reference.

It had taken more than an hour to get Nousaine to admit he *suspected* his current human protégé, Michael Beck, of the crime. And that he *thought* the man might have a trace of Nephilim in his ancestry, and he *imagined* Beck was trying to become more Nephilim and less human by feeding psychically on the teens' terror.

He also *guessed* Beck was choosing his victims from among the underage humans who constantly sought access to some of the city's more popular vampire clubs. Though he couldn't be *sure*, he *believed* he'd spotted Beck outside a club in the Tenderloin on Mission a couple of nights back.

He provided them with a vague description of Michael Beck but couldn't provide a photo. Beck didn't work in the tower, after all, and didn't visit Nousaine there, so there was no surveillance camera footage of him, either.

Pressed to it, Nousaine had reluctantly admitted to losing all physical and psychic contact with the man at some point over the last week.

Luc felt his jaw tighten. Jinx and Senn didn't believe anyone human, even one with latent Watcher–Nephilim DNA, would be capable of "disconnecting" from an Ekoa Krillu as powerful as Nousaine. But, as Luc pointed out, the rules governing humans had clearly changed—especially given the things Rory had demonstrated she could do.

He pictured the blond man who'd been among those who'd been drawn to Rory the night she'd crossed the city in her sleep. The description Nousaine had provided of Michael Beck fit that man.

In the end, and for want of a better plan, Jinx and Senn had agreed to help Luc comb the clubs in the Tenderloin and question bouncers, patrons, and staff to learn if they'd seen the man.

Which, despite the fact that it was really too early for patrons, was what they were doing now.

"Sounds like a guy calls himself Erra," a waitperson at one of the darker clubs along Mission told them.

"The plague god?" Jinx made an *are you kidding me,* face and got a shrug in response.

"He ever with anyone?" Senn asked.

Another shrug. "He's usually got a couple of kids with him, I guess."

"You *guess?*" Luc felt himself getting hungrier and angrier by the instant. He needed to feed before he did real damage by pulling energy from the entire area. Who the hell let a guy who fancied himself the god of pestilence and plagues near underage kids?

Senn put a hand on his arm. Luc jerked away to loom over the server who backed up, fear radiating from him. He breathed deep, hoping the small amount of emotion he took from this guy would be better than nothing. "You *guess?*"

"Hey." The waiter held up his hands and backed away. "You asked. I've only seen him in here a few times, and he's never been a problem."

"Thanks."

Senn produced a sizable tip while Jinx stepped in front of Luc and forced him to back away from the man.

"What do you think?" Senn asked when the waiter was gone.

Jinx shook his head. "I don't like it."

Again, Luc pictured the arrogant blond man who'd wanted to challenge him outside Rory's studio. "I've seen this guy," he said grimly.

"You're sure?" Jinx asked.

He nodded.

"Where?" Senn.

"That night—*aahh*!" There was a physical wrench in the region of his heart, then the tracker he'd included with Rory's tattoos stuttered and went offline. The pain was intense, disorienting, something he'd never experienced before. He hunched, trying to breathe while he attempted to locate her telepathically. If she heard his silent call, she didn't respond.

"Luc?"

Senn reached for him at the same moment that Jinx caught his collar to prevent him from faceplanting the pavement.

"It's Rory." Anxiety hummed through him. He tried to focus on his shield stone, on the amethyst's connection to Rory's tattoos. "Can't reach… She's gone."

"Gone?" Senn's voice was sharp. "What do you mean, gone? Gone *where*?"

"Don't know." Luc tried to straighten, only to be smacked sideways again by the pain. "Can't feel her." Again, he touched the crystal in his chest, spread his fingers until he could his access connection to her. No matter what was happening to her, the link between them should have remained uninterrupted unless…

Fear jolted him. Unless she was dead. But even then, his mark should have allowed him to trace her body.

Not happening, he assured himself. Couldn't. Had to be something else. A supernatural storm, perhaps. One that had caused the link between them to disconnect the way Internet connections were disrupted by atmospheric disturbances. Whatever, he didn't like it. It felt exactly as though someone had amputated half of him.

She's messing with you again, he assured himself. *Testing the link and her boundaries.*

The thought didn't make him feel better.

Trying to rub the burning sensation from his chest, he staggered erect. She had to be screwing with him. "God damn it, Rory."

"Rory?" Senn was on top of him in a second. "What the hell, Garard?" He made a gesture that encompassed the evident pain Luc was in. "She's nowhere near here. You don't think she could do this—"

Luc pulled his shirt up so he could see his chest. A mark the shape and size of *Gebo* twined with *Luceire* branded the skin over his heart. He huffed a disbelieving laugh and side-eyed Senn, grimacing.

"Shit." Senn shoved his hands through his hair, took another look at Luc, and laughed without humor. "Fuck me."

"Thanks, no," Luc said, wincing. "We're both fucked enough already."

"We wouldn't be if you'd just done what I asked."

Luc snorted. "You *gave* her to me and told me to—"

"I didn't *give* her—"

"Children, children." Jinx got between them.

At the same time, Rory's voice in Luc's head was sharp. *Boys.*

Luc saw Senn start and look around wildly before glancing at him for confirmation. When he nodded, Senn mouthed an obscenity. Jinx eyed them both as though they were crazy. Luc ignored them.

"Where are you and what did you do?" he asked aloud.

Jinx did a three-sixty, scanning the area. "Who are you talking to?"

Experimented, she said. *Something's wrong with the girl I saved, and I'm making sure she's all right. See you later.*

"Don't do anything," Luc barked. "It's not safe. We think we know who's—"

But her voice, her presence, winked out of Luc's head, leaving him feeling hollow and uneasy.

"What the…" Senn began, then shook his head. "Rory, where are you?"

Luc shook his head. "She's gone."

"Where?"

"Hospital, I think."

Senn swore. "We have to get to her."

He started toward Jinx's GX 460, Luc two steps ahead of him.

Jinx unlocked the vehicle before they reached it, slid into the driver's seat. "I'll drop you at Luc's Rover then head back to the club and Google this Michael Beck."

Feeling slightly woozy, Rory stepped out of the ether and into the tiny office she used at Kate Cavanaugh & Associates, Pediatric Therapy. Was there a correlation between the dizziness and the number of times and people she'd brought through a doorway with her in the last twenty-four hours? Or the fact that she was so new to the ability?

Of course, maybe she was just dehydrated. She couldn't remember the last time she'd paused for a glass of water. Or food, for that matter. While this office was more comfortable and private, if she'd been at Sunshine Dance, she could have sent across the street for tapas takeout to boost her energy. A case of water sat on the floor near the desk. She twisted open a bottle and gulped the water down. Took a second bottle and opened it. Set it down before drinking it. It had been an incomprehensible few days what with meeting Luc and finding out she had powers. Even so, nothing could have prepared her for bringing a dead teen back to life.

A thrill of exhilaration coupled with heart-pounding dread ran through her when she looked at her hands. She'd brought a dead person back to life, and she had no idea what that meant for either her or the teen. She needed someone to help her sort it out, step by step. That person needed to be Luc, not anyone else, because everyone from her parents to Senn, Solaya, and Kate had all skipped right over telling her what she to expect when her abilities manifested. Luc was the only one who hadn't lied to her or evaded any part of the truth. He'd simply jumped in and done his best to—

Keep her from imploding when things started to happen.

Movies, television shows, novels—all of them suggested that the dead came back as something other than themselves. True-life accounts suggested that a few minutes spent in the afterlife—or maybe simply suspended from this one—didn't seem to make any difference, other than perhaps to make the revived person more appreciative of the life they had. But those who'd been dead longer, the way this teen had undoubtedly been…

Consequences, she thought. *Every action costs* something, *even when the intention is good.*

All at once, the scene in *The Princess Bride,* where Miracle Max had pronounced Westley only *mostly* dead played over and over in her mind. Maybe that's what had happened—the kid had only been *mostly* dead all day, meaning that she might have been slightly alive, and there would be no bad aftereffects.

A bubble of hysterical laughter, quickly stifled, fizzed through her. It was done, and she had no time to worry about consequences now.

Without further thought, she shut and locked her office door then sat in the rolling chair in front of her desk. Within three seconds of closing her eyes, the room felt far too close and she opened them again.

She pushed herself upright. She'd never be able to meditate in here. When she'd left her body at Luc's, she'd needed to concentrate then visualize him. She had a feeling it would take far more focus to do what she had in mind now.

Thoughtfully, she studied the room. The heavy purple yoga mat propped in one corner caught her eye. It would be a tight squeeze for the limited floor space, but possible.

It was the work of a moment to pile the chair on top of her desk, unroll the mat, remove her skirt and shoes, and stretch out. Her mind raced before her years of training took over. She stilled and visualized the girl from the sewer tunnels.

Moments later, she was in the hospital's emergency treatment area.

The rooms were enclosed in glass, quiet areas where the motorized beds were high and machines pulsed and beeped information about the state of patients' lives. Scrub-clothed personnel chattered in hushed voices, moving between patients and rooms, tapping notes into their tablets.

The walls were painted either an unobtrusive, utilitarian shade of sage green or an overripe pear brownish yellow. Heavy, room-darkening curtains in soft stone and sand hues were drawn across the bank of windows across from the nurses' station to give patients privacy while staff worked on them. Open, the glass allowed staff to keep an eye on patients without intruding unless necessary.

No one looked at Rory, and she did not see her reflection in the bank of glass. She allowed herself a single fist pump before she cautiously propelled her spirit about in search of her quarry.

The voice she associated with the girl from the cells found her once more. She turned to see Kate Cavanaugh, who must have been called to attend in her capacity as a pediatric counselor, and Celeste Fury outside one of the rooms, heads together as they conferred in low tones. Rory drifted nearer—and stopped when the head of the Council of Light shivered and looked directly at her.

Shit. Maybe she was invisible but detectable by someone who was sensitive to the unseen.

Before she could decide what to do, Celeste gave the area where Rory hovered a puzzled look and motioned to a nurse. Rory looked behind her when Celeste pointed at the spot she bobbed in front of. Relief swept her when she saw the clock the cherubim motioned at as she issued instructions to the nurse. He nodded, made a note on the small tablet he carried, and headed for a door with reinforced windows behind the nurses' station.

Apparently satisfied, Celeste returned to her conversation with Kate. When they moved to the next room, Rory dove down to peer into the room they'd left. The teen in the bed was not the girl she sought.

The cry for help came again, from the direction opposite the one Kate and Celeste had taken. An ooze-like cloud hovered outside one of the doors. There was something familiar about it that she recognized from somewhere else. Like…

The tunnels, she realized suddenly. As in, the girl who'd been dead that she'd revived.

Or thought she'd revived.

If there'd been air inside Rory, it would have whooshed out to make room for panic. Oh hell. Dead kid. Resurrection. Conse-freaking-quences.

Mess with the natural order of things and shit happens.

If she'd had a throat in this form, she would have gulped. What had she done?

The cloud dissipated and moved closer to Rory, coalescing into the face of the girl from the cell. Her mouth was open and she appeared to be trying to speak—or at least make herself understood. Simultaneously, a portion of the outer edge of the haze seemed to be trying to point toward a treatment room two doors away.

That's. Not. Me.

The mouth formed the words three times before Rory understood them all. She regarded the face in the mist with horror—and suspicion. Preventing someone or some*thing* else from taking up residence in her body was a large part of the reason Luc had wanted to tattoo her, and Solaya had agreed. That meant the…*face's* assertion had merit. But—and it was a large *but*—what if it was lying to her?

Who then? she thought at the image, but it dissolved without responding.

Determination flowed through her when the dark fog re-formed then paused as though waiting for her to see it. When she blinked in its direction, it faded into a smoky tornado-like spiral that drilled its way through the door and out of sight.

Curiosity, dread, and guilt riding her in equal measures, Rory followed.

The quake that rolled beneath his feet as he and Senn parked near the Council's entrance at a local hospital felt different to Luc.

He concentrated on it for a moment. *Not Rory. Not the new kids. Not crystals. Not…local. Not Cali.* He tipped his head. *Out of state. South-southeast.*

"You feel that?" Senn sounded uneasy.

Luc nodded and slid from behind the steering wheel. "Yep." He side-eyed Senn. "Surprised you can. Most wizards aren't that in tune."

Senn ignored the jibe. "It's not local. Not Rory. Not the kids the Council is keeping an eye on."

Luc alighted from the vehicle and shut his door with a quiet *snick.* "Nope."

Together they started across the lot toward the hospital at the same moment that a colorfully dressed man appeared as though from nowhere, bullhorn in hand.

"The end is nigh," he declared to the uniformed and lab-coated people also hurrying into the medical center. A few glanced his way, then ducked their heads in a clear effort to avoid the madness that rolled off of him in waves. He paid no attention, only turned his head to point the bullhorn at Luc and Senn. "Beware the final battle. The fallen are rising, the watchers are everywhere. They feed on the souls of the innocent. They feed and are nearly upon us—"

His rant broke off abruptly when a pair of women, one tall and blond, the other short and redhaired, approached him. When they were close to him, the redhead reached out and gave his hand a light stroke in passing. The hand holding the bullhorn went slack, as he watched them go. For a moment he stared after them as though dazed, then he visibly shook himself and brought the bullhorn back to his mouth.

Senn gestured at the man. "He seem familiar to you?"

Luc nodded, attention sharpening. "Civic Center. First time Rory opened a door. Two women approached him and he shut up." He jerked his head toward the women, who had almost disappeared. Under other circumstances, he might have pursued them, but not now. "Those two women, in fact."

"What did we miss?"

The question echoed Luc's thoughts. He shook his head, touched his chest. The mark Rory had left there still burned. His thumbs prickled, breath felt tight in his lungs, stomach seemed to drop as though he'd driven over a mountain at speed. *Rory.*

He'd done everything he could to protect her, but her abilities had charged ahead regardless. The runes he'd designed, along with the specially prepared ink, were meant to ground her, prevent her body from being invaded by unwanted entities and her energy from being hijacked by Nousaine and his sycophants. Her ink not only exceeded but exploded his intentions.

Whether by natural progression, the nature of the runes, or both, her abilities were far more advanced than he'd anticipated. But her ability to resurrect the dead teen was something he hadn't anticipated. Regardless of the strength of her gifts, that was something she shouldn't have been able to do. The very idea of it, and the possible significance of her being able to breathe life into death, terrified him. The talent was not something either the Council of Light or the Brotherhood of Shadows would take lightly. Once they figured out what she could do, she'd be in more danger than she already was—not only from San Francisco's rogue vampire factions, but their enemies, as well.

The sudden need to find her, make sure she was safe, overwhelmed him.

Senn close on his heels, he strode into the hospital. They'd barely reached the Council's wing when Celeste accosted them.

"We're getting some strange, low-grade energy readings off some of the children," she said without preamble. "Something not human." She grimaced. "Someone…" Her eyes narrowed. "Some*thing* that shouldn't…*be?*"

Senn's face contorted with disbelief. "Like *what?*"

Celeste's mouth worked too long on more thought, warning Luc to be wary of the coming pronouncement.

"Was anyone—any*thing*—else in there with those kids before we arrived on scene?" She turned to look directly at Luc. "Did anything…odd happen before we arrived?"

Bingo.

Schooling his features to shutter his suspicions, Luc glanced over her head at Senn, who gave his head the tiniest shake, then back at her. *Sidestep the Rory issue*, the sorcerer's body language said. *Tell her anything else.*

Like about Athan having been there before them.

Not gonna happen. He owed the Council nothing and preferred to deal with his son himself. Still…

"Someone was in one of the cells with three of the kids before we arrived," he said coolly, electing to compromise. "I read Nousaine on him."

Her eyes narrowed even more on the evasion. "This isn't Nousaine. We all know his signature. This is something I've never encountered before." Her jaw worked again before she glanced over her shoulder at Senn, who avoided her gaze. "I want to know what it is," she said flatly, "but for now, I want an investigation. Whatever it is, it's unnatural."

A chill ran down Luc's spine. He ignored it. "We're all fucking unnatural, Fury. None of us should be here. Be specific."

"Not this kind of unnatural." She turned her head to eye the curtain-shuttered rooms across from the nurses' station. "We were created. Put here to do a job. What I'm sensing is a perversion even by our standards, Garard. It shouldn't exist—anywhere. Take it to Falken." She gave him a hard look. "The Council sees it as a threat and wants it eliminated. With prejudice. Today."

Turning, she strode into the nearest treatment chamber. The moment she was out of sight, Senn looked at Luc. "Rory."

Heart sinking, he nodded. "Maybe."

"What the fuck did you do to her, Garard?"

"You know exactly what I did, Lawton," Luc said more mildly than he felt. "You told me to protect her. I did. The same as you would have done under the circumstances."

"The hell I would have." Angrily, Senn gestured for Luc to follow as he put distance between them and the trauma rooms. "Protect her, yes, but not the way you did." He huffed out an angry breath. "I realize you probably couldn't help it. You think you're working the redemption track, but you're still a freaking demon on a good day. You corrupted and impregnated a seraph. You spent millennia as that devil Nousaine's right hand." He ran his hand through his hair. "What the fuck was I thinking, sending you to her? Doesn't matter what your intentions might have been, it's the fact that *you*—and not Solaya or I or someone *not* you—devised the means to protect her."

"The hell does that mean?"

Senn's lips twisted into a snarl. "You flagged her to the Council, asshole. By trying to make it so the 'Krillu can't touch her, you made her visible."

Bewildered, Luc regarded him. "Visible? The Council's been working with her for years. She was already visible—"

Senn loosed a sharp laugh. "Not like this. Hell, I'll bet Solaya doesn't even know about this."

Fed up with the intrigue, Luc stepped in close and grabbed the shorter man by the shirt, lifted him off his feet. "English," he said, "Like what?"

Senn looked down at the hand wrapped in his shirt, up into Luc's face. "They thought she was only human."

"The hell—"

Realization was slow to set in. When it did, everything about Rory and her abilities clicked into place in alarming detail. His gut churned. He gave Senn a little push and opened his hand to drop the sorcerer on his ass. Even though he was already sure of the answer, he asked anyway, "She's not a crystal, is she?"

"No."

"Fuck." Luc shut his eyes, cursed himself back to the hell he'd crawled out of. Desperate but hopeful, he said, "Maybe Celeste isn't picking up on her."

Doubt mixed with hope lit Senn's eyes. "Who else?"

Luc looked at him. "Fish. Magpie. The baby."

Senn swore.

Luc nodded.

"Shit."

Luc grimaced. "That." The Brotherhood of Shadows's primary mission was to protect the course of *human* evolution at all costs. It wouldn't matter to them what Rory's part in that evolution might be. If she was more—or less—than human, they would send someone to kill her the moment they found out. If they didn't already know. And as the Brotherhood's enforcer, he was the one they'd send. The one they'd already sent. Any which way he looked at it, she was targeted for dead. "Who else knows?"

Senn got to his feet. "Me. You."

"You knew her abilities were coming in. You knew that once they did, I'd be assigned to do something about her." He turned to walk away. He needed to find her before that freaking *angel* Celeste talked to Jinx about fuck all and they put it together with Rory. "You set me up."

Senn caught up with him and shrugged. "I had to do something. I already told you I thought she'd be good for you."

"What am I supposed to be for *her*?" Luc asked viciously. "Her fucking executioner?"

The hunger he'd managed to contain since he'd left the tunnels resurfaced, brutal and unrelenting. He needed to feed. Soon.

"Yes," Senn said simply. "But I figured once you met her, you'd change course and walk through hell to keep her safe if you had to."

Luc snorted. Hadn't he just thought the same thing? Without responding, he stopped short and looked around. Something about the atmosphere seemed familiar. A scent, an energy…a faint, almost electric glow. "We have to find her."

"Yep." Senn side-eyed him. "Any ideas?"

"Maybe."

He touched the spot on his chest that had begun to burn and sting again. Images played in his head that he couldn't quite grasp. Hoping they'd come clear, he headed back into the trauma unit. Following the burn.

Chapter Fifteen

Astral Warriors are spiritual soldiers who are able to leave—and later return to—their physical bodies in order to move about the ethereal world at will. It is their calling to fight evil on the psychic plane and to dispatch it with extreme prejudice by whatever means necessary.

—from *The Lightway Codex, Appendix i: Defining the Players*
by McCleron O'Connell, Indigo Lightworker

The activity in the Council of Light's special emergency wing of the hospital seemed intense but controlled when Rory sifted through the walls and into it. Other than her mostly wish-thinking trip at Luc's house, this was her first deliberate attempt at astral travel. It had been a good deal more difficult and taken greater concentration, than she'd anticipated to leave her body while keeping her person intact. She wasn't entirely sure what she hoped to accomplish now that she was here. Checking on the kids, yes, but if they really needed something? She wasn't sure if she'd be able to help. Although thinking back to Luc…

A sly grin infused her spirit. Well, she'd managed there. Could here be much different?

Other than circumstances and intent, of course.

She looked around, getting her bearings. Celeste Fury stood inside the nurse's station, reading a chart. Nearby, Kate Cavanaugh leaned against the charge desk, talking avidly to someone on her cell phone. Two people in multi-colored scrubs were righting an equipment cart that appeared to have collided with a med trolley and picking up pills, med cups, and sealed hypodermics and other disposable paraphernalia that had been scattered across the floor. Snatches of conversation reached her.

"Going to need ten milligrams of…"

"Did you order the CAT scan for bed one…"

"Celeste really thinks she'll need to be stopped…"

Rory halted, startled, and wafted as close as she dared, trying to get a better idea of whom Kate was talking about. As she did, she saw Celeste turn on her heel, clearly angry, and head toward the pediatric psychologist. Close by, a shadowy specter made itself part of the sage-colored wall, exactly as she'd initially seen it. No one but her seemed to realize it was there. Uncertain of its intent, she watched it carefully, alert to possible danger, hoping she'd be up to the challenge should things go haywire.

"Talk to her," Celeste told Kate, interrupting her phone conversation. "The situation is getting dangerous—you felt that quake, the ongoing cluster. The girl's got to be kept out of here, away from these kids. If we don't stop her now, the entire city's…" Her voice dropped when Kate turned to her. Heads bent together, they continued the earnest conversation at a level below Rory's hearing.

"The girl" who had to be stopped, Rory realized with a start of misgiving, must refer to *her*. She wondered who was on the phone with Kate. Who Celeste wanted made aware of the situation.

Her senses, more acute in this form, focused on the question. Definitely someone else. Someone with a larger agenda than the Council could…

Something skittered at the edge of her awareness. Something cool, almost foggy, barely there, slipped into the atmosphere behind the psychologist and the Council's director. It loomed nearby, apparently unfelt and unseen by anyone but astral-Rory.

Uncomfortable and wary, Rory did her best to listen in on more of the discussion between Kate and Celeste. She'd trusted Kate for ten years, wanted to give her the benefit of the doubt before jumping to conclusions. Kate was the one who'd shown her the way out of the dark place she'd been in at fifteen. She'd trusted the psychologist implicitly. Now she wasn't so sure. Not when both Kate and Director Fury seemed to think Rory might be a threat to the entire city.

"No." At the charge desk, Celeste jerked out of her *sotto voce* conversation with Kate. "The girl in treatment three had the equivalent of a cardiac event and possibly an out-of-body experience. We need to make sure nothing took her over—"

Celeste leaned in closer to Kate and spoke directly into her ear, so Rory was unable to hear. Intuition made her itch. There was something wrong with the partial conversation she'd overheard, something that whispered to her of lies and betrayal. Made her doubt every one of her close personal relationships, including what she had with Senn and Solaya.

Unwilling to think about what the Lawtons might be hiding from her—or that they might be working against her—Rory flowed along the corridor beside the desk, looking into every room she came across. A shadow hovered at the corner of her eye, appearing to follow her. Something about it seemed almost familiar, but she wasn't sure. Male, big—possibly as big as Luc, but more slightly built. Hair kind of spiky, features indeterminate due to being translucent. Not a ghost, though, merely ghostly. Aiming to be a Big Bad but failing miserably. The sense of danger that had manifested when Luc had first walked into her studio didn't even *blip*. She was experiencing no impulse to throw whoever this was across the room—or, more to the point, take his specter apart and destroy it. In fact, she kind of wanted to make friends with him, which was just weird. Comfortable, touchy-feely without being sexual friends. Totally bizarre. Especially since he was hardly corporeal enough to be friends with.

Of course, neither was she.

Nonsensically, she wondered what it might be like to dance with him. It. Whatever. Aside from still being slightly worn out from astraling, she was so hopped up on the energy she'd pulled upon when she'd revived the kid that her entire being felt like it was sizzling.

The need to discharge the excess was electric. Pushing what she could into Luc before he left the apartment hadn't been enough—especially since he'd refused to accept it. She understood he hadn't wanted to feed and leave her empty—the heroics, in light of what he was, were laudable. But what he didn't seem to understand was that trying to contain as much power as she'd absorbed made her feel reckless, invincible. She *needed* to disperse it or at least foist off more of it where it would do some good. And after what he'd fed into her in the cells so she could bring back the girl, Luc had to be starving for it. The tight rein he kept on that craving both humbled and amazed her.

Memory *pinged*. Running through the streets being chased by multiple varieties of vampires. Throwing a blond man who appeared energy drunk into the outside wall of the restaurant across from her studio. Popping the lock on the studio's exterior iron gate—using her hands to solder it closed. Dancing, *flying* on feet that felt as though they were on fire.

Tattered wings opening wide behind a dark silhouette that she knew far more intimately than a few hours could possibly account for.

Luceire…

He excited her entire being in ways she wanted time to explore in full. Unfortunately, everything she'd done with him so far had resulted in night flights, injury, chaos, near-death experiences, and a great deal of confusion over the extravagant and unearthly new "gifts" she hadn't yet had time to digest.

Get a grip.

She didn't have time to indulge in thoughts of Luc, given she'd ether-walked her way over here for a purpose. Resolved to find the girl she sought, she drifted to the ceiling and tried to decide on a direction. Farther along the hall, the other Mostly Ghostly floated outside a bank of curtained windows. She flowed in that direction. He glided away.

Keeping an eye on him as he floated down the corridor, Rory peeked into the treatment bays until she found the one that held the most beeping equipment, then slipped inside.

The room was darker than she'd expected, especially given the number of monitors surrounding the bed. The still body beneath the sheets was a gray silhouette against what little light there was. Above it, the girl's frail spirit hovered, looking worried.

Rory knew how she felt. She had no idea how to fix what had happened, or even what to do about the situation. Being told that something or someone other than oneself could take over one's temporarily vacant body was one thing. Being the one who'd caused the takeover to happen…

If she'd been in her body right now, she'd throw up.

Practicality set in. Since she wasn't in her body, and ralphing wasn't an option, she needed to find a way to correct the appalling mistake she'd made in her sorrow and ignorance. Whatever was inside the girl's body had to be removed or destroyed, and the girl's soul released.

Doubt filled her. There were no auric cords to cut the way there'd been in the morgue or when she'd gone through the web to Vegas. Given what had happened the last time she'd acted on instinct, she wanted Luc to back her up, but he wasn't here.

For a split second, she wondered if she could enter the girl's body herself and oust the thing that was inside her that way. Then something alerted her to another presence in the room besides hers, the girl's, and whatever occupied her body, and she got distracted by an energy she recognized…

In the shadows, just outside the treatment bay occupied by the formerly dead girl, Athan hovered, a smoky, insubstantial version of himself. As translucent as he was, he nevertheless waited until Celeste Fury's back was turned before slipping after Rory's spirit. She floated near the bed as though uncertain of what she was doing, her ghostly arms held wide from her body, palms hovering about three inches above the teen in the bed. For an instant, she froze. Then she turned and planted her phantom self between him and the bed.

"I know who you are," she told him. "I can read your energy signature. You were in the tunnel just before we found the kids, too. You didn't hurt them, but you have something to do with this. I want to know what."

The assertion nearly startled Athan into responding. It was, in fact, an effort to remain silent, which made him wonder if she was somehow trying to compel him to reveal himself. If she was powerful—and untrained— enough to cause the cluster of small earthquakes he'd felt running beneath the city since the moment she'd met Luceire, then she was undoubtedly strong enough to compel almost anyone to do almost anything. In other words, as potentially dangerous to both mundane and supernatural crea‑ tures as he'd been advised.

Except there was something about her—or at least her specter—that seemed about as threatening as burned toast while at the same time being more like him than he'd imagined.

One of a kind, the almost constant presence in his ear reminded him. *Shouldn't exist. Kill it.*

For a moment, they stared at each other, protective astral presence to shadow-being sent to render her nonexistent. In the span of a breath, she seemed to assess why he was there, his silence and his intentions. Then she turned away to once again focus on the other out-of-body specter in the room. Dismissing him as benign.

Foolish of her.

Or perhaps not.

As Athan watched, Rory plunged a spectral hand into the body in the bed and yanked. A dense, viscous mass rose from the body and coalesced above it before advancing on the cowering ghost to whom that vessel belonged. Before it could reach her, Rory plunged both of her spectral hands into it and tore it apart, twisting and flinging it into the floor beneath her.

The colors of the aurora borealis swam about her while at the same time, hot orange-yellow fire engulfed her spirit. Her otherworldly fingers glowed with blue-white flames, burned into the sludge-like accumulation, and reduced it to something resembling ash. The residue disintegrated to nothing.

Athan gaped. *What the ever-loving fuck?* Even he couldn't do—or perhaps hadn't thought to try to do—what she'd just done, and he'd had centuries to learn to manipulate and control his abilities.

No wonder *they* wanted her dead.

But it wasn't for the reasons he'd been given. That bull about the world not being ready for the onset of human evolutionary change. It was because she was hella more dangerous to them—the Council, the Brotherhood, the Nightkeepers—than he'd ever dreamed of being.

The black slurry she'd just dispatched had been a Watcher.

Which meant what he'd been told was true. Kartchner was ruptured and the Watchers were rising.

The prospect horrified even him.

The apparition of the woman he'd been sent to kill if his father—if *Luceire*—did not was moving about the room in a sweeping motion, cleaning up whatever dark residue might remain. Finished, she turned to the spirit lingering above the bed.

"You can return to your body now," she said even as one of the monitors attached to the body began to *ding*.

There was a sudden flurry of activity outside the room, the sound of hurrying feet and the rattle of wheels, rushed voices. A voice over a loudspeaker announced, "Code blue, trauma three. Code blue, trauma three…"

The girl's specter seemed to hesitate, confused by the commotion.

"You're my responsibility." Rory's voice was urgent. "I did this to you without meaning to. I want to fix it, and I can help you, but it has to be now."

"You did…what?" the girl asked faintly. Then, doubtfully, "Will it hurt?"

"I don't—"

"Yes," Athan said harshly, unable to remain silent any longer. Someone had to say something. This whole thing had Bad Idea written on it in giant, neon letters. As he understood it, once a body had been used by a Watcher it would be permanently tainted—and so would the soul it belonged to. "It will hurt. You were in pain before you died. You'll be in more pain if you come back. If you aren't, you probably won't be yourself anymore."

"What does that even mean?" Rory asked, surprising him. "Probably. What is this 'probably' you speak of? It means 'might be,' Negative Nellie."

Before Athan could gather his shocked thoughts enough to respond, she turned to the uncertain spirit of the girl. "You make your choices, you take your chances, same as anybody. But it has to be *your* choice." She pointed at the girl's body. "And it has to be now."

In the same moment that the girl shuddered and nodded, Council medical personnel filled the room, Celeste Fury among them. He'd wondered why he did it later, but in the moment, Athan spread the shadow of his being wide, masking Aurora Montgomery's presence from the Council director's sharpening gaze. Instead of spotting Rory, she flicked a glance at Athan then focused on the teen's spirit. She reached into the air and gave her wrist a quick twist. Her hand made a grasping movement then slapped, palm down, into the heart center of the body's chest.

Stay behind me but get out. Athan shoved the thought at Rory, hoping Celeste couldn't pick them up. *Get back to your body before she sees you.*

He saw her ignore him long enough to glance at the girl, who'd returned to her flesh at Celeste's insistence. Then she glided out of the room and drifted away.

Uneasy, Athan drifted after her.

No wonder Luceire was intrigued by her. She was designed to drive him crazy.

And no wonder the Council was afraid.

Curiosity about her plagued him more than ever. He had no idea what she was, and couldn't begin to guess. The brief he'd been given had described her as human, but if she was, she was unlike any other human with whom he'd ever come into contact. Witness the fact that she'd been able to resurrect a kid Athan knew without doubt had been completely and utterly deceased, for example. Not one of the supernatural beings he was aware of, including those of the seraphim or cherubim classes, would have been able to accomplish that feat. It was a God-only gift and, to Athan's knowledge, there had ever been only the one Lazarus. What she'd done in the tunnel should have been impossible.

Was impossible.

Experimentally, he stuck out a finger, scooped up a sample of her residual energy, and tasted. The spicy-sour-sweet tang hit his tongue. His nose wrinkled. Good thing he didn't have to live on borrowed energy, or he'd wind up dieting. She didn't taste right. Or the way she'd tasted when he'd first encountered her energy signature in the tunnels.

She also didn't taste strictly human.

Or human at all.

The thought brought him up short. Of course, she was human—she had to be. Hadn't he just acknowledged to himself that she was nothing on the supernatural hierarchy? But if she was something else, something *other*, more, and unique in the universe like he was, no wonder the entire supernatural world was wary. It would certainly take something—some*one*—matchless to have his *pater familias* ready to tear apart worlds to protect her and be near her.

Though he'd shadowed Luceire in some form for centuries, this was the first time he'd witnessed uncertainty in his sire. The first time he'd seen Luceire roused from the almost somnolent but efficient way he performed his tasks for the Brotherhood. But there'd been nothing drowsy or detached about the man who'd followed the tiny blonde into her dance studio the other night. Even the way Luceire's eyes had narrowed and his mouth had flattened before he had finally gone inside spoke volumes. That look—that quickly masked evidence of his sire's hunger—made the juvenile and vindictive side of Athan want to poke the beast, play with the lady, see how far he could go before Luceire's iron will deteriorated and all hell broke loose.

His mouth formed an idle curve. More than one interested party wanted to pay him to keep an eye on the girl and report back. Maybe it was time to get close to her as well, let the old man know what chaos was really all about.

One thing human ERs were full of was people who often needed to have the edges of pain, grief, and anxiety muffled. That was why so many of the Ekoa Krillu worked as healers of one sort or another—as their patients benefited, so did they. By the time Luc and Senn reached the center of the Council's trauma unit, hunger was gnawing a hole through Luc. It had been a long time since he'd experienced a near-ravening emptiness, but there was a tacit "no poaching" agreement among the 'Krillu. In territory that belonged to the hospital psi vamps, he had to do his best *not* to suck it up. Especially when instinct told him he didn't have time to sip even a little emotion off the top. He had to find Rory.

Fast.

He gave Senn a pointed look. The sorcerer returned a wordless nod and peeled off to head down the hall on the right side of the unit while

Luc took the left. Moments later, an unusual and overwhelming sense of anxiety and dread encompassed him. He stopped, gave the energy a circumspect once-over.

Not Rory. He'd know the taste of her life force anywhere. Further examination told him the distress came from the teens who'd been imprisoned in the tunnel. The one Rory had jump-started back to life seemed particularly anxious. As quickly and unobtrusively as possible, he breathed in that apprehension, searching for its source.

The first flavor to hit him was the one he associated with Athan. It caught him off guard, made him physically finger the atmosphere. But the scent wasn't fresh…more like something carried in by someone who'd passed close to his son on the way here. Still, if Athan was anywhere close to the immediate vicinity, Luc couldn't let himself get distracted. Not when he had Rory to find.

Of necessity, he let Athan's presence go for the moment and tried again.

Almost at once, a nearly impenetrable darkness filled his lungs. Startled, he took a step back. It had been more eternities than humans could count since that particular tang had met his tongue. *Watchers.* They were still supposed to be sealed in caverns deep beneath the earth. If they weren't…

What the hell was going on?

A more pressing knowledge struck him. If the Watchers had surfaced, Rory—and kids like Fish and the baby, and no doubt Magpie, too—would be the energy source they needed to rejuvenate. And if Celeste knew they were out, it would explain why she was willing to get her hands dirty in the killing game. She'd feel it incumbent upon the Council to destroy the energy source the Watchers needed to fully rejuvenate.

It also meant she'd realized—or was close to realizing—that, as far as the entombed leeches were concerned, Rory would be the power source to end all power sources.

Anger, instantly contained, seeped along his nerves. Dispatching humans or near-humans in the war between heaven and hell was neither the cherubim's duty nor her calling. It had not been M's duty or calling, either, but he'd led the Fall. The Watchers, envious of humanity's standing in the eyes of their Creator, had simply taken up the cause. Luc wouldn't be able to live with himself if he allowed Celeste to sanction any action that might lead to Rory's death—or the deaths of any of the special children.

Like the ones already in the morgue.

Not on my watch.

The passion and intensity of the thought was as new and startling to him as his instant reaction to Rory the first time he'd seen her in her dance studio. But he'd explore it later—if he bothered to explore it at all. He'd lived long enough to understand that some things just *were*, and this was one of those things. Rory was one of those things.

Rory, goddammit. Where are you?

A light mist and delicate scent, cool and welcome, wafted around him, seeming to caress his face before drifting away. Immediately on its heels, a commotion rose outside a room across from the charge desk. Luc's mouth curved in a wry grin. Of course. The teens. Where it appeared there was a problem. That was where he'd find her. Working her magic.

And, no doubt meddling.

He headed toward the point where healer 'Krillus dashed about collecting equipment, shoving it toward a single treatment bay opposite the nurses' station. The gentle vapor trailed him, gathered insistently about his face, clouded his vision.

Other way.

The command was less than a whisper of thought, barely there. Following its lead, he stepped off to the side out of sight and turned to look in the direction the fragment of scent had gone.

C'mon. It's being handled. Let's go. Now.

What the hell? *Rory?*

Yes. Don't think so loudly, they'll hear you. It *will hear you. The director… don't let them see you.*

The energy in the area changed. Celeste Fury's authority charged the hallway with irritation and anger.

Where's your body?

He felt mist-Rory slip beneath his shirt and settle atop the burn mark on his chest. A skirl of pleasure ran through him at the same moment that his hunger lessened. It didn't fully abate, but his link to Rory returned in full.

Go, he thought at her. *I'm right behind you.*

There was another instant of connection and she was gone. He wasn't sure where she was going, only that he'd be able to follow the tether between them and find her when he was finished here.

He returned his attention to the malicious energy in the unit. More carefully than before, he tested the atmosphere to verify his previous impression, but came up short. He squinted into the middle distance, puzzled. Watcher, but also not. There was something else in the mix, another signature, also familiar but somehow not. He considered the flavor. Nousaine mixed with Watcher, mixed with…

Recognition hit him with the force Rory had used to throw him out of her studio the first day. The extra something belonged to the blond man who'd been outside Sunshine Dance the night Rory had done a barefoot runner in her sleep. The distantly Nephilim one Nousaine thought was responsible for kidnapping the kids and trying to feed on them until they died. His essence was still human, but stronger. Less than supernatural, more than mundane. Hungrier than ever and ready to devour—

Rory.

Wrath filled him. Wondering if Nousaine knew exactly what his human protégé was capable of, and knowing he'd have to find out, Luc spun about and strode out of the unit. Wherever Rory and her body were, he needed to get to her now.

Rory slipped back into her recumbent body and gave herself a moment to settle in. Her physical form was exactly as she'd left it—she glanced at the clock above the door—nearly an hour ago.
Funny how much longer it seemed.

And how sluggish she felt despite the adrenaline running through her veins. Despite feeling wider awake than she ever had in her life.

And despite trying to push some of the energy overload into Luc when he'd arrived at the hospital looking for her. He'd been hungrier than she'd yet seen him, and she'd both wanted and needed to help. She tucked an arm up her back, feeling for the invisible tether. She could feel that hunger through the renewed connection even now.

Worrying about him, she got to her feet and chugged two small bottles of water then dug into her gym bag for the box of protein bars she kept there. Her movement therapy class would begin to arrive in less than thirty minutes. She had just enough time to shower, change, and get out the day's equipment.

A few minutes later, the energy bar had begun to take effect and she was dragging balance balls, bells, hoops, ribbons, and mats into place with more force than necessary. She couldn't get the things she'd overheard Celeste tell Kate out of her head.

Everything she thought she knew about her mentor had been turned on its head. She'd trusted Kate for a long time, and now she wasn't sure if she should—or could. From the current of intimacy between Kate and the Council of Light's director, to the idea that Celeste knew more about Rory than she was comfortable with—it all smacked of betrayal. Possibly even pillow talk wherein Kate had shared confidential details of her sessions with Rory with Celeste.

Why she might have done it didn't matter, except that Rory had come to think of the psychologist as a friend. If that wasn't how Kate saw their relationship…

Then maybe it wasn't Kate she couldn't trust, but herself.

Misgiving assailed Rory. Kids, new and possibly catastrophic abilities, the shadow guy only she could see. The…*thing* that had come out of the kid in the treatment room and that she hoped she'd disposed of permanently. Intuition told her she hadn't really seen anything yet.

Later, she advised herself as the first of her students, a ten-year-old with Down's syndrome, arrived with his mother. She could hear more arriving in the hall.

Telling herself she'd done all she could, that it wouldn't be healthy for anyone if she obsessed over a what-if that hadn't yet happened and might never, she stepped out to greet her charges.

An hour later, as her second group of dance movement therapy clients were starting to arrive, unease ticked along Rory's pulse and throbbed against her temple. Beneath her breast, disquiet beat a syncopated tattoo. Something— more things than those she'd already encountered over the last however many days—was *off*.

She was off. Didn't feel quite…

Herself.

She was usually even tempered, especially around the kids, but now she felt edgy and impatient. Between the energy overload and the feeling that some*thing* had returned from the hospital with her, everything felt wrong. She couldn't put a finger on what the "wrong" was, only that she'd be more comfortable if whatever *it* was would stop bothering her.

Actions have consequences.

The phrase, the judgment, whispered against her mind, making her crabby.

"No, like this," she snapped at a girl with cerebral palsy whose balance left her faltering over a new move. Hurriedly, she corrected the placement of the girl's legs and arms, causing one of the DMT interns who worked with her to give her a look that plainly asked, *Are you okay?*

Rory swore softly. Make that *very* crabby.

Stooping quickly, she framed the child's face with her hands. "I'm sorry for being so impatient," she said, offering the girl a contrite smile. "You're amazing and you're doing beautifully. Truly."

The youngster nodded, gave her a tremulous smile and a hug in response, but the damage was done. After that, most of the children in the class were agitated and rambunctious, unable to focus for the rest of the session. Even those who'd made huge strides since starting to work with her shied away, retreating inside themselves to someplace safe, or moaning and screaming.

Aggravated with herself and the situation, and not sure how to correct it, she tried to continue with the session even though none of them—her, kids, the interns—were able to concentrate on what they were doing.

When her hands unexpectedly took on a sunny halo less intense than they had in the tunnels and at the hospital, it only added to her young clients' distraction. They stopped being weirded out by her and came forward to touch her fingers, her palms. Like cats, they slipped under her hands or raised them to their faces and rubbed against them. For an all too brief moment, Rory felt ease flow through her and into them. The moment they calmed, however, the glow subsided and the hyper returned to her system with more insistence than before.

Again, the kids withdrew from her.

She was futilely attempting to calm a frightened, often difficult, child with whom she normally had a special rapport when a sense of dread scudded through her. On the other side of the room, a shadow crossed her doorway. She glanced up to see one of the practice's participating doctors lean into the doorframe.

"Dr. Beck." Surprise colored her voice. Michael Beck looked weak and grayish, a sharp contrast to his usual almost feverish appearance of health and all-American boy-next-door blondness. She also didn't remember ever noticing how uncomfortable he made her when he looked at the kids in her care. Or the fact that he seemed somehow familiar from someplace else, as some*one* else. An image percolated about the edges of her mind and flitted away. "Are you all right?"

He gave her a grimace and shrugged. "Just this flu thing that's been going around."

"Maybe you shouldn't be here with the kids then," Rory said firmly, moving to put herself between them and him. "Don't want them to get sick, too."

"It was urgent that I see you." He winced and thrust himself away from the lintel, took a step forward, only to stumble back, gasping and wearing a look of pain.

Alarmed, Rory started toward him, but a powerful invisible *yank* pulled her back. Puzzled, she stopped and made a quick check of all her telepathic connections. She sensed something, but the link was so vague as to be almost nonexistent.

Again, she stepped forward. Again, that unseen presence stopped her.

Trying not to be obvious about it, she looked around. In the corner of her eye, a shadowy someone gestured at Beck and shook his head. What the heck? Mostly Ghostly from the hospital was stalking her now?

In the doorway, Dr. Beck seemed to make a grab for where she would have been if she hadn't stopped moving. With an ugly but quickly masked scowl, he visibly pulled himself together, flapped a hand at her in a shaky good-bye.

"Please see me later," he said. "It's vital." His voice hardened. "To both of us."

Then he eased slowly away in the direction of his office.

When he was gone, she gestured at the interns to carry on with the class before swinging around toward where she'd seen the phantom. This was going to be a mess that Kate would hear about. She'd be lucky if she was allowed to continue working even one day a week with the kids here.

Glaring at the specter she said, "Haunting me? Really?"

A silent wave of smirking laughter coupled with an exaggerated shrug of "*You caught me*" rolled over her.

Exasperated, she looked at her clients, now even more freaked out and cowering. They were all wide-eyed, watching the spot with which Rory seemed to be conversing. Great. One more thing she'd have to deal with if she was ever going to regain their trust.

"Okay." She clapped her hands and glanced at her puzzled interns, gestured toward the area where parents and caregivers waited for the session to conclude. "I think that's enough for today. I'll see you all next week. We'll do something fun!"

Without waiting to see how they took this additional disruption in their routine, she helped shepherd them out. Then, exasperated, she turned and took a couple of steps toward Mostly Ghostly.

"What do you want? If you're here to talk to me, come out of the woodwork and do it. If not, go away. You scared my students."

Again, response was more sensation than the sort of telepathic communication she shared with Luc. *You scared your students.*

She snorted. "No shi—" A glance toward the door, where a couple of parents were still helping their children into jackets, made her swallow the expletive. "No kidding," she managed instead. "Tell me something I don't know. Like how not to."

A shrug from the shadows. Then she felt another warning.

Doctor friend is dangerous. Be careful.

Doctor friend? Her gaze slid toward the doorway Dr. Beck had recently vacated while her thoughts flitted back to the hospital where she'd last seen Kate. He wasn't a friend, but Kate…

She turned back to the corner, but the sense of presence was gone.

And Luc was in her doorway.

Just like that, everything inside Rory settled. The edgy excess energy still flooded her, but there was an eagerness about it now, a knowledge that soon it would have somewhere to go, someone to benefit. On the heels of that recognition, a lazy warmth filled her. Her nipples pebbled, hard and visible against her midriff-length turquoise dance bra. Her belly seemed to liquefy and drop, her clit tightened. The thread that tied her to Luc began to vibrate. Hunger, carnal and intense, flared in his eyes, overpowering concern as she watched.

"Hey," she said, unable to stop herself from leaning toward him as he strode across the space between them.

"Hey." He reached her and bent toward her— —and Senn swung around the doorframe and into the room in a rush.

"Damn it, Rory," he said. "Which part of 'Stay. Put.' didn't compute?"

He'd entered the second level of hell, he knew it.

Hunger, raw and ungovernable, filled Luc the moment he saw her. She glowed with energy. It washed around her in waves, beckoning him. Caused greed to quicken in every pore, run through his veins in molten rivers.

Everything but Rory vanished.

Beyond anything else, he lusted. Needed. Wanted.

To feed on her. Replenish her. Meld into her.

Bury his cock deep *deep* inside her.

Fill her. Spill his seed into her humid earth.

Awareness of her was excruciating. His feet carried him toward her. He felt his jaw go slack, his breathing quicken. Was he drooling? He felt like a slavering beast hungering after prey.

Or a mate.

His nostrils opened wide, smelled the air. Jealousy flooded him at the taste of the others who'd been in the room with her. Not the children, but the fair-haired man he hunted. Hated. And, faintly, the son from whom he was estranged.

He tipped his head and sniffed. Athan was merely a hint of a presence. He would keep. But the blond… *He* had been here, in the room with her, looking at her and the children she taught. Focused on *her*. On acquiring her. That made him the one who mattered right now. Protecting Rory. Finding the blond man and making him dead.

He stopped in front of Rory, reached for her. She came to him eagerly.

"Damn it, Rory."

Senn barged loudly into the room, interrupting the claiming, the hot freaking sex that would have inevitably happened right after Rory touched him. The moment he touched her.

"Which part of 'Stay put' didn't compute when we left you at the apartment?"

Breathing hard, Luc spun about to give Senn a look of pure jealous male guarding his hard-won mate.

"Whoa."

Hands wide to the side, Senn took two steps back, frowning at Rory— who was, Luc's beast was pleased to note, regarding the sorcerer with supreme displeasure.

She was also glowing a fiery orange red. *Shit.* That could only mean bad things for someone.

She walked over to stiff-finger Senn's chest. "What"—poke—"are"— jab—"you"—poke—"doing here?" Poke-poke-jab.

"Looking for you—"

"You need to leave so Luc—"

"He was here, wasn't he?" Luc cut in, stepping between her and the sorcerer. Hoping Senn didn't notice him distracting Rory from expending that irritated energy where it might do damage. Clearly, she needed to get rid of it safely. He was just the man to help her—some other place. When they were alone. "Beck."

"Yes." She swiveled her head to give him a quizzical look. Some of the orangey red glow faded. "He looked weak. Sick." She stepped away from Senn and toward him, thinking about it. "I didn't like the way he was looking at the kids. Or me. He might have gone to his office. He said he wants to talk to me about something important."

The thing inside Luc growled. Audibly. "Did he touch you? Any of you?"

"He looked too sick to do anything."

"Not the point," Luc ground out. Again, he gave the atmosphere a silent sweep with his senses, concentrating on isolating Beck's energy residue. All he found were the trace remnants that told him Beck was gone. "The point being—"

"You were worried about me." She grinned suddenly.

"Damn straight. He's—"

Dimples popped into her cheeks. "That's so *cute*."

"—dangerous," Luc finished, grimacing. "I'm protective, not cute."

"Cute," Rory purred and touched a hand to his torso.

He flinched and sucked in his stomach, away from the less than innocent contact. Too aware of where he wanted that hand to go. Aware of what she wanted to do, too.

"Not"—he cast a sideways glance at Senn—"here."

"Where?"

"Fuck." Exasperated, Senn stepped forward to grab Rory's arm and drag her toward the door. "I do not want to see this."

Rory dug in her heels and yanked out of his grasp. "Then go away."

"No." In his best overbearing-big-brother fashion, Senn caught her again. "Not until we get you back to the apartment. Where you were supposed to stay. Why didn't you?"

"Bored. No one to play with. Had a DMT session to lead."

Despite his concern and his clamoring appetite, Luc bit back a grin when she looked over her shoulder at him. He'd remember that the next time she needed to be kept out of the way. Give her something to do so she wouldn't come up with something more interesting on her own. He followed them out the door, listening.

"Solaya—"

"—is afraid of babies," Rory said. "But she's a healer, so Kessie wanted her to stay in the room anyway. They all stayed with Magpie but kicked me out. I don't know why. Then I remembered I had things that I couldn't cancel at the last minute and no one to take over for me. So, I went."

They stepped outside as she made this pronouncement. Luc did his best to remember the gravity of the situation as he tried not to laugh. Senn sent him a withering look, then glanced at the evening sky.

"We have to get her out of here," he said.

Rory stopped short and peeled the sorcerer's fingers off her arm. "*Her* is right here," she said.

She did not, Luc noted when Senn winced and looked at her in surprise, do it gently. Or with any apparent effort. He had the feeling he should be disturbed by her show of physical strength, but he wasn't. Maybe later.

"Hey." Senn rubbed his fingers.

Beyond the buildings and trees, twilight sat at the city's horizon, dragging long shadows across the asphalt. Here and there, early stars printed a sky studded with gray clouds.

"Rory." Luc held out a hand to her, palm up. "We need to go."

"I want to walk." She looked up at him, face anxious. "Get rid of some of this." A flutter of her fingers at the electric aura surrounding her sent sparklers of light flittering into the dusk. "If I don't…" She shook her head. "I don't know. It feels dangerous. If *they* could take some, if I can give it, maybe—"

"No."

His voice was sharper than he'd intended, but the very idea of the night-feeders feasting on what she offered scared him silly. She would stand out to the unholy creatures, a lighthouse beacon in a stormy sea. He could feel them already, waiting in the deepest shadows. The fair-haired man with the physique of a bodybuilder was out there among them, lingering. Salivating.

Wanting her.

He couldn't let them have any part of her.

Wouldn't.

Even as he watched, two or three crept from shadow to shade, grasping for the stray bits of energy froth she'd flicked from her fingers. He shut his eyes for a second, glanced at Senn, looked back at her. Beck was something he'd have to deal with later, because the distress in her expression almost took him to his knees.

"No," he said again, more gently. "You can't feed them like this. If you do"—he hesitated, trying to find the right way to explain it—"if you do, they'll hound you, turn what you offer against you. Against others, like the kids you teach. They'll never leave you alone until they've bled them—bled you—dry."

"I thought that's what the tattoos were for. To prevent that."

"They are." Luc rubbed a hand across his face. He didn't know how to tell her. Didn't want to be that brutal. "You're getting more and more powerful, but—"

"Your tats only protect *you*," Senn said harshly. He shoved Luc aside and hunkered down into her face. "Do you understand? Not the kids you work with, not anyone around you. They don't act as a shield for anyone but you. And how well they work on *you* could change if you invite those *creatures*"—he almost spat the word—"past them."

Hurt filled her face, causing Luc's hands to fist instinctively. She stayed the one he would have used to punch Senn.

"Do you really think I'm so naïve and thoughtless not to know that?" she asked, turning to regard the dusk. "I know what's out there. I know what they want. I can feel it. Them. I don't want anyone else hurt because of me, but I can't let *might* stop me. I can't…quit just because you all"—she made an openhanded gesture that encompassed Luc and Senn as well as those who weren't with them—"think I'm something dangerous that needs to be swaddled in bubble wrap and stuck in the back of the closet the way my parents tried to do."

She swiveled about, eyes suddenly blazing, her entire being shining so brightly that Luc had to avert his gaze, and Senn's jaw dropped. He stepped back.

"Rory…"

"No." She slashed a hand through the air to cut him off and stepped up to the Range Rover's driver's-side rear door, pulled it open. Turned abruptly back to him. "I know you think you were protecting me, but they fed on me for *six months*," she said softly, vehemently, "and you and Solaya did *nothing* to stop them. Said *nothing* to me, just let them *feed* even though you had to have had some idea what was happening." Her mouth tightened. She looked at Luc. "Luc is the only one who did anything. Made it *stop*." Turning her back on Senn, she stepped up onto the running board and slid onto the seat. "I'm pretty sure that means you're the one who has no clue." She shut the door in his face.

Devastated, Senn eyed Luc.

"Don't look at me," Luc said, voice hard. "I agree with her. You didn't tell her anything, but she's learning faster than you can imagine. Faster than any of us can think. Get used to it."

Then he shoved the Rover's keys at Senn and got into the back seat with Rory.

He was pretty sure that "with Rory" was the only place he'd ever want to be.

Chapter Sixteen

Lightworkers of both the divine and human realms work for right and crave light. They despise the Ekoa Krillu and the Dugo Balang, who originated from a being tumbled from the divine realms and cursed to an eternity of darkness. With few exceptions, these entities not only cannot live in the light, but prey unforgivably upon it.

—from *The Lightway Codex, Appendix iii: Relationships* by McCleron O'Connell, Indigo Lightworker

The trip back to the penthouse apartment was fraught and silent, the tension between the front and back seats palpable. Rory leaned against the seat and gazed out the tinted window, trying to still her jittery pulse and quiet the manic energy coursing through her. Beside her, Luc was both too near yet not near enough.

She could feel his hunger, the control he exerted not to breach the short space between them either physically or mentally. Her own self-control was frayed-thread thin, her fingers twisted tightly in her lap. Only her seatbelt and the fact that Senn kept glancing at them in the rearview mirror as he drove kept her from crawling across the car to straddle Luc's lap, open his fly, and ride him until the frenzied energy inside her stilled and his need to feed abated.

Getting out of the vehicle and away from prying eyes couldn't happen soon enough.

They arrived at the club as the twilight was fading to full dark. Though Carpe Noctem was not yet open, muscular bouncers had set up the velvet ropes in front of the doors in preparation and clubgoers had begun to line the building's front wall. The air was restive, rife with anticipation mixed with laughter and an undercurrent of lust and hedonistic greed. Senn's jaw tightened and he shook his head at the scene, drove them to the door in the alley behind the club. Jinx met them. He scowled at Luc and Senn as they alighted, gestured one of the security guards with him toward Rory.

"Escort her upstairs," he told the guard, then barked at Luc and Senn, "Office. Now."

Rory gaped at him for a moment, then snapped her mouth closed. She sidestepped the guard to plant herself squarely in Jinx's path, arms akimbo. He gave her a look that clearly said, *Out of my way, little girl.*

Emphasis on the *little.*

She tapped her foot, glanced at Luc, who winced. Senn groaned.

"Luc needs to feed," she said. "Badly."

Jinx lifted a brow and stared at her. She stared back until Luc got between them and stooped to look her in the eye.

"You could take him"—the corner of his lips kicked upward when she turned her glare on him—"but show of force later." He brushed her mouth with the pad of one thumb, causing her lips to tingle and her pulse to whisper *please.* His eyes went black with desire. "*Us* later."

His promise, vibrated through her, blocking out everything else. She struggled with need, conquered it. Touched a palm to the side of his face. He closed his eyes, pressed into the touch.

"If you're sure," she said.

When he nodded, she withdrew her hand and followed the guard to the elevator. Before the security door closed behind them, she heard Jinx's incredulous voice, "What the hell, Garard. She can *take* me?" And Luc's emphatic response, "Believe it."

Warmth filled her. When she stepped into the elevator, she was smiling.

At the top of the building, the apartment was as she'd left it, still and silent, if not quite empty-feeling—until Solaya burst from the birthing room at the end of the back hallway.

"*Gaaah!*" When Rory eyed her askance, she shook her head in dismay. "It's never going to end. *Never.* I can't take it."

Rory snorted. Why Solaya had been gifted with a healer's talents to go with her warrior skills was unfathomable. At a noise from down the hall, the sorceress turned, wild-eyed, as the door she'd just slammed shut reopened and Kessie emerged.

"Magpie wants French fries," she told Solaya then leaned back into the room, listening. Stuck her head back out. "Good ones, not the frozen kind. Fresh."

"She's in *labor*," Solaya shouted after the fairy. "They can't be good for her."

"Get a double order and hamburgers," Kessie countered. "Fish needs to eat, too."

The door closed again before Solaya could lob the witchflame she'd conjured at the fae doula. Swearing, she squashed the witchflame into her fist and strode toward Rory.

"Damn woman could speed things up if she wanted to, magically goose labor along, but nooo," Solaya muttered. "She says that would be *bad*, that some things need to be allowed to take their *natural course*. And now I have to find *freaking fresh French fries*. God!" She steamed past Rory and into the kitchen.

"Call downstairs," Rory said, picking up the house phone and holding out the receiver. "Get them to send something up."

"You thought I'd peel, cut, and fry potatoes myself?" Solaya snatched the phone out of Rory's hand. Paused. "Jinx and everyone still gone?"

There was an edge of longing on Jinx's name. Rory tilted her head, wondering about that. "I think he, Senn, and Luc are down in his office." She gave it a beat. "He's very…autocratic, isn't he." It wasn't a question.

"Jinx?"

Rory nodded.

Solaya shrugged, looking suddenly lonely and tired. "He kind of has to be, given what the Brotherhood are." When Rory raised her eyebrows, Solaya said, "Bad guys looking for redemption." She turned away and squinted at the list of plastic-encased numbers beside the phone, punched one into the handset. "There's a duffel bag in one of the bedrooms." She flung a hand toward the hallway. "Wasn't sure what you'd need for how long, but I brought you some clothes and stuff." She held up a finger at Rory to say into the phone, "Yeah, hi. Penthouse 2. We need some fried food."

Instead of waiting for her to finish, Rory went down the hall, poking her head into each room until she spotted the bag Solaya had mentioned. Though still wired to the gills, she was emotionally exhausted. In all the years she'd known him and Solaya, she didn't remember ever arguing with Senn. She'd thought she knew him well, but his outburst as they were leaving the pediatric clinic suggested otherwise. That, coupled with what she'd seen and overheard during her astral outing to the hospital, made her wonder how well she knew any of the people she'd spent the better part of a lifetime being close to.

Mind churning, she dug through the duffel bag without seeing what was there, wondering how the girl in the hospital was doing and what the thing that had come out of her body was. Even though Rory had felt intuitively competent to deal with the situation in the moment, now that the moment had past, she had no idea what she'd felt competent to deal with.

Actions—all actions, regardless how insignificant or well-intentioned—had consequences. She had no idea what kind of life after death, resurrection, possession, and exorcism the teenager from the tunnels could have. Helluva lot of supernatural shit for one kid to go through in a single day.

Despair filled Rory. What the hell had she done?

And what the hell had she been thinking?

She hated second-guessing herself.

Don't think. Luc's voice was in her head.

But…

No "buts." Just don't. Second guesses can get you killed.

She took a deep breath. *I'll try.*

Good.

Where are you?

Hunting bad guys. Don't know how long it'll take.

A feeling of dread ran through her. *Don't eat them!*

His chuckle of response was dry. *The only person I plan to eat is you.*

A shiver of anticipation coupled with a sigh of relief ran through her. *Good. Be careful.*

He laughed, gave the link between them a tug, and was gone.

A tickle of warmth ran through Rory. It was ridiculous how much better that little telepathic tweak made her feel. She was still concerned about what she'd done, but it was no longer quite so overwhelming. She was responsible for her actions, both deliberate and instinctive. If worse came to worst, she would deal.

She'd spent a lifetime already dealing.

Listlessly, she looked at what Solaya had stuffed into the bag for her. Unwashed dance togs mingled with practical lingerie, T-shirts, club wear, jeans, toiletries, and a weirdly eclectic assortment of shoes. She began to sort through the detritus, separating the pieces. Her *Dancers Do It Better* cami fell into her hands along with a cropped tee emblazoned *When you stumble, make it part of the dance* and a sleep shirt telling her to *Dance 'til you drop.*

A smile formed when she remembered Luc's reaction to the first top. The second was something she continually reminded herself about, but the third…

The third was a call to action.

Dance 'til you drop.

She held out the vibrant aqua shirt and regarded the message, then looked at the tiny but sparkly black dress crumpled into the middle of the pile. Solaya must have just grabbed whatever came to hand when she'd packed for her. The dress was hardly something the sorceress would have chosen for Rory if she'd been paying attention—especially not while Rory was staying in an apartment above Carpe Noctem.

Cut to ride high on her thighs, low to the small of her back, and with a deeply plunging neckline that exposed a lot of her bosom, it was more daring than most of the clubbing dresses Rory owned. One of the flimsy spaghetti straps still bore the sales tags from the boutique in which she'd found it because she hadn't had a chance to give the barely there number a workout yet.

A vee formed between her eyebrows. Maybe all she needed to do to shed some of the excess energy rattling through her was to put on the dress and follow the shirt's advice. It was just too bad she couldn't get Solaya to come with her—

Before she'd even finished thinking it, there was a commotion that sent her hurrying to the bedroom door to look into the hall. Solaya burst from the birthing room, Kessie hard on her heels.

"Out. *Out!*" the fairy shouted. "You're driving me crazy and you're scaring the girl. If we actually need you for this, we'll call. Just go away!"

"You didn't need me in the first place," Solaya shouted back. "You just wanted my med and herb kit." Fuming, she turned to stalk toward Rory as Kessie slammed the birthing room door shut. "Damn fairy needs her head examined by a woodcutter. I need a drink."

Rory dangled the little black dress at her. "How about dancing?"

Solaya's mouth gaped. "You are not going anywhere in that. Where did you get it?"

"You packed it for me."

A flush climbed the sorceress's face. "I didn't—I couldn't—you can't—"

Rory smiled at her. "There will be booze. And boys."

Solaya paused opposite her, considering. "I want a man not a boy."

Holding the dress against herself, Rory danced in place while Solaya thought about it.

"Fine," Solaya said finally. "Let me see if I brought anything to wear." She turned to continue down the hallway, calling over her shoulder, "Find some-place close that's PG-rated because I'm not going dancing with you here."

She slammed the door of the room she was using behind her.

Rory stared after her, grinning. She had no intention of locating another club for them to go to. Carpe Noctem allegedly catered to everyone but teens, which would have to do.

She looked at the dress in her hands. It was too bad her "Disco Tits" paint and faux gems and sparklies kit wasn't in the bag so she could really go all out, but she'd make do.

Reentering her room, she cast aside the three T-shirts and laid out the LBD to finish rooting around in the bag. A lacy black thong joined the dress before she looked to see which shoes Solaya had grabbed for her. Though some were only one half of a pair, both of her favorite silver dancing heels had been included. Picking them up with the dress and the nearly nonexistent lingerie, Rory headed for the en suite bathroom to shower and change.

Daring, dangerous, and different—that was who she needed to be tonight.

Luc glared at himself in the mirror above the ice water-filled sink in his bathroom. Energy hunger carved ugly lines across his features, made them ripple with something he'd always considered the source of his downfall. Emotions that contained six of the seven deadlies—wrath, greed, gluttony, pride, envy, and lust—littered his expression, warning that implosion was imminent if he didn't feed soon.

Sipping from a boisterous crowd at the Pier wouldn't cut it this time. He was just too damn hungry. If he didn't suck down some surplus anima soon, he'd be back where he started when he came out of the pit, devouring whatever energy came to hand. The last time he'd let himself go like that, hundreds of years ago, he'd taken out the entire population of Roanoke without leaving a trace.

Yeah. That was the kind of history for which he sought redemption.

Swallowing self-recrimination, he turned off the tap and buried his face in the frigid water. Emptiness, dark and insatiable, filtered through him.

The night of extreme thuggery he, Senn, and Jinx had embarked on had not gone as planned. He didn't remember ever before being so wiped out by one of Jinx's "goon squad expeditions." No doubt that was because he usually fed on some of the energy of a situation to calm it while Jinx occasionally fed on the creatures the Brotherhood and the Council sent them after.

Not so tonight.

They'd backtracked to the pediatric clinic where Luc had last sensed Beck's presence. The little that remained of Beck's essence trail took them to the emergency wing the Council maintained at the nearby hospital where the victims from the sewer cells had been taken.

Things had started to go sideways when one of the teens had awakened, screaming, from a sedative-induced sleep and torn out her IV. The resulting blood spatter had caused Jinx's pupils to dilate and swirl, his fangs to descend.

The kid's screaming had practically caused Luc himself to salivate, but he'd managed to grab Jinx under one shoulder while Senn took the other. Jinx had struggled, forcing them to drag him bodily from the unit.

They'd made a quick stop at a Brotherhood-owned pharmacy for blood packs before resuming the chase. Jinx had sucked down three units before his appetite dulled. Luc had slapped a fourth unit into his hand and ripped him a new one when the club owner admitted to trying to wean himself of his need for human blood by spending the previous six months subsisting on Council-synthesized plasma only.

The incident only served to reinforce Luc's opinion that committing extreme thuggery was a lot like grocery shopping while hungry. If you didn't eat properly first, the slightest provocation could turn you into a raving lunatic in the doughnut aisle.

Luc was only grateful that he hadn't been the one to need to binge-feed first—especially after a night spent wrangling Jinx. Nevertheless, he needed to feed soon.

Given how long it took to get Jinx properly fed, they'd lost not only time, but Beck's energy trace as well. At Luc's suggestion, they'd driven into the Tenderloin hoping to find the doctor around one of the vamp clubs he apparently frequented. The search had been hampered by Jinx, who was now so hopped up on a blood-gorge high that he was rowdy, raucous, and ready to throw punches whether or not they needed to be thrown. It had taken Luc literally sitting on him to contain that outburst. If he could have tapped into blood-happy chi, he would have. Unfortunately, sang energy was anathema to psis.

Senn had finally attempted a locator spell. Unable to remember if he'd ever met Beck, and without something belonging to the man to use as a focus, the sorcerer was dubious about the spell's usefulness. But they managed to get multiple hits at some of the larger parks where many homeless tented up at night.

With little else to go on, they made the tour, with Jinx singing bawdy songs at the top of his lungs through most of it. Trace was spotty, but Luc thought he tasted Beck on the breeze in Golden Gate Park. Unfortunately, all they found was a world of hungry psis and sangs, and more emotionally and physically hollowed-out victims than he cared to think about. Some bore Nousaine's feeding signature, others the tang of unrepentant Fallen with whom Luc and Jinx were both familiar.

Among these living casualties were those that were so empty they were all but dead. All were marked with the flavor of something *other*, a stench akin to what Luc had smelled at the hospital earlier in the day.

Watchers.

Even as he'd thought of them, the ground had trembled beneath his feet. The grass he, Jinx, and Senn stood on had visibly rolled. Not far away, asphalt had crumpled, and he'd have sworn the earth seemed to roar.

He straightened and looked at himself in the mirror again. Had to be his imagination, right? Even though he was pretty sure he didn't have one.

Grimacing, he pulled the plug to empty the sink just as the beast inside him growled. His hearing sharpened until he heard shouting and crying—a domesticate dispute, dangerous for anyone but him to get involved in. The participants were practically bleeding emotions. Begging to be calmed. He could do it, but if he accidentally overfed…

Hating to do it, he found his phone and called the police, then closed his eyes and let energy deprivation shudder through him. Every part of him begged to tug on his connection to Rory, know that she was safe, to *feel* everything she felt. To fuel himself, *feed* himself, on her spirit. Force of will alone prevented him from doing it. Before he went anywhere near her, even telepathically, he needed to feed.

Now.

There was only one place in the city that he could find energy perverted enough, saturated with enough lust, greed, gluttony, pride, and envy to safely sate him in this state—Carpe Noctem, the club Jinx owned where special rooms were set aside for consenting adults so the locusts or psis like him could "dark feed." Above which, Rory waited for him.

Grimly, he made a twisting motion in the air in the region of his heart, knotting the string that tied him to Rory. Better safe than having her accidentally connect with him, see who and what he really was when he needed to eat.

Carpe Noctem wasn't like any other San Francisco nightclub Rory had been to, and she'd been to most of them. Dark, light, grungy, sexy, LGBTQ, it didn't matter. If there was good music and dancing, she was on top of the scene, usually with other dancers with whom she'd worked local shows. Tonight, she needed something different.

She'd never been to the mostly private club, but one of the dancers she often went out with had called Carpe Noctem dark-sex-edgy and chaotic. Another had complained that the supes in charge took a hard "no-drugs" line—and enforced it. And the third had simply referred to it as a "must." Rory knew that sequestered levels of the club catered to an untold variety of sexual appetites in degrees ranging from old-fashioned chaste to BDSM to orgiastic vampire feeding lounges where only those who consented to be fed from could enter.

The club wasn't listed online, but numerous Yelp reviews referred to it as IYCGI—If You Can Get In. Rory took that as a challenge.

Direct access should have been simple, given that she currently resided in one of the club's VIP-only penthouses, but as with the various club levels, that elevator, too, required a special keycard. Advice from friends suggested she "dress hot" and take a "hot sorceress" with her if she could.

Solaya had given Rory an incensed "No, you're not old enough," when she'd learned they were going downstairs to Carpe Noctem to which Rory had furiously responded "Twenty-six. Adult." Solaya had thrown up her hands and shouted, "You're not adult enough for this. Don't say I didn't warn you, but fine. Let's go!"

Rory thought Solaya had seemed relieved to give in. She'd certainly managed to find the right clothes for the occasion, looking smoking hot in six-inch fuck-me stilettos and a backless, cleavage-baring red leather dress. The sides were cut out, little more than crisscrossed laces from thigh to breast that left less to the imagination than Rory's own skin-revealing outfit.

She also thought she'd overheard Solaya talking to herself as she dressed about needing to wear something that would get her screwed senseless by *mumble-mumble*. Her voice had dropped, and Rory hadn't been able to catch who she wanted to be screwed senseless by. Whoever it was, Rory doubted he'd be able to resist Solaya at any time, but particularly not when she wore That Dress.

Getting sexed up and banged senseless sounded like a fabulous idea to Rory. She was a bit choosy by whom (Luc) but felt out of control enough energy-wise not to care where or when at this point. Not only did she want him, but Luc would be the only one who could safely handle the power she had to vent.

When they were finally dressed and in the elevator with Solaya giving Rory's barely-there ensemble her scariest look, Rory decided it was probably a good thing she hadn't gone with the disco tits ensemble. Especially after the security guards at the private, back-alley entrance seemed to need their eyes returned to their sockets when she and Solaya stepped out. The sorceress gave the male and female sentries an appraising once-over. Then, dismissing them with a curl of her lip, she'd linked her arm through Rory's and dragged her around to the front of the building.

The main club entrance was located just shy of mid-block. There, twenty-ones and up were vetted for admission by a pair of muscular bouncers dressed in unrelieved black. The male bouncers' heads were shaved clean, the females' close-cropped. All of them seemed to sport identically bulging left biceps encircled by blood red armbands bearing the Carpe Noctem security logo.

Why did beefy bald guys always look tougher than those with hair, Rory wondered as they approached. She followed Solaya when the other woman nodded at the men and passed under the discreet sign to enter the club without waiting to go through the queue held at bay by red velvet ropes.

An overwhelming sense of dark, sweaty need engulfed her the moment she stepped into the club. The atmosphere screamed *SEX*, dripped with its muskiness, causing her to stagger and clutch at the pipe banister on the stairway down into the club's entry-level sanctums. For an instant, panic filled her. She'd always been empathic, experienced other people's emotions as a sort of virtual reality, but this was different. Closer, more intense. Clear and present rather than distant and virtual.

Every nightclub she'd ever been in had reeked of sexual possibilities, every dance company she'd ever been part of had been a hotbed of hormones, hookups, breakups, and lust. None of them had affected her like this. As though something inside her had been ripped wide open and screamed with want. She couldn't *not* feel what was happening around her, what clubgoers were doing to and with each other.

Dancing in a troupe could be sexually charged, but this was flat out sex, lust, dark fantasies given life…

Catching on to Rory's discomfort, Solaya gave her a smug, purely evil grin that said, "I told you so." Wishing she could ignore the sorceress, Rory reached for the runes along her back in a frantic attempt to center herself. Between the runes themselves and the crystal and amethyst-imbued ink they were made of, she should be shielded from this sort of thing. Right?

Right.

No way did she want to admit Solaya had been right about the sexually charged atmosphere being too much for her. She was a dancer, damn it. Sexually charged was part and parcel of what she did.

Though perhaps, she admitted to herself, not to quite this degree.

Trying to control her emotions, Rory looked around. Dimness was broken only by the occasional muted spotlight or candlelight. The club was darker inside than out where streetlights and neon marquees chased the darkness into the shadows. She took a shallow breath and tried to get her bearings. The club was crowded. Bodies were packed together both on the dance floor and among the small round tables and narrow iron chairs on the raised platform that ran three-quarters of the way around it. An additional three stories of private entrance balconies that overlooked the dance floor, bar, and stage also appeared packed.

A restless shiver coursed along her skin when someone a level above the dance floor gasped in ecstasy. She tried reaching for the runes along her back. When they failed her, she tried to ignore it when every touch, move, sigh, and plea filtered through her defenses, causing her to experience everything.

Her skin was on fire, electrified, and every millimeter of it itched with anticipation. The air seemed to have fingers that teased her *everywhere*. She couldn't think, couldn't move without sensation driving her wild. Was it the place or the supernatural patrons, or had something more than she'd already realized happened to her in that tunnel?

Another glance at the shadowed upper balconies showed her that many of Carpe Noctem's patrons didn't care where or when, either. They also didn't appear to care with whom. Sensation crawled through her, spilled into her belly, fizzed to life between her thighs. She flinched and gasped when someone on the tier immediately above where she stood came hard. Heat coiled and tightened in her abdomen, sent her staggering against a railing as the scrap of fabric that covered her cleft grew damp.

Solaya *had* been right. She was not prepared for this.

Shuddering, Rory tried to collect herself when someone nearby also climaxed. *Holy—!*

Squirming with too much awareness, and too conscious of her own need, she again reached for the protective runes along her back. Tried to locate the one that might put a barrier between her and *this* as several more balcony revelers came in unison. Maybe…

A sharp tug at her arm made her wince and caused the tide of sexually charged emotions to recede until they only sparked lightly but insistently along her nerve endings. Gratefully, she looked at Solaya.

"Come on." The sorceress shouted to be heard above the cacophony of music and voices. She gestured toward the bar. "Let's get a drink and check things out." She dragged Rory down the steps to the edge of the dance floor—

—where the prickly awareness of sex being had or about to be had returned and immediately went from bad to worse.

Everywhere, bodies undulated together, brushed against her and each other, heightened her awareness, elicited her body's response. Her skin tingled and burned, her nipples hardened. Her clothing was too confining, her breathing grew harsh in her lungs. The wicked little *ping* of want between her thighs grew flagrant with need, her knees turned to liquid.

Breathe, she told herself. But the deep breath she drew filled her throat and lungs with the pungent flavor of sex and made things worse. This had been a Really Bad Idea.

Dance with me.

The murmur touched her ears, both from within and without. She knew that voice. *Ghost.*

A chuckle of response made her turn. Solaya's grasp on her arm loosened as she did the same. Behind them stood one of the tallest men Rory had ever seen in person—aside from Jinx and Luc, who always seemed about twice her five-foot-two-inch height. His hair was lighter than Luc's, more blond than brown, his physique muscular but slight. He was too big to be a professional dancer, but there was an inherent grace in the way his body swayed with the music.

There was also something more than his nonverbal *"Dance with me"* that made her think they'd met before. She didn't recognize the sulky mouth, but the jawline and the demeanor… There was a lot more smartass in his face, but…

Recognition sent a shiver through her and she took a step back to look up into his eyes. Wild and dark, as murky and blue as the Bay in a storm, she knew them. Luc's eyes.

His mouth formed a wry twist. He shrugged. "Can't choose your parents."

Before she could react, he grabbed one of her hands and the club's insistent atmosphere of sex, Sex, *SEX!* faded slightly. She still felt everything, but it was buffered by a thin veil. Startled, she looked up. He gave her a rogue's grin and caught one of Solaya's hands, too, twirled them both into the crooks of his arms.

Later, he cautioned Rory. Then aloud, "Let's dance."

Solaya cast a glance upward, toward a point three levels above and behind the stage. Following the direction of her gaze, Rory saw a tall, blondish man with a cleft chin and a scruff of facial fuzz staring at them. Jinx. In response, Rory watched as Solaya's teeth glinted, her tongue flicking forward to touch her upper lip. Her mouth formed a wicked smile. She leaned into their would-be partner's embrace.

"Why not?"

In moments, they were among the other dancers, him sandwiched between them, twisting and grinding to the heavy bass beat as a threesome.

Above them, Rory saw Jinx's features contort with an emotion akin to jealousy coupled with despair. Then it was as though a shutter came down. His expression turned bland and he turned his back on the floor as though dismissing—or trying to—Solaya as just one more partier in a herd.

So that was the guy Solaya not only wanted to torment but be screwed senseless by.

Thoughtfully, Rory turned and allowed their partner to draw one leg high to fit around his waist. Her upper body relaxed into a graceful dancer's arch while her lower body gyrated with his in provocative simulation. Behind him, Solaya slid an arm about his waist and hooked one of her own legs over his other hip and matched their rhythm. Together, they bumped and whirled, thrust and parried until Rory's skin felt too tight, her energy rose, and the heat inside her threatened to burst free and engulf them all.

Chapter Seventeen

Luc entered Carpe Noctem through an almost invisible entrance reserved only for members of the Brotherhood of Shadows. Even at the outside edges of the club, dark energy roiled and coalesced, an almost living entity. He sucked it deep before heading into the interior areas to join Jinx on the balcony outside the private fifth-floor offices overlooking the action.

"Damned witch," the Brotherhood's leader said, jutting his chin toward a point on the dance floor below.

Luc needed no explanation. The Dugo Balang had been in love with Solaya Lawton since her first incarnation nearly four thousand years before. Luc wasn't sure what had happened between them at that time, but Jinx had alluded to being cursed and doomed to repeat his love affair with Solaya about once a century. Every single time her incarnation fell for him, she died in battle, heroically, as the warrior she was. No matter what he tried, Jinx couldn't *not* fall for her. He'd also never yet been able to work out a way to a) keep her alive and b) get her to remember him when she reincarnated.

This was just the latest of many lifetimes Jinx couldn't forget and Solaya didn't remember.

Scowling, the other Fallen pulled his attention off the dance floor and glanced sideways at Luc.

"You know what's coming, so why don't you just tell her?" Luc asked.

Jinx huffed a laugh. "How many times have you seen this play out? You know how it works. She never wants to know."

"Yeah. Then you don't tell her and disaster happens. She dies, you go dark and kill things. People."

The blood vamp looked away. "Can't change the past."

"We're talking present—"

Jinx cut him off with a slash of a hand. "Look to your own troubles, 'Krillu."

Luc narrowed his eyes. So it was like that. Jinx was spoiling for a fight, and Luc was always the one he could count on to give him one.

Irritation crawled into his bloodstream, smoldered. He wasn't going to fall for the locust's bullshit tonight. The club's atmosphere was starting to soak into his pores. Instead of abating, the hunger that coursed through him was rising. Transforming. Mutating into something dark and out of control. He'd be ravening soon. Feeding on everything and everyone within range. And here, where lust, greed, and envy coupled with a furious undercurrent of wrath, that meant he'd lay waste to the club and everyone in it.

From the looks of it, Jinx's blood leviathan would be right alongside him. Which would be nothing but bad.

With an effort, Luc short-chained his beast to the floor.

Jinx eyed him, clearly struggling to bring his own monster to heel. "Did you locate Nousaine's protégé?"

"Only the trace you know about." Violence edged his voice. "Elusive little shit."

"Is Nousaine hiding him?"

"To what purpose? Wouldn't buy him anything. He's got to at least appear respectable. Something like this would shoot the shit out of tha—" He gasped and rocked back at the sudden sensation of a bludgeon punching him squarely in the center of his chest. Energy, darkness, need—his own, someone else's—weakened him. He staggered into the balcony rail, gripped it hard to keep himself on his feet.

Jinx eyed him sharply, spun to make a visual sweep of the area. "What?"

Luc shook his head, trying to reclaim his breath. He'd deliberately blocked his ability to distinguish individual auric signatures before he'd entered Carpe Noctem. It was always better to maintain some distance from those he fed on, keep it as impersonal as possible so he'd have no regrets later. But this…

This was something he'd never experienced—and how often had he had to admit that since meeting Rory? This was deeply personal and potentially toxic—almost as though the energy he'd planned to consume had suddenly turned on him, slammed itself into him, and was beating him to a pulp before trying to drown him. He couldn't seem to catch a breath before whatever or whoever it was shoved his head under again.

Struggling to keep it together, he did his best to raise his head above the suffocating miasma. He touched the tip of his tongue to the club's musk-filled air. Flavor, pungent and powerful, hit him. Steadying himself, he tried to sort individual signatures from the overpowering cocktail. The cinnamon-spice tang of sorceress, mixed with Solaya's personal essence, was the only individual taste in the muddy mixture. He twisted to find her in the crush.

"I thought she was supposed to be upstairs."

"Way she feels about birthing rooms? The way she's felt in every single incarnation about babies and the stickier emotions?" Jinx snorted. "She's scared to death of the whole thing. Kessie called down to say that the baby won't arrive for hours and that Solaya needs to chillax." He shrugged when Luc gave him the side-eye. "Her term."

Huffing a laugh, Luc returned his attention to the floor, still trying to pick apart the jumble of energy signatures that had hammered him. None of it belonged here, now or blended together.

Beside him, he felt Jinx go rigid as they watched Solaya roll her pelvis into the backside of a tall male who reached his hand back to hold her hips close to his. There was something familiar about him, his life force, but Luc couldn't get a good read. Something muddy and foreign stained him, and everyone around him. Luc sipped the air. Tasted of…

The answer fled when something crackled and glowed in front of the male. Luc squinted, trying to get a better look while attempting to figure out how he knew the guy. As he did so, the man moved slightly, revealing the tiny woman in front of him. Energy sparked about her like lightning when the man wrapped an arm around her middle and appeared to fit her bottom closely against his gyrating crotch. She wrapped a hand back to hold onto one of his arms, bring him close. Her face lifted, mouth parted in either a gasp or a laugh, and Luc stiffened when he recognized the last person he'd expected to see down there.

Rory.

Hollowness preceded the fury that ripped through him, releasing the knot he'd put in the rune-tether to prevent himself from feeling the dancer while he set about trying to assuage the hunger riding him. Sensation flooded him, washed him in Rory's scent and sexual need, heightened to extreme by the activity in the club. He felt rather than saw her eyes widen, breath grow shallow as the runes along her back flared to life. She swung her face in his direction. Tension sang between them, razor wire strung tightly enough to break and do serious damage to everyone around them if one of them didn't do something about it.

At the same time, the male between her and Solaya looked directly at Luc before pulling Rory more tightly into his pelvis. He grinned in challenge.

Goddammit. Athan.

The move was clearly a blatant attempt to goad him into a confrontation. In some distant, reasoned part of his mind, Luc knew that. But he also remembered what he knew of Athan's part in the Great Fire of London and other devastating incidents over the century and a half before it. Remembered Athanarius's blatant disregard for humanity.

The edges of his temper frayed and snapped. In a blur of movement, he was over the balcony railing, dropping the five stories to make a three-point landing in the crowd surrounding the trio. The other dancers shrieked and moved to accommodate his unexpected intrusion. Athan shifted Rory and Solaya almost protectively away from himself. Arms wide from his sides, he turned to face his father as Jinx landed lightly between them. The Brotherhood's leader put a hand on Luc's chest and leaned hard into him, holding him back.

"Not here," he warned Luc then snarled over his shoulder at Athan, "Get out. Now."

"As you wish." Affably, the thing that should not be held up his hands and backed into the crowd, toward the exit. As he went, he called to Luc, "I like her, but they've got her scent now. You don't deal with it, they'll send me." He gave his sire a fingertip wave and turned to go.

Rage roared through Luc. No one was getting near Aurora Montgomery while he existed. No one. Not the Council, not the Brotherhood, not Nousaine and his ilk, not the Watchers. She was not a chess piece to be won, lost, or played by *anyone.*

"Chill," Jinx warned him. "You have no idea why he's here or what all's going on. Bigger things—"

Luc's lip curled. The look he turned on the other Fallen was filled with fury. "Back off, Falken. What happens here is not up to you."

Blood and the thirst for it thundered in his ears. He shook off the blood vamp, *blinked* through the crowd, and grabbed Athan as he reached Carpe Noctem's exit. His son did nothing to prevent it when Luc slammed him into the wall hard enough to make the building shake. A few revelers jumped out of the way, but most simply ignored the testosterone-filled threat of violence, returning quickly to more pleasurable pursuits. A couple of bouncers headed in their direction, but Jinx intervened, waving them away. Athan laughed when Luc put a forearm to his throat and pressed hard against his windpipe.

"Stay away from her." The low, animal growl that accompanied the statement left no doubt about the implied *or else*.

Jinx put a hand on his shoulder, tried to tug him off. "Don't let him bait you."

Conscious of Rory picking her way through the crowd toward them, Luc shook him off. "Tell them to back off," he told Athan.

Athan laughed at him. "You have no idea who you're dealing with."

"No." Luc's voice was deadly. He applied crushing force to Athan's throat, staring into the stormy eyes that twinned his own. "*They* have no idea, and neither do you."

"Do it," Athan wheezed. "Try. I am what you made me, Father, and you know you can't. You didn't even have the courtesy to make me mortal enough to die."

"Maybe not," Luc spat, "but ritual is your enemy, and I know the one that will put you down."

He couldn't be sure, but Athan's eyes seemed to take on a distant, almost pleading look when he responded quietly, "I hope so."

"*Luc!*"

Again, Jinx tugged at him, and the moment between him and Athan was gone before Luc could wonder if it had been real. Jinx pulled him back far enough for Athan to eel out from under his arm, laughing derisively.

"You know what you need to do, Daddy," he shouted. Then, with a salute to someone behind his father, he turned and elbowed his way out of the club.

Pain and despair filled Luc. He'd been here before—allowed emotion and the whisper of something that sounded like reason to drag him toward the precipice of his original Fall. Sophiel had offered him a choice, a chance to redeem himself, and he'd shattered any hope of accepting the chance she'd offered in favor of seducing her and begetting Athan.

It didn't matter that, this time, both his options and his reasons were different. He was still at the cliff's edge, still about to make a choice, his betters felt could destroy not only mankind, but annihilate heaven and hell, as well. All in order to keep a single, exquisite, not-quite-human woman out of the affairs of angels.

Behind him, he felt rather than saw Rory push her way out of the crowd, Solaya close on her heels. Athan's mocking laughter ringing in his ears, he shook her off when she reached for him and swung around to stride through the oblivious crush of revelers toward the back exit. He had to get away from here, from Athan, and especially from Rory. From the images in his head of his progeny fitted to her bottom, sandwiched between her and Solaya. Of the sight of Rory's arm wrapped back about Athan's neck as he crouched over her, holding him to her as the three of them undulated together to the music's throbbing, sexual beat.

Of the pleasure on Rory's face as she participated in the dancing emulation of ménage.

From the memory of Rory grinding her cleft against the ridge of *his* cock, riding *him* in sleep-sex.

From the sudden and damning thought that it probably wouldn't have mattered who he was that night. That anyone with an engorged penis would have done…

Jealousy was a savage beat in his pulse. The scent of lust filled his nose. Everywhere around him, clubgoers gyrated and writhed together, fondling one another or dry humping right there on the dance floor. He shook his head, unsure if he sought to clear the rage from his brain or to suck in the sexual haze. To feed on it. To drown himself in it. That's why he'd come here, after all. And anything would be better than reliving the image of Rory and Athan undulating together with Solaya, or remembering what he, the enforcer, was supposed to do.

Use Rory to find the child and its mother, then kill them all.

Fury suffused him, want crawled inside him like fire ants swarming and biting whatever disturbed their hill. His senses bristled. Need and something more ravaged him. He didn't want to—*couldn't*—imagine killing her. Fucking her—and by default getting himself fucked—senseless, yes. *God, yes.* But no matter how compelling the argument was in favor of murdering her, the child that was about to be born, *and* its mother, he could not, *would* not, imagine that.

Especially not when he believed—no, he *knew*—she could save them all. He might be immortal, but if he followed orders and killed her, having to live with what he'd done would destroy him.

The need to commit violence engulfed him. He plowed his way through the dancers to the curtain that separated that back-alley exit from the club's interior. As he pushed the curtain aside to step through, a slender hand touched his arm. His senses scalded, body strung taut, cock sprang to painful life against his fly. He swung about and grabbed Rory, lifted her bodily against the wall, and let the curtain drop, hiding them from the dance floor.

"What the fuck do you want from me?" he snarled.

She clasped his shoulders, wrapped her legs around his waist. Planted her scantily clad privates tight to the burgeoning erection behind his fly. "Exactly that. Fuck me, Luc."

He grasped her thighs, held her away. Her tiny dress hiked above her hips, revealing the silky scrap of nothing that almost covered her. "Like you let *him* fuck you, Rory?"

Heavy-lidded eyes considered his. She shoved at him, trying to drop her legs and get away. "What?"

He held her fast, wrapped her legs back around his waist, and brought the engorged cock behind his zipper to the wetness that soaked her thong. "Did you let him touch you, get under your dress and finger-fuck you while you danced, Rory? Did you let him—"

"You unbelievable bast…"

Her throat arched, and she gasped when he pushed his erection against her then withdrew. She tried to press forward, to slide her silk-covered folds against him. Bared her teeth and tried to tilt her head forward so she could bite his neck. He shoved her away.

"Did you, Rory?"

Vibrating with anger, she reared back to give herself the best leverage she could and slapped him. Hard.

"Wake up, Luc," she said harshly. "Dancing is *fun*. And dirty dancing is a freaking turn-on. Any other night like this, I'd go home and wear out the batteries on my vibrator. But it wouldn't be your fucking *son's* face I'd be seeing while I did that, it'd be yours. The only dick I've ever wanted touching my clit or finger-fucking me is *you*. The only prick I want inside me is yours. I need *you*. I want *you*. Here. Now. *Hard.*"

Breath ragged, she looked him in the eyes. Her own were wet. "Not only that, you giant ass, if I don't get rid of the excess power I'm carrying, I feel like I'll explode and take this building and everyone inside it with me. It'll be worse than what happened in the tunnels because it'll hurt everyone. You *know* that. And that's what you do, isn't it? Suck off the excess to feed yourself and keep the world from imploding?"

"Rory…"

She closed her eyes, shuddering. Opened them and took his face between her hands. The air around her crackled with lightning, making her glow. There was desperation in her voice when she said, "You need this as badly as I do, I can feel it, feel *you*. I'm begging you, Luc. Please. I don't want to hurt anybody. *Fuck. Me. Now.*"

Her despair unnerved him. Her need sent him over the edge. He ducked his mouth to hers, plunged his tongue recklessly inside it. Tasted the power, drew it in. Came up gasping for air. The waters she inhabited were deep and charged with electricity, with the sustenance he needed to recharge himself and keep her from torching the entire city.

Another deep kiss and her breasts were free of the plunging neckline of her dress, rising into his palms. He teased her nipples with one hand while the other worked his zipper down. He shoved his pants open and his cock lifted free, prodded the silk of her thong. Impatiently, she leaned back against the wall and reached between them, tried to fit herself over him, to shove the scrap of fabric between them out of the way. But the sleek stuff was soaking wet and stretched tight, refused to give to her plucking. Luc lifted her away from the wall even as she twisted in his arms.

Stumbling backward, he found the edge of a table and turned to plant her on its surface, facedown. The thong's string snapped beneath his fingers, her bottom lifted to him. At the same time, she pushed herself back, and he speared his fingers into her cleft to find her opening then slammed forward to seat his cock deep inside her.

There was no finesse, only the hard, fast, fucking they both wanted. Needed. Her breath sobbed in her lungs. His grunted out of him. He gripped her hips in iron fists, filling her and withdrawing, plundering and retreating.

The table and the wall it stood against rattled and shook. The air around them sputtered and hissed audibly, spitting with power. When the curtain they'd come through was shoved aside, Luc felt the wings he'd thought he'd lost thousands of millennia before unfurl and close around them protectively. Within their shielding embrace, he lost himself in Rory. Took her until his name came out of her on a guttural scream, her inner muscles clamped around him, and the anteroom they were in erupted with light.

Strength surged through him. His cock filled to bursting with cum. His seed jetted into her—

—and then they were no longer in the back room of Carpe Noctem, but collapsing into the sheets of a rafter-hung swing-bed on the exterior balcony of an apartment on one of the club's upper levels, wrapped in his wings.

At the very moment the earthquake struck and the air sputtered and hissed with power, several other things also happened:

Jinx and Solaya acted on their "with benefits" clause, coming together violently against a wall in Jinx's office.

Senn walked into the Congress of Principles and slammed Celeste Fury against the wall by the throat and said, "What the fuck have you done?"

At the center of the long conference table around which the now-shocked congress was seated, Luceire Garard's one-time paramour, Sophiel, curved her lips into a viciously triumphant smile and sent a sideways glance toward the room's deepest shadows. Without acknowledging his mother's silent command, Athanarius let himself fade to something less visible and more transparent than mist and disappear from the room.

And upstairs, in the penthouse's makeshift birthing chamber, Kessie yelled, "Push!" Magpie shrieked to high heaven, a terrified Fish buried himself in a corner, hugging his arms around his head and ears…

And the baby that had started this whole chain of events slid into Kessie's hands, opened its eyes, and took its first breath in the world.

Inside his crystal-encrusted tower sanctuary, Savitri Nousaine leaned forward with anticipation. The energy discharge that lit the night sky was formidable the way a gas explosion was: powerful, uncontrolled, and destructively pretty to look at. Occasional tracer-like energy rockets veered off the original flare, lighting the sky like fireworks. He braced himself when the percussive wave hit, ready to absorb the power tsunami—and recoiled in surprise when the energy bounced off the unrepaired structure without coming anywhere near him.

Uncertainty riffled through him for the first time in eons. That shouldn't have happened. *He* was the city's master. The city's power belonged to *him*.

A surge of anger whispered through him. Perhaps he'd become too complacent, depending upon others to find his meals for him. Allowing himself to become too respectable to hunt and feed where it would do him the most good, make him strongest—among those who were his human partners, his upper-crust clients, the people it wouldn't pay him financially to feed on. To kill.

Wrath filled him. With all of his senses, he reached deep, feeling for the power threads he could see leaching into the air from the explosion point. Again, they eluded him, almost shoving him away. He could see them but not touch, either physically or mentally.

He let his eyes glaze slightly, trying to see precisely what was happening. Found the opalescent, dome-like barrier that covered the city in all directions, stopping just beyond his broken window. Moving to the window, he put a hand into the night and poked the bubble. It sagged inward like a balloon, then snapped back, pushing his hand away.

From the offices outside his door and the floors below, he sensed movement, routine, people he'd never before considered consuming either in whole or part. Even now, he hesitated, reaching out with his senses, looking for his protégé, Beck. The not-so-good doctor was his surrogate, his fuel base. He'd signed a contract in blood that allowed Nousaine to feed on him whenever and wherever. Now only a null came back to Nousaine, a void so profound it was as though the man had never existed.

Nousaine's gaze narrowed. Fine. If that was the play…

On feet made heavy by denied hunger, he moved to the door of his office, opened it, and stepped into his secretary's space. He smiled at the man's querying brow before stepping to the desk and grabbing his human servant from behind it.

Then he fastened his mouth over the struggling man's and started to eat.

Deep beneath an abandoned warehouse—the very warehouse, in fact, that had housed Fish and the pregnant Magpie—bell jars lined row upon row of wooden shelves the height and length of the space's painted concrete walls. Between the rows, tall glass cylinders rose toward the ceiling in a more haphazard fashion, as though scattered wherever they might fit.

Michael Beck or Erra, as he preferred, wandered the aisles between the shelves and containers, occasionally reaching out to stroke a jar or tank with his fingertips. Everywhere he looked, mustard yellow etheric cords infected by thin vines of gray, brown, and black trailed from the cylinders to the jars and back. Additional creepers ran from the containers to the floor where they wove together into one massive cable that fed into a storm drain sunk into the lowest section of the floor. The tanks contained the bodies of special children he'd stolen. The jars held the souls siphoned into them. The creepers bore those souls into and through the pipeline he'd devised to provide his ancestors the nourishment they required to rise.

Giddiness ran through him as he checked the tangle to make sure there were no kinks. He had done this. Where others had failed, he was succeeding.

In the center of the place, well away from the crowded shelves and cylinders, a single, glass-enclosed, body-sized unit stood upright. A gelatinous liquid engineered to imprison but sustain a single human life filled it. *Her* single human life. All he had to do was take her.

He wrapped his arms around himself, giggling. The pair of eighteen-year-olds he'd found at the blood club he'd gone to earlier had charged his batteries in ways they'd never imagined when they'd set out on their evening's adventure. They were hardly his usual choice of fuel, but his appetite had been voracious, and they'd been available. Having learned his lesson from the adolescents retrieved from the sewer tunnels, he'd used then killed these girls, left their bodies where they were unlikely to ever be found.

Dragging a hand along the glass, he circled the gel-filled container, admiring his handiwork. Somewhere outside himself, he could feel Savitri Nousaine hunting him. The master psi's demand to know where he was and what he was doing glanced off him, as though he wasn't there. Ecstatic, Beck embraced the circular unit. Amazing! For the first time, his mentor couldn't find and feed on him whenever he wanted. Along with immortality, it was exactly what Beck had been prostituting himself for.

And it was only part of what he stood to gain by toadying up to those beings unjustly incarcerated deep within the earth. What he'd earn by abetting their escape and resurgence into the world from which they'd been banished.

He, whose DNA was 97.5 percent human and only 2.5 percent "other," had bested the self-proclaimed Ekoa Krillu master at his own game. Euphoria filled him. *They* said that you couldn't serve two masters, that it didn't pay. But what did *they* know? *They* hadn't apprenticed to one badass vampire while working for the imprisoned Watchers. *They* hadn't learned everything Nousaine had to offer and turned it on him. *They* had no idea how powerful he'd become, how deserving of his birthright.

Nousaine was only a Fallen, after all. One of heaven's rejects, *M*'s minions. But Beck would be more. Watchers had walked the earth, bedded humans, and become so powerful that the Almighty had his angels, his warriors, entomb them. When Beck brought them Aurora Montgomery, whose full powers he could feel manifesting—whose full powers the entire western half of North America could feel manifesting, whether they understood it or not…

When he deposited her in the container, harnessed the power of her spirit, and spliced it into the souls of the extraordinary children he'd already collected…

When he did that, the Watchers would regain their bodies and powers, and leave their tomb. And he who'd orchestrated their release…

He would become their *god!*

But he had to take her first. And given how rabidly that 'Krillu and his locust and sorcerer friends had been guarding her when Beck had spotted her outside the psychologist's offices, he had a fair idea of where she might be.

And if Nousaine's former protégé, Luceire Garard, thought he could keep Aurora Montgomery from the destiny Erra had chosen for her, well…

Everyone had just better think again.

Chapter Eighteen

So that Guardian Thug thing for when stupid lands on your doorstep? Yeah. Not a guideline. It's a rule.

—Aurora Montgomery, Crystal Elder Philosophies from *The Lightway Codex, Appendix vi: Quotations* by McCleron O'Connell, Indigo Lightworker

He couldn't get enough of her. One taste led to the need for more.

Mindless of where they were and how they got there, Luc plundered Rory's senses, fed on her energy, filled her with his own.

Again, she came. Again, her dancer's stamina met and bested his immortal strength. He fed on her cream, devoured her sex, toyed with her clit until the sheets beneath them were saturated with her juices. Her hands twisted the sheets, pulled them askew. Her back bowed nearly double as she tried to get closer, get *more*. He lifted her knees over his arms then his shoulders, and raised her higher, tongued her more deeply while she squirmed and moaned—and finally sat upright against his mouth, twisted to angle herself down along his torso, and took his erection into her mouth.

His smothered-in-pussy gasp *"Fuck me"* as he fell backward against the nightstand, the wall, and finally the bed, was as much plea as prayer. Her own muted moans vibrated along his already near-to-bursting cock, causing it to flex and tighten and thrust. When her orgasm coiled spring-tight and rocketed through her, she loosed a strangled scream, opened her throat, and dragged him deep. Sucked him until his brain fried, his body strained, and he came.

And came. And came.

Around them, the walls shook, the furnishings rattled, the lights flashed. And when Luc finally caught his breath enough to raise his head, it was to see her pulsing with light, with fire—with the colors of the borealis. And he knew, without a shred of doubt, what he'd already begun to suspect.

Aurora Montgomery was not remotely human.

He couldn't begin to guess where she'd come from or who had sent her to her human parents, but she hadn't been born of them, he was sure.

She was energy incarnate, power made flesh, a gift to be cherished and guarded. And that was why the Council wanted her dead. Because between her, the children who were *dead but not dying*, and the babe from Magpie's belly, the Watchers could rise and feed. Harness her to their own ends. Which would give them the resources they needed to enslave not only humanity, but the Fallen, the earthbound angels like Celeste, and the rest of the earth's supes and elementals and Fae, as well.

In the glow that suffused the being who'd given herself to him, fed him, and empowered him—who'd given him back his wings—Luc faced the overwhelming realization of what had just happened. Of who, and *what*, Rory was.

Knowledge. Life. Love.

Redemption.

He should have been awed. He should have been afraid. He should have been…

But then she opened her eyes and she looked up at him, her mouth curved in a pleased grin, her lips still glistening with his cum, and "should have" fled. Instead, pleasure swept through him, desire filled him. He swooped down on her as she laughed and reached for him. His cock, already rising, prodded her belly. She wrapped her legs around him and took him in. Held him.

Loved him.

Less than two hours later, Luc woke in darkness, feeling unusually happy but groggy, disoriented, and wholly unlike the creature he'd been since the Fall. Replete. Different. Better.

Different and better.

Overwhelmingly replete.

Somewhere outside the not quite soundproof room, music played loudly, clashed with the rumble of hundreds of voices talking, laughing, groaning in pain and ecstasy. For a moment, all he could do was lick his lips, try to work moisture back into his dry mouth. Blink until memory came tiptoeing back then roared into his awareness.

Rory.

The unprecedented, unbelievable return of the wings he could even now feel tucked neatly—and a little painfully, after so many millennia without them—into place within his shoulder blades.

Him, his wings, bringing them…wherever *here* was…between one flutter of his eyelids and the next.

Being inside her.

Worshipping her.

Feeling as though he'd been cherished beyond his wildest imagination in return. And, when he had one, his imagination was ancient and wild.

Lovemaking—to the point where he was just a little high from all the energy they'd shared.

His wings, his wings, *his wings*!

And Rory.

His arms were tucked along her sides, his hands upturned beneath her shoulders. He moved his head and his cheek slid over the silken skin of her lower abdomen, chin brushed into the spiky triangle of blond curls over her sex. His mouth curved. If he turned his head just so he could wake her—

An alarm screamed suddenly, shrill and painful in his head, echoing through him, making him cringe. Senses keyed, he jerked upright, trying to figure out where the noise came from even as he gathered Rory into his arms to bring her with him.

She lifted her head, startled, eyes going wide and wild as she tried to sort out what was going on. Luc felt her tense as she connected with his pain, brought her hands up to cup his head. She winced, turtled her head into her shoulders as though she experienced everything he felt. Then just like *that*, the pain eased.

"Are you all right?"

He grimaced and loosed a short laugh. "Aside from needing that"—with his chin he gestured toward the ceiling—"to stop?"

He thought she sketched a symbol in the air over each of his ears before the alarm's shriek receded to manageable levels. He worked his jaw, trying to figure out what she'd done to his hearing. Somewhere below the room they were in, the warning buzzer continued to sound.

"What happened?" Her voice sounded muzzy and strained.

He glanced sharply at her as he swiveled to the edge of the bed. "Not sure. Sounds like a fire alarm."

The *blaat-blaat-blaat* came closer, flitting from one room detector to the next until the one above the bed they were in screamed. A harsh red glow permeated the darkness, showing them the room's door.

Rory struggled out of his arms and staggered a bit, putting out her hands to catch her balance. They landed low on his belly and his cock stirred. He quelled it. Gonads served their purpose, but they were no substitute for brains in a crisis. As though recognizing the direction of his thoughts, she looked up at him. Her face looked pinched in the crimson light. He opened his mouth to ask her about it, but she shook her head and grabbed a sheet off the bed. Quickly, she wrapped it around herself, looping the excess over one shoulder and under the other, and tucking it securely together.

"Where are we?"

Concerned, but unable to detect the exact nature of the problem, Luc found his pants and stepped into them. "Looks like one of the apartments above the club that Jinx leases to members."

"Carpe Noctem has memberships?"

Trust Rory to pick up on that amid everything else.

Lips kicking up, Luc stepped to the door and laid a hand flat near the knob, checking for heat. Beside him, Rory flattened her entire body against the door. He tipped his head to look at her. Anxiety was a living thing, coursing through her and into him.

"What?"

"Something's wrong," she murmured just loud enough for him to hear.

He started to crack the door open. "No heat—"

"Don't!"

He heard the sharp exclamation at the same time he was flung across the room and onto the bed by invisible hands. Hers. A moment later, the door exploded inward.

Inside that instant, the world as he'd come to know it stopped.

"Rory!"

Even after so many eons, using his wings to catapult himself upright and reach for the heavy door was automatic. Flames licked in through the open portal as he pitched the door aside, searching for her.

"*Rory!*"

Smoke curled into the room with the flames, obscuring his vision. A cacophony of screams and shouts from below filtered through the fire's roar.

"Rory!" he shouted again. "Answer me, damn it!"

Nothing.

The link in the center of his chest twitched. He reached for it, tried to grab hold of the intangible connection. It withered and died beneath his fingertips.

"*Shit!*" Fear, stark and unaccustomed, seized him. From the moment they'd met, he'd violated every Brotherhood rule by giving himself one job only—to keep her close, to keep her safe, to make her his. "Rory," he pleaded, not caring that he'd never begged for anything before in his overlong existence, "please. Tell me where you are."

Around him, the conflagration bellowed and the club's overhead sprinkler system fought a losing battle. Water droplets sizzled and popped as they fell into the blaze. Then he heard it.

Okay.

The whisper shivered beneath the hair on the back of his neck, chill but welcome. He shut his eyes, feeling for her.

Here.

He opened his eyes and turned in the direction he thought her voice came from, found her silhouetted by flames. He stepped toward her. "No…"

She held up a hand and moved backward, into the fire. Her aura took light, blazed red-orange-yellow. Made her part of the inferno.

It's about the kids, he heard her say. *I have to get the kids.* She pointed at the wall of flame, the howl of shouts and screams and fire behind him. *You help them.*

Then a portal opened behind her and, in a shower of sparks, she was gone. The connection between them severed.

"No!" he shouted.

Too late.

For a moment, he stared after her. The declaration Kessie had made when she'd arrived in the penthouse that *they* could find and follow her if she manipulated the energy required to tesseract made him queasy—and frustrated.

One of the things he'd realized almost as soon as they'd met was that Aurora Montgomery had no sense of self-preservation. Some part of him wanted to rail and curse, ream her from one end of the universe to the other to get her ass back where he could stand between her and all comers. The other parts of him knew that he had to trust her to find her own way. To use who and what she was to fulfill her purpose in the world.

Regardless of his.

Along his shoulder blades, his wings twitched and unfurled, impatient to be used. He was wasting time while people in the main part of the club were likely dying. Time to move.

Without another thought, he vaulted through the fire and over the balcony railing outside the bedroom suite's door. There was a moment of exhilaration when his newly returned wings supported him. Then he sailed down into the smoke and chaos, and moved as quickly as he could to get people out.

Smoke filled Rory's vision when she stepped through the opening in the ether and into the penthouse apartment Jinx had lent them. She couldn't be sure, but the haze seemed thicker here than it had however many floors below. Freaky. Possibly not as freaky as looking down at herself and discovering she'd become part of the fire, but still.

"Laya," she called, coughing and flapping a hand at the cloud of smoke in front of her face. It was hard to breathe. "Solaya!"

From somewhere to her right, she thought she heard someone call her name. Between the unearthly chatter in the web and the dull thudding in her ears caused by the explosion, it was difficult to be sure. She tried batting the smoke aside, to no avail. Her eyes stung. Blinking to clear them didn't help. They were dry as dust and filled with grit. She turned and, feeling the way with her hands, took a step in the direction she thought the voice had come from.

"Laya!"

Barely able to hear her own voice, she worked her jaw this way and that, trying to relieve the pressure in her ears. The move worked too well. There was an audible pop as the pressure released, then her ears buzzed, head filled with the disjointed chatter of those who populated the nexus. Some of them were screaming, others crying or shouting so loudly the message was jumbled.

Please, she told them. *I can't understand you. There's been an explosion. Where are you? Tell me.*

It took a moment, but last the cacophony separated into distinct voices.

Get out, get out! she heard. *Help, get help!* Then an echo of her question, *where are they, where are they, where are they?*

Don't know don't know don't know. Gone…gone…gone…can't find…

She staggered under the weight of the voices, the throb of premonition, the sense of emptiness running through the apartment. The choir in her head was shrieking now, the sound echoing and bouncing until she thought she'd go mad. She couldn't hear anything outside them.

Something's wrong…wrong…wrong… Get the baby, find the baby, don't let them take the baby. Dead but not dying, save the souls, free them. Let them go…go…go…

Find him…

One hand to her forehead, the other to the base of her skull, she tried to disconnect from them the way she'd done before, but they were having none of it. Then, out of nowhere, a single voice separated itself from the others, came through sharp and clear.

"In the world of the prairie, the world by the sea, beneath the old shed, the undying dead cry Help me, help me…"

Behind the rhyme, the chorus chanted, *Help me, help me, help me.*

It took a second repetition of the whole for Rory to understand what she was being told. When it finally sank in, she sucked a lungful of smoky air and started to turn toward the back hallway. The place felt empty, but she had to be sure.

"They're gone," someone rasped. A hand latched onto her arm with bruising force.

Through the haze, she could just make out Michael Beck's fair hair and too-handsome face. She felt heat and power gather into her hands—the same power that had coalesced inside her when she'd thrown Luc out of her studio. Before she knew him.

Don't, don't, the voices urged. *He knows where they are. He uses them. Don't hurt him…don't…*

Steeling herself against the instinct to do something to him, she contemplated his hand on her, lifted her gaze to his face, and blinked. Luc wouldn't think twice about killing him for this.

Good thing he's not here, then, someone suggested. Possibly it was her. *Can't afford to kill him…*

Yet.

She had other things to consider first. People.

The baby. The *child*.

"Dr. Beck," she said quietly. Rasped, really. The smoke was getting thicker, being sucked into her lungs with every breath. How had she stood in the fire before and not been burned? "What are you doing here?"

He acknowledged her recognition with a nod. "Hello, my dear," he said. "Where is Magpie and her babe? They belong to me, you know. I don't suppose you can tell me where they went?"

Eyes watering from the smoke, Rory stared at him. Somewhere inside her, a flame of understanding licked to life. She caught it and held it close, while in the back of her head, the voices quieted to a single thought. *He knows, he knows, the undying dead…*

He knows.

If she could get him to show her what he'd done…

"Even if I knew, I wouldn't tell you. Or anyone."

"That's unfortunate."

He slapped his free hand onto the arm he was holding, and she felt a sting. She started in surprise and tried to yank away, but a strange lassitude was already creeping along her limbs. Her jaw went slack. Even after the ghost at the clinic—Athan—had warned her not to trust Michael Beck, it had never occurred to her that he might drug her to ensure her cooperation. Stupid, but there it was.

The last thing she felt as she slumped was being lifted and carried. The last thing she heard was, "Now I suppose you're the one who'll have to help me."

Twenty miles away, Keile Raeburn wheeled another not-quite-lifeless body into the Council of Light's autopsy wing. Sharp on his heels, Celeste Fury followed, dragging a cart full of instruments and a mishmash of blinking and beeping electronic devices. Kate Cavanaugh brought up the rear.

"Celeste, this is wrong. Don't do this," Kate pleaded. Her voice shook with fear as though she'd been pleading with Celeste for a while. "You can't—"

"Who is she?" Celeste ignored her, leaning in to attach patches from one of the monitors to the dead girl's temples. "She's older than the others."

"No idea." Keile gave them a questioning side-eye, but only shook his head. "I'd say she's at least five or six years older than the others. Mid-teens, maybe." He pulled back the sheet covering the body and glanced sideways at the director. "I'd also say she recently gave birth. *Aiiieeee.*" He made a motion at the victim's torso. "Or rather, a baby was cut out of her at the same time her soul was harvested."

"Oh God," Kate whispered. She shrank to the side of the room and slid to the floor against the compartments where bodies were stored at the same time that Celeste exclaimed, "What?"

She leaned in to look at the brutal wounds that cross-patched the body's belly area. Her expression turned ugly. "Not one of our people, then. And the Nightkeepers wouldn't need to be so"—her mouth worked—"careless."

She adjusted the monitors, added a patch and a lead to the body's throat, and flipped a couple of dials.

"Don't!" Kate begged.

"We'll never learn what they know if we don't," Celeste said harshly. "Aurora Montgomery can't be the only one able to speak with them."

She punched a button and the body's mouth opened. A belch of air issued from it.

"Good." Celeste patted the victim's arm, leaned in close to its ear. "Tell me who took your baby," she whispered. "Help me find him."

Chapter Nineteen

On the theory that Christ told the thieves on the cross, "Repent and you will this day be with me in heaven," the Fallen members of the Brotherhood of Shadows each begged forgiveness of their Creator and swore to spend eternity in service to the humans He valued so highly. Regardless, many among the higher angelic orders remain skeptical that the Fallen will honor this vow...

—from *The Lightway Codex, Introduction: Overview*
by McCleron O'Connell, Indigo Lightworker

"Where is she?" Luc shouted.

He, Senn, and Jinx had come directly from the explosion's aftermath to the Lawton residence where Kessie had transported Solaya, Fish, the exhausted-from-birthing Magpie, and her newborn to get them out of reach of the fire.

Thirty-eight people had died in the blaze, including two members of the band playing at the club and the deejay. The club's manager had been trying to free another of the band members from beneath the collapsed stage when the wall behind the platform gave way. The band member had survived. Carpe Noctem's manager had not.

That the explosion had been timed to go off when the club's business was at its evening peak did not help matters. Neither Senn nor Jinx were in the mood to be gentle now that Rory was missing. And Luc...

Luc was nearly out of his mind with worry. Senn had given her to him to keep safe, and he'd done everything but.

When Solaya continued to stare at them looking devastated and guilty, and despite Senn's restraining hand, Luc stooped nose-to-nose with her and ground out, "She's not with me, she had to be with you. Where is she?"

"I don't know!" Solaya shouted, rousing from her exhausted disbelief at last. "Last time I saw her, she went after *you*, and Jinx stopped me from following her. We thought that maybe when you were done with her, she came here."

When he was *done* with her? Anger ran a swift and destructive course through Luc. He would never be *done* with Aurora Montgomery. His hands curled into fists. "You—"

"She went to make sure y'all were safe." Arms held wide, Jinx stepped between her and Luc, bodily separating them. "Nobody's seen her since."

"What?" Solaya's face said *WTF, I don't believe this shit, what the hell have you people been doing.* "What are you talking about?" She turned on Luc, punched him in the chest. "You were supposed to look after her. You let her take the stairs, twenty flights, *by herself*, during a fire? What the everlasting *fuck*, Garard?"

Luc pressed his lips together, looked away. Damn him for the fool he was. "She didn't take the stairs."

"What?" Solaya's eyebrows flew, her brow distorted with confusion. "You let her out of your sight when—"

"I don't think it was about *letting her* do anything," Senn told her mildly. "You have no idea what she's capable of."

"And why is that?" Solaya turned to glare at him. "Because you think I can't handle knowing what she does when you think I'm not looking?"

Senn took a step back. He looked at Luc, who swore and said, "She opened a door before I could stop her. Look, this isn't getting us—"

"After I said not to?" Kessie entered the room as though on cue. When Senn and Jinx stood mute, and Luc gave her a pointed look, she muttered something colorful under her breath and said flatly, "If she did that, *they* have her."

"What are you talking about?" Solaya asked, confused. Her gaze bounced from Kessie to Senn to Jinx to Luc and back to Senn. She planted a quick, hard punch to her brother's chest and looked sharply at Kessie. "*Who* has her?"

"Them." The fairy's eyes widened. "You know. *Them.*"

"Them." Solaya's lips thinned as realization set in. "Watchers." Her jaw worked. She looked at Senn, covered her mouth with a hand when he gave her a clipped nod. "That's what this is about?" She glanced toward the hallway, toward where Magpie and her child rested on a couch in the library. "This is the *child* you wanted Rory to find? This—"

"Look," Luc said, interrupting her. "I don't know what the Council has told its people, but yes. Kartchner ruptured. It's leaking Watchers or their wraiths. And this"—he made a gesture that encompassed them all—"is a freaking waste of time—"

Before he could finish, Fish exploded into the room, charged forward, and reached high to slap a hand over his mouth.

"No," he pleaded, wide-eyed and trembling. "Stop. If you're not quiet, they'll find it. Her. *Us.*"

Senn eyed him sharply. "Who—"

Fish put a finger to his lips and shook his head hard. "No," he pleaded. "No."

Though clearly unsettled, Senn simply nodded and glanced over the boy's head at Luc. Fish turned to Luc, too.

Find her, he mouthed. *She needs you.* He turned and shoved a crumpled piece of paper into Senn's hand. "You need this."

Luc grabbed Fish's shoulders, stooped to eye level. *Where?* A question without sound.

The boy shook his head, tapped his brow. Luc narrowed his eyes. Fish tapped the side of his own head again, reached over to thump his forefinger repeatedly against Luc's head. Then the boy glanced at Jinx. The bloodsucker nodded, and a dialogue balloon appeared in Luc's mind. *Maybe. Try it.*

Luc turned back to Fish. *Can you hear me?*

Fish nodded.

Do you know where she is?

A grimace followed by a shrug.

Where do you think *she is?*

The boy's face contorted in what looked like agonizing thought. Then he shut his eyes. There was a pause while the fingers on one of his hands seemed to twiddle an invisible dial in the air as though seeking a radio frequency. For several minutes, the room was completely silent before the sound of wind filled Luc's head. A moment later, he heard a bullhorn's *blaat*, followed by the voice of the crier he'd heard twice before.

In the world of the prairie, the world by the sea, beneath the old shed, the undying dead…

It took a heartbeat for Luc to register what he was hearing. When he did, his soul sank to his toes, and he knew where she was.

Rory came out of the drug-induced sleep feeling sluggish but strangely lucid. The only thing she was completely aware of was being naked.

Not the least discomfited by this realization, she opened her eyes to find herself suspended within some sort of translucent, viscous solution inside an upright, glass-enclosed, tube-shaped container. She gasped, fighting the emulsion for a moment before realizing it didn't prevent her from breathing normally. She wondered why—the same way she'd wondered why she hadn't been affected by the flames when the room she and Luc were in was engulfed in flame. Then the realization she was surrounded by glowing cylinders that appeared identical to hers distracted her. The containers were all filled with the same luminescent fluid, allowing her to see into those closest to her. Every one that she could see contained a small, human shape. Most of the figures hung limp within the fluid. Others thrashed frantically, pounding on the thick glass walls or kicking upward to tug or push at the top of the chambers in an effort to escape. Their eyes were wide with panic, their mouths opening and closing as though gasping for air until, one by one, their struggles ceased. Their eyes turned glassy, bodies drooped.

That was when the screaming started.

It was the same piercing, inhuman shriek that had sucked her into the crystal nexus at the start of this odyssey. That had taken her out of her body, to the dead-but-not-dying children in the Neon Boneyard. The sound went straight to her hind brain, made her tuck into herself and grab her ears, trying to block it. To no avail. The keening scraped at the inside of her skull, leaving it raw and bleeding. She wrapped her arms about her head and gasped, inhaling some of the gelatinous material. Coughing and choking, she tried to spit it out again. Her entire body seized, hands and feet thrashed against the spherical container, trying to break her out. The stuff inhibited her efforts. Every attempt to shatter the glass was cushioned and rebuffed by the substance. The shrieking inside her head did not let up.

Panic flowed through her, and her attack on her prison grew more frenzied. Some part of her understood that she should be able to control the volume of the screams she heard, that she had, in fact, done so before, but the present situation was so foreign to her she'd lost the ability to think.

Stop, a voice in her head urged. *Be still. I'm coming.*

Not Luc. She couldn't feel her connection to him, and that frightened her. She looked around wildly, looking for the voice's source, too rattled to realize it was in her head.

"Ghost?" No sound breached the jelly encasing her, only bubbles stirred up by her attempt to speak. She took hold of her terror, repeated silently, *Ghost?*

Yes.

Luc's son. A connection to hold on to. Her mind had not entirely deserted her.

Athanarius, yes. The response sounded strained—and more than a little insolent. Then, in his normal thought voice, *Don't think. Others can hear you, too. Breathe normally. You'll be all right.*

How—Rory caught the word before it finished forming. Instead, she nodded once in acknowledgment. It took everything she had to remember and reach for the runes along her back. To close her eyes and feel them, pull on the harmony and balance they represented. The moment she succeeded, the dreadful screaming dulled, allowed her to force back her own fear and grow still. Her breathing returned to normal. Power fizzed through her veins, pooled in her fingers. She didn't know what had happened to her when she'd coupled with Luc, and after that, during the fire, but she'd never felt quite so fiercely herself. Not even dancing had ever made her feel quite so powerful.

Or so impatient to use the abilities she could feel coursing insistently through her.

She reached for the container walls, intent on rupturing them.

No!

She paused.

Look, the ghost voice—Athanarius—commanded.

She felt a slight push against her consciousness and turned her head in the direction it seemed to indicate.

Though the gel made the world outside her prison appear murky and distorted, Rory could see figures weaving back and forth among the cylindrical cells. She couldn't tell what they were—man, woman, other—as they appeared to be identically dressed in dark, hooded robes. Their faces were covered except where holes had been cut for them to see through, making her think of executioners. Unidentifiable and anonymous. And frighteningly appropriate, given the number of dead in the surrounding tubes.

As she watched, each worker paused to attach filaments wrapped in sinew-like tendrils to an apparatus at the top and bottom of the units surrounding hers. When that was done, they carefully unrolled the bundled strands and laid them out like sun rays with her unit at their center. Each bunch gave off the same dirty ochre light she'd first seen attached to the soulbound dead inside the nexus the day Luc had found her. Here and there, the murky yellow-brown was laced with the blue-white glow Rory associated with the souls she'd released.

She shuddered. Whoever these people were that Beck was associated with, they appeared to be getting better at harvesting soul energy. She still didn't understand why it was being harvested or how it would be used, but the dread that filled her told her that she would. Soon.

Outside her prison, one of the workers completed laying out the filament bundle, glanced up, and caught sight of her watching. The figure immediately turned and began gesturing toward her. The information was passed from hooded figure to hooded figure in a series of frantic gesticulations. Moments later, a dark shape at the fuzzy limit of Rory's line of sight separated itself from the others and approached to stare at her. Motionless, Rory stared back, shocked by what she saw. Images of the souls she'd released in the Neon Boneyard, the Council of Light's morgue, and later, in the sewer tunnels, flashed within the cut-out holes in the figure's mask. Streaks laced with red pain whirled and fled across the same screen. The figure lifted an arm, reaching toward her.

Sound breached the walls of her container. Not the voices in her head, but tangible, external, noise.

Please. The unfamiliar voice came from outside the nexus, directed at her by the creature outside her prison. *You have to die. They'll stop if you die.*

Rory stared at the hooded shape, perplexed. She had no intention of dying, and she was honestly beginning to wonder if she could. Whatever had happened when she and Luc joined, something about her had irrevocably changed. She was alive in a tank full of goo when the prisoners in the other tanks were…

…dead but not dying…

The phrase slipped into her mind, circled it, left pain in its wake. She had to do something to free the children and their souls, and she had to do it *now.*

Die, Athanarius's voice whispered.

Die…die…die… echoed the distant chorus inside the web.

Rory cocked her head and twisted her lips into a grimace that she hoped conveyed *What the fuck* to Luc's son. She could almost see a Cheshire Cat grin form and disappear. Almost.

Pretend, he suggested. *Buy time.* Then, when she failed to understand, *If you're dead, they can't use you.*

Rory stilled. What? If she was dead…*use* her? How? To what end? And why?

The hairs at the back of her neck, even plastered to her scalp by the jelly encasing her, stood on end. A patchy and imperfect light dawned. Of course. It had to have something to do with her increasing gifts. But what?

She sensed the ghost-being's approbation. *Yes.*

Bewildered, and unwilling to fully trust him, she goggled her eyes in question. At the same time that Luc's son started to tell her *They don't know what you are*, another hooded form joined the first.

For a second, it merely studied her. Then it stepped closer to the tank and pulled off its hood and mask. Dr. Michael Beck, the man to whom parents had entrusted their fragile children's psyches—the man who'd abducted her—smirked and tapped the glass in front of her face. In one arm, he carried a bell jar filled with blue-white light.

Soul light, Rory thought, heart sinking.

Sadly, she watched as Beck turned to the tanks surrounding hers. Instantly, the gelatinous substance inside the tanks churned and changed color—frightened colors, red, orange, fuchsia, puce, all streaked with the menacing ochre—then mashed itself to the back of the cylinders, as far from Beck as it could get.

Ask him what he's doing, Athanarius prompted as though the question might not occur to her, and Rory got the sinking feeling that he already knew the answer, and she wouldn't like it. *And who he's doing it for. And why.*

She narrowed her eyes then, on an exhalation of gel-bubbles, acquiesced. Before she could phrase the questions, however, the terrified screeching in her head got worse. *Please. Please, stop. Please, make it stop. Stop him…stop him…stop…*

As though he, too, heard the soundless cries, Beck smiled wider and stooped to pick up one of the filamented hoses. "Watch," he mouthed to her and connected the sinew-wrapped fibers to one of the connectors at the top of her tank. A nearby worker attached a second line to the bottom.

At once, Rory felt a push from the top of her cylinder, then a rush as the mustardy light and energy she associated with *tortured soul* filtered through the connection and into the tank. Into *her*. An instant later, she experienced a sucking wrench in the vicinity of her toes. A fizzing sensation ran through her from head to toe.

Emotion that was not her own filled her—despair, dread, humiliation—anger then demoralized acceptance. It bubbled and sizzled inside her as though she were a cauldron coming to a boil while its contents morphed into something new. Something…edible. Then the transmogrified substance sank out of her and back into the tank, transmuted from the sickened ochre to a new and brilliant lavender-white.

Devastating loss filled her. As she watched, the altered energy was dragged through the bottom filament-wrapped hose and into a receptacle attached to its far end. Clearly certain he'd accomplished what he'd set out to do, Beck smiled big and turned to speak to the workers around him, making a twirl-hand "quick-quick" gesture. They rushed to couple the remaining hoses to the top and bottom of her tank.

The screaming in the web took on desperate proportions. *Help us, helphelphelp! Killing us, changing us, stop him…stop…*

"What are you doing?" she gasped—or tried to. The gel filled her mouth and throat. She struggled instinctively against the choking, drowning sensation until she once again realized that she was neither choking nor drowning. As Beck watched with puzzled interest, she spat out what she could of the substance and repeated, "What are you doing?"

The question sounded garbled to her ears, but Beck seemed to understand it. Face alight with fervor, he said, "Feeding the earth's rightful masters. Helping them to rise." He waved toward a dark spot just outside the ring of cylinders Rory hadn't noticed before. Dark energy swirled and seethed at its center. "Taking my place among them."

Turning, he twitched a finger at the hooded workers, and her tank was suddenly filled with scores of terrified, mustard-colored souls. They battered and buffeted her, coalescing into a dirty cloud near the top of the cylinder only to be dragged down into her, one by one, until she was bursting with them. Something inside her refused to struggle, let them come in. Encouraged it. Absorbed them and their terror.

Amalgamated it into the rage building inside her.

Power gathered in her veins, traveled down her arms, into her hands. The evil bastard had stolen not only their lives, but their souls, and now he was torturing those same souls, feeding them to…

Well, she wasn't sure to whom because what he'd said didn't make sense. Which didn't matter. Because he did not deserve to live. He did not deserve to die. An eternity of torture in this life then the afterlife would be too good, but it was something she was pretty sure she could deliver.

Even if she wasn't sure how.

Or why.

She put the fingers of one hand to the glass in front of her. Saw Beck recoil in shock then collect himself. Clearly curious, he mirrored her action by putting his opposing hand to the outside of the glass while gesturing to one of the workers with him.

At once, Rory heard Athanarius shout, *No!* and saw an indistinct shadow start to materialize behind Beck. The souls inside her shrieked with fury, and the glass beneath her fingertips started to crack…

Savitri Nousaine surveyed the hilly park in front of him. The homeless tent city resembled nothing so much as the kiddie forts he had no personal knowledge of but had seen in photographs. Everywhere he looked, cardboard boxes, tables, chairs, and hastily built structures were tented over by blankets, coats, tarpaulins, and sheets to create a colorful and pathetic sense of "home" and privacy. He licked his lips. Energy pulsed everywhere. Apathy, fear, jittery paranoia, despair, defiance…

And madness. The tastiest of all emotions.

Hunger howled through him, keen-edged, sharpening. If he bled these people dry, the city might notice, but no one would care enough to launch an investigation. The spring night air was unseasonable chilly. Hypothermia would be an issue. Energy theft would never be considered a cause of death until overworked human pathologists were shown what to look for.

He raised one hand to the air. Felt the life drain from a pair of humans in the middle of the park without any assistance from him. It would have made for a paltry but necessary meal. Now it was wasted fuel sucked into the ether where it would do him no good.

He turned and started downhill toward the car that awaited him, debating how he wanted to proceed. His driver stood beside his Lexus, staring into the middle distance, a muscular monolith devoid of personality or opinions. Nousaine pursed his lips, nodded to himself. He would have—

Awareness buzzed through him without warning, a physical sensation he could not ignore. He halted and turned in a slow arch, tracking the cause. Suspicion filled him when he caught the direction of the signal, then the energy source. Beck but not Beck. More than the human doctor, less than…

Nephilim. Watcher.

Traitor.

Realization filled him. Fast on its heels was anger. He reached out with a mental fist and backhanded his too-ambitious protégé—only to be one-two punched in return by someone, some*thing*, far stronger and more dangerous than Beck could pretend to be. His head rocked hard on his neck. Off balance, he stumbled, and the side of the hill seemed to rise to meet him. Blood spurted from his nose to the half-parted seam of his lips. He tasted iron and salt, the bitterness of humiliation.

Inside him, the always careful, never-dirty-your-own-hands persona he'd cultivated since arriving in San Francisco snapped. The beast he was snarled awake, destroying the civilized shroud he'd worn since arriving in the city just less than two centuries ago. This was *his* territory. *His* city. *He* was its master. No one else. Only his. Past time he reminded himself and everyone else of that.

On that, he opened his mouth, spread his arms wide, and roared.

Throughout the park, people, animals, plant life turned, startled, in his direction, then fell, withered, and died. The grass upon which he was sitting turned to dust and blew away.

And still he roared.

Night birds fell from the sky, dehydrated and shriveled, littering the newly powdered soil around him. He planted his fingers deep into it. Heat flared around them, spread outward. Desiccated trees toppled, flamed briefly, and were reduced to ash in a breath.

A vicious smile traced his mouth. He stopped roaring and breathed deep. Anything and anyone still alive in the park died on that inhalation, both life and soul sucked forcibly from them and out of existence.

Intoxicated, he feasted on the energy of death until there was not even a memory of it left to haunt the park—or the people who would eventually pass by. He was Savitri Nousaine, master of this city, and he'd finally remembered who he was and what he could do.

From the corner of his eye, he saw his driver head toward him at speed, unaffected by either the energy drain or the memory manipulation because he, too, was one of the ancient, though far less powerful, Fallen. Watching him, Nousaine pushed himself off the ground and brushed a fleck of nothing from his suit. A gob of blood filled his mouth and he spat it onto the scorched earth. Long-unused power coursed through him, exhilarating and awful at once.

Use it or lose it, a voice inside him whispered. *Use…use…use…*

A sneer traced his features. He beckoned to his driver even as the bones in his jaws, his arms, and his legs cracked and elongated. The skin along his shoulder blades and back split, releasing great, leathery wings. The demon he hadn't allowed loose for centuries discarded his skin and came out to play.

A few feet below him, his driver stopped. Wariness then fear distorted his features as he watched his master *become*. He swallowed visibly, spun about, and started to run.

Nousaine's toothy demon smiled. The old saying was true. It *was* more fun when prey ran.

It was also true that *immortal* meant neither *indestructible* nor *inedible*. It only meant the immortal would continue to live in whatever horrifying mess of a shape Nousaine left him.

In a blink, he caught his driver, ripped out his throat, and consumed blood, flesh, and energy. Dropped what was left to flop about on the desiccated earth, undead, and flicked his newly forked tongue out to lick what now passed for his lips. *Tasty.* It had been too long since he'd fed properly. Too damn long.

Almost sated, he savored the air, raised his creature countenance to the sky. From across the city, he could sense the rising Watchers, feel their need. Feel Beck's glee over the souls he'd stolen to feed the creatures that had once been humanity's helpmates and guardians. Felt Beck's greed over the bargain he'd struck with the Watchers to help them rise in exchange for the increased power "owed" to him as his birthright.

Nousaine laughed at the very thought of the Watchers granting such a thing. At the idea that they *could* do such a thing at all. They were *Watchers*, not God. Not creators. Not wish-granters or miracle workers of any kind. As far as he was concerned, they were scum. Traitors. Betrayers of God, of man, and of their own somewhat less than angelic kin. Before their banishment, their power had been limited by the necessity for them to walk among humans without disturbing the status quo. They'd been capable of assisting humans with feats that resembled miracles but were more about the Watcher being in the right place at the right time. Until, like the Fallen before them, they'd rebeled—then been entombed by angels like Celeste Fury and the Council of Light.

He smiled a grotesque smile. Council of Light. *Bah.*

He stooped to sift through the living debris of his former driver, came up with the cell phone he sought. It took a minute for him to scroll through the contacts list until he found the one he was looking for, and hit CALL.

As though the Council was any less corrupt than he and the legions who were more comfortable in the After Dark. His side was simply more direct and less scrupulous about how they went about defying the creator.

Nevertheless, he and the Lightkeepers and the Brotherhood of Shadows were on the same page when it came to keeping the Watchers imprisoned.

The rise of those specters of disorder signaled the beginning of the end, not only for humanity as it was, but for the supernatural classes, as well. And he'd be damned—again—before he allowed that to happen.

Though at least this time, the Council would be damned along with him.

His teeth gleamed in a grotesque demon smile as his call to Celeste Fury's office went through.

Chapter Twenty

Ancient legend speaks of a single extraordinary child who will become a bridge to a greater understanding among all men, and who will guide humanity into the next stage of human enlightenment. A contradictory rumor alludes to the birth of a second extraordinary child who will grow to oppose the first and lead humanity to its destruction. No corroborating evidence points to the existence of this second child.

—*The Lightway Codex, Appendix xxiii: Myths, Legends, & Rumors* by McCleron O'Connell, Indigo Lightworker

He didn't think, merely acted. Even as Senn picked up on what he was doing and shouted, "Wait!" Luc grabbed Jinx and dragged him through the ether to the concrete and weed-infested field just outside the warehouse Fish had shown them the first time Rory had folded the space between one place and the next. He neither knew nor cared how he managed it. If his wings were back, why not at least some of his other lost abilities, too?

Jinx swearing at his heels, Luc headed into the rotting warehouse.

In the world of the prairie, the world by the sea, beneath the old shed, the undying dead…

The refrain looped in his head. He understood it now—or most of it, anyway. The Council's desire to contain or eliminate Rory altogether. To contain or eliminate Magpie's baby, as well. It was the only way they thought they could prevent the Watchers from rising. But everything in Luc told him they were wrong. That they had no idea who—or more to the point *what*—Aurora Montgomery was or what she was capable of. Luc was pretty sure he didn't know either, but he would damn sure do his best to be at her side when—

The ground beneath his feet rumbled, then pitched and rolled. Jinx grabbed his arm to steady them both.

"What the ever-lovin' fuck've you gotten us into, Garard?"

Luc ignored the question and stepped into the warehouse. Daylight peeked through more than windows. The floor heaved. Dust, boards, and wooden beams showered them. He dodged or batted aside the projectiles, intent upon reaching the groove in the floor he'd seen when he'd been here with Rory. If he was right…

He stumbled but caught himself when he fell into the partially grated drainage trench he'd been looking for. Awareness washed through him. Beside him, Jinx went stock still before reaching up to scrub hard at the back of his neck. Eyes narrowed, he looked at Luc.

What the hell, he mouthed.

Luc nodded. His lips moved without sound. *Exactly.*

Rubbing at the tether point over his heart and wishing he could feel Rory, pinpoint her exact location, he paced forward as quickly as he dared, alert for the slightest change in atmosphere that would indicate they were close to where they needed to be. A few steps to his left, Jinx coughed and flapped a hand in front of his face when another shower of dust and debris shrouded them. Looking for breathable air, Luc pulled the collar of his T-shirt up over his nose and kept moving. There was nothing he could do about the grit stinging his eyes except gut it out.

He squinted at the concrete flooring. The drain followed the floor toward the opening through which he, Rory, and Fish had exited the first time he'd been here. A striped dimness, created by the gaps in the warehouse's broken siding, stretched around them. Grime coated the air as the earth rocked and what was left of the wooden building broke apart. He and Jinx kept pace, senses keened to any change in the air as they went.

When they were about halfway along the drain trench, the air thickened to the consistency of sludge. Luc found himself leaning into it the way he might a heavy wind, trying to power his way forward. At the same time, it felt like something or someone had stuck suction hoses into him and was trying to yank out his soul.

It was oddly comforting to realize that he had a soul for this to happen to.

Then reality returned.

"Watchers're feeding." He tilted his head toward Jinx as debris stung his face. "We don't put a stop to it, we won't be able to recover any of the souls Beck stole for them."

The blood vamp nodded and pointed to a spot to their right where a thick cloud of dust formed a tornado-like vortex. Loose rubble flew across the building's expanse and collected inside the growing maelstrom. Ahead of them, the twister's tail looked like it was trying to drill a hole into the floor—and was succeeding.

Luc reached for the coalescing power. Gave it a tug. It bowed toward him for a second before snapping back into its funnel cloud shape. The tail punched through the concrete floor. Energy and debris poured through the opening even as the mushroom cloud widened to yank in asphalt, scrub grass, and concrete from outside. Jinx ducked when a chunk of sidewalk sailed past his head. Luc jerked his head toward the center of the turbulence and pointed down. Jinx grimaced but nodded. Together, they crossed the warehouse and allowed themselves to be sucked into the storm.

The whirlwind launched a physical assault on Luc, pummeling him, trying to siphon out of him everything he'd worked so hard to become.

Rory, he reminded himself. *Have to get to her.*

He shut his eyes against the sensation of thousands of needle-like fingers trying to burrow into his body and imagined himself nothing more than vapor swept along inside the melee.

A few moments later, the funnel spat him and the cursing Jinx into a seemingly endless space crowded with upright cylindrical chambers and shelves lined with bell jars. There was no time to get their bearings or to examine the compartments. A feral battle cry sounded, and they were attacked from all sides by dark, faceless shapes. The assault was undisciplined and ineffectual, clearly meant to delay and distract rather than to harm.

"Go. Find her," Jinx shouted, flinging aside one shapeless form after another. "Get her out. I've got this."

Luc nodded, threw one of the formless things out of his way, and started toward where the bulk of the commotion seemed to come from.

"*No!*"

Rory. The horrified shout made him alter direction. Every instinct he possessed told him she would be at the center of what was happening wherever that cry had come from.

A deafening *crack* reverberated through the facility. Cylinders and bell jars splintered, glass went flying. Bodies and translucent goo flooded the concrete floor and nearly knocked him off his feet. On an instinct so long untapped that it should have been forgotten, his shirt shredded as his wings unfurled to lift him above the mess, carry him forward at speed.

"Rory!" he shouted. If anything happened to her, eternity would be the hell he'd have to spend not only living with his failure to keep her safe, but without her love. Without being able to give his back to her.

Of course, he *was* dealing with Rory. She had an uncanny knack for taking life into her own hands and bending it into new shapes.

Which, judging from the bellows of rage coming from somewhere ahead of him, was exactly what she was doing now. He started toward the chaos.

"Luc!" Jinx shouted.

In a blur veiled by the haze of ahead of him, Luc turned to see Beck roar with rage as he slipped about in the goo while a naked Rory stumbled out of a shattering container. Before Luc could move, she collected herself and strode purposefully toward the child psychiatrist, gathering something that resembled lightning into her hands as she went. At the same time, a full-on demon burst through the ceiling, followed closely by Council of Light soldiers led by Celeste Fury.

Fear and loathing shot through Luc when he recognized the demon. "Nousaine!" he snarled.

His former mentor gave him a freakishly toothy grin and dove at Rory. "Too late, Garard." The whisper fluttered into Luc's mind, invasive and unwelcome. "She's mine now. The Council gave her to me as payment for my help against the Watchers."

"The Council doesn't own her. She's not theirs to give—"

"Think again, fledgling."

Luc's blood ran cold. He'd known from the start that the Council was of a mind to eliminate rather than work with beings like Rory, but he hadn't wanted to imagine how far Celeste might go to remedy what she saw as a problem.

With a snarl, he folded his wings close to his back and plunged into a steep dive, intent on putting himself between Rory, the incoming hell's spawn, and the Council's less-than-angelic warriors. If she displayed her growing abilities, he was pretty damned sure Celeste would feel no compunction to keep her alive so neither Nousaine nor the soul-eating Watchers could use her.

From below, he heard Rory call, "To me, to me, to me," and saw her hold out her arms.

Everywhere he looked, souls released from bodies and containers screamed and scattered, trying desperately to reach her. Grayish, wraith-like figures swooped into view, coating the blue-lit souls in a sickly yellowish-green sludge before sucking them completely out of existence. Behind them swooped the "angels" the Council counted as its soldiers. Luc's stomach turned when he recognized several as former comrades from the host of Principalities. Unthinking thugs, the lot of them, unwilling or unable to think for themselves. Like the person he used to be.

Before Rory.

And who—according to his designation as the Brotherhood's enforcer—he was still supposed to be.

Mindless. Unthinking. Thug.

Not anymore. He looked at Rory and the kind of raw, electric power he hadn't felt or been able to access since he'd Fallen surged through him. Satisfaction and something more sizzled through his veins. He reached out and tore apart a pair of smoke-like wraiths, then intercepted one of his former brethren who was trying to beat Nousaine to Rory.

The Legionnaire laughed at him. "You were never a match for me, Garard," he said and aimed a kick at Luc's head.

Never taking his eyes off Rory, Luc punched him twice in the throat, temporarily collapsing his windpipe, and let the choking angel fall.

Below him, Rory dashed into the midst of the descending angels and howling wraiths. Still shouting, "To me, to me," she began to pluck souls from the air, seemingly absorbing them the moment she touched them. Instead of disappearing as had happened when the phantom Watchers whipped through them, the souls coalesced, lending and gaining light and strength as they merged with her. The lightning forming in her hands grew brighter. Palms out, she sent bright white bolts at a group of Council angels who appeared to be trying to shred the gathering souls. They fell back, stunned, their wings singed, as they dropped like rocks. When they were down, some of the souls detached from Rory and descended on them, lashing them to the floor with cocoon-like filaments.

Shit. Luc's jaw dropped even as he dodged a pair of Council soldiers, then in rapid succession, shredded three wraiths that had begun to shimmer into more Watcher-like form. And he'd been worried about Rory displaying her new abilities in front of the Council. Clearly, she could take care of herself *and* the souls she meant to rescue. Whatever it cost, he would back her play every step of the way.

Again, he headed toward her and her latest group of Council directed attackers in time to stick out an arm and clothesline the nearest before it could tackle her. She turned her face up to him when she saw him and offered him a blazing smile then pointed behind him and to his left before returning her attention to the battle.

Luc looked over his shoulder in time to see Athan stick his hands all the way through two solidifying watchers and *yank*. The Watchers dissolved, leaving Athan holding the souls they'd been attempting to eat. Then, even as his eyes turned demon red with hunger, Athan knelt between the goo-coated bodies of two adolescents and slammed a palm into the heart center of each of them.

The exact same way Rory had slammed the girl's soul back into her in the tunnels.

When the blue-white energy around Athan's hands refused to dislodge, he smacked the bodies again. This time, the souls slipped from his hands and melted back where they belonged. One after another, the teens heaved in great, gasping breaths and rolled onto their sides, coughing.

Growling, Athan leaped away from them, as though afraid of what he might do if he lingered. Luc understood all too well. Hunger, painful and mind-stealing, rode his son, causing him to crave the energy those souls could give him almost as badly as the Watchers did. Except Luc had never known Athan to devour souls. Toy with and torment them, yes. But not destroy them.

"Garard! Look out!"

Below, Senn charged into the melee, Solaya on his heels. What appeared to be at least a legion of Council troops followed close behind. Half-turning, Solaya sent burst after burst of yellow-orange hex flame into the trailing Legionnaires. The smell of burned flesh rose. Voices screamed and cursed in pain wherever the spell landed. At the same time, Senn conjured basketballs that bore a striking resemblance to mini black holes. He pitched them into the oncoming troops. As the blackness touched them, two and three at a time disappeared.

"Stay out of the shadows," he shouted at Luc.

Ironic, Luc thought, given what he was. Hands first, he touched down onto the warehouse's concrete floor without responding and somersaulted into a half-dozen of his former comrades, felling them. In an instant, he'd rolled onto his feet and headed toward Rory, bowling through anyone in his path.

"To me, to me!" she called and spread her arms wide, welcoming a new *swoosh* of incoming souls.

Luc was two wing strokes from her when Nousaine landed and grabbed Rory from behind. Laughing with disbelief, she spun toward him as Beck also broke through the tumult and made a grab for her.

"Minion."

Sneering, the demon version of Nousaine backhanded Beck, the stunned would-be god, straight into Athan's waiting arms. Chest heaving, Athan cupped Beck's chin and the back of his head between his hands and twisted. There was an audible *snap*. For a moment, the psychiatrist hung there, rag doll limp. Then Athan tossed aside his body, discarding him.

Almost simultaneously, Rory twisted out of Nousaine's grasp and swung to face him, and Luc landed behind him. Before the demon Nousaine could react, Luc wrapped an arm around his throat and hauled him back into the crook of his elbow. He caught that elbow in his other hand and bore down. At the same time, wings spread for balance, he wrapped his ankles around Nousaine's, effectively hobbling him.

"You're outmatched," he snarled into his former mentor's ear.

Nousaine's horned brow raised incredulously. Then he laughed—or tried to. Breath whistled out of him when Luc tightened his grip on his windpipe.

"You were never a match for me, Garard," he wheezed.

"Not me." Luc nodded toward Rory. "Her."

"Human or demon?" she asked the astonished Master of the City.

Nousaine's derisive laugh short-circuited when Rory spread her hands wide and planted her palms on his breastplate. Just that quickly, the demon began to gag and choke, and Luc felt a *push*. He staggered as a rush of energy pulsed through him and, as he watched, Nousaine shrank and back into human form. *Shit, Rory!* Luc had never seen anyone able to do that before, let alone someone who...

Used to appear to be human, and who was now...

What?

She winked at Luc, glanced at Nousaine. "Human it is—"

"Um, guys?" Hex flame in either hand, Solaya reached them, panting. She spun to put her back to them at Luc's left elbow as a new group of angelic soldiers appeared from nowhere. "Maybe not the best time—" She glanced at Rory and halted, her eyes widening. Quickly reabsorbing the hex balls, she snatched off the leather duster she'd worn to the club and attempted to muscle her housemate's arms through the sleeves and button it closed. "Where *are* your clothes?"

Senn arrived at Luc's other elbow to face their opponents. He lobbed a pair of mini black holes into the horde of wraiths and angels following him. "Time to get the hell out of here," he shouted.

"Fight another day," Jinx concurred, taking up his position at Luc's back. "Fun as this is, we need to shut it down—"

"She needs to close the rift, shut the Watchers in."

Eyes now a smoky amber-red that appeared to spin, Athan planted himself at Rory's back and looked over his shoulder at her. She held his gaze for a moment then nodded. Luc opened his mouth to object, but his son beat him to the punch.

"It has to be her." Athan's growl was harsh. Breath shuddered out of him. His body seemed to take on height and bulk as he stood there, filling out his clothing until the seams strained. Luc tensed, recognizing the change for what it was—Athan doing his best to contain his near to ravening demon. "This won't end until the rift is closed. Can you seal it?"

Luc's hold on Nousaine tightened. Below his chokehold, Rory's hands glowed against his former mentor's now human-sized chest. The energy she pushed through Nousaine and into him nearly made Luc giddy. He had no doubt she could do it, but what messing with all that vengeful energy might do to her in return—

"There's got to be another way."

A wheezing chuckle thrummed through the wrist he'd pressed against the master psi's trachea.

"Mighty warrior afraid of what might happen to a puny human woman?" Nousaine rasped.

"No," Rory shot back before Luc could say anything. Again, she smacked Nousaine in the chest with both hands. A split second's surprise flickered across the master psi vamp's features before he sagged, unconscious. "He's afraid of what *this* puny human woman might do to *you*."

Luc lifted an eyebrow at her then dropped Nousaine to the floor.

"Fine." He blew out a harassed breath and, ignoring the maelstrom that swirled around them, tossed his hands high, glaring at her. "I forgot. Mad skills. Don't need protection. Get it done then."

She laughed, a light musical sound that pricked at the part of his brain that her singing had affected when they'd first met. He shook it off when she tucked a hand into his and brought it to her mouth. Luc felt the electric sizzle of her kiss everywhere.

"I do need protection sometimes," she told him softly. "Just not here and now or"—she inclined her head toward the Legionnaires and wraiths who'd backed away when she laughed—"from *them.*"

Jinx butted Luc in the back of the head, gestured toward the spot where they'd been sucked into the warehouse. Below that point, the cyclone reversed flow, eddying tighter and faster, pulling more and more wraiths out of the earth's depths and into the *now.*

"Saccharine as this crap is"—he whirled to kick a pair of incoming Council soldiers toward Senn, who pitched his black holes at them while Solaya flung hex flame everywhere—"we need to seal that rupture and get the hell out."

Everywhere Rory looked, there was an ongoing battle. In one direction, what she assumed were Council members fought solidifying Watchers, even as her allies did their best to stay between all of them and her.

In another direction, smoke-gray wraiths dived and rolled, trying to cover and absorb the blue-white souls that tried to escape by rushing in screaming waves toward, and into, her. She welcomed each and every one of them, but allowing them entry wasn't without cost. Her entire being felt full to bursting with them and yet she couldn't tell them to stop. Couldn't turn them away.

Couldn't tune out the chaos that promised to drown out everything she needed to hear.

She shook her head, trying to get rid of their continual, discomfiting shriek. Their fright made her irritable. Solaya's much-too-long coat was confining. She ripped at it, shrugging it off.

"Rory!"

Solaya's prudish admonishment in the midst of battle made her want to laugh. It wasn't the first time she'd been naked in front of an audience. The only difference was that she wasn't simply an anonymous member of the chorus here, but part of the main attraction. But there were no voyeurs in this crowd, and she could move so much more freely without that coat.

More uncertain than she let on, she headed for the vortex at the end of the hoses Beck's flunkies had connected to the now-shattered glass cylinders. Souls, wraiths, specters, and winged soldiers rushed about at the edges of her concentration as she approached the void. The darkness within it was nearly overwhelming—sinister, debris-filled, howling. She half-turned then hesitated, wanting nothing to do with it. Luc caught up with her and wrapped his arms around her from behind.

Everything inside her stilled as his energy, his life force, mingled with hers. She felt her heart center tug at his, felt the intensity of the connection when his responded. The amethyst-imbued runes along her back flared and ignited, steadying her, linking to the one in his chest.

The cacophony in her head subsided.

You've got this, he murmured.

She closed her eyes, allowing her mind-heart-soul to couple with his. In her mind, she saw his wings surge out from his shoulder blades, still black, but whole and untattered. Felt them close protectively around her.

I don't know how to do this, she whispered.

You do. Just let go and trust yourself, Aurora Montgomery. I've got you.

He released her, and Rory took a deep breath, nodded. She could do this. She could—

Insubstantial shapes spun out of the vortex and smacked her in the face. A tracing of invisible plumage across her cheek followed it quickly. Without thought, Rory reached out and made a grab for whatever she might catch. Her hand first brushed through the cold, ghoulish thing, then snagged in the winged thing and came away full of brilliantly colored feathers. The first being spun away, shrinking from her touch. The second gasped with pain and blinked into existence as an impossibly beautiful creature whose existence Rory was barely able to comprehend. Simultaneously, Athan's and Luc's shocked voices filled her head.

Mother.

Sophiel.

Chapter Twenty-One

According to rumor, there has ever only been one Soul Singer, a true immortal ousted from the ranks of the seraphim for fraternizing with a Fallen. The Soul Singer's purpose is to conduct the souls of the dead and dying home to their eternal rest...

—*The Lightway Codex, Appendix xxiii: Myths, Legends, & Rumors* by McCleron O'Connell, Indigo Lightworker

Everything paused—or seemed to.

The whatever-it-was seemed to fill the space between Rory and the open rift. A sense of insignificance filled Rory as the creature peered a long way down at her. An angel of some sort—a seraphim—if what Luc was thinking was any clue.

"Soul Keeper," the being said.

As though in response, the congregation of souls inside Rory huddled together in a seething mass, seeming to try to fit into some nonexistent hiding place behind her ribs. Not caring for the souls' frightened response, she regarded the unknown creature with impatience coupled with displeasure.

"You're in the way," she said.

Rory, Luc groaned.

Rory felt him wince even as Athan snickered. The being—Sophiel, according to Luc's thoughts—laughed at her.

"Show some respect, littling," the winged giantess chided.

A rude noise snorted out of Rory. "You first." She tipped her head back to give Sophiel a cursory once-over before continuing toward the rift in the floor. "What are you, anyway?"

Athan's snicker became a full-blown laugh. *You've got balls,* he thought at her. *Big ones.*

Rory ignored him, looked expectantly at Sophiel.

Who tilted her head thoughtfully and glanced at Luc, who'd moved a couple of paces in front of Rory, and at Athan, who still had her back. "The singer to your keeper, Aurora Montgomery," Sophiel said.

As one, Luc, Jinx, and Senn muttered "Shit," while Solaya's brow wrinkled and she said, "What the hell are you talking about?"

Athan snorted. *Told you. Did you listen?*

Rory ignored them, standing her ground. "The what to my what?"

"Singer to your keeper," Senn said grimly. "You're the Soul *Keeper*, she's the Soul *Singer*. She's here to take the souls from you."

Everything inside Rory stilled. Then a protective rage took her over. "Not gonna happen," she said flatly.

Out of the corner of her eye, she saw Celeste Fury closing in on them.

The seraph glanced toward Celeste, then nodded. "It will." She gave Celeste another dark look that caused the director to retreat from them at full speed. Turned to Senn. "And that is *almost* correct, sorcerer."

She returned her attention to Rory, who detected a note of sadness in the creature's voice. It was hard to tell, given the roar of chaos around them.

"Their very existence—*your* existence—destroys the human evolutionary timeline," Sophiel continued, seemingly oblivious to the battle. "It is my purpose to correct that."

Rory gaped at her. "What? You—"

"Explanations later," Solaya shouted, penetrating Rory's disbelief. "We need to shut this sucker down *now*—"

Even as she spoke, the rift exploded open, releasing a new horde of wraiths that swarmed over the legions of Council troops. Both groups fell back, stunned, as Sophiel opened her mouth and began to sing.

Immediately, the souls sharing space inside Rory began to writhe uncontrollably, fighting the call by latching onto every tendril of Rory they could grab. She clutched her head, wrapped her arms around herself, and fought the pain for as long as she could.

Then she screamed.

Luc made a diving tackle at Sophiel, hoping to knock her off balance and shut her up. The invisible tether with which he'd bound Rory to him brought him up short, snapped him back to her. Heat seared his chest, burned when he pressed a hand to the spot. An exact replica of the runes he'd tattooed in the center of her spine was burned into his palm.

Seeing what he was trying to do, Jinx went high, Athan low, trying to catch Sophiel off guard. Senn and Solaya rushed to try and help Rory, but she flung them aside and doubled in on herself, shrieking with pain.

Luc crouched over her. He could feel the souls of the children she'd collected punching and kicking against Sophiel's power, leeching their keeper's strength in the process. His breath caught when they latched onto his energy as well, attempted to pull it out of him and through her, into themselves.

Scream weakening, Rory slumped in his arms, her strength waning. He gathered her to his chest, tried to send his energy reserves into her through their link. Instead, the souls inside her latched even harder onto him, desperate to remain where they were rather than heed the Soul Singer's call.

He flinched as they fed on him through Rory. Nothing he'd experienced before could have prepared him for this invasion, the accompanying physical weakness. Nor was he prepared for Sophiel's reappearance or the possibility that she might work with the Council against them. It had never occurred to him she could, given that the seraphim choir were supposed to be neutral observers who did not meddle in the affairs of men.

But Sophiel had never been neutral. Or particularly seraphic. And to his knowledge, she was the only heavenly being of any sort who had ever borne a child. Or been able to.

He certainly should never have been able to sire one.

A glance to his left showed him that "child," his son Athanarius, had managed to get behind Sophiel and clamp a hand over her mouth. The action didn't stop her song, but it did muffle it.

It was almost enough.

The rift, Rory whispered, rousing slightly when the souls she carried loosened their death grip on her chi. *Get us there. Open the nexus. They'll help…*

In his depleted state, it took Luc a moment to grasp her meaning. Then he told her, *Hold onto me.*

He waited until she'd slipped her arms about his neck before crawling forward until they were within inches of the widening crack in the warehouse floor. He felt her mind touch his. A broken image of the lighted web he'd fallen into with her the day they'd met appeared. A faint array of pinpoint illuminations flickered into existence—and promptly faded when Rory made a feeble attempt to reach them.

Faintly, Luc heard Sophiel's song cut off and Athan growl, "Do it," then someone else—Jinx?—yelling something unintelligible. A moment later, the souls inside Rory stopped trying to bleed her energy and reversed course, attempting to push it back into her. Instead, she grew heavier in his arms.

Desperation filled him. He could feel Rory's spirit dwindling, dying no matter how hard he tried to hold her in place. His own energy reserves were in the red, but he offered them to her, covered her mouth with his, and breathed everything he had into her.

It wasn't enough.

From the corner of his eye, Luc saw one of Jinx's dialogue bubbles pop up. It was filled with comic book images. The first illustration showed a vague representation of a glowing Doctor Who-like weeping angel with fang marks in its neck. The second held a gleeful-looking cartoon vampire whose bloody fangs dripped with blood. An explosive burst filled the third along with the all-caps caption, "AHAHAHA! OVERLOAD. TAKE SOME."

If he'd had the strength or inclination to laugh, Luc knew he would have. In typical over-the-top fashion, Jinx had determined that the way to solve the psi's energy problem was to fang Sophiel. He had no idea how that would work out for Jinx in the long run, but gratefully extended a hand toward the offered vital force. Slowly, he closed his fingers into a fist and pulled Jinx's energy surfeit into himself.

Inside the protective cover his body provided, Rory stirred and touched his face. As usual, she was once again trying to feed back to him everything he offered her.

Just take it, he told her, *accept it.*

But—

Accept, he said firmly. *You can't save us all if you're dying or dead.*

He felt her half-amused, mostly exhausted grimace against his lips. *You saying it's up to me to save the world?*

A strangled laugh escaped him. *Only this one time. I promise.*

"Yeah, yeah," she mumbled aloud, but settled back and allowed Luc to channel Jinx's gift through them both.

Strength returned in quick stages. As it did, Rory slid out of Luc's arms and angled her way into the rift's energy field, stretched across the floor, and reached both hands into its center. She flinched when Jinx hit the floor beside her with an unholy roar, collected himself, and scrambled back into the fray. She took a deep breath, settled herself, and re-focused her attention on the crack that was leaking wraiths at an alarming pace. When Sophiel shouted with triumph and once again began to sing, that pace grew even more frenzied.

It was almost as though, this time, the Soul Singer's song called to *them* instead of to the souls Rory carried.

She side-eyed Luc, wondering if he felt it, too. He gave her a clipped nod. *Not imagining—*

There was a sudden inhuman snarl, and a larger-than-life Athan plowed through the swarming wraiths, leaving a sizable hole in the mass.

Close it! Athan thought-shouted at Rory. *Hurry. Do it now!*

Doing her best to ignore the sensation that the Watchers' wraiths were trying to invade her in order to access her passenger souls, she lunged through the yowling horde and smacked her hands deep into the void's energy field. Sweat poured down her face at the sudden onslaught of heat. Her muscles seized, lungs seemed to petrify, heart paused between beats. The sensation passed just as quickly. Relief filtered through her. She reached inside herself, searching for the power that, until now, had only manifested by accident or instinct when she was under duress.

She had never been under more duress.

It took a moment—and a gentle energy nudge from Luc—but then her hands started to glow. Pale yellow turned to gold, became the pulsing colors of the aurora before turning a brilliant, blinding white. Warmth flared into searing heat, crackled alive with flame.

As though it was being welded shut, the rift began to close. In panic, the rising host of Watcher-wraiths tried to either retreat or to run. Satisfaction flickered to life. She could do this. She *was* doing this.

From the corner of her eye, she saw Luc grab for the fleeing wraiths and stuff them into the slowly narrowing fissure. Somewhere beyond him, Sophiel's song changed pitch, dropped a couple of octaves.

The effect was immediate. The passenger souls inside Rory struggled for an instant then went dormant. A moment later, they began to dribble out of her like a pack of zombies drawn to brains.

Focus deserted her. Gathering the souls had been only mildly disconcerting, momentarily uncomfortable. Losing them tore at her, touched every nerve and scraped it raw. She was barely aware when Athan grew to exaggerated heights and slammed a grossly oversized fist into Sophiel's chest. The Soul Singer's song stuttered but didn't end.

As though from a distance, she felt Luc crowd in behind her, cover her body with his, filling her with warmth and solace.

I'm here, he whispered for her alone. *You've got this.*

I don't know—

"Sing," he said aloud.

It hurts you.

"Doesn't matter," he said. "Just *sing*."

She hesitated. He pressed into her with his heart, body, soul, touching all of her.

Sing.

Swallowing, she nodded. Then she collected all of the pain, fear, and uncertainty to which she couldn't allow herself to succumb into her throat. She opened her mouth.

And sang.

The song wobbled at first, so Luc pressed himself more tightly against her, trying to bolster her confidence. To tell her how much he believed in her. She settled. Her voice steadied, took on depth and volume.

Her song became an unearthly descant that sent pain ricocheting through his head and nearly undid him. He turned his head to tuck one ear into the hollow between her neck and shoulder. It didn't help much, but he'd promised her everything he had. He couldn't, wouldn't, let go.

Around them, Council troops clutched their heads and dropped to the floor or staggered about in apparent agony. Jinx shook his head as though to rid himself of the pressure then paused only long enough to find something in his pockets that he stuffed into his ears before launching himself back into what remained of the fray.

Nearby, Luc saw Celeste glance their way in shock then drop to her knees, too, while a gleeful Athan yanked his fist out of his mother's chest and stepped back. Surprise and disbelief colored Sophiel's face as she looked down to see the gaping hole her son had left in her. Her song fell apart as she collapsed into a stunned heap on the floor and didn't get up.

Rory's song changed to a haunting rendition of "Kyrie Eleison"—Lord, Have Mercy. Her hands shifted position over the fracture in the ground. Wraiths shrieked. Watchers solidified only to fall in agony. Both appeared to be sucked backward toward the fault—then into it. They scrambled at the edge, wisplike fingers scrabbling to maintain a purchase in the human world, only to lose the battle and fall through the crack. Distantly, Luc saw a few angelic troops fall in, too. Then, suddenly, the fissure closed.

Rory stopped singing. Debris rained about them as the entire warehouse crumpled in on itself.

And then everything went still.

Chapter Twenty-Two

And there will come among you one who is neither human nor inhuman, neither of this world nor the next. Some will call her Soul Keeper, others may call her Crystal Elder. Yet others may come to refer to her as the seventh element, the mistress of space and time. By whichever name she is known, she will always be more than she appears. She is the living bridge between the mortal and immortal worlds...

—*The Lightway Codex, Appendix xxv: Prophecies*
by McCleron O'Connell, Indigo Lightworker

"**G**et off me."

Half-smiling, Luc rolled aside when Rory shoved at him as she tried to squirm out from under his protective embrace. Together, they got up and surveyed the battlefield that had once been a warehouse. Rubble lay everywhere in a mishmash of Council soldiers, Nousaine's remaining demons, and the pulverized remains of the warehouse and its containment tubes, as well as the bodies of those who had been housed within them.

From various points within the wreckage, Jinx, Senn, and Solaya picked themselves up and looked around. Celeste pulled herself up to all fours and shook her head as though to clear it. Savitri Nousaine moaned and tried to move but couldn't quite manage it. Red-eyed, hands clenched, and breathing hard in what appeared to be a valiant effort to control himself, Athan towered over the fallen Sophiel. For her part, his mother tried to pull herself into a sitting position as the hole he'd punched in her to stop her singing closed over and faded.

"Wow," Rory breathed, head swiveling to take it all in.

"Yeah." Luc swallowed and looked down to where the top of her head was barely level with the lower part of his ribcage. Given what she'd just done, it seemed there should be more of her, that she should be taller, more

257

imposing. But she was as she ever was—short, curvaceously well-endowed, solid, dancer lithe. In short, Rory. His Rory.

He crouched so their faces were level. Regarded her glorious, unself-consciously naked, goop-coated body. Brushed a length of goo-matted hair behind her ear. "Just…yeah."

He leaned in to touch her mouth with his, trace the seam of her lips with his tongue. Assure himself she was there. Real. She slid her hands into the mass of hair at his neck, dragged him forward, parted her lips for him. Tangled her tongue with his. Reluctantly, he removed her hands from his hair, got up, and cupped her face in a palm.

"Later," he promised as Jinx, Senn, and Solaya joined them.

Then he stepped back and turned on Sophiel, who was just pulling herself together, and dragged her upright to face him.

"Why are you here? Who are you working for?"

He started to shake her, but Athan stepped up and grabbed his mother by the arms. Shook her until Luc swore he could hear Sophiel's teeth rattle.

"Who gave the order to wake the Watchers," Athan snarled, "and *why?*"

The seraph jerked an arm free and tried to elbow Athan in the side of the head. His mouth quirked at one corner when he simply shook his head and took Sophiel's arm again.

"No." His voice was a gravel-hauler rumble deep in his chest. "Not the biggest bad here, *Mom.*"

Sophiel flinched. She glanced first at Rory then at Luc—then at Celeste, who stood at the group's periphery. The Council's director shook her head. Sophiel bowed her head.

"I cannot say," she said simply. "I can only sing the souls I'm told must hear the song." She cast a glance at Rory. "The same way I was told *she* would try to hold them." She sent a grimace of respect in Rory's direction. "But you are not who you are supposed to be."

Rory shrugged. "Bad at 'supposed to be.'"

Luc suppressed a laugh. Senn rolled his eyes. Jinx lifted a brow but remained silent.

"You are the *worst* at everything 'supposed to,'" Solaya confirmed.

"As I said." Sophiel's tone changed, took on the same musical lilt it had when she'd sung to the souls.

Luc saw Rory flinch at the shift in timbre, fold her arms across her chest. Her skin seemed to jump as though she were being pulled out of herself. Then she rallied and drew herself erect.

Her lip curled as she threw out her hands, knocking Sophiel back with a bolt of light. The Soul Singer staggered and would have fallen if Athan hadn't kept her on her feet. Sneering, she caught her breath and opened her mouth. Without remorse, and before Sophiel could utter a sound, Luc punched her in the throat, silencing her.

Celeste darted forward, protesting the move, but Solaya caught the weakened cherubim and held her back. The Council's director lunged against the sorceress's iron hold.

"You overstep your limits, *shadow*," she spat at Luc. "This is Council business and not your concern."

He gave her a look of derision. "If it involves Aurora Montgomery, it is my *only* concern." He turned to regard Sophiel. "You're done," he told her. "Quit. No more."

"Not—" Sophiel coughed and cleared her bruised throat, tried again. "Not quite yet." She looked at Rory. "You still need to lose the souls."

"Not *lose*," Rory responded quietly. She side-eyed Celeste. "*Return*."

Celeste stared at her, aghast. "You can't—"

"Yes." Rory nodded. "I can."

"But the bodies—"

"Are still warm." She made an all-encompassing gesture around the warehouse battleground. "Still have beating hearts. Still have working minds." She made eye contact with Celeste, who looked away. "Still have families waiting for them to come home."

Celeste blanched. "You *can't*."

"Going to," Rory told her firmly. She looked from Luc to Athan then at Sophiel. "Wanna help?"

Luc choked. Jinx smothered a grin and sent Luc a text bubble that read *I like her*. Luc sent him a frowny face in reply.

Sophiel laughed, coughed, put a hand to her sore throat, and laughed again. Looked Rory up and down. "I don't know what you are, little girl, but you've got brass."

"I'm a dancer," Rory said. "We're flexible."

Eyes alight, shoulders shaking, Sophiel looked from her to Luc. "This one could save you."

Luc's chest tightened with an emotion he planned to name just as soon as he had Rory to himself. He nodded. "She already has."

Rory blew him a kiss. One corner of his mouth kicked up in response.

"Let's do this," he said.

While Solaya continued to detain Celeste, Senn held the remaining Council guard at bay. Jinx positioned himself next to Sophiel after making sure Nousaine was still unconscious. The Soul Singer's brows raised high, stating as clearly as if she'd spoken, *You really think you can take me, little man?*

Jinx gave her a fangy smile in response.

Ignoring the byplay, Luc and Rory moved to the center of the space that had held the glass prisons, and where the largest concentration of bodies lay. She took a deep breath, and then, arms wide, nodded at Sophiel. The seraphim closed her eyes and stood quiet for a moment. Then a calm, prayerful tune, different from the others she'd employed earlier, issued from her.

It took several minutes, with Rory weaving a soft contralto into the composition, before the first blue-white soul emerged. It paused as though perplexed about its purpose, then suddenly flared bright in ecstasy and made a beeline for a nearby body. Other souls followed, faster and faster, until the air was filled with their radiance. One by one, the bodies they'd chosen heaved wracking breaths, shuddered to life, and sat up.

Within thirty minutes, the reunion of bodies and souls ceased, supernatural light dimmed. As soon as they were done, Sophiel simply faded from existence. Shortly after, the souls that had been released from the bell jars rose toward the heavens and winked out, one by one.

Not sorry to see Sophiel go, Luc surveyed the aftermath. One hundred eighteen teens and preteens looked around themselves in puzzlement. Another forty-three would never revive, souls consumed by the escaped Watchers. Thirteen bodies remained warm but empty, their souls having either abandoned them or gotten lost or simply…loose somewhere.

It was the report about the missing souls that caused Celeste to start struggling again in earnest.

"This is what happens when amateurs think they can do your job," she shouted at Solaya. "This is *my* job. Let me take them. Let me *help* them."

"Help them *how*?" Solaya's voice was scornful. "If you'd done your job in the first place—"

"Stand down, Laya," Senn said sharply. He sent a questioning glance at Luc, who lifted an eyebrow at Rory, who nodded. "Nothing we can do here but squabble over who made what mistakes. Let them finish."

Solaya's mouth tightened, but she released Celeste. Growling something Luc didn't catch, the Council's director jerked free of the sorceress and strode into the debris, motioning her remaining troops to join her. She said something to a pair of them. Immediately, they took the still-insensible Savitri Nousaine, spread their wings, leaped into the air and disappeared. Another of the soldiers handed her a phone, into which she immediately began barking orders. Among the commands Luc overheard was, "Get 'em out and finish razing this place"—a plan he heartily approved.

Not long after, a crew arrived to set up a system for entry to and exit from the underground warehouse-slash-lab via a platform mechanism that could be raised and lowered from the surface. Once that was done, H.E.A.R.T. arrived to do triage. On their heels, Keile Raeburn and the Council's morgue team appeared and began clearing up bodies. They took special care with the thirteen "dead-but-not-dying" children, treating them with gentle reverence, wrapping them for transport in clean white sheets rather than body bags.

Once they were finished, forensics took its time, moving in to fine-tooth the area before the underground warehouse could be emptied, nonessential personnel sent packing, and the demolition crew moved in.

In the interim, and at Celeste Fury's insistence when Luc, Solaya, Senn, and Jinx himself refused to be debriefed by the Council, Jinx called in the Brotherhood of Shadows's investigative team to interview them about events. As a neutral liaison between the Brotherhood and the Council, Senn could have refused to answer questions, but spoke with both groups regardless. He simply declined to say much.

When it was Rory's turn, she listened to the first few questions, then raised a brow at Senn and Luc and ignored both interrogation teams. When the cross-examination continued regardless, she simply turned around and wandered away. Luc snagged an extra sheet from the pile left by Keile's team and followed her. Restless and distracted, she avoided his attempts to drape the sheet around her. Turning in circles, she looked around as though searching for something—or someone.

"Where is he?" she muttered. "He needs help, I can feel it."

"Where's who—" Luc started, and stopped when he realized.

Athan had disappeared, too.

Uneasiness rose. The last he'd seen, Athan had been a hair's breadth from turning into the monster Luc had been when he'd first escaped the pit. Luc wrapped his arms around Rory with the sheet, causing her to still. She hugged his forearms tightly about herself, tipped a worried face to his.

"He's dangerous."

Luc nodded, wishing he'd had time to do something before Athan had gone missing. "To himself and everyone else right now."

"We have to find him." Anxiety washed her features.

"Can you sense him?" Jealousy over the intimate connection she had with his son surged but abated quickly. She'd come after *him* at Carpe Noctem, not Athan. Him. Her connection with Athanarius might have begun as a way for his son to get back at him in some fashion, but it wasn't that now. "Feel where he is?"

She bit her lip and moved out of his embrace to turn in a slow circle. Stopped. Her eyes narrowed thoughtfully. "I think—"

She went bowstring tight. Luc looked where she pointed.

Eyes alight with demonic fire, Athan strode out of the twilight toward them, fists opening and closing at his sides. His entire being seemed to pulse, features and body wavering back and forth between his more human-looking mien and the beast of his otherness.

"Shit." Shoving Rory behind him, Luc faced his son. "Athan— Athanarius—no. Please. Stop."

"Begging, Father?" The sneer in the unholy being's voice was unmistakable. "That's not like you. You demand. You take. You *use*." Breathing hard, Athan swept his hands up in a sweeping motion that physically pushed Luc to the side and back several steps. "You're not worthy of walking her path. Get away from her."

The pronouncement smacked Luc in the heart, tightening the connection between him and Rory. He glanced sidelong at her sheet-wrapped, sunshine-filled glory. She smiled at him and his entire being sang. No, he wasn't worthy, but she'd chosen him, and he would not let her down.

He hardened his jaw. Athan might, in all truth, be physically stronger than he was, but this thing with Rory made Luc more than he'd ever before been. He planted himself in front of her again and squared his stance, refusing to be baited. Been there, done that. It had always ended badly.

"No."

"Luc," Rory said quietly. Hands crackling with unspent power, she moved several paces to his left and forward, until she was a short stride ahead of him. Tipped her head side to side, regarding them both. Settled her gaze on Athan. "What do you want?" she asked. "What is it you *need* from me?"

Athan flinched from her stare. "Your energy," he said hoarsely, putting out a hand toward her, curling it back with an effort. "All of it."

Then he turned, took two running steps, and disappeared into the ether.

"*No.*" Luc instinctively put out an arm to keep Rory from following.

As if he'd ever been able to keep her from doing anything.

Without appearing to think about it, she pursued Athan through the ether, yanking Luc after her by their heart connection. He was still trying to catch up when the sensation of being escorted by a thousand unseen beings hit him. It was a new and disconcerting at first. Finally, he felt Rory's hand on his arm, and warmth filled him. The invisible essences became welcoming pinpoints of light, guiding his journey.

They exited the void at last to find themselves on an abandoned pier that jutted well into the Bay at the city's edge. It was covered in the usual seals, sea lions, and a family of otters. A solitary, worse-for-wear fishing trawler was moored to it. Athan was bent over the engine, trying to get it to catch. He swore and straightened to face them as they approached.

"Stay back."

Luc regarded him. Athan was breathing hard, still bulked up the way he'd been the first night Luc had seen him at Pier 39. The fire in his eyes was banked, and he seemed in control of himself for the moment, but Luc was intimately acquainted with how easily that control could snap. He put out an arm to prevent Rory from going closer.

Yeah, right.

"You don't need to feed." She cast a chiding sideways glance at Luc, and then, attention locked on Athan, she pressed Luc's arm gently out of her way and shifted nearer to his son, the monster in the man suit. "You're not that kind of creature. Why do you want to feed?"

Luc's head snapped around. He looked down at her, startled. She spoke as though she knew what she was talking about. A glance at his son told him she knew what he had forgotten—that Athan was both the sum of his parents and far more than either of them.

His heart clenched with guilt over the actions that had brought them— him and Athan with Rory acting as buffer—to this. How could he not have realized?

Perhaps it was only Rory and the way he felt about her that allowed him to realize it now.

"I am my mother's *creature*. My father's spawn." Athan closed his eyes. He swallowed and half turned, as though attempting to retreat. Twisted back, as though full withdrawal was physically impossible. He stared at Rory. "Your energy is so"—the tip of his tongue tasted the air, withdrew, and he shuddered—"shiny." An involuntary swipe of his tongue across his lips. "Pure."

His features distorted with pain, the effort it took to contain a ravening Luc understood far too well. "*Necessary.*" Another convulsive swallow, another pleading glance at her. "Unless you stop me, I'll feed until you're gone. I don't want to. I like you. I don't want to hurt you."

Athan made a jerky gesture toward a fifteen-by-eight-inch intricately carved, wooden casket that sat on the deck behind him. A harsh breath escaped Luc when he saw the ritually rune-etched, iron-wrapped sarcophagus beside it. Pain shot through him when he gazed into the flame-red eyes Athan turned his way.

"Stop me."

Chapter Twenty-Three

One of the unpleasant duties with which the Brotherhood of Shadows is tasked is the policing of immortals. Since a true immortal cannot be killed, the Brotherhood must maintain the balance between humans and supernatural beings through ritual. If an immortal goes rogue, becoming a danger to either the mortal or supernatural worlds, it is up to the Brotherhood to deal with the threat by piercing the heart of the offending creature with the Soul Dagger. This is followed by imprisoning the immortal in a coffin designed to contain it in the deepest part of the ocean for at least one thousand eons...

—*The Lightway Codex, Appendix xii: Rituals* by McCleron O'Connell, Indigo Lightworker

"**N**o!"

Rory made to dart between them, but Luc and Athan were both faster. While Luc caught Rory around the waist and hauled her close, Athan kicked open the wooden casket and snatched up the dagger within it.

"Stay back."

Anguish rifled through Luc as Rory struggled to escape his hold and Athan pressed the tip of the ritual weapon called Soul Dagger to his own chest. Luc had put his son into that sarcophagus once, centuries ago. He didn't want to be the one to do it again. Didn't want to have to.

But Athanarius's hunger, his deeds, were still Luc's responsibility. Luceire's deeds had created the monster that crippled his son. That monster remained his to destroy, want to or not.

"I don't want to hurt you, Aurora."

The hand gripping Soul Dagger trembled. Rory stilled, turned a distressed face to Luc, then back to Athan.

"You won't hurt me. I know you tried before, but you *stopped*."

"That was then." He choked on a sad laugh. "Now I'm bound by their orders—my *mother's* orders. She won't release me. I may not be able to stop myself."

He turned to Luc. Motioned at Rory. "She's the one." He struggled to speak, as though something or someone tried to prevent him. To choke off the words before they could leave his throat. "The Soul Keeper."

His voice grew hoarser. "You are the Guardian. She is Time's mistress." He gripped his throat, yanked at an invisible binding. "The Aurora—the light. The guide." He turned a pleading gaze on Luc. "They want her dead—the Watchers, the Council, the Nightkeepers. They think she shouldn't exist. They think if they kill her, if she's gone, they can change the way things are. The way it's supposed to be."

His features twisted. He made a strangled sound then yanked himself erect. His voice strengthened. "It won't work that way, though. If she's gone, chaos—"

His jaw worked, voice cut off. He pulled the dagger away from his chest and flipped it end over end. Caught it by the blade and offered it butt first to Luc. "You have to do it," he said starkly. "Put me down before I kill her. When it's done, take her away. Hide her where they can't find her. Keep her safe."

For a moment, Luc hesitated, glanced at Rory. She shoved away from him to position herself between him and Athan again, arms spread. She planted a palm on his chest, the other on Athan's. Keeping them literally at arm's length from each other and from her.

"No," she said furiously. Light glowed around her hands, hot, burning. "I won't have it. *Nobody* dies for me."

"You're right," Luc said quietly.

Rubbing his chest and grimacing, he stepped out from under her hand because *ouch*. Something that might have been a gurgle of painful laughter issued from his son, who also removed himself from the fiery heat of her palm.

"Nobody dies. We"—he waved a hand between himself and Athan—"can't die. Immortal, remember? Only ritual can—"

"—knock me down," Athan finished. He shrugged. "It's kind of like putting me away for safekeeping."

Rory gave them both dubious looks. "For how long?"

Luc winced. Straight to the crux of it, as always. A glance at Athan. "Ahm…"

"Long enough," Athan said sharply. He grabbed Luc's hand, slapped the dagger into it. "Do it. If you don't, I swear I will be unable to contain this hell-sent hunger and she will die—as will the others." He bent to get in Rory's face. "I know you don't want other deaths on your conscience." A sideways glance at Luc. "Either of you. End this. Now."

Reading the hunger that was causing Athan's creature self to reach for Rory, Luc closed his fist around the dagger. Before Rory could object or stop him, he gave the Soul Dagger a sudden, upward thrust, slamming it under Athan's sternum and into his heart.

Rory screamed. Athan's eyes closed.

"Thank you," he whispered, and fell.

When Athan's body had been wrapped and shackled into its coffin, Luc piloted the trawler out of the Bay and into the deep Pacific. Rory sat in the stern, arms wrapped around herself, face wet with tears.

One eye on the sea, Luc studied her. He hated himself for being the instrument of her pain, which was what he was, despite her sobbing assurances to the contrary. If there'd been any other way…

But there hadn't. And he would do it again and again if he had to. If it would keep her safe.

Wondering what Athan had meant about being bound by Sophiel's orders, Luc cut the trawler's engine and went to hoist Athan's coffin onto the deck rail.

Rory appeared at his elbow. "I'll help."

Knowing she was a great deal stronger than she looked, Luc gave her a curt nod. Together, they lifted the sarcophagus and positioned it to go over the side, headfirst. For a moment, Luc let the casket teeter there.

"He never had a chance," he said hoarsely. "Not with me as his sire or Sophiel as his mother. We satisfied each other's cravings at the time. He wasn't even an afterthought."

"He never wanted to be bad," Rory said softly, reaching across the sarcophagus toward him. "He did everything he could to protect me when I didn't listen to you and went off on my own. He warned me about Dr. Beck. Kept me safe from that demon thing in the warehouse until you got there. From the Soul Singer. Sophiel."

"I know." Luc puffed out a sad breath. Looked at her. "This is a shit way to repay him for all of that, but it's what has to be done. It's all I've got."

Then he slid the sarcophagus forward, let it overbalance, and dropped his son into the sea.

After

Late October. Somewhere in a quiet neighborhood in northwest Oregon. Pre-dawn.

The wind undressed the trees with the hands of a voracious lover—much as Luc's hands had removed Rory's clothing only a couple of hours before. Her hands had been equally voracious, her touch both healing and passionate as she impaled herself on his cock and rode him until they both climaxed—several times, in fact. And he was ready to wrap himself in the cocoon of her body and repeat that ride again.

The last five months had been filled with discovery. As it had from the start, every mating changed both him and Rory. The abilities he'd had before the Fall continued to return. Rory's gifts had grown and expanded to the point Luc had no idea where they might end. Together, they were stronger than they were apart.

Lifting the gauze curtain away from the window, he watched the leaves fall—maple, oak, aspen, birch—and wondered, as he had often since the night they'd commended Athan to the ocean, if they could have done anything differently. If Sophiel's or the Council's plans—whatever they were—could have been stopped or delayed any other way.

It had been months since he'd had more than a bubble dialogue with Jinx, weeks since his and Rory's last contact with Senn or Solaya. In keeping with Athan's insistence that Rory would only be safe if they kept to the shadows, Luc couldn't be sure what was going on anywhere in the supernatural world they and their friends inhabited.

He knew only what Jinx could tell him—that Carpe Noctem remained closed for renovations but would reopen before New Year's. That Fish, Magpie, and Magpie's baby had disappeared, no one knew where. That the

Council of Light had severed all cooperative ties with the Brotherhood of Shadows and banned Senn from their chambers. Savitri Nousaine—Luc's mouth curved, and he sent a wondering glance toward the sleeping Rory—had somehow lost his psi-ness, been rendered merely human, and was supremely unhappy about it. Keile Raeburn had managed to get a message to Senn that the Council of Light believed that one of the bodies they'd recovered might be that of a mother of a second missing infant that Celeste Fury wanted found.

A shiver, alien and uncomfortable, ran through him. So many plots to unravel. So many possible outcomes. And every one of them seemed to involve the woman who shared his life and his bed.

As though she'd heard him thinking, Rory slipped from between the sheets and pressed herself, naked and warm, to his back. She wrapped her arms about his waist.

"You did what you had to," she said. "We did. We are."

"That doesn't make it easier." He twisted to look down at the top of her shining head, marveling at her ability to glow in the dark. For him. "I can't even die properly, but it would kill me if anything were to happen to you."

"I know." She pressed a kiss just below his left nipple. "The same is true here. But if we go back now—"

"If we go back now, it starts all over again." Luc nodded, pulling her close. "The Council tries to take you and everyone we know is endangered if they try to hide you. Us. If we stay out, they might hunt us, but your connection to the web helps to keep us—you—hidden. We can continue to find and help the children you connect with, help them to become who they're meant to be. And we can search for that baby…"

"We can. But right now…" She eased herself around in front of him, stood on her tiptoes, and ran her tongue across his right nipple. It pebbled tight for her, so she licked it again. When Luc groaned, she leaned across his torso and did the same thing to his left nipple. Tilted her head and looked up at him. "Have I mentioned that I love you?"

Luc swallowed. "Not in so many words," he rasped. "No."

"Well, I do." She pirouetted out of his embrace, returned, and slid a hand along his hardening cock. "Always and only. You."

"Yes." Heart squeezing tight, he caught her hand and lifted it to his mouth. Planted a kiss in her palm, then licked it. The corresponding mark on his palm tingled. "Always and only. Love you."

He bent to pick her up, but she laughed and did a grand jeté onto the bed. "Now that we've got that sorted…"

"We always had that sorted." One stride brought him to the edge of the mattress. "If we hadn't, none of that stuff in the foyer of Carpe Noctem would have happened."

"That was fun," she said dreamily. "We should do that again."

"Maybe." He reached for her. She evaded him. "Right now, I'm more interested in—"

"You know what I've always been interested in?" She shimmied toward him, breasts swaying. "Sex dancing."

He opened his mouth. Closed it. It was always hard to concentrate when she did that. "What?"

"Sex." She brought the apex of her thighs to the growing erection jutting out from between his. "Dancing." She wrapped one leg around his hip, tipped her hips to slide moist heat along his cock. "I've always wondered if it's possible to have you inside me while we"—her hips undulated, bringing the tip of his sex in contact with the entrance to her heat—"dance."

"I don't know." He caught her thigh in one big hand, positioned her, then while her belly rolled against his, he slid into her, then out. In, then out. "I've never sex danced before, but we can…" His breath caught when she made a small movement with her hips that made his cock surge. "Ah hell, *yes*! Just like that, baby. Just like—"

His muttering grew incoherent. His knees turned to jelly even as his hips pumped harder and harder into her. He'd known the night that he'd found her sleepwalking, sleep dancing, that making love with her would be incredible. But her inventiveness, this…

He fell back against the wall and simply held onto her while she slow danced them both to sweet, sweet oblivion.

Meanwhile, somewhere in the warm waters of the southern Gulf…
In the Stygian darkness of his sarcophagus, Athan's eyes opened.

Authors' Notes

FISHERMAN'S WHARF: For story purposes some liberties were taken with what Luc and Rory might see from the warehouse loading dock. Apologies to purists and to those who know the city and its history better than I do.

SOMA / South of the Slot: Liberties have been taken with the location and appearance of areas of San Francisco to fit with the story. The alternate San Francisco in which this *Brotherhood of Shadows* title is set bears a resemblance to present-day San Francisco but should not be mistaken for it.

TRANSAMERICA PYRAMID: Four-sided pyramid, at this writing the tallest building in SF, exterior concrete embedded with quartz to make it look pure white.

Cast

Aseneth Lawton – Senn; sorcerer; twin brother of Solaya Lawton; incarnated many times; neutral liaison between the Brotherhood of Shadows and the Council of Light.

Athanarius – Athan; unknown quantity; son of Luceire Garard and Sophiel

Aurora Montgomery – Rory; Soul Keeper, seventh element, dancer, Dance Movement Therapist

Celeste Fury – Director of the Council of Light; cherubim

Fish – the teenage Indigo (a guard or warrior being) who protects Magpie and her baby

Jinx Falken – Jinx; leader of the Brotherhood; Fallen from the Order of Principalities; Dugo Balang (blood vamp or sang)

Kate Cavanaugh; pediatric psychologist; owns Kate Cavanaugh & Associates

Keile Raeburn – crypto-forensic enigmalogist. Similar to a medical examiner but for the supernatural world; Mal'akh

Kestrel Sundstrom – Kessie. Woodland Fairy (Fae). Doula. Runs Kids Kare / Karing Kids

Luceire Garard – Luc; Enforcer; Fallen from the Order of Principalities; Ekoa Krillu (psychic vampire or psi)

Magpie – believed to be the teenage mother of the child the Council, the Brotherhood, and the bad guys are seeking

Michael Beck, Dr. – aka the self-named plague god Erra. Nousaine's protégé. Nephilim heritage.

Savitri Nousaine – Master of the City. Ekoa Krillu

Solaya Lawton – Laya; sorceress; twin sister of Aseneth Lawton; incarnated many times

Sophiel – Leader; Soul Singer; disgraced seraphim

Organizations

Brotherhood of Shadows

Council of Light, occasionally known as Lightkeepers

Nightkeepers

Places in Alternate San Francisco

Blood Simple

Carpe Noctem

Voodoo Roost

Glossary

Angelic Classes:

Cherubim: hold the knowledge of God. They are often sent to earth to perform the greatest of tasks and are second in rank only to the seraphim.

Mal'akh: messenger angels, once considered to be members of the Sons of Life or Twilight.

Order of Principalities: directly responsible for watching over the mortal world and for guiding and protecting nations, cities, and towns. This is the primary group from which Fallen Angels are derived and are part of both the first and second "falls."

Seraphim: also known as "fiery serpents." They often give off a light that is so intense, not even other divine beings can look at them. They are the angels closest to the throne of God and are the highest ranking of the angelic orders.

Astral Travelers: Astral warriors and travelers utilized the otherworldly bond to keep spirit connected to physical self. Like Hansel and Gretel's breadcrumbs, the bond ensured the out-of-body traveler a safe and easy return when the trek was finished. While the traveler was "away" it also acted to ensure the body against uninvited take-over by anything that didn't belong. An inexperienced traveler—or one shaken involuntarily from the body by shock or trauma the way Aurora had been—sometimes lost the thread. The road home was more difficult then, sometimes required external help to prevent the temporary out-of-body experience turning into a more permanent one. Astral Warriors are spiritual soldiers who are able to leave—and later return to—their physical bodies whenever necessary and move about the ethereal world at will. It is their calling to fight evil on the psychic plane and to dispatch it with extreme prejudice, by whatever means necessary.

Crystals: Kids; Elders; etc. These people are loving, giving; natural huggers (like Rory.) They are thought to herald the coming of a kinder, gentler humanity.

Draugr: in this instance used to describe any undead vampire.

Dugo Balang: literally "blood locust," in this instance used to describe immortal, living (as opposed to undead) sanguinary vampires. They are easily distinguished by their fangs and the darkness that colors their thirst for human blood. Some sangs are able to control their feeding urges and are capable of injecting healing antibodies into those suffering from often fatal human ailments, including cancer.

Ekoa Krillu: an invented term to distinguish the difference between immortal psychic vampires and their human counterparts. They are nearly indistinguishable from humans except for their intense energy and the way their eyes appear to be imbued with lightning or electrical sparks when they feed. They are also far larger and taller than sangs and most humans. A 'Krillu who is able to control its needs can distill the anger from mob energies. They can also heal illness, emotional imbalance, and pain in humans by drawing off the illness, imbalance, or pain by feeding on the energies those things generate.

Fifth Element: similar to the one depicted in the movie *The Fifth Element*, and representing unconditional love

FRT: Forensics Retrieval Unit

H.E.A.R.T.: Healing Energy and Retrieval Team

Hex Flame: yellow-orange ball of flame that burns what it touches, and that Solaya can use to kill her enemies.

Indigo Children: Fish. These children (and adults) are surrounded by a deep indigo aura and possess special and often supernatural abilities. They are frequently considered strange, but are usually leaders, protectors, and guides for the people they choose to be around. They are drawn to those who need their protection.

Lightway Codex, The: legends and prophecies that the Council of Light and the Brotherhood of Shadows refer to for guidance. A guide to the spiritual and supernatural worlds these supernatural creatures inhabit.

Magic: A volatile term when it came to angels because it suggests that a wave of the hand or the wiggle of a nose can change things in whatever manner the wielder chooses. Though there may be practical and symbolic shortcuts, the only way to get what you want is to work for it.

Mayday: May 1, the date the Council of Light learns that Kartchner, the deep cave wherein the Watchers are imprisoned, has ruptured and it's only a matter of time before the watchers escape.

Mini black holes: about the size of a basketball; conjured by the sorcerer, Senn/Aseneth Lawton; when the black hole touches someone, it causes them to disappear; can take out two to three enemies at a time.

Nephilim: generally considered to be the offspring of the mating between a human woman and a Watcher. In Chapter Two, Solaya uses the term incorrectly as a slur.

Nightkeeper: so named because they kept what shouldn't be known from coming to light.

Repha'im: are the descendants of the Nephilim "sons of God." As the generations got farther declined, they were called Anakim and later Rephaim.

Seventh Element: Rory is thought to be the mistress of space and time, a living bridge between the mortal and immortal worlds.

Sixth Element: alleged to be the embodiment of awakening knowledge, and the next step in human evolution

Soul Keeper: One who keeps the souls of the dead-but-not-dying children so they can be returned to the bodies intact.

Soul Singer: similar to a banshee, the Soul Singer calls the souls out of the body.

Tesseract: a means to "fold" time and space in order to shorten the distance through both. Luc refers to it as Rory being able to open a door in space so as to immediately step between one place and the next.

Watchers: also known as souleaters or the "sons of life or of twilight," at one time they were direct intermediaries between God and man, and put on earth to aid humans. When their envy over God's love of humans became too much for them to bear, they set about trying to corrupt humanity for their own ends. Rebuffed, they went rogue and began feeding on and digesting human souls until those souls are gone from the world and cannot move on to the next phase of existence.

Witchflame: a pinkish orange ball of flame a few degrees more potent than witchlight. Can burn whomever it's thrown at without doing permanent damage.

Witchlight: cooler than both witchflame and hex flame, it is a blue-white used to give someone a painful shock or to light a path.

Sigils, Runes, Symbols, & Marks

Rory's Tattoos in Order

Algiz – protective

Ehwaz – communication and travelling between worlds

Laguz – travelling of the soul and the unconscious mind

Gebo – for harmony and balance
Luceire sigil – entwined with Gebo to mark her as under his protection

Uruz – union of energy and mind

Perdhu – to keep her down to earth.

Sowelo – combats dark energy

Luc's Sigil (tattooed onto Rory as well) – means "Find & protect in all worlds."

Brotherhood of Shadows Logo with Luc's Sigil

About the Authors

Cathryn Marr is the pseudonym for the writing team of Terese Ramin and Dawn Johanson.

Terese Ramin is the award winning, bestselling author of ten romance and romantic suspense novels, numerous short stories, and the creator/editor/author of the charitable collaboration *Bewitched, Bothered & BeVampyred*. She co-wrote the medical-legal thriller *The Whistleblower's Daughter* with David Wind. Her autobiographical essay, "Two-Puppy Theory", is included in the anthology *The Sound and the Furry*, sales of which benefit the International Fund for Animal Welfare. Aside from writing, Terese has worked as an editor, a ghost writer, a book doctor, and a paranormal investigator. She resides in Michigan with her husband and (usually) four dogs.

Dawn Johanson worked as a counseling psychologist in both the private and public sectors for 25 years. Dawn's years of working with exceptional children led her on an unexpected and thought-provoking journey exploring the phenomenon parapsychologists refer to as the new generation of psychic children, often called the Indigo, Crystal, and Rainbow children. Thousands of websites and numerous non-fiction books later and all with fascinating information regarding these unique children finally coalesced into story ideas for the fictional *Brotherhood of Shadows* series.

Dawn has always been fascinated by labyrinths and is a member of the International Labyrinth Society. Number one on her bucket list is 'walking' as many world labyrinths as she can.

When she's not working with her writing partner, Terese Ramin, on their paranormal romantic suspense series, *Brotherhood of Shadows,* Dawn can be found playing with her grandkids and working on her labyrinth designs.

Dawn lives with her husband and two dogs in northern California where she's inspired daily by the magic of the redwoods and power of the Pacific Ocean.

Please visit Ms. Marr's website: https://cathrynmarr.com
Facebook: https://facebook.com/Cathryn.Marr
Twitter: @CathrynMarr
Instagram: Cathryn Marr
Pinterest: Cathryn Marr